MILA
2.0

LA

2.0

DEBRA DRIZA

KATHERINE TEGEN BOOKS
An Imprint of HarperCollins Publishers

Katherine Tegen Books is an imprint of HarperCollins Publishers.

Mila 2.0
www.epicreads.com

Library of Congress Cataloging-in-Publication Data
Driza, Debra.
  Mila 2.0 / Debra Driza. — 1st ed.
    p. cm.
  Summary: A teenage girl named Mila must escape from the CIA
and rogue operatives when she discovers that she is an experiment in
artificial intelligence and that her scientist mother kidnapped her from a
secret laboratory when she was found to have human emotions.
  ISBN 978-0-06-209036-2 (trade bdg.)
  [1. Science fiction. 2. Identity—Fiction. 3. Androids—Fiction.] I. Title.
II. Title: Mila two point zero.
PZ7.D793Mi 2013   2012005248
[Fic]—dc23   CIP
                                                                AC
                    Typography by Erin Fitzsimmons

     13 14 15 16 17   LP/RRDH   10 9 8 7 6 5 4 3 2 1
                                ❖
                          First Edition

For Mom and Dad, and for Scott—who believed even when I didn't

PART ONE

ONE

Beyond the eastern border of Greenwood Ranch, orange poured across the sky, edging the clouds like flames.

Flames.

I clenched handfuls of Bliss's silky-thick mane and squeezed my eyes shut, searching my memories for the black haze of smoke. For the smell of burning wood and plastic, of smoldering Phillies shirts and baby photos. For sirens and screams. For anything at all that hinted at fire.

For Dad.

Beneath me, the horse snorted. I sighed, relaxed my grip, and smoothed her mane back into place. Nothing. Once again all I'd conjured up was a big fat bunch of nothing. Over four weeks since the accident that had ended my father's life, and the memories still resisted my every attempt to unlock them.

I opened my eyes, just as something flashed in my mind.

White walls, white lights. A white lab coat. The searing aroma of bleach.

My skin prickled. From the hospital I'd been taken to, maybe? After the fire? It was the closest I'd come to remembering anything so far.

I grasped at the images, tried to drag them into view, but they vanished as fast as they'd appeared.

Now that my eyes were open, what wouldn't disappear was the picket fence blocking our path, its white posts stabbing upward and bisecting an unrelenting sprawl of green, green, green.

The other thing that wouldn't disappear, as much as I dreamed otherwise? Good old Clearwater, Minnesota—my new home as of thirty days ago. Land of grass, trees, dirt, of scattered old ranch-style houses tucked between plots of farmland. Home of work trucks and the thick, earthy stench of manure. A town so tiny, it didn't even have its own movie theater. Or a McDonald's. A place where, according to Kaylee, the sole listing under Yelp's Arts and Entertainment section was Mount'em Taxidermy.

Nothing said good times like a stuffed mammal.

Bliss snorted and yanked her head away from the fence, back in the direction of the stables. I couldn't blame her.

The fields and lakes and quiet that Mom accepted so readily held nothing for me, either. They couldn't. Not when every good memory had been created back in Philly.

At least the ones I could still remember.

I rubbed my cheek against green-and-tan flannel—Dad's shirt collar—seeking comfort in the soft fabric. Dad had worn this shirt as he guided me through throngs of Phillies fans inside Citizens Park, his hand gentle on my elbow while the aroma of popcorn and hot dogs and overheated bodies surrounded us.

The hollow widened in my chest. How was it that some memories played so vividly behind my eyes, like DVDs complete with sounds and smells, while others, not at all?

Mom said anxiety following a traumatic death was normal, that it did odd things to our brains. A nice way of saying I wasn't crazy, just because I could recall the exact layout of our old house and the way Dad pumped one arm in the air when he cheered for his favorite team, yet couldn't remember something as simple as my favorite brand of jeans. Or if I liked to go on bike rides. Or if I'd ever been in love.

Mom assured me it would all come back. Eventually.

My dad never would.

I dug my nails into the leather reins and drew in a deep, shuddering breath. Everything, burned to ashes along with our old house.

Everything except for one pathetic shirt.

Bliss pawed the ground, kicking up a clump of grass. She whinnied in anticipation of escape.

I knew exactly how she felt.

I steered Bliss away from the fence before nudging her into a trot, her body swaying rhythmically beneath me. A chilly breeze brushed over my face. I threw back my head and allowed the grassy-sweet gusts to grab at my hair, my shirt, the painful ache that lived where my heart should be. If only the breeze could pick me up and carry me back in time.

The ache behind my lungs grew, like it was trying to metastasize to the rest of my body.

"Let's go!" I dug my heels into Bliss's sides.

The mare didn't need to be asked twice. All fifteen hundred pounds of horse surged forward at once. Power roared up from her legs and slammed into me, and I leaned lower, pressing my body as close to the mare's as possible, relishing the snap of her mane whipping into my face.

The faster we went, the more the ache in my chest seemed to subside, as if my pounding heart and each one of Bliss's hoof strikes hammered the pain into a smaller and smaller ball.

I urged Bliss even faster.

As we raced back for the stables, boulders rose before us, part of the decorative wall that meandered through a small portion of the twenty-five-acre property. I was already defying Mom by venturing above a speed of painfully dull.

Jumping was out of the question. Especially since I'd never done it before.

Or had I?

The rocks grew closer and closer. Either I veered away now or carried out a split-second and idiotic attempt to slam my memory back into gear.

I let the reins slip through my fingers. Idiotic it was.

The mare's powerful muscles gathered beneath my legs, and our soar into the air felt amazing, like I was part of Bliss and the two of us were flying.

Until the stirrup gave under my right foot. Until the saddle slipped.

I lost balance, slid sideways with the loosened saddle, saw the rocks rush toward me. I pictured my head splattering open like a broken egg while my pulse pounded a terrified drumbeat in my ears.

You're a goner flashed through my mind.

And then my hands lashed out, quicker than I even knew I could move. I grabbed hold of Bliss's mane, pulled myself upright with remarkable ease—just as Bliss's front hooves crashed to the ground.

"Yes!" An exhilarated laugh exploded from my mouth. So I hadn't conjured up my past, but I did feel more alive than I had in weeks. Like the whole world had burst into high definition.

Plus—I had wicked good reflexes. Maybe one day Mom

would tell me if sports featured prominently in those missing chunks of my life.

"Mila!"

Speaking of whom . . .

Busted.

I slowed Bliss to a trot. My stomach clenched as we drew closer to the willowy figure who stood near the gravel driveway.

Of course, the expression on Mom's heart-shaped face was as poised as ever; not even a single blond hair strayed from her usual neat ponytail. The wiry arms crossed under her chest hinted at annoyance, but that was all the reaction I got. Disappointing, but hardly shocking.

Nothing fazed Nicole Daily, not one of the critically injured horses she tended or an impromptu move to a new state, and certainly not one slightly rebellious, hugely heart-broken daughter.

When I pulled the horse to a stop, Mom's dark-blue eyes remained neutral behind the square frames of her glasses. "I'm sure I've told you not to ride faster than a walk. Was there a point to that?"

I dismounted and patted the blowing horse on the neck. My shoulders hitched back. "No point."

Her eyebrows arched over her lenses, accentuating her surprise. Then her lipstick-free mouth flattened into a thin line.

The spurt of satisfaction I felt wasn't nice.

"I see." An abrupt shake of her head, followed by her slender fingers rubbing the spot between her brows.

With a start, I noticed her hand was shaking when she extended it toward me, palm up. An uncharacteristically pleading gesture. "No, I don't see. Mila, please, you can't do this sort of thing. What if you'd had an accident, and then—"

She broke off, but it didn't matter. The flannel shirt I wore became heavier, burdened with the weight of words left unsaid.

And then—maybe I'd lose you, too.

For the first time since the move, I threw my arms around her and buried my face in the comforting bend of her neck. "I'm sorry," I said, my words muffled against skin scented with a combination of rosemary and horse liniment. "Only slow rides from now on. Promise."

When Mom stiffened, I gripped her all the tighter. I wouldn't let her slip away. Not this time. Her hand patted the spot above my left shoulder blade, so soft, so hesitant, I almost thought I'd imagined it. Like after this past month, she'd forgotten how.

And maybe I did imagine it, because she untangled herself from my grasp a moment later and stepped away. I tried not to let the hurt show on my face while she adjusted the wire-framed glasses that only intensified the intellectual glint in her eyes. People said Mom didn't look like a stereotypical veterinarian, not at all, not with those acres of blond hair and her petite frame and delicate features. She eschewed makeup as a waste of time, and her bare face only seemed to enhance her natural beauty.

We looked completely different, the two of us. I was shorter, sturdier, with natural muscle like my dad and his brown hair and eyes, too. The quarter horse to her thoroughbred. But I liked to tell myself I had Mom's heart-shaped face.

And her stubbornness.

"You have to follow the rules, Mila. I need you to be safe."

She hesitated before tucking my wind-blown hair behind my ears. As her fingers grazed my temples, her eyes closed. A tiny sigh escaped her lips.

I stood frozen in place by the unexpected sweetness of her gesture, afraid that any sudden movement might startle her back into the present. I so, so wanted this version of Mom back, the one who dispensed hugs and kisses and comfort as needed. But up until this moment, I'd been convinced that the old version hadn't made the trip to Clearwater. That maybe the old version had holed up somewhere in Philly—along with the missing pieces of my memory.

Mom pulled away all too quickly, her right hand flying to the emerald pendant dangling around her neck. My birthstone. A necklace Dad had given her when I was just a baby.

After his death, Mom heaped more affection on the symbolic version of her daughter than she did on the real thing.

Her abrupt swivel kicked up dirt. I watched the dust plume upward in a small, tangible reminder of her rejection, a cloud that thinned and thinned until it finally dissipated into blue sky. What would it be like, to disappear so easily?

"Go walk Bliss out and rub her down. I'm going to check on Maisey," Mom called over her shoulder, her swift stride already carrying her halfway to the barn.

If only I were as efficient at leaving things behind as she was.

"Oh, and Kaylee called. She wants to pick you up for a Dairy Queen run in half an hour. You can go there and nowhere else, understand?"

"Yes," I said, barely suppressing an eye roll. Come straight home after school. No going anywhere without approval. Never let anyone besides Kaylee—who'd gone through a rigorous prescreening process—give me a ride. You'd think we lived in the slums of New York City or something.

Not that it mattered. I didn't have anyone else to go with—or anywhere else to go—anyway.

I leaned my head against Bliss's lathered body, taking comfort in her warmth, in her musky horse smell, before straightening. "Come on, Bliss. Let's walk you out."

She snorted, as if in approval.

I started a slow trek in Mom's footsteps, letting my eyes wander over the grounds that practically screamed country. Everything here screamed country.

Like the gravel driveway to my right, and the dirt trail that sprouted off and led to the guesthouse ahead. Our new residence was a smaller, more modest replica of the vacant eight-thousand-square-foot, L-shaped main house that sprawled another half mile back. The same white paint with green trim, the same covered porch. No lounge chairs with their wrought-iron backs crafted into the shape of horse heads, but we did have our very own bronze horse-head door knocker.

The dirt path continued from our guesthouse and led to the tall, A-framed building to my right. The stables; part of the reason Mom and I were here. Apparently the owners had a sick relative in England and had to stay indefinitely, so Mom had been hired on as the resident vet and caretaker.

Lucky me.

I supposed some girls would be thrilled to move to a big ranch away from the city, to help care for the horses, to make a fresh start.

I rubbed Bliss's oh-so-soft muzzle. So far, the horses were the only thing working for me.

TWO

"Do these colors look right together, Mila?"

Kaylee's high-pitched voice, so close to my ear, plucked me right out of a memory with Dad—a good one.

He'd been walking through Penn's Landing, hand in hand with Mom, while I ran up ahead, taking in all the tourists and the skaters, the historic ships and the musty scent of the Delaware River. The air held a chill, in spite of my red-mittened hands, but his bellowing laugh had warmed me.

When I opened my eyes to the brown-and-tan interior of the Clearwater Dairy Queen, loss ripped through me. Back in the memory, I'd felt loved, a sense of belonging. A feeling that was hard to come by in a fast-food restaurant in a strange town.

Kaylee wiggled her alternating Purrrfectly Pink and Purplicious fingernails right under my nose, bouncing the entire booth with her enthusiasm. I forced my fists to unclench and fought back the urge to bat those colorful fingers away.

"They look great, right?" In typical Kaylee fashion, she jumped in and answered her own question before I'd even had a chance to respond.

"They look awesome," Ella answered from across the table, genuine enthusiasm lighting up her narrow, mousy face.

"Awesome," I echoed. Actually, I couldn't summon even a speck of interest over nail polish colors and top coats. "How'd you get that scar on your pinkie?"

Kaylee stopped the finger wiggling. She frowned as she inspected the little fingers on both hands, squinting at the white line I'd noticed, near her first knuckle. "This tiny thing? I have no idea." She shrugged. "Maybe I pricked it with a needle in my sleep—hoping I'd fall into a coma and wake up somewhere besides Clearwater."

From across the table, Ella sighed. "Don't forget the prince and the magic kiss."

"As if." Kaylee's overzealous snort made Ella burst into laughter, and even I couldn't hold back a smile.

Ever since the day I first met her four weeks ago, Kaylee Daniels had operated at that same breakneck speed. She'd been the first person at school to introduce herself: a leggy, freckled dynamo in high-heeled boots. After latching onto my arm in homeroom, she'd practically dragged me to the desk next to hers.

I remembered the exchange verbatim.

"You're Mia Daily, right? The one who just moved into the guesthouse at Greenwood Ranch? The one from Philly, which, oh my god, has to be a billion times more exciting than here? I'm Kaylee Daniels, and I'm going to tell you everything you need to know about Clearwater. Which, unfortunately, isn't much. First and foremost—we need more boys here. More. Boys."

Once she paused to take a breath, I'd corrected my name—my parents had shortened Mia Lana into Mila as a nickname years ago—and then let her babble flow over me, even welcomed the distraction.

"So, what's the emergency?" Back in real time, Parker's Vanilla Skies perfume preceded her clomping, platform-shoed arrival. She carelessly tossed her fringed purse onto the table, almost taking out Ella's Butterfinger Blizzard before she collapsed into the booth next to her.

Parker? Kaylee had invited Parker? I tried not to groan.

Beside me, Kaylee's Purrrfectly Pink index nail tapped her Coke float cup. "Um, hello—ice cream?" But out of the corner of my eye, I saw her not-so-subtle head jerk in my direction.

"Ahhh," Ella said knowingly. Just before a trio of pitying smiles landed on me.

I scuffed my Nike on the sticky floor under the table, wishing I could slide down and join it. Kaylee had tricked me. This trip to Dairy Queen wasn't really about her satisfying a sudden urge for ice cream. It practically screamed intervention.

Mila Daily, charity case, that was me. Those pitying smiles followed me whenever people found out about Dad, along with awkward silences. As if they were terrified the wrong words would crack me like a broken mirror—and nobody wanted responsibility for picking up the pieces.

My sneaker rubbed the floor again while I tried hard to look uncrackable. Since I wasn't sure I succeeded, I did the next best thing. I deflected.

"I like your haircut, Parker."

Parker's hand flew to the ends of her long, painstakingly flat-ironed blond hair. But instead of the smug preening I expected, she frowned. "Okay, single white female. Leslie only trimmed it a quarter inch."

Kaylee waved away Parker's snark. "Oh, whatever. You'd be pissed if no one had noticed," she said, elbowing me. She pushed a Diet Coke across the table. "Here. You must need the caffeine."

"You're a goddess."

"I know."

As I watched the exchange, the grateful smile I shot Kaylee for her save faded. What must it be like, to have friends who knew you so well they could order for you? At this point, I could barely order for myself.

"So listen—" Kaylee started.

The squeak of the door interrupted Kaylee. For a moment, the smell of asphalt and manure mingled with frying chicken and grease. Two teenage guys walked in: one blond with a small U-shaped mole on his forehead, the other dark haired with a tiny red stain on his shirt collar.

That made customers ten and eleven since we'd been here.

"Ugh, just look at Tommy . . . those scruffy old work boots?" Kaylee said, scrunching her slightly crooked nose and talking loud enough to be heard over the whir of a blender. "Atrocious. An affront to feet everywhere. And Jackson isn't much better. Did you know he plans to stick around once we graduate, so he can help his parents run their store? La-ame."

Ella and Parker nodded in agreement.

"Plus Jackson dresses like he's the founding member of the Carhartt shirt-of-the-week club," Kaylee continued in real time, shaking the booth with one of her typically over-the-top shudders. "Logo shirts—also lame."

I tried to drum up similar disdain for the yellow logo on Jackson's shirt but instead saw my dad cheering on the

Phillies from our old living room. Wearing his red tee with the white, stylized P logo in the top right corner.

I pulled the sleeves of Dad's flannel shirt over my hands and rubbed the worn fabric between my fingers. The feel of it was so familiar by now, I could probably recognize the shirt blindfolded. He'd been forty-three when he died thirty-five days ago, yet all I had left of him was this and a handful of memories. It wasn't enough.

An insistent tug on my baggy sleeve made me look over, to find Kaylee staring at me. All of them, staring at me.

"What?"

Kaylee glanced at my shirt-covered hands, cleared her throat in a not-so-delicate *ah-hem*, and then flashed me her brightest smile. "We brought you out here because we thought you might need to get out a little more."

Ella nodded while Kaylee continued. "You know, a break from the ranch, your mom . . ."

"That shirt," Parker muttered under her breath.

I stiffened, but no one else seemed to notice what she'd said.

". . . things," Kaylee finished.

Dad dying. Summed up as "things."

Suddenly the vinyl seat felt like a trap. I'd made a mistake, after all. A mistake in thinking that an outing with Kaylee, with anyone, would help. At least back at the ranch, the horses didn't think I could be fixed with a Blizzard.

I winced as soon as the thought formed. They were trying, at least. Okay, not so much Parker, but Kaylee. And Ella, in her quiet, don't-rock-the-boat way.

They were trying. They just didn't understand.

"Thanks," I finally murmured. I just wished they'd focus their collective interest on something besides me.

Luckily, the door by the cashier squeaked open. "Who's that?" I asked, mentally apologizing to the boy, whoever he was, for nominating him as diversion-of-the-minute. He eased into the restaurant, a tall, lean frame topped with a mass of dark, wavy hair.

Kaylee's brown eyes widened. "Dunno. But *day-yum* . . . I'd like to."

Parker feigned a yawn. "You'd say that about any guy who wasn't local and had a pulse. Actually, nix the pulse part." But when she craned her head to look over the back of the booth, she puckered her lips and let out a short, off-key whistle. "Not bad."

Not to be left out, Ella craned her neck to peer at the newcomer, who was now placing his order with the young, pimpled cashier. "Maybe he's from Annandale?" she said, naming the next closest high school.

I shook my head. "He said he just moved here when he ordered."

Parker curled a pink-glossed lip at me while she swirled her straw in her Diet Coke. She always made at least three revolutions before each sip. "Right. Like you could catch that from all the way back here."

"Mila's quiet. She notices things," Kaylee said, taking the sting out of Parker's words. And then she laughed. "But maybe she does have some high-tech hearing aid stashed away in there." Her fingers reached out to yank playfully at my earlobe, and the sensation triggered a series of images.

White walls. A blurred image of a man in a white lab coat. His fingers reaching out, jabbing deep into my ear.

In my lunge to escape, I jolted the table and knocked over my Blizzard cup. I was out of the booth and on my feet before I even realized I'd moved.

"Jesus, Mila. Don't be such a spaz," Parker snapped. "Seriously, someone tell me why we hang out with her?"

"Shut up, Parker—she's cool. I mean, at least she's lived somewhere besides this godforsaken place. Where were you born again? Oh, that's right—Clearwater."

I stood by our table, dazed. For once, Parker was right—I was acting like a spaz. Based on the stares and giggles from around the restaurant, everyone else thought so, too. Including the new boy. Up by the cashier, he studied me with blue eyes so pale, they looked almost translucent.

A crease formed over Kaylee's nose as she waved her hands at me, palms out. "I swear, I had no idea you were an ear-o-phobe. No more ear touching, promise—but try not to make us look lame in front of cute boys, okay?"

Forcing a smile, I sank back into the booth. Even if I

wanted to explain what had happened, I couldn't, because I didn't have the faintest clue. Unless this had something to do with the hospital, post fire. Maybe the doctors had performed a procedure on my ears?

Ella's giggle rescued me. "Hey, the new guy's still looking this way."

"Thanks to Mila, everyone's still looking this way," Parker muttered. But of course our heads swiveled toward him.

Old denim, I decided. His eyes were the color of old denim.

His long-sleeved white tee was paired with slim gray pants. And on his feet—checkered gray-and-black Vans.

"No work boots," I pointed out, for Kaylee's benefit.

"Duh. That's the first thing I noticed."

I bit back a smile. Of course it was. Me, I'd noticed lots of things—as always. The gray along his jawline that hinted at five o'clock shadow. The way he leaned against the counter, poised but standoffish, his hunched shoulders not inviting anyone to chat. The way the left side of his upper lip was slightly higher than the other, saving his mouth from perfection in an intriguing way.

And then a worker handed him a drink, and he was out the door.

Kaylee broke the silence by banging her fist on the table, making our collection of cups jump. "Now that's what I'm talking about. That's exactly the kind of fresh blood we need at Clearwater."

"Too bad Mila scared him off with her booth dive," Parker sniped.

Kaylee jumped in, pointing out that any attention was better than none at all. While the girls' chatter went from mystery boys to favorite actors, I burrowed into Dad's shirt. My gaze found the window, but instead of pastureland, I summoned more memories, pored through images of Mom and Dad smiling and dabbing my nose with tomato sauce while we assembled a homemade pizza. Images of all three of us, curled up on our navy-blue sofa, playing a game of gin rummy.

Kaylee's fake swoon into my shoulder stole them away. "Oh my god, he was hot in that werewolf movie. But I still liked him better in *Tristan James, Underage Soldier.*"

I stood up. On purpose, this time.

"I've gotta go," I said. Knowing Mom would probably be upset that I was breaking the rule by walking, and not really caring.

I took off before Kaylee could even finish her startled good-bye or Parker her second eye roll. And then I was outside. Alone. Away from the girls, from the fried food smells, from the strangers and plastic booths and everything that wasn't Philly.

Away from any interruptions to the memories I continued to parade through my head.

THREE

Kaylee burst into homeroom the next morning in a bigger frenzy than usual, her brown hair fluttering behind her as she practically sprinted over to my desk. Only after she had smoothed down her homemade black dress—the girl could sew like anyone's business—adjusted her sparkling aqua tights, and rubbed her index finger across her top teeth to erase phantom lipstick did she collapse into her spot next to me.

"Have you seen him yet?" she hissed, craning her head to check out every corner of the room.

"Him who?"

When I performed my own room inspection, I didn't see anyone—or anything—out of the ordinary. Same chalkboard spanning the opposite wall, same bulletin board full of colorful flyers advertising SWIM TEAM TRYOUTS! and FREE TUTORS! and YOUTH GROUP CAMPING TRIP TO AJ ACRES! Same twenty desks, lined up in four rows of five across the green industrial carpeting, the color supposedly picked in an administrative spurt of school spirit. Same group of students settling into those desks. Same ammonia-mixed-with-sweaty-feet smell.

Same sense of being stranded in a room filled with strangers. Kaylee assured me that Clearwater High was small compared to tons of schools, but since I'd been home-schooled back in Philly, the words did little to soothe me.

"No fair." She sighed, letting her backpack slip from her fingers and smack the floor.

I ignored the typical Kaylee drama and pulled a pen from my backpack. "Who are you talking about?"

I heard .rather than saw Kaylee stiffen. "Oh my god, Mila, look!" she said, knocking my arm as she whirled in her chair. The pen flew out of my hand . . . and headed straight for the instigator of the "oh my god, Mila, look" comment's chest.

In a reflexive motion, my hand whipped out, snagging the pen-missile midair. Great save, until the hand connected to the gray shirt knocked into mine as it sought to do the same. The pen sprang loose and clattered to the floor.

Shaggy dark hair. Lean face. Faded blue eyes—the color of Kaylee's favorite old jeans—that widened briefly. I had just enough time to register the images before the boy from Dairy Queen dropped into a crouch behind my chair.

He didn't say anything as he extended the pen to me. Kaylee cleared her throat in a totally obvious *um-hum*, but I ignored her. I was too busy shaking my hair forward to hide what had to be a brilliant display of red spreading across my cheeks.

So I was correct—the Dairy Queen boy didn't go to Annandale. And, in a spectacular display of idiocy equaled only by my booth dive yesterday, I'd just assaulted him with a writing utensil. Well played.

"Here you go," he said in a surprisingly deep voice.

After accepting the pen and placing it on my desk, I turned around, an apology on my lips. It died as I watched his broad shoulders retreat. Smart choice. All the safer from the weird girl and her incredible flying Bic.

"Okay, now that's a voice I could totally wake up to in the morning," Kaylee whispered, staring unabashedly.

"Kaylee!" I said, half appalled, half amused. Even though I tried not to follow in her ogling footsteps, my peripheral vision had other ideas. I caught the slump of the boy's six-foot frame into a chair on the far side of the room, the top of his head level with the bottom of a baby-blue BOOK FAIR! poster. Only fifteen feet of space to escape us, and he'd utilized every available inch.

Obviously my attempted stabbing hadn't amused him.

From across the room, I noted how only four wavy strands of hair actually grazed the top of the olive buttondown that flapped loosely at his sides, jacket style. The same way I wore Dad's flannel. Once again, his slim-fitting pants—black this time—hinted at skater rather than farmhand. Today's black-and-yellow Vans—Kaylee would be in heaven—pretty much clinched the nonlocal look. Still, there were all types at our school, even in the middle of rural Minnesota, so he wasn't completely out of place.

The bell rang to mark the beginning of the period, a prolonged, discordant groan inciting the usual snickers from students.

Mrs. Stegmeyer cleared her throat before slapping the attendance file onto her desk and resting her clasped, multi-ringed fingers on top of it. Four of her rings were the same as always, but I noticed she'd traded the thick silver one on her right index finger for three thin gold bands, stacked one on top of the other.

Once the chatter ceased, her syrupy voice filled the room, a thick drawl that suggested southern roots. "All right, y'all. Before we move on to roll call, we have a new student to introduce. Hunter, please stand and say a few words about yourself."

Hunter scuffed his Vans against the floor. His hunched posture said giving an impromptu monologue was about the last thing he wanted to do. I could relate. I'd had to deliver my own less than a month ago in this very room. Back when everything had been too new and weird and overwhelming.

Come to think of it, things really hadn't changed all that much.

Hunter swiped at a strand of hair that covered one of his eyes, the wavy fall of his bangs making him bear a passing resemblance to the neighbors' dog, a shaggy briard that kept their horses company in the front yard.

I'd always thought the briard was cute, too.

He stuffed his hands into tight pockets and rose to his full height, his gaze skimming past everyone without really sticking. I flashed him a sympathetic smile as it slid over me.

"Yeah. Hey. I'm Hunter Lowe from San Diego," he said.

After one more ineffectual swipe at the dark waves grazing his eyelashes, he slumped back into his chair.

"Is that all?" Even Mrs. Stegmeyer seemed surprised at the brevity of his speech.

He shrugged, a loose-limbed, eloquent gesture that almost made words unnecessary.

Kaylee leaned toward me. "It's okay—no one expects him to be a genius when he looks like that," she whispered.

I remembered back to my introduction—I hadn't said much either. Was that the assumption then, too? That I was lacking in brain cells?

I could feel my smile wilt around the edges when I

glanced back over at Hunter. Not that he could tell. He was staring out the window, a view with which I'd become intimately acquainted over the past month. I let my line of sight follow his, wondered if he was doing what I did. If he stared beyond the football field, beyond the slow country street behind it, and wished himself back into another place and time.

Every so often during homeroom, I'd sneak a peek at Hunter. And each time, his head was turned toward that window.

When the bell rang, Kaylee jumped out of her seat like the sound had triggered an electric shock. Her eyes were glued to the spot under the window.

"Mila, hurry!" she said, flapping her hands at me.

"What's the emergency?" But I shouldered my backpack and stood anyway. She nabbed my arm and plowed us between the rows of desks, almost tripping over Mary Stanley's purple peace sign backpack and taking out Brad Zanzibar as he stooped over to tie his shoe.

Her trajectory led us straight to Hunter's desk.

"Hi! I'm Kaylee, and this is Mila." I tried to fade into the background, but she grabbed my arm and yanked me forward. "We figured you might want some help finding your next class."

While Kaylee bounced on her toes and beamed, I froze. *We* figured? Since when?

My head whipped to the side. I hoped to stare her into a spontaneous confession, but she either didn't notice or deliberately ignored me.

Hunter stood, hoisting his red North Face backpack over his shoulder before shoving his hands into his pockets. His eyes flitted from Kaylee to me and back again. He shrugged.

Of course that was all the invitation Kaylee needed. "Perfect!" she said, giving two baby claps. "Follow me." As she scurried ahead, she used her left hand to inconspicuously flatten down the sides of her hair.

I stood there awkwardly, shifting my weight from foot to foot, wondering who was supposed to follow next, since the row was way too narrow for both of us to fit through together. Hunter glanced at me then, his eyes lingering on my face for three excruciatingly long seconds. Seconds in which I realized that in different light, his eyes lost their translucent quality and looked more opaque. Still that sky blue, but a weightier, more substantial version. "You first," he finally said.

The combination of deep voice, slight smile, and offhanded invitation had a peculiar effect on my lungs, like I'd suddenly released a breath I hadn't known I'd been holding.

I hurried after Kaylee and hoped that breathing in the hallway would prove less of a challenge.

Yeah, not so much. Students streamed both ways along the corridor, some rushing to class, others meandering. All of them varying degrees of loud. And with the exception of the few I exchanged hellos with in class, virtually every one of them was a stranger.

Plus there were no windows in this particular hallway, just rows of chipped forest-green lockers and classroom doors. Between the lack of natural light and the narrow space, it felt like we'd been thrust inside a long, narrow trap.

"Where to?" Kaylee said as Hunter emerged. After he told her where his next class was—Room 132, Mr. Chesky—she tucked her hand into the crook of his elbow and tugged him along like a reluctant pull toy. I followed on her other side as she navigated us down the hall.

"So, you're from San Diego? What's it like there? Awesome, I bet. Do you surf?"

I peeked in front of Kaylee and watched Hunter tug his earlobe before responding.

"Yes," he said solemnly. "If you don't surf, you don't graduate."

Kaylee's eyes widened. "No way, really?"

A twitch of his lips gave him away. She squealed. "Oh my gosh, you're evil! Mila, can you believe this guy? He's barely here for three seconds and he's already teasing me!"

And now all of Clearwater High knew about it, since Kaylee's voice echoed down the corridor.

I coughed to cover my laugh. For all her good grades, Kaylee could really act dim-witted around boys, but they usually never called her on it.

Until now.

In her typical babble-a-thon manner, Kaylee managed to quiz Hunter on everything from whether he owned a pet—no—to his favorite singer—Jack Johnson—before we'd even turned the corner. Of course, his monosyllabic answers gave her plenty of time to talk.

Instead of listening to her, I watched him. He walked gracefully, like an athlete. He had a tiny mole on his left cheek, just where a dimple would be, and whenever Kaylee asked him a question that seemed this side of too personal—like did he get along with his parents—he looked down at the ground before responding.

About five doors away from his drop-off spot, she finally abandoned the one-sided questioning and launched into telling him all about us.

"I'm from here, born and raised. Sad, isn't it? But Mila's not. Poor thing moved here from Philly a few weeks ago, when her dad died. We've been buds ever since," she said, hooking her arm through mine and resting her head on my shoulder.

"When her dad died . . ."

I stiffened. Great. Unintentional or not, she'd managed to up my pathetic quotient and spew private details of my life, all in a few breezy sentences.

"Right," I mumbled. Hunter stopped walking, which had a domino effect since Kaylee currently linked the three of us into some kind of crazy human chain. Kaylee jerked to a stop first, then me. I looked up to see Hunter staring at me over the top of her frizzy head.

"Sorry."

Sorry. That was all he said. It was what he didn't say that spoke volumes. He didn't try to change the subject, or make hasty excuses to leave, the way Kaylee's friends usually did.

For once, I didn't feel like having a dead parent was contagious. "Thanks."

The slam of a nearby locker interrupted us.

"Come on, we're going to be late." Kaylee's voice sounded this side of sulky while her hand tugged on us, prompting the human chain back into motion. "Oh, look. There's Parker and Ella." If possible, she sounded even less enthusiastic than before, and I watched in surprise as she ducked her head. Too late. The girls saw us.

Hunter's head whipped up. I had a sudden impression of a deer in the headlights. I guess the idea of two more girls converging on him was too much to bear. Not that I could blame him, I thought, watching Parker flounce over in skinny jeans, while Ella trotted her shorter legs to keep up. It was kind of like watching a pack of piranhas descend on a particularly tasty fish.

"My classroom," Hunter said before breaking free and loping ahead.

"Hey, will we see you at lunch?" Kaylee called after him.

He mumbled something about "dunno—forms to fill out" before escaping to the sanctuary of Room 132.

The instant he disappeared around the corner, Kaylee

turned on the girls with a fierce scowl. "Less obvious next time, okay?"

I blinked. How could they be any more obvious than Kaylee herself?

But I held my tongue as Kaylee launched into a blow-by-blow of our march down the hall, instead following Hunter's lead and slipping away to my class. Only, unlike with Hunter, I don't think anyone noticed.

Until Parker pulled away from the group and followed me, a sly smile on her face. While I paused in surprise, she leaned in close, like she wanted to share something special.

Oh, it was special, all right. "See that?" she whispered, wiggling her fingers at someone in greeting. Even when she was talking to me, I didn't have her full attention. "It's happening already. Kaylee's interest in new toys only lasts so long. You got extra mileage because you were from out of town, but now that Hunter's around . . ."

She straightened, and her smile widened into a careless grin. "Let's just say I'll give you a week, tops, before you're sitting at your own lunch table in the corner. Even less if you keep looking at Hunter like that. Kaylee doesn't like to share."

And then, with a satisfied sigh, she whirled and disappeared down the hall.

I shook my head and entered my classroom, wondering for the billionth time what Kaylee saw in her.

FOUR

When the lunch bell rang, I decided to ditch the hordes of ravenous students and head outside. Even on a good day, I hated the cafeteria, with its crowds and fluorescent glare—every time I walked inside, I instantly felt on display. And after Parker's extreme cattiness earlier, well . . . let's just say my enthusiasm for group dining had fallen to an all-time low.

I reached the door that led to my escape path, to the lone bench in the completely ignored courtyard. No other kids to deal with there, just a patch of grass, three overgrown trees, and a slightly lopsided rendition of the school's cartoon lion mascot.

When I pushed open the door, frigid air blasted my cheeks. The news had called for an uncharacteristically dreary fall week, and so far, the weather was cooperating. A bonus for me, since chill and drizzle never bothered me but seemed to lock the rest of the student body inside.

Well, all except for one.

The door clattered shut behind me, a noise that announced my arrival with gunshot subtlety to the lone figure commandeering *my* spot.

I inspected him from behind drooping tree branches, completely conscious of the curious eyes peering back at me through a kaleidoscope of red-orange-brown. Hunter didn't sit on the bench like a normal person. Instead he perched on top of the backrest, his feet planted against the blue boards that made up the seat. His jacket hood was pulled up over his head, his elbows balanced on his knees. Cradled between his hands was a battered book. So much for those papers he had to fill out.

Okay . . . now what? I scanned the tiny oval courtyard for potential escape routes, for any other seating destination that wouldn't make me look like a giant stalker. But there was nothing, unless I fancied sitting on the wet grass or the dirty and equally wet concrete—neither of which were particularly tempting.

Just when I'd decided that waving and then bolting for the door would be my least embarrassing option, Hunter spoke from beneath his black hood.

"Did I steal your spot?"

"Technically, no. I mean, it's not my spot. It belongs to the school."

Heat rushed into my cheeks. Wow. Okay, so yes, *technically* my words were true, but that didn't mean I had to go all dork and say them.

Hunter's soft laugh floated through the courtyard, loosening the knot in my stomach. A second later, my laugh joined his. "I come out here to get away sometimes, but obviously you were here first, so I'll just leave," I said.

He scooted over to the far edge of the bench, leaving a gaping expanse of blue wood on the side closest to me. "Plenty of room."

I caught my lower lip with my teeth. Tempting. Especially considering the alternative—the sense of isolation that ironically grew more pronounced in a crowd. "You sure?"

He shrugged, a rise and fall of broad shoulders meant to convey disinterest. Only his fingers gave him away. They drummed against his knee, hinting at whatever lurked beneath his seemingly apathetic exterior. That tiny burst of motion—of lean, restless fingers striking worn denim—somehow demoted him from intimidating to approachable.

I remembered the way he'd stared out the window in homeroom, his quiet contemplation a huge contrast to the loud voices that echoed throughout the hallways.

"Okay." I ducked under the tree branch and followed the brick-lined path to the bench. No big deal. I'd sit on my edge of the bench, he'd stay on his, and we'd ignore each other.

Great idea in theory. Hard to execute in real life. Because as I positioned myself on my half, I was aware of the steady rate of Hunter's inhalations and exhalations, the way he smelled like laundry detergent and something spicier—sandalwood—and how he tapped his foot on the bench beside me while he read. Twenty-two times per minute.

I snuggled into Dad's shirt. My plan had been to let the memories roll through my head, but I don't know. I felt strangely exposed with Hunter sitting next to me. Instead, I closed my eyes and tried to count the individual drizzle droplets as they landed, feather soft, on my face.

After an unproductive three minutes, Hunter's book crinkled. "You're Maya, right?" he asked.

An unexpected disappointment stabbed me. I opened my eyes. "Close. Mila."

"Sorry. Mi-la." The way he carefully drew my name out gave it a mellifluous quality I'd never heard before.

He nodded absently, his fingers drumming away on his left knee. I waited for a follow-up question. Instead, he hunched his shoulders and stopped tapping to turn the page on his comic.

I tried to shift my attention back to the courtyard, my shoes, anything besides Hunter, but the six-foot figure of damp, mussed, and brooding boy proved just a little too potent to ignore. I had a sudden craving to hear him say my name again, with that same melodic tone.

Mi-la.

I stifled a groan. Perfect. Kaylee's boy-crazy ways must be rubbing off on me.

Hunter tilted his head up to the sky, closing his eyes and letting drizzle dampen his cheeks and eyelashes. Any other guy at our school would have looked silly in that position, like he was posing or something. Hunter just looked . . . peaceful. "The rain doesn't bother you?" he said, seemingly half asleep.

I glanced up at the drifting mass of gray. The clouds blocked out any trace of brightness, casting the entire school in a haze of blah. "It's actually a relief."

He shot me a sideways glance, the curious rise of his eyebrows making me want to retract my words. I'd revealed too much. Any second now, and I'd get the pitying look. Any second now . . .

Instead his mouth softened into a smile. "Yeah" was all he said before closing his eyes again.

Just *yeah*. Nothing more. But that one *yeah* hinted at more understanding than a whole hour of lunch-table babble with Kaylee's friends.

That one *yeah* unburdened me, like maybe I'd finally stumbled upon someone who could accept me as I was. This post-Philly, post-Dad version of me—not some happy, unfettered, whole version that everyone seemed to want. Including Mom.

Maybe here, at last, was someone I could talk to. Only, as luck would have it, I couldn't think of a thing to say.

I fumbled for a suitable conversational topic. Horses came to mind, but I had no idea if he rode or, like Parker, thought they were "smelly giants with big teeth." No, I needed something he was interested in.

What did I know about him so far? Not much. He was new, he was from San Diego. He smelled a thousand times better than the guy who sat next to me in English. My gaze fell to the book in his lap. Instead of rows of words, it was full of pictures.

"What's that about?"

"*Ghost in the Shell*? The usual. Good guys versus bad. Major Motoko versus the Puppeteer." He coughed, nudged his backpack with his shoe. "I should probably put it away. The rain . . ."

Before he closed the book, I peeked at the graphics. I saw a girl with wild hair and a futuristic outfit, holding a big gun, standing in front of a weird-looking machine. Interesting, and definitely not the usual sort of thing students carted around with them here.

I pulled my knees to my chest and watched him unzip his bag and stuff the book in.

"Are you a fan of manga?"

I hugged my legs tighter and wondered how to respond. "Don't think so" was what I settled on. Not a total lie, but not an uncomfortable truth, either. "But I do like to read. Did you bring that with you in the move?" I couldn't imagine he'd picked it up in Clearwater.

"Yeah. We had a great bookstore back in San Diego. They kept a manga collection, special ordered anything they didn't stock."

His slow sigh triggered an echoing wistfulness in me. Oddly enough, the knowledge that I wasn't the only one longing for the past made my loneliness dissipate, just a teensy bit. Even if that longing was only for a bookstore, it served as a reminder. I wasn't completely alone in this feeling. Hunter had been forced to leave favorite things behind, too.

With one arm still cradling my knees, I pulled the other up to rest against my cheek. To breathe in Dad's flannel, searching for the minuscule trace of his scent that remained, the smell of sweet, pine-scented cologne. Every day it faded, leaving me terrified of the day the smell would disappear completely and I'd lose that last link.

"Gonna have to trek to Minneapolis to find a decent bookstore." He paused, then added. "If you ever want to come with . . ."

"Okay," I murmured past the giant knot clogging my throat. His kindness, losing Dad; my feelings were all blending together into one big explosive concoction. Who knew which emotion would burst free at any given time?

"Hey. You okay?"

I swallowed hard, nodded, not trusting myself to speak.

"That your dad's shirt?"

I nodded again.

"He died . . . recently?"

I cleared my throat, forced air into my lungs. All this time, I'd been complaining about how everyone tiptoed around Dad's death. Only a hypocrite wouldn't answer.

"Yeah. In a fire."

I heard his shoes scrape wood as he shifted positions. "Rough. Were you there?"

Supposedly. I sifted through my memory again, seeking flames, smoke, anything. Like every other time, nothing came.

And then I heard a scream. In my head, a girl's scream.

The sound made the hair on the back of my neck prickle. But the only images to accompany it were those same white walls, a white lab coat. The smell of bleach.

Still no fire.

"I don't remember."

I felt his surprise more than saw it, because as soon as the words came tumbling out, I closed my eyes. I couldn't believe I'd said that, and yet . . . instant relief.

The weight of his hand on my shoulder shocked me. "You okay?" he repeated. Softly.

"Yeah. But I don't really want to talk about it anymore."

When I peeked up between a few loose strands of hair, I was stunned to see that he wasn't giving me one of those "what's her deal?" looks, one of Parker's specialties. "No problem."

He closed his eyes. This time, the silence felt companionable. If I could have sat out there for the rest of the day, just feeling normal in someone else's company for a change, I would have done it in a flash. But after a while, the warning bell stuttered its crazy ring, signaling lunch's end.

Hunter groaned. He stretched his long arms over his head, an act that pulled his shirt tight across his chest and accentuated the fact that muscles existed there. I felt my cheeks flush and looked at my feet, whereas Kaylee would have squealed. Not that I couldn't appreciate his physical attractiveness, because apparently I could. A lot.

But what was really compelling about him was his sensitivity. Something that none of the other girls even cared enough to discover before deciding he was potential boyfriend material.

That notion made me want to stuff him into my backpack and hide him away.

"Want to trade cell numbers? Just to talk and stuff," he said.

I ducked my head before he could see my smile widen into an obnoxiously goofy grin. I gave him my number as I pulled my phone out of my bag. "What's yours?"

My hands vibrated two seconds later.

Our gazes locked while I pushed send and lifted the phone to my mouth. "Hello?"

"Now you've got it," Hunter said. In stereo. He ended the call, tilting his head as he studied my phone. "A Samsung ie80? They still make those? No surfing for you, huh?"

I sighed, glaring at my phone. "No. My mom's sort of anti-internet. Anti-computers, really. She won't even let me get a laptop."

He looked startled; the same look everyone gave when they found out Mom chose to shun modern technology. One girl had even asked if I was Amish. "Parents" was all he finally said, though. With a knowing smile.

We headed up the path leading back into school, side by side.

"What class do you have next?" he asked, just before we reached the door.

"Pre-calc. You?"

"AP chemistry."

See that? Not even remotely dim. "Cool."

When we reached the door, he leaned across me to open it. The brush of his arm across my shoulder sent a shiver rushing through me. I stepped into the congested hallway and fumbled to put a name to the strange feeling, just as a familiar voice rang out.

"Hey, Mila, there you are! And . . . you *ran into* Hunter?"

Kaylee stood a few feet away, arms crossed over her chest, forming a platform-heeled, long-legged obstacle that students veered to avoid hitting. Her emphasis on "ran into" wasn't lost on me, even in the din of chattering voices and footsteps as kids rushed to their next class.

Her gaze touched on me, lingered longer on Hunter and even longer on the cell phones we still clutched in our hands. I shoved mine into my bag, even though I wasn't sure why, exactly. I hadn't done anything wrong.

She stepped closer, her grin flashing fewer teeth than usual. "So what were you guys doing out there? Was Mila helping you fill out your forms?"

Hunter shrugged and shook his hair out of his face. "Something like that," he said. And then he winked at me before merging into the flow of students and ambling down the hallway.

Kaylee pressed a hand to her chest and watched his retreat. "Mysterious guys are so hot."

But the second he was out of sight, her playfulness vanished. She whirled on me with her hands on her hips. "Is that why you ditched us at lunch today, so you could get Hunter all to yourself? What, are you some kind of stalker now? Oh my god, Mila, that is so uncool!"

Red blotches erupted on her cheeks, and her voice rose with each question, loud enough to garner sideways looks from the kids passing by. Two girls from our homeroom started whispering, while a trio of boys poked one another and laughed.

"Shhhh!" I said.

"What, am I embarrassing you?" she said in an even louder voice. "About HUNTER?"

More kids turned to look, triggering that trapped feeling again. My muscles tensed. I wanted out of the public eye. *Now.*

In a quick movement hidden by the position of her body, I grabbed Kaylee's upper arm. Then I pulled her to the door and yanked it open. My momentum propelled both of us outside, away from the streaming students and their way-too-curious eyes.

"Mila, you're hurting me!" Kaylee tugged against my grip.

With dawning horror, I looked down to see I was squeezing her upper arm. I released my grip, and her other hand immediately rubbed the spot. "What's your deal?" she said, her stare all brown-eyed accusation.

I shook my head, dazed, gaping at the way she cradled her arm to her chest. Seriously, what *was* my deal?

I couldn't believe I'd just grabbed Kaylee like that, out of nowhere. What a terrible thing to do.

"Kaylee, I'm so sorry. I didn't mean to hurt you. There were all those people, and I just . . . get a little claustrophobic sometimes. I didn't think."

Between the jump with Bliss and my booth dive at Dairy Queen, there seemed to be a lot of that going on lately. Too much.

"You're a nut, you know that?" she said, still clutching her arm.

My chin whipped up and down in my enthusiasm to agree. "I'll work on it, promise."

"Do that," she said, shaking her head before walking off.

I tried to dismiss the incident. Really, I did. But a tiny, niggling worry made it difficult. The truth was, I hadn't even been trying to grab Kaylee's arm with any real degree of force. I definitely hadn't been trying to hurt her.

So how on earth had it happened?

FIVE

The worry still niggled at me after dinner that night, when Mom's yell summoned me from my book.

"Mila, come here!"

With a sigh, I jabbed my bookmark into the middle of *The Handmaid's Tale* and rolled off the green-and-gold quilt that came with the room and always smelled faintly of mothballs and lavender. Rain tap-tapped an offbeat rhythm against the window. Figuring she wanted me to check on the horses, I slipped my feet into my discarded Nikes and headed down the hall.

Mom waited by the coat rack, practically drowning in the brown fleece blanket she'd tossed over her shoulder. An unusually wide grin spread across her face. The sight of that smile, aimed at me, melted away any residual craving for

Atwood and my bed. That was a smile from the old days. A smile that banished some of my loneliness and promised good things to come.

I almost didn't want to say anything, in case talking broke the spell, but curiosity won out. "What are we doing?"

She pulled the front door open. "We're going to watch the storm."

I swung my legs back and forth against the rickety porch edge. Mom's suggestion to go outside and experience the storm had sounded crazy at first, not to mention extremely un-Mom-like. But I couldn't say no. Not when the invitations were so few and far between.

Raindrops splattered against my upturned palms. As usual, Mom was right—there was nothing quite like experiencing a Midwest storm firsthand. The sky's vivid light show, the thick humidity that made my jeans cling to my legs, the smell of electricity and damp dirt, it enveloped us.

"Isn't this amazing?" Mom asked.

In a stun of disbelief, I watched her peel off her boots and toss them over her shoulder. They hit the porch with a thud while she wiggled her bare toes under the drizzle. Her sigh was pure bliss. Yep. Decidedly un-Mom-like.

"You should try it."

My shoes were stripped off before she could realize the storm had addled her brain. Under the dim light and mist, our naked skin glowed a ghostly white.

"Feels great, doesn't it?"

The tiny drops felt wet more than anything, but her enjoyment was infectious. What really felt great was her acceptance. "Definitely."

Another diagonal of light cracked the night sky. For a moment, all of Clearwater was illuminated, like someone had switched on a giant spotlight. Just as quickly, the brightness was snatched away and darkness returned, broken only by the glow from our kitchen window.

"One one thousand, two one thousand, three one thousand, four one thousand, five—" A deep rumble overhead cut off Mom's strange chant.

"What's the counting for?"

"Just something . . . we used to do together."

My legs stopped moving. Mom rarely talked about the past, especially not in the context of things we'd done together. I got the distinct impression that she wanted nothing more than to wipe the slate clean. To start completely fresh here in Clearwater.

Too many questions to name spiraled through my head. In the interest of starting small, I latched onto one of the most innocuous ones.

"Did I use to like nail polish? I mean, before?" I asked, thinking back to Kaylee's Dairy Queen convo.

I knew I'd made the right decision when even that

simple, fluffy inquiry caused her to flinch. I held my breath, half expecting her to ignore me.

"Yes. When you were little. But . . . but only toenail polish, and only if your dad and I would wear it, too."

She started off hesitantly, but the longer she talked, the more the story gained steam. "In fact, this one time, your dad forgot to take it off, and then he went to the gym . . . well, you can imagine the looks he got."

She reached out to squeeze my shoulder, laughing. "Can't you picture it? Your big, manly father . . . sporting pink sparkle nail polish."

And with her words as my guide, I could picture it. My stout, dark-haired father. Standing in his gym shorts in the locker room and shaking his head at his sparkling toes. I reveled in the image for a moment before pressing on. Her laughter, the shoulder squeeze, had made me bold.

"Did the doctors do anything to my ears, after the fire?"

The second her hand dropped away, I knew I'd made a mistake, pushed too far. But I pressed on. "I have this memory. Of a man, in a white coat. And he did something to my ear. . . ."

It was no use. Even in the dim light, I could see her lips press together. She wrapped her arms around her waist, angled her head away from me, did everything short of slapping duct tape on her mouth and flashing a DON'T ASK sign.

"Why won't you answer me?" I whispered, even as the

familiar weight of rejection settled on my shoulders. "Please. This has been hard for me, too." I hated the beggarlike quality to my voice, but I couldn't help it.

Her hand lifted, like she might stroke my cheek, the way she used to in Philly every night before bed, back when her nails weren't brown from horse grime or pungent with liniment. I caught my breath while seconds built up between us. While my heart pounded out its yearning for a return of that nighttime ritual.

She shoved her hands into her lap and turned back to the storm.

I curled my toes to subdue the building scream. Had my faulty memory erased some terrible thing I'd done—was that it? Was that why Mom couldn't resurrect even a tiny piece of our old relationship? Why I'd somehow lost both parents when only one had burned in the fire?

Under the cover of my hair, I pressed a trembling hand to my own cheek, half expecting to touch something repugnant. Instead, my skin felt normal. Slightly slick from the moisture-filled air, but warm and soft. Nothing that should scare a mother away.

"Why don't you love me anymore?" I whispered, to no one, really. Because I knew she wouldn't answer.

I rose. Though the storm still raged overhead, its allure drained away as surely as the water that dripped from my hem and pooled at my feet.

"The counting gives you an approximation of how far away the lightning really is. Five seconds for every mile."

Mom's steady voice paused me after only one step. Was this her deluded attempt at an olive branch? *Sorry, Mila, can't hug you, but I can inundate you with random facts about storms.*

Gee, thanks.

I didn't have to listen to this.

Anger fueled my short walk to the door. I opened it, determined to escape to the safe haven of my room, where Atwood and my smelly quilt awaited.

"The thunder comes after the lightning, but it's an illusion. It just seems that way because the speed of light is faster than the speed of sound."

My grip tightened on the doorknob. I'd asked for her love, and instead got the speed of sound? Really?

"Also, the lightning bolt we see doesn't really originate from the sky. It comes from the ground up."

That did it. The door slam echoed in the night. I whirled, glaring at the sight of her slender back and that sleek, serene ponytail. "Why are you telling me this?"

I don't care about the origins of lightning bolts and the speed of sound! I wanted to scream. *I care about things that matter.* About my missing memory and her missing love, about the wrenching pain in my heart that never went away. Not about some stupid storm in the middle of stupid Minnesota.

Not about—

Another white line forked across the sky. I caught a flash of sagging porch and Mom's hand clenched around that stupid birthstone necklace before darkness reclaimed them. It couldn't reclaim my spark of intuition.

"Are you trying to say things aren't always the way they appear? What, Mom? What isn't how it appears?"

Boards creaked and thunder rumbled, but there was no reply.

No reply. Right. Just like there was nothing I could say to change anything. Still, I took a grim satisfaction in correcting her. "You don't even have your facts right. Not everyone sees lightning from the top down. I don't."

Before I could head inside, something interrupted my brilliant exit.

I cocked my head. "Did you hear that?"

"What?"

"A noise. From the barn." Over the patter of rain, I'd heard it.

Clank.

"There it goes again."

Mom was on her feet in an instant. Barefoot, she raced for the front door, shoving it open so hard that the bottom smacked the doorstop and bounced back. She darted inside and reemerged seconds later, wielding the giant Maglite she stashed in a kitchen drawer for emergencies. Weapon in hand, she leaped off the porch and ran for the barn.

"Mom?" When she didn't look back, I sprinted after her, my feet slapping the wet path while muddy water squished between my toes. I rounded the corner of our guesthouse in time to see Mom reach the oversized barn door, to hear the nickers and snorts that burst within at her arrival. Louder than usual.

Someone had left the door ajar.

My neck prickling, I pulled up behind Mom as she yanked the door open.

"Hello?" she called out, flipping on the light.

Her voice echoed back through the rafters, as even-keeled as ever. But in her right hand, the super-long, super-heavy Maglite was clenched and at the ready. Shoulder level, like a baseball bat.

Nothing but silence followed, except for the intermittent raindrops that drummed against the vaulted roof. And then a high-pitched whinny, and straw rustling under restless hooves.

Mom took four careful steps inside, half crouched like some kind of jungle cat. I knew I shouldn't be surprised, that Mom was ultracapable under any circumstance. Still, the transformation from mild-mannered veterinarian to prowling tiger was a little terrifying. Why would a few strange noises make her react this way?

Everything seemed normal. The sweet-sour smell of hay

and horse bodies mingled into its familiar musk. The rows of pine stalls on either side of the empty corridor looked as tidy as ever, and the stall doors were all closed, as they should be. Since we tended to leave the green-barred windows open, a few inquisitive horse heads poked out over the tops. Also normal.

And yet . . . there was almost no way Mom had forgotten to latch that door. Not after the minilecture I'd gotten when we first moved here. Plus she was so vigilant about locking the guesthouse, you'd think we stored diamonds in our beds.

Mom peered over her shoulder and spotted me. I could see fear in the wide blue eyes behind her rain-splotched glasses, in the way she stabbed a finger toward the door.

"Outside," she mouthed.

I clenched my jaw and shook my head, even though squeezing air into my ever-tightening lungs had become tricky. No way was I leaving her here, to deal with . . . *whatever* . . . on her own.

I must have had my determined face on, because she didn't bother with a second hopeless attempt to send me fleeing. Instead she motioned me toward the stalls on the right side of the corridor, while she crept to the left.

She leaned her upper body into the open window of the first stall, looking for what, I didn't know. But her paranoia was contagious. Feeling wound up enough to explode at the slightest sound, I peered into the first stall on my side. Gentle Jim's quarters. When the big roan gelding saw me, he lumbered over and nosed me in the forehead, hoping I'd slip him a carrot from my pocket. The stall was empty except for him. Leaning over, I quietly grabbed his tin feed bucket and a steel-clipped lead. Just in case. Not my first choice in weaponry, but they were better than nothing.

I checked the next two stalls. Nothing but groggy horses.

Clank.

Loud. Just like I'd heard it before. Coming from the row of stalls around the corner.

Mom's head whipped toward the noise. I tiptoed across the concrete floor, dodging unswept pieces of hay but ignoring the growing collection of grit and other unsavory substances on the balls of my bare feet.

As soon as I was close enough, Mom grabbed my head with one firm hand. My heart galloped as she pressed her mouth close to my ear. "I'm going to check it out," she whispered. "Wait here. If you hear anything, run."

I tried to shake my head, but her grip tightened, pressing me even closer. Her breath hissed between her teeth and collided with my earlobe, which I swear was already jumping from the *thud-thud-thud* of my pulse. "Mila. Please."

As soon as she let go and rounded the corner ahead, I took off on stealthy feet after her, clutching my makeshift weapons like they were swords rather than random barn utensils.

When I reached the corner, I noticed the first three stalls in the next corridor had their green-barred windows tightly shut. Empties. There were a lot of those, space vacated by the boarders who came when the Greenwood family was actually in residence. Mom stalked past them. She moved so quietly, so smoothly, that her blond ponytail barely bobbed behind her.

She was only three stalls from the end of the row when we heard it again.

Clank.

Our heads swiveled as one toward the last stall on the right. My breath hitched in my throat. If there was a crazy stalker or horse thief in there, he or she could probably hear my heart slamming against my rib cage by now.

But under the rapid-fire beat of my heart lurked something else. An anticipatory tightening of my muscles, an unshakable determination to help Mom.

No matter what.

I traced Mom's careful footsteps as she picked out a silent path that led to that last stall. I watched while those slender, capable fingers wrapped around the handle, squeezed, and eased the door open.

Maisey let out a startled whinny when Mom leaped across the threshold, Maglite poised for action.

The long black flashlight lowered an instant later.

"What the . . . ?" I heard Mom say as I leaned into the

stall. Maisey was the lone occupant.

My heart decelerated to a gentler rhythm while I scratched the mare's soft muzzle. Meanwhile, Mom performed an itemized inspection of the stall's contents, running her hands along the walls. She stopped on the feed bucket attached to the wall.

Slipping farther inside, she reached over and pulled the bucket away from the wall, then pushed it forward.

Clank.

"Silly girl. Was that you, playing with your bucket? Mrs. Greenwood warned me about that," Mom said, her laugh flowing like water; the easiest, purest laugh I'd her from her in ages. The sound released the tension from my limbs, like a valve had opened up and drained it all away. Part of me wanted to join in. The other part worried. This type of reaction, it wasn't Mom. Had Dad's death finally sent her over the edge?

But when Mom slipped her arm around my shoulder and smiled at me, I gave in to the laughter, pushed aside the niggling voices.

Like a squirrel, I felt compelled to store every spare scrap of affection I could find. You never knew when winter would strike and make the scraps scarce again.

It wasn't until we reached the barn door that Mom's smile slipped.

I followed her gaze and realized what she was thinking.

"I'm sorry I left the door open. I was in a hurry and forgot."

Her brows lowered at that news. And then she laughed it off. "Actually, I'm relieved it was you. This time," she tacked on hastily. "You need to be more careful in the future."

The thing was, I was pretty sure I had closed the barn door. But as we ran from the barn back to the house, the tiny lie felt worth it. There was no sense in making Mom worry unnecessarily. I mean, despite her obvious jitters, we were in Clearwater. What could possibly happen here?

The question I should have been asking myself was, how had I possibly heard Maisey banging her feed bucket from so far away? But the thought didn't even occur to me. Not until it was way too late.

SIX

The next morning, I felt the happiest I had in weeks. My newfound camaraderie with Mom made my smiles come easier and the hallways seem less overwhelming. Kaylee snapped her fingers just as we reached her locker. "Shoot, I left my economics book in the car—I wanted to try to study for that quiz during homeroom."

Yesterday's weirdness seemed to have blown over. I hadn't mentioned her little freakout, and in return, she hadn't brought up mine.

"Do you want me to go with you?" I said, just as the warning bell rang.

She speed-walked toward the main door, fast as her three-inch heels would allow. "No, you go ahead," she called over her shoulder. "I'll only be a second."

I settled into my usual spot in homeroom. Even though I purposely tried to ignore the students already in class, apparently that was too big a challenge for my analytical brain. Five boys, three girls. None of them Hunter.

I smiled at all of them anyway.

I busied myself digging a notebook out of my backpack. Still, I sensed Hunter's presence several seconds before he dropped into Kaylee's spot next to me.

"Hey," he said in his soft voice, those blue eyes fixed on me beneath a sweep of messy hair.

"Hi." Nervous flutters kicked up inside me. Silly. He was just a boy. Okay, not entirely true. He was a boy Kaylee happened to like.

Kaylee, who'd be back any second, expecting to sit in her spot.

Nervous flutters or not, the boy had to sit somewhere else.

Just then, Hunter dropped his backpack on the desk and laid his head against it. Closed his eyes.

My heart softened into what felt like a big, mushy pile of goo. He looked so tired, young even, with his dark eyelashes fanning across the tops of his cheeks. His mouth softened, too. I had a sudden yearning to trace that lopsided top lip with my finger.

Whoa.

I was so caught up in that crazy thought that the footsteps

I'd heard clicking in the hall didn't register at first. The kind of clicking made by high-heeled shoes.

Oh, no.

I straightened. "Hunter, you need to—" The final bell cut me off, as did the tiny gasp I heard from the open doorway behind me.

Kaylee stood there, freshly glossed lips parted in surprise. She took two steps toward her occupied desk before pausing to smooth her purple tunic dress uncertainly, gaze flitting from Hunter to me.

"Kaylee, hey! Hunter was just hanging out here for a sec—" I started, only to be cut off again, this time by Mrs. Stegmeyer.

"Ms. Daniels, please take an empty seat if you don't want to be marked tardy," our homeroom teacher said over the top of her magazine.

Kaylee's gaze lingered on her usual spot for a millisecond longer, prompting me into action. "Hunter," I whispered. His eyelashes swept open. The task of kicking him out of the seat became a hundred times harder under that sleepy blue stare. "Um, would you mind moving? This is where Kaylee sits."

He sat up, glanced at Kaylee like he was seeing her for the first time, then swooped up his backpack and stood. "Yeah. Sorry," he said. His sheepish grin was the best parting gift he could give, because I could tell it practically melted her on the spot. He loped over to the empty desk he'd sat in last time.

She slid into the vacated seat with a huge sigh, while Mrs. Stegmeyer tapped her nails on the desk impatiently. "He warmed it up for me," she whispered, pretending to fan herself with a notebook. "At this very moment, I'm being warmed by Hunter Lowe's body heat."

A huge wave of relief hit me, prompting a louder giggle than I intended.

"Girls, please. It's time for the announcements," Mrs. Stegmeyer admonished.

Sure enough, the intercom screeched, followed by the overly peppy voice of our student council president.

I listened absently to news about an upcoming car wash fund-raiser while I whispered to Kaylee. "He just sort of . . . sat down. Uninvited."

Though, truth be told, I hadn't exactly fought him off with a stick.

She waved her hand. "Please. It's fine."

Fine, everything was fine.

"Girls . . . shhh!" Mrs. Stegmeyer tapped her lips and glared.

But as soon as the teacher looked away, Kaylee leaned over to whisper in my ear. "Really, don't worry. Nothing wrong with a little healthy competition."

What?

"Kaylee," I started. Only to be interrupted by the loud whack of the manila attendance file as it slapped the desk.

"Last warning before I separate you," Mrs. Stegmeyer said, her drawl thickening the way it did when she was upset.

I slouched into my chair and kept my mouth shut the rest of homeroom. But Kaylee's comment spun through my head, over and over again.

Healthy competition? Over Hunter? I didn't like the sound of that, not one tiny bit.

SEVEN

Kaylee's decrepit old truck bounced us down the dirt road, away from Clearwater High. Between the tires crunching over uneven terrain and the ancient engine's stuttering roar, the noise level was pretty high. Inside the cab, though, the silence was deafening. Kaylee clutched the zebra-striped steering wheel cover and refused to acknowledge me, her gaze directed straight ahead.

"Kaylee, I swear—I had nothing to do with Hunter transferring into my English class." Of course, I'd been pleading my innocence for the past ten minutes, and none of it had yet to make a dent in Kaylee's stony expression.

So much for her "healthy" competition.

I sighed and looked out the passenger window. From far off on the hillside, I saw flickering black strands slap a gleaming mahogany neck. The gorgeous stallion threw his head again before rearing up and launching his massive body into an explosive gallop.

Horses. Horses were one of two things that had kept me from losing my mind when I first moved here.

The other thing was Kaylee.

I peeked at her face again, but her usual smiling mouth remained tight and silent. I couldn't remember a single ride in this truck without a soundtrack of relentless Kaylee babble to make me laugh. Not until now.

A perfect image of Hunter's face, with his careless fall of soft brown waves framing a pair of intense blue eyes, crystallized in my head. Stupid. Picturing him right now only made this harder. But even if Hunter Lowe was the most interesting thing to happen to Clearwater in, well, ever—at least since I'd lived here—a silly crush couldn't take precedence over a friendship. That wasn't the kind of person Mom had raised me to be.

I needed to put a stop to this. I wanted babbling Kaylee back. After all, she was the only thing that had kept me from being a complete outcast at school. Surely I owed her for that.

"Look, this is ridiculous. We shouldn't be fighting over some guy . . . just because he's not into Carhartt and partying down by the river," I added, to lighten the mood. Though there was much more to Hunter than that. Something about the quiet way he studied me with those blue eyes when I talked, like he really cared about what I was saying, made the rest of the world just melt away.

And I needed that right now, the world melting away. But not at someone else's expense.

I thought I saw Kaylee's death grip on the wheel relax, just a teensy bit. Springs creaked as she adjusted her position. But no smile.

"I'm not sure, Mila," Kaylee said, finally glancing my way. "How do I know I can trust you?"

"Look, I swear—I did not tell him to switch to my English class. You can ask him, if you don't believe me."

While I would have loved to believe that he'd transferred because of me, he'd told me the move was solely based on his desire for a more ambitious reading list.

She released the wheel with one hand to smooth the neck of her aqua cowl-necked sweater, one of her amazing do-it-yourself creations. "Please. He'd think I was an idiot." But her voice didn't hold quite the edge it had just moments ago.

She peeked at me, nibbling her lower lip. Then her shoulders deflated. "Though I'm doing a pretty good job of acting like one on my own, aren't I?"

"Hey, me too," I said. Not thinking so much of Hunter as I was that time when I'd grabbed her arm.

Her smile was timid, not the carefree Kaylee smile I was used to. Nevertheless, I'd take what I could get.

"So, let's just—wait! Oh my god, there he is!" Kaylee yelled.

For an instant, my logic deserted me. No . . . she couldn't mean . . .

My eyes flew open as the brakes squealed. I turned my head, searched for the object of Kaylee's pointing finger. Confusion hit first, followed by a flood of disappointment. Hunter. She'd meant Hunter.

Of course she had.

I grabbed hold of my fleeing composure while we bump-bump-bumped our way to the side of the road.

"Roll down your window, hurry!" Kaylee said, finger combing a few flyaway pieces of hair into order. Hunter was just turning to see who approached, his hands rammed into the pockets of black cargo pants.

I couldn't prevent the rush of excitement at the sight of him. Even though I gave myself stern orders to play it cool. I cranked the old rotor window down, the one that stuck for Kaylee's little brother and her mom but never gave me any problems at all.

Without the glass as a barrier, the smell of manure grew even headier.

"Hi, Mila," Hunter said. As usual, I noticed the way his lopsided smile upturned his lips, the left side just a little higher than the right. When he tilted his head, the hood of his black long-sleeved shirt pulled loose, unleashing that now-familiar tumble of brown waves. Waves that looked incredibly soft and practically begged for my fingers to run through them.

Okay, I really needed to stop. Kaylee and I had a deal.

I commanded my voice to sound nonchalant. "Hi, Hunt—"

"Hunter!" Kaylee squealed. "Hey, why don't you come with us? We're on our way to Dairy Queen, and you seriously don't want to pass up one of the best things this town has to offer!" Kaylee leaned across me for a better view, forcing me to smash my head against the crunchy old headrest if I didn't want to inhale a mouthful of her grapefruit-scented hair.

And wait . . . since when were we on our way to Dairy Queen?

I managed to wrestle my head out from behind hers. Hunter's blue gaze immediately captured mine, searching. I got that the-world-is-fading sensation all over again. Despite my best intentions, I felt a goofy smile crawl onto my mouth. "Sounds good," he finally said, still focused on me.

Meanwhile, Kaylee's smile faded. She watched him watching me, and her eyes narrowed. This time, her excitement seemed forced as she bounced up and down on the seat, sending the springs into a squeaky chorus. "Yay! Mila, you jump in the back so that Hunter can sit up front, okay?

We don't want to scare the new guy off by making him ride in the back of a pickup!"

Ha ha, very funny. "Good one, Kaylee, but how about I just squeeze closer to you?"

The edges of Kaylee's mouth fell. She lowered her voice. "What, so that you can be all pressed up against him like a saddle on a horse?" she hissed.

Seriously? "You told me less than two minutes ago that you were acting like an idiot. Well, guess what? You're doing it again," I whispered back.

Kaylee glared at me before gesturing to Hunter. "Wait a second—Mila was just getting out. She wanted some fresh air, anyway."

I gawked, trying to convince myself she was only acting crazy because Hunter had caught her by surprise. Later we'd laugh at her insanity.

Until she lowered her voice and said, "My truck, my rules. Get in the back or walk."

Okay, so laughing wasn't an option.

"You can't be serious."

"Out."

More than anything, it was the sudden tension in my hands that made me open the door and hop out. I couldn't be sure I wouldn't use them to grab Kaylee again.

Possibly around her neck this time.

When I leaped onto the grass before he could get in,

Hunter's smile fell. "Are you leaving?"

"No, just getting in the back," I said. Feeling like an utter moron at the surprised rise of his brows. "It's, uh, nice to see the landscape from a different perspective sometimes."

After letting loose with that little bit of ridiculousness, I clamped my big mouth shut and stomped around to the back of the pickup, climbed onto the dented rear bumper, and vaulted into the bed with a little more force than necessary. The stupid Chevy groaned.

"That's crazy," Hunter said. "Why don't I—"

"Nope, I'm good. I like it back here. It's nice." It was much easier pretending when I didn't have to look at him.

"Are you sure?" He sounded doubtful.

"Yep. Totally."

After another few moments, the front passenger door whined its way shut. The truck started lumbering down the road.

I scrambled across the bed so I could slump against the cab. Never in a million years would anyone have forced me into the back of a pickup truck in Philly. It was almost barbaric. Not to mention illegal.

I stamped my foot on the bed, hard. So hard that I managed to chip the paint.

Served her right. Kaylee had a lot to answer for later. No wonder she and Parker were such good friends.

The truck gathered speed. I had to throw my hands up to

keep from eating my hair. The road noise was pretty loud, but I could still catch the conversation going on inside the cab. The back window must have been cracked.

"Are you sure she's okay back there?" Hunter asked. I pictured him craning his head to look at me in the truck bed and kept my eyes on the trees fading behind us. He didn't need to see me with my face all red from the wind or my hair flapping around like it was alive.

One of the first things I'd learned in Clearwater: no one ever looks good with truck hair.

"Oh, she's fine. Like I said, she loves to ride in back. Must be a Philly thing."

I glared at the tailgate.

"That's right, she's from Philly. When did she move here again?"

"About a month ago."

"I've heard Philly's got a great art scene. Did she love it there?"

"Yeah, I guess." Even from the back I could hear the annoyance coating Kaylee's words like the fine layer of dust that coated the truck bed, and now, by virtue of my new seating arrangement, my jeans. "Hey, here's something fun that you can't do in a big city like Philly . . . practice your drag-racing skills. C'mon, let's see what old Butch here is really made of!"

And then the rest of her words processed. Drag racing?

Drag racing? Had she totally forgotten me back here?

"Hey, Kaylee!" I was just reaching around to rap on the window and get her attention when the truck bolted forward. My body lurched and my palms smacked the metal bed. Kaylee's whoop from up front was followed by an even bigger burst of speed. I grabbed for the side of the truck with my left hand.

My hair whipped my face as the truck went faster and faster, bouncing over the pockmarked road on less-than-optimal suspension. I could hear Hunter urging Kaylee to slow down, hear the thrum of the engine as she gunned it harder, and feel the truck accelerate. But under it all, I started to feel something new, something unexpected: a tiny thrill of exhilaration. The rush of embracing something dangerous started to eclipse the fear, sort of like when Bliss had taken me over that jump.

This was actually kind of fun.

The wind caught my gasping laugh and yanked it away as I slowly released my hand. Maybe this is what happened when you moved from big towns to tiny rural hole-in-the-walls . . . maybe it turned you into an adrenaline junkie. It was like my body was preparing for something it was meant to be doing. This really *was* fun. Great, even. I hadn't had this much fun since—

The slide to the left was sudden. So was the hard jerk to the right that followed. My arm scraped metal . . . just before I felt a surge of nothingness as my body went airborne.

One second I was flying, and the next, the scream tearing through my throat was silenced by the crushing impact.

I landed arm first on something sharp, felt a strange tearing sensation. Then I was tumbling. The world careened in a crazy spin as I bounced once, hit the ground again, and continued to roll. Tiny visual details repeated themselves—leaves, grass, blue sky—while I flipped around and around.

I landed at the bottom of the hill, staring up at a low patch of white clouds. Clouds of the stratocumulus type, if I wasn't mistaken.

My lips moved, but no sound came out, my voice strangled by the same shock that glued me to the ground. Shock, that had to be it. What else could explain the fact that I was lying here, analyzing types of clouds instead of massively freaking out?

Other concerns ripped through my head. Like, what on earth had just happened? Why wasn't I even the tiniest bit out of breath? Or—oh, god—why was I barely feeling any pain? Had I damaged my spine? What if I couldn't walk?

I wiggled my fingers, then my toes. So far, so good. I climbed to my feet, stunned to discover my dignity felt more damaged than anything else. I'd been unbelievably lucky.

"Mila!" Hunter's sure strides quickened his descent

down the hill, Kaylee tripping after him as fast as her black platform boots would allow. That's when the anger started to flare. "Kaylee Daniels, what is wrong with you? When your mom finds out, you are going to be grounded for life! You could have killed me!" I brushed at the grass clinging to my sweatshirt. Grass stains, I was going to have grass stains, I thought, somewhat clinically.

"Oh my god, Mila! Are you okay? I'm so, so sorry!" Kaylee sobbed, still several yards away. "Lie back down! You could have a back injury or something!"

Hunter raced to my side first. "She's right, you need to sit down. Are you hurt anywhere?"

"I . . . I don't think so," I said. Which really didn't make any sense, but I wasn't about to complain. "But my left arm feels kind of weird. On the outside, above my elbow."

"Here, let me see." Hunter cradled my wrist and lifted the flap of shredded material that used to be my sleeve. Since I was watching his face, I saw when his expression morphed from concern to shock, saw his eyes widen. "What the . . . ? *Mila?*"

This couldn't be good.

"Is it really that bad? Or are you just the type of guy who gets all squeamish at the tiniest drop of blood?" I twisted to get a better look at whatever had turned Hunter into a frozen, gaping statue, just as Kaylee stumbled up.

"I was so scared—I was sure you'd landed on that rusted

hunk of metal and killed yourself!" she said, pointing at the mangled remains of a car door near the top of the hill. "Thank—" Her shriek accompanied the hiss of my inhalation.

"Mila? Oh my god, Mila!" she said. "What—what is that? Because it isn't—"

"—blood," I breathed at the same time.

All three of us stared at my arm. And stared. And stared. It was like none of us could believe what we were seeing.

My arm wasn't bleeding at all. There was a huge, gaping tear in my skin, but no blood. No blood. No blood because instead of blood, a thin film of red had ruptured, allowing some disgusting milky-white liquid to leach from the wound and trickle down to my elbow.

And it got worse. Inside the cut, inside *me*, was this transparent tube with a minuscule jagged fissure shaped like a row of clamped teeth. And inside that? Something that looked like wires. Tiny silver wires, twisted like the double helixes we studied in biology.

No. No, no. I was hallucinating. I'd hit my head, after all, and I was hallucinating. That was the only explanation that made sense.

I snatched my arm away and glanced from Kaylee's horrified face to Hunter's shocked one. Of course, if I was hallucinating, so were they.

My hair whipped the air as my head shook side to side. I didn't understand any of this. "I can't . . . I don't . . . this is— Kaylee?" I lifted my hand, the one attached to my good arm, toward her. Only to watch her flinch away.

"Shhh, Mila, it's okay. Let's get you back in the truck," Hunter said, wrapping a tentative arm around my waist. "Can you walk if you lean on me a little?"

"Hospital," Kaylee blurted. "She needs to go to the hospital."

My head shook faster. "No, no hospital! How can I go to the hospital, when . . ." We all looked at my arm again, and we could all fill in the rest. How could I go to the hospital when I was such a freak? When they'd ask me questions and I'd have no answers? "No hospital," I repeated grimly. "No, no, NO!"

"It's okay, calm down. Kaylee? Kaylee! Could you help us out here a little? Come make sure she's steady on her feet."

For a second, I thought Kaylee was going to refuse. She looked ready to bolt. "Fine."

She arranged herself flush with my side, her reluctance evident in the way her arm slipped around my waist without actually touching me.

As soon as he saw Kaylee had me, Hunter stripped off his black hoodie, revealing a thin gray shirt underneath. He carefully wrapped the hoodie around my wound. Unlike Kaylee, his hands were firm and steady. He didn't so much as flinch.

"There you go—that should be okay for now." He gently

tugged me away from Kaylee, wrapped a firm arm around my waist, and started leading me up the hill.

The ride home was as silent as the ride out had been. The entire way, Hunter cradled my hand in his and watched me with hard-to-read eyes. Eyes that were probably trying to hide his stark horror over finding out I was some kind of freak of nature, a horror that echoed my own.

Kaylee refused to say a word. Actually, she wouldn't even look at us.

And all I could think was: *no blood*.

By the time we pulled up into our driveway, I was desperate to escape, even as dread crept through my chest on spiderlike legs. Because if anyone had answers, it would be Mom. And while part of me clamored for those answers, a tiny part, deep inside, whispered that maybe I was better off not knowing.

I scrambled out the door before anyone could speak, mumbled, "See you later," and tumbled into the late-afternoon air, a chill sweeping over me that hadn't been present before. Because even if the tiny part of me was right, it didn't matter. I had to know the truth.

As I rushed through the guesthouse front door, I told myself, *You're blowing it all out of proportion, Mila. Mom will explain it, and everything will be fine.*

I couldn't have been further from the truth if I'd tried.

EIGHT

I closed the door quietly behind me and just stood there in the entryway, staring right at the empty green-and-tan plaid couch without really seeing it. Dazed, and wishing there was a way to rewind the last hour of my life. Rewind and erase.

With a deep breath, I shoved open the white swinging door that separated the kitchen from the rest of the house, to find Mom rummaging in the white walk-in pantry.

The sight of her slim, jean-clad figure, shuffling through cereal boxes and containers like today was any other day, gave me a sudden urge to shake her. My arm looked like something out of a nightmare, and she was looking for a snack?

When she turned around, a bag of her favorite dried

pineapple in hand, she smiled and said, "Hey, honey. How was school today?"

I just stood, wordless, staring into Mom's familiar face. It was so hard to wrap my mind around the fact that sometime, somewhere, she had started keeping things from me. But when? Why?

Was she sheltering me from something she didn't think I could understand? Not that it mattered. It was like I could feel the fragile bonds of last night's reconciliation snapping around us under the strain of her lies.

By the time I opened my mouth to ask, her astute gaze had fallen on the hoodie wrapped around my arm. Hunter's hoodie. "Oh no," she breathed, her eyes closing as if to block out the sight. Her sharp inhale pierced the room, a harbinger of bad things to come. But when she opened her eyes, efficient, capable Mom was back. The Mom who hunted noises in the night with flashlights. The Mom who didn't let anything, not even the knowledge that she'd just been trapped in a lie, faze her. "Show me."

Show me? Didn't she know she was doing this all wrong? She was supposed to tell me everything was going to be okay.

Why wasn't she doing that?

"Show me," she repeated, louder, when I didn't move.

Slowly, I reached over and untied Hunter's hoodie with my free hand, let it collapse onto the cheerful blue-and-white tile floor. Contrary to my fervent wishing, the alien parts protruding from my arm had not disappeared. The white liquid had ceased leaking, but the twisted wires, the plastic—they were still there, like the guts of a child's mechanical toy.

Mom gasped. "What happened? To do this kind of damage, you would have had to hit something sharp at an incredibly high velocity!"

When Mom said "something sharp," Kaylee's words clicked in my head.

I was sure you'd landed on that rusted hunk of metal.

"I was thrown from the back of Kaylee's truck," I murmured, but Mom wasn't listening. She was too busy inspecting my arm. I scrutinized her expression, searching for even a trace of the shock I'd felt when I'd first seen my injury. The shock I still felt. But there was nothing. No exclamations of disbelief, no sobs, no cries of horror. Nothing at all to indicate that the interior makeup of my arm was news to her.

The flare of hope that maybe, somehow, Mom hadn't known about this, known that my arm was completely freaktastic and had just failed to mention it to me, smothered to death, right there, in my chest.

Mom's own chest rose and fell under her soft blue tee. She reached for my hands. "Mila. I know this is hard, but I need you to listen."

I allowed her to take them. And waited. Waited for an

explanation that could make sense out of this. After all, a simple, logical explanation had to exist. It had to.

Mom's cheeks showed an uncharacteristic pallor. "How many people saw this?" she demanded. When I just stared at her, dumbfounded by her reaction, she grabbed my shoulder and actually shook me. "How many?"

"Just . . . just two. Kaylee and another friend."

"Are you sure?"

"Yes! You're starting to freak me out—please, just tell me what's going on!"

Her grip on my shoulders eased. Resignation settled over her face. "Follow me."

That simple command gave permission for the dam inside me to burst, unleashing wave after wave of craziness and anxiety. I followed her down the hallway, and by the time we arrived at her bedroom, it was a wonder I wasn't shaking.

I wanted to turn and run. To tell her to forget that I'd just demanded an explanation, to forget the whole thing. We could tape some kind of permanent bandage over my arm, pretend it didn't exist.

I wanted to run. Instead, I followed her into the master bedroom.

She headed for her antique mahogany dresser and squatted before it. The bottom drawer, always obstinate, finally popped open.

I stared blankly at the assortment of colorful folded T-shirts, wondering what on earth they had to do with my alien arm. Then Mom yanked the drawer out completely, set it aside, and peered into the dresser. I squatted next to her and immediately saw her target. In the very back corner, a bit of silver gleamed under a piece of masking tape.

A key.

Once she had the key in hand, Mom led me into the laundry room, halting just in front of the door to the garage. Finally she turned, smoothing my hair away from my cheek before dropping her hand back to her side. "Mila, before we go any further, I need you to know that I really do care. In fact, I believe now, more than ever, that you're worth all the risks."

Those words froze me to the core.

Inside the garage, she led me to a bunch of empty moving boxes, arranged neatly against the far back wall. Or at least I'd assumed they were empty. After dragging down the top three, she reached inside the bottom one and withdrew a shiny silver metal box by its handle. An oversized toolbox.

As she turned to carry the box into the house, I flinched away to avoid touching it. My body's reaction to knowing, without a doubt, that whatever was locked away inside that innocuous-looking container was likely to change my life forever.

When we reached the living room, Mom set the box on

the coffee table and pointed to the overstuffed green couch. "Have a seat, Mila. This is going to take a while."

I sat. The silver key headed for the lock. Three seconds until my life exploded.

The key turned. Two seconds.

The lid opened. One second.

And . . .

Whatever crazy ideas I'd had about the contents of the box, I could say with certainty that none of them involved a silver iPod and matching earbuds. Which were exactly the items Mom withdrew.

"Here. Listen to this while I fix up your arm. It will explain everything."

Mom looked away, her strong, capable fingers brushing quickly under her eyes. Then she extended the earbuds toward me. Two round white circles, only a quarter inch in diameter each. Nestled like tiny bombs in her upturned palm.

I hesitated. Did I really want to know? Really? Because whatever was on there was bad enough to make Nicole Daily cry.

No, the truth was, I didn't want to know. But I had to.

My fingers curled around the earbuds. I shoved them into my ears before I could change my mind. Mom withdrew more items from the box—a pen-sized laser, a pair of crazy-looking tweezers, goggles, and a tiny screwdriver—tools that seemed perfect for servicing a broken laptop. She saw me staring and managed a faint smile. "To fix your arm," she said, sounding like it was the most normal thing in the world.

Uh-huh, I thought as I eyed a screwdriver. Totally normal.

"Don't worry, it won't hurt."

Then she hit play on the iPod, flooding my ears with a deep male drawl, and everything else fell away. Well, everything except the lingering thought that Mom had lied. Because while there wasn't pain in my arm, the words spewing from the stranger were another story.

They hurt. They hurt like hell.

NINE

The very first words the man with the matter-of-fact Southern drawl uttered made my entire world shatter.

"MILA, or Mobile Intel Lifelike Android, is the military's current experiment in artificial intelligence. The MILA project is cofunded by a special top-clearance segment of the CIA and the military, so as to produce a supercovert robot spy that can infiltrate sleeper cells and then record all of their movements and intelligence."

I groped for the pause button, pushed it. Stared into space as the words penetrated. Mobile Intel Lifelike Android. Android. My name wasn't a shortened combination of Mia and Lana, it was an acronym. And it meant . . .

No way. There was no way. That was ridiculous, unbelievable. The stupidest thing I'd ever heard.

I went to yank the earbuds out, consumed by an urge to chuck the iPod at the wall, to smash it into a million pieces . . . and then my gaze fell on my mom. My mom, who was currently using a laser to seal the tube in my arm shut.

And just like that, it hit me. Destroying the messenger would do me no good. Not when I couldn't escape the reality unfolding right in front of my eyes.

I hit play, and the voice continued its detached monologue.

"Although the MILA 2.0—" The! THE! Like I was an object, a thing! And 2.0? What did that even mean? "—is physically indistinguishable from an ordinary sixteen-year-old girl, its brain is a reverse-engineered nanocomputer, a complex mix of transistors and live cell technology that gives it unique capabilities. These include exceptional reflexes and strength, superhuman memory skills, and the ability to hack computer systems, among many others. It can also evoke appropriate emotions, based on environmental and physical stimuli."

I . . . what was this? A nanocomputer? Evoke appropriate emotions? *Evoke?* This person couldn't possibly be trying to tell me . . . he couldn't be saying . . . there was just no way. Of course my emotions were real. I felt things all the time.

My throat constricted, as if to confirm my belief.

"The rest of its structure is also a conglomeration of

human and manmade, but mostly synthetic. Its body is comprised of cyberdermis, synthetic tissue infused with a polymer hydrogel lying just under bioengineered skin that is exceptionally strong and resistant to injury and also holds receptors to carry sensation signals to the nano-brain—though pain receptors are very sparse, only one one thousandth of the amount found in a typical human."

I recalled the fall from the truck, my worry that I'd damaged my spinal cord. Suddenly Mom's insistence on slow horseback rides made complete and terrible sense. She hadn't been terrified that I'd hurt myself—on the contrary. She'd been worried that I'd fall and the whole no-pain thing would lead to questions. It was amazing it hadn't happened before.

Wait a second. How had it not happened before? How, in sixteen years of life, had I not noticed that I had little to no pain sensation?

That's when the brutal wave of reality really hit. The voice had said that the MILA 2.0 was physically indistinguishable from a sixteen-year-old girl. Meaning . . . he was also saying I'd never been any age other than sixteen.

Meaning . . . those memories I had of being younger? Lies. All of them.

According to him, I'd been "born" exactly as I was now.

Nausea flooded me. Which, given everything I'd just heard, made no sense. None of this did.

I was human. I *was*.

"Its endoskeleton mixes tightly woven braids of fiber optics encased by tubes of transparent ceramic hybrid that is very difficult to break and easy to repair, and its body utilizes a unique technology that meshes human with machine by way of embedding nanotransistors into live cell membranes. Instead of a heart, Mila has a sophisticated pump to supply energy to her partially organic cells, which can generate their own oxygen. Breathing for it is just a computer program to simulate human function."

No heart? I had *no heart*? No, that was absurd. Ridiculous. I could feel it there, in my chest, beating away.

Unless . . . unless that was the "sophisticated pump" the voice was talking about. My hand flew to my chest, my fingers spreading across my shirt and pressing inward. A second passed, and then I felt the faint upward motion. Beating. Something under there was definitely beating. I hoped the action would soothe me, but instead of the fist-shaped, vein and artery-covered organ I'd seen in biology class, all I could picture was a pool pump. A bit of machinery stuck under my ribs, masquerading as life.

Of course, that was assuming I had ribs to begin with.

I hit pause again, my gaze flying to Mom, but her goggled head was bent over my arm, her focus on aiming the laser's bright-red line at a spot within it.

It felt like no more than a tickle.

I hit play.

"In an especially exciting development, the MILA 2.0 goes one step beyond just approximating feelings. By using experimental data on living girls, we were able to store the visceral and physical sensations that emotions produce and re-create them. Thus, the MILA 2.0 actually feels the same things that humans do, which we anticipate will facilitate blending in with subjects and add authenticity to her cover."

Cover. Oh my god. Did he mean . . . my cover as a *human*?

"MILA contains just enough human cells to simulate biological functions, but it is in reality a machine. The launch date for this exciting project is August twenty-second."

The recording cut off, but the ramifications of that last sentence remained. August 22. Just five days before Mom and I arrived in Clearwater.

I couldn't even move, couldn't breathe. Guess that not-needing-air thing really came in handy. The thought made me laugh, a gasping, hysterical gurgle that made Mom drop her tools and grasp my hand.

Mom. Just another lie in a whole string of them.

The pain in my chest, in my nonheart, was excruciating. Whoever had worked on "evoking appropriate emotional responses" had done a bang-up job.

Maybe I was dreaming. Maybe I would wake up and realize this was just a nightmare.

Maybe I'd even wake up back in Philly, with Dad still alive. A man who, if I believed the voice, had never been a part of my life.

As for "Mom"—well, according to the voice, I was more genetically related to our toaster than I was to her.

Another gurgle erupted.

"Is this all true? It can't be, right? Please tell me it's some kind of sick joke. Please!" But when Mom looked up from packing away the tools, all I saw was the sadness in her eyes. No matter what, I knew this was real to her.

"Mila, I'm so sorry. . . . I wish—"

"I don't care what you wish," I said, jumping to my feet. "Just tell me what's going on. Where did I come from? Why am I here? And how—how could I not be real?" I whirled and faced a watercolor of a horse, wrapping my arms around my waist. I immediately wondered if that action had been programmed, too.

"You are real," Mom said in her soothing calm-down-and-listen-to-me voice. I bet she didn't know that, right now, it had the opposite effect. It made me want to jump up and down, scream bloody murder, and shake that poise right out of her. "That's why I stole you from the military labs. I worked with you every day, Mila. Actually, I'm the bioengineer who helped create you. I know that you aren't just a weapon . . . you're too human for that. So yes, I stole you—to keep you safe. You deserved more than what the army had to offer."

Stolen. I was stolen goods.

Mom's hand smoothed my hair aside before gently stroking the nape of my neck. Everything inside me wanted to believe her, to know that she really did love me, that I really was part human. She'd always been there for me, when I was little, when Dad died . . .

. . . except—none of that was real. But how was that possible? I could see the memories etched in my head, so perfectly clear, playing out behind my eyes like detailed videos.

Like videos.

The pressure of her fingers on my neck went from comforting to oppressive in an instant. I jerked away and whirled to face her. "How did you do it? All those memories I have?"

Mom—no, *Nicole*—sighed, her shaking fingers reaching up to remove her glasses so she could rub the bridge of her nose. "I programmed them. The reason some of them feel especially real is because I created them using a virtual reality program, which allowed me to actually insert you into the memory."

Programmed. My entire past, everything I'd understood to be true about my life, my family, what had formed me as a person. Stripped away with one simple word. Programmed.

"And the fire?" I whispered. "What kind of a person

makes that up? And wait—is your name even Nicole?"

"Yes, it's Nicole, but Laurent, not Daily." Mom—*Nicole*—sighed and rubbed her head. "I was just trying to buy us time, to figure out a way to tell you! My first priority was to keep us safe. The only way I could make sure to protect you was to make you think you were a real girl. There's no doubt in my head that the government is searching for us, with every resource they have at their disposal. Why do you think I chose Clearwater? I disabled your tracking device, but that doesn't mean they won't find us."

And it was just going from bad to worse. Tracking device, like I was some kind of runaway dog. Except—at least dogs were truly alive. Whereas I was some kind of monster. Part living cells, mostly hardware.

All freak.

She made another move to touch me, but I batted her hand away. "Don't! I don't even understand how . . . how can any of this be true? Manufactured emotions?" A tight ache squeezed my throat—programmed? Real? How could I possibly know?—and I lowered my voice to a whisper. "If I'm not human, why does this hurt so much?"

"It's a little like phantom limb syndrome . . . only for emotions. You might not have the same parts as a regular human, but you can still sense the feeling in those parts when you're in an emotional state—pressure, warmth, chill, visceral, all of it. Phantom sensations, if you will, copied from the feelings of a teenage human girl. Via an elaborate neuromatrix, we prewired your brain to believe you were formed just like a human body, so it would accept all those sensations as real."

Prewired. Neuromatrix. It was too much.

"And what about Dad's shirt?" I sneered, using air quotes around the word "Dad." "Was that just to buy us time, too? And that stupid necklace?"

Before she could grasp my intentions, I'd lunged forward, grabbed the emerald around her neck, and yanked. The fragile chain snapped, and when it did, I chucked the entire thing across the room.

"Mila!" she gasped before scrambling after it.

I raced down the hall, rushing into my room and locking the door behind me, desperate to escape before I burst into tears.

I threw myself facedown on my bed as the first sob hit, felt the warm tears pool under my cheeks. Tears I wasn't even sure were real. Were they made up of some weird solution, prompted by "appropriate" environmental stimuli? Was I really sad, or was a computer program telling me to feel sad?

One minute I was a normal girl, the next . . . a monster.

That thought urged me to my feet and over to the oval-shaped mirror topping my white dresser. Frankenstein did not stare back at me. Just my own face. Were my eyes a slightly-too-improbable shade of leaf green? I reached up to slide my fingers through my hair. And my hair—how did it grow? Or didn't it? Those memories of haircuts I had . . . they must all be fake. Not Mom—*Nicole*, I corrected once again. But even knowing what I did, calling her by name just didn't feel right.

Next I touched the wetness on my cheeks. The liquid felt like real tears, but then, how did I even know what real tears felt like? How could I believe anything ever again, when everything I knew about myself was completely false?

Even my face, my familiar heart-shaped face with the extra-wide lower lip and the tiniest smattering of freckles fanning out from my nose. Not real. Not real.

Not. Real.

Before I knew it, my fist flew forward, my urge to destroy that phony reflection eclipsing everything else. Glass shattered and a jagged avalanche spilled across the dresser like a cascade of lies. Glittering lies, strewn in front of me as a reminder of everything I'd lost. Of everything I'd never had.

Once the rush of emotion faded, I surveyed the damage. Stupid. Not only had I made a huge mess, but the act hadn't done anything but reinforce my otherness. No blood seeping through cuts in my knuckles, and only the faintest of pink scratches. Worst of all—no pain in my hand to speak of.

No, the only pain I was allowed was choking the

nonexistent life from my fake heart.

Sweeping the shards onto the floor, I stormed over to the bed and slid between the sheets. Threw the pillow over my head in an effort to block out the world.

But I couldn't block out the memories, false or not. Couldn't block out the internal pain I shouldn't even be able to feel.

Couldn't keep those annoying phony tears that felt so, so real from flowing.

TEN

Later that night I was slumped in Bliss's stall, knees bent, my left cheek resting against my pajama bottoms. Just staring at her dark leg like I might find the answers lurking there.

The familiar, musky scent of horse engulfed me, along with the slightly sweet smell of hay. It was quiet inside, except for the occasional snort or shuffling of hooves.

Quiet, but not safe.

Less than twenty-four hours before, this barn had been my refuge. A place where I could come to recover from Dad's death in peace, under the nonjudgmental eyes of the horses. In my grief-stricken state, I'd never once believed that something worse could happen.

I'd never once imagined that discovering Dad hadn't

really died would haunt me in ways that his death never could.

Nowhere felt safe anymore.

"Why couldn't I be a horse?" I asked, the sound of my voice making Bliss swing her massive head toward me, her huge oval nostrils snuffling at my hair. That simple gesture made my throat tighten.

At least she didn't care if I was a freak.

I reached behind my head to rub her soft muzzle, ignoring the stupid tears that refused to quit welling up. "You wouldn't even understand if you weren't . . . normal. Not that any of that's true, right? I mean, look at me—I'm asking a horse a question. Could it get any more human than that?"

Outside the barn, only a few stars escaped the thick cover of late-night clouds, leaving the sky dark and depressing. Besides the rustling of horses, an occasional cricket chirped. An owl hooted from a nearby tree. But I refused to go back to my room until I was sure my mom—*Nicole*—was sleeping. Once she'd poked her head in and swept up the disaster I'd made of the mirror, she'd taken to hovering.

Yes, hovering. As if acting like a stereotypical teen's mom would make everything better. Right now, the sight of her slim, capable figure and concerned face filled me with violence: simultaneous and disparate needs to rage against more mirrors and to break down and sob in her arms.

Break down in the arms of the person who'd betrayed

me—that would never happen. Still, with both of us occupying the guesthouse, I found it impossible to sit still, let alone sleep.

Sleep. About that. Did I actually sleep? Or was sleeping for me just another one of those "humanlike programs" that someone had had installed? Like a new version of Windows?

It would explain why I woke at the slightest motion or noise, perfectly lucid and alert.

I buried my head between my knees, taking deep breaths to combat the panic-induced dizziness. None of what Mom said made sense, I told myself. If I were an android, why did I feel dizzy in the first place? And how could deep breaths help, when, according to iPod Man, I didn't have any lungs? When I combed my fingers through the hay, how could I feel the exact scratchy texture with fake skin? Suddenly, all of it seemed like an elaborate scheme. A sanity test. If it weren't for my stupid arm . . .

My mind shied away from that topic. From that and my quick reflexes, my strength. And mostly from the explanations that Mom had offered. I didn't want to think about any of it for too long, afraid that if I did, I'd start to believe.

I just wanted to pretend today had never happened. Go back to being regular Mila. A girl fumbling her way through a loss in a new town.

The high-pitched notes of my ringtone yanked my head up.

I rescued my cell phone from the hay and glanced at the screen. And stared, my eyes scanning the number over and over again in case I'd somehow made a mistake.

Hunter.

I'd actually brought the phone to the barn to text him, but I'd chickened out and texted Kaylee instead. No response from her.

I scrambled to press send. "Hello?"

"Hey, Mila."

Just the sound of his voice, that quiet, husky voice, made the entire debacle with Mom feel less real. Hunter Lowe— A. Real. Boy.—was calling me. The military, the CIA? Secret android project? *Really?*

"Hey."

"You took off earlier. I was just . . . worried. You okay? Your arm?"

The concern in his voice leached through the phone, flooded me with an unexpected warmth. I latched onto that feeling like it was my savior. "It's fine." True enough. It was just the rest of my life that was a disaster.

"This might sound weird, but I'm in my car and was wondering if . . . can I come by, to check on you?"

Come by, *now*? To check on me?

I pressed my eyes shut, hesitating. Earlier today, I would have been beyond thrilled to have Hunter call and ask to see me. But with the click of an iPod button, everything had changed. My past, my parents, the nature of my entire existence—all of it called into question by a faceless man with a southern drawl.

"I don't know . . . it's late, and I'm pretty sure my mom wouldn't be thrilled."

Not that I cared what Mom thought at the moment. Still, the last thing this night needed was more drama.

"Could you sneak outside?"

I walked to the door and pushed it open, emitting a wedge of light. Besides that, nothing softened the darkness except the glow of a few determined stars. The unlit house windows suggested Mom had finally climbed into bed.

Bliss nickered. A reminder that while horses were nice, I could really use a friend who talked.

"Meet me in the barn."

"Okay. See you in a few."

As soon as I hung up, I realized what I'd done.

I craned my neck, brushing clinging strands of hay off my butt and tugging down the short-sleeved shirt where it had risen over my stomach. Ducks. Hunter was coming, and I was wearing flannel ducks. Then I realized how ridiculous I was being. If only greeting a boy I liked in silly pajamas was my sole worry.

After a futile attempt to comb the pillow-inflicted knots from my hair, I dropped my hands and waited. Hopefully, the sliver of light would act like a beacon.

Less than three minutes later, the muted rumble of an engine cut through the night air in the distance. It was another thirty seconds before I saw the dark shape of a Jeep heading down our street. No headlights—it had to be Hunter, in an attempt to be stealthy. Sure enough, the Jeep turned into our driveway, the tires crunching on gravel.

He turned off the engine at least twenty yards from our house. I could tell he was trying to be quiet, but even so, I caught the slight click of the car door as it opened, and again as it closed.

A few moments later he stood in front of me, his hands shoved deep into his pockets and an uncertain smile hovering at his mouth.

"Hey," he said. Softly.

"Hey." Also softly, since my voice wanted to freeze up at the sight of him.

The faint glow from the barn picked up the damp strands of hair clinging to the collar of his gray sweatshirt and his clean-shaven cheeks, marred only by a tiny red dot on the left side. Right above his jawbone. He smelled like soap mixed with sandalwood.

Freshly showered, definitely. Which suggested he'd used the line about being out and about anyway as an excuse to see me. That realization sent a flutter of . . . something . . . through me. Something that felt warm, alive, and very definitely human.

I put one finger to my lips and beckoned him to follow, swinging the door gently closed behind us.

Amid the rustle of horses, who snorted at the scent of a newcomer, I led Hunter farther into the barn. And then we stood there. The pair of us. Saying nothing.

"Um, do you want to sit?" I finally asked to break the silence, glancing around even though I knew a chair or a couch wasn't about to appear out of nowhere.

"Sure." Hunter slid down the wall next to the first stall until he reached the floor. Then he smiled and patted the spot next to him.

I sat, careful to keep space between us. Even so, I found his nearness distracting. The way his bare knee peeked out of the frayed fabric of his jeans. Even the look of the fingers that tapped away at his knee, long and lean and gentle. I wondered what those fingers would feel like, interlaced with my own.

Fearful that my expression would give my thoughts away, I traced a yellow duck on my leg to avoid looking at him.

"So . . . ," he said, pausing.

"So . . . ," I echoed. When he still didn't continue, I felt a pressure inflate my chest, rising with every silent second that slipped by.

Why wasn't he saying anything? Did he already regret coming here? Was it my arm? Maybe he was wanting to ask me about it but didn't know how. I should just tell him.

Well, tell him the fabricated version I'd come up with between his phone call and his arrival. Get the ordeal over with already.

With a bravado I didn't feel, I forced myself to turn my head and look at him. He did the same thing at the same exact time.

"So—"

"So—"

Our words competed again, and we both broke off. The corners of his mouth twitched up. I felt mine follow. A second later, our laughter comingled in the barn, echoing off the lofty ceiling and concrete floor.

"So you wanted to check up on me?" I said, giving him the perfect opening.

Then wished I hadn't when he stopped laughing. His eyelashes swept low as his gaze fell to my arm. "Yeah, I did. You seemed really upset when you left."

As Hunter continued to stare, that trapped sensation, the one from school, rushed over me. Maybe inviting him over had been a mistake. If I were smart, I'd stand up, tell him I was tired, then send him away. Tomorrow at school, things would be safer, once the memory of the accident faded and there was a hall full of kids to distract him.

But my feet neglected to cooperate. My head, my heart, everything balked. Smart was good, but right now, I needed Hunter around. Right now, he kept me anchored to the world of the living.

"So your arm, is it . . . fixed?"

Here we go. "It is, actually. No permanent damage or anything." I rotated my wrist so he could see it from every angle. Amazing, the way Mom had fixed it with a few random tools. All that remained was a thin pink line, like a long scratch, but Mom said even that would fade within two days.

What I wouldn't give for a scar.

He reached out to stroke the inside of my elbow, his fingers warm against my skin. Panic mixed with flutter—lots and lots of flutters.

See that? Perfectly normal teen response. Okay, maybe not so much the panic, but definitely the flutters.

"May I?" he said.

"Um, sure."

Ever so gently, he clasped my wrist. When he traced the scratch with his other hand, I swear something inside me flipped over completely. Somersaulted. Performed an entire circus act in less than five seconds.

No way could a covert nanocomputer android spy feel like that.

"Amazing. Not really sure how it's possible, but it's definitely amazing. How did it happen?"

The protective way he cradled my arm sent a ball of warmth careening through my stomach. His blue eyes connected with mine, tempting my lips to swallow the lie and release the truth. I could chuck the fabrication. Get another take—his take—on the whole unbelievable thing. Because right now, it still felt surreal. The two of us, we could figure it out. Together.

Of course, there was the other, way more probable scenario to consider. The one where I told him the truth and he laughed. Right before he backed away, ran for his Jeep, and alerted the entire school that I was a nutjob of epic proportions.

The iPod Man's drawl whispered through my head, conjuring visions of jail cells and labs and other places I wouldn't allow my mind to go. I shivered. No one could know. Ever.

Besides, I wasn't about to chase off the one person who made me feel the most human. Sticking with a lie was my best bet.

"My arm is a prosthetic," I said, disappointment making my voice flat. "I was in a car accident a year ago. It's so realistic, I almost forget it's fake sometimes."

"I'm sorry."

Yeah, me too, I wanted to say. *For lying, for your completely unwarranted sympathy.*

I needed a distraction. Something to steer his attention away from my arm, my past, the questions I couldn't answer.

I pushed away from the wall, cocking my head. "Did you hear that?"

Hunter shot to his feet like his Vans were spring-loaded. "No, what was it?" he said, his eyes trained on the barn door.

My hand flew to my mouth to cover the smile that threatened to spill across my face. Hunter Lowe, who seemed so carefree and cool. Scared of a little bump in the night.

We both waited, him listening for a sound to follow the first imaginary one, and me pretending to listen. A horse snorted, followed by a solitary cricket chirp.

"Guess it was nothing," I said a few seconds later.

"You sure?"

"Yeah, probably just one of the horses."

His eyes flicked from me back to the door. "If your mom woke up . . ."

This time I was unable to stifle a small giggle. So that was it. Hunter was scared of being busted by Mom.

His shoulders relaxed. "Either way, I'd probably better go. Just to be safe."

I led him to the door with slow steps, savoring every remaining moment. Once he vanished back into the night, the barn would feel empty again, robbed of his comforting presence. It would be quiet and still and lonely. "So were you really terrified of running into my mom back there? Disappointing." I tsked.

He paused just as his lean fingers encircled the door handle. Out of nowhere, he turned and grabbed my hands.

I jumped, sending a strand of hair slipping forward into my eyes. Acutely aware that the space separating us had dwindled to mere inches.

"Yes, terrified . . . of being busted and ruining my chances to make a good first impression," he said.

And then he stepped closer, and the entire world went still. I felt the soft swish of air on my forehead as his hand reached for my face. The warmth of his skin as his fingers slid down my wisp of stray hair. The sensation of my heart stopping as he leaned closer . . . only to pluck a loose bit of straw from the top of my head.

The smile that sprawled across his lips may have been a tinge smug as he tossed the straw to the floor. But he still didn't make a move for the door. Instead, his hand slid under my chin, tilting my face up. My stomach coiled, my eyes closed. This, this was exactly what I needed.

One kiss, to turn my horrible nightmare into a fairy tale.

One kiss, to prove I was normal, once and for all.

One kiss, to give me a real story to tell.

But before his lips could so much as brush mine, a slamming door shattered our perfect moment. Our front door.

Mom.

Hunter released me and leaped back. I froze. For all my earlier teasing, the thought of Mom discovering I'd allowed someone onto the property at night made me slightly panicky. I couldn't handle one of her lectures. Not tonight.

"Back door," I whispered, pointing.

"See you tomorrow," Hunter said. And then he bolted, running to the far end of the corridor, unlocking the latch, and slipping into the dark.

I hurried over and relocked the door behind him, turning just in time to see the other doorway frame a familiar figure.

"Mila? It's late. You should come inside."

Mom peered at me blearily. The red streaks in her eyes startled me, but I refused to soften. Especially not when I saw the emerald pendant peeping above her blue pajama top, restored to its former prominence around her neck.

Wrapping my arms around my waist, I padded over to her silently. I made a deliberate, conspicuous effort to duck the hand that reached for my shoulder, to avoid contact completely. She'd had plenty of opportunities for that kind of comforting before the big reveal. She'd chosen to pass them up then.

Now it was my turn to return the favor. Especially when every touch felt like a lie.

With the darkness surrounding us, our silent walk to the house was like a cruel parody of our return from the barn last night. With Mom smiling at me, her arm linked through mine, I'd felt like part of a real mother-daughter duo for the first time in months. Or so I'd thought.

Little had I known it'd been the first time, period.

Mom lagged a few paces behind when I turned and slammed my bedroom door in her face.

I sprawled on my bed in a spent heap, realizing the tale I'd manufactured earlier was probably delusional. Somehow I'd come up with the notion that Hunter could set me free. Like some twisted version of Sleeping Beauty. But instead of saving me from an evil spell, his kiss would save me from the iPod.

I'd convinced myself, in that tiny space of time, that Hunter's kiss would make me human.

ELEVEN

When I woke the next morning, I experienced one perfect moment of peace. One serene, crazy-free moment, until yesterday's events slammed me with avalanche force: iPod Man, neuromatrices, programmed memories. A false past, a false mom and dad.

Everything about me, false, false, false.

It was like being buried alive in a landslide of hopelessness and despair. Except I wasn't alive. That was the problem.

I dug my fingers into the mattress, squeezed my eyes shut, gasped in tiny, frantic breaths that, according to some stranger, I didn't need, but that felt as natural to me as the sun rising. If I let these feelings consume me, what would I have left?

Nothing.

I needed to focus on something positive. I needed to get dressed, go to school, and try to get on with my life . . . whatever that entailed. Talk to Kaylee, talk to Hunter.

Hunter.

The memory of the almost-kiss flooded me and, despite the horror of yesterday and the questions flashing through my head, I felt the stirring of those same crazy flutters.

If I could feel that same breathless hope and anticipation over a boy Kaylee and Ella and even Parker talked about, then surely I was more teen girl than Mom thought? Someone, somewhere, had gotten it wrong?

Ultimately, those were the thoughts that propelled me out of bed and into my closet to forage for clean clothes.

After getting dressed, I followed the scent of warm toast into the kitchen. See? Hunger pangs. So normal, there couldn't possibly be a reasonable explanation for a nonhuman to feel them.

"MILA contains just enough human cells to simulate biological functions."

The voice could not have been referring to food and . . . stuff. No way.

My plunk into the chair at the counter made Mom spin around from the refrigerator, wielding a jar of strawberry preserves. "Good morning," she said, her voice wary. Like she was testing the waters to see if my mood was stable.

Though she was dressed in clean jeans and a blue long-sleeved tee, and her hair was pulled back into that tidy ponytail, the hollows under her eyes looked deeper than usual. Her walk to the back counter to grab the plate of toast lacked her usual efficient pep.

"Morning," I replied in a neutral tone and spread jelly on my toast.

Mom settled into the chair next to me. She yawned before propping her chin in her hands, watching me devour my breakfast. "How are you feeling this morning?" she asked.

Hunter. Think about Hunter and seeing him at school. Nothing else. "Great," I said, taking another bite.

Her mystified stare followed my movements as I chewed and swallowed. Obviously "great" wasn't the response she'd been expecting.

Her lips parted, but no sound came out. She gave her head a tiny shake instead, slapped her hands on her sensible, faded work jeans, and stood. "Good. But if you change your mind and want to talk . . ."

"I won't," I said, wiping my mouth on a napkin.

I placed my empty plate in her outstretched hand and watched her carry it over to the sink. "I understand that you're not ready yet," she said. "But when you are—"

"Ever." My voice was steady even as my insides trembled. "I don't want to talk about yesterday ever."

Amid the clank of dishes and the smell of green apple

soap, I looked up at the pig-shaped clock that Mom called kitschy and I called lame. Then I wondered—was that the real me who'd come up with the term, or the programmed me? Or were they one and the same?

I closed my eyes and managed to block out the clock, but not the uneasy train of my thoughts. "Can you do those after you drop me off at school? I don't want to be late."

The clanking paused for a moment before resuming. "You aren't going to school."

The words blindsided me. I sat there, speechless in my shock until one crucial question surfaced. "Today?" I said, fighting off the gut-twisting burst of panic. "Or ever?"

"I'm not sure yet."

"What? *Why?*" That last shriek was probably twitching the horses' ears back in the stable.

Hunter's face popped into my head, and I clung to the image with everything I had. No school meant no Hunter, and I couldn't give him up. I wouldn't.

My question didn't interrupt Mom's steady scrub-rinse-dry cycle of clearing the stained porcelain sink.

As the pile of cheerful daisy-rimmed plates and silver-ware grew on top of the rooster-print dish towel, so did my urge to smash them to the ground. How could she drop a bombshell like that and not even bother to look at me?

The screech of my chair interrupted the cycle. Mom dried her hands and finally turned to give me her full attention.

As I looked at her, I wondered how it could all be a lie. Her slim, wiry figure, her blue eyes, the sound and smell and feel of her. The way she fiddled with the nosepiece of her glasses on the rare occasion she struggled for words, like she was doing right now. All of that felt so real, like I'd known her for so much longer than months.

"I'm sorry, but after what happened yesterday, we just can't take the risk. Not now."

"You mean the risk that I might actually have a semi-normal life—that risk?"

She yanked off her glasses and rubbed her eyes. "I know this is difficult. But we're in a very precarious situation here."

"And whose fault is that? Not mine, but I'm the one being punished!" I stopped, took a deep breath. Reason, I had to reason with her. "Anyway, you're being paranoid. Who's going to come looking for us in the middle of nowhere?"

Mom's hands froze on her eyes for the briefest of moments. When she replaced her glasses, her voice was quiet. "You have no idea . . . and I'd like to keep it that way. But we need to take precautions. Then, if it's safe, you can go back."

She turned back to the pile of dishes, patting away non-existent wet spots with a dish towel. Pretending.

Both of us, always pretending.

The sight of her, returning to some mindless, completely insignificant activity instead of actually talking to me, pushed me over the edge. "You're lying. You're never going to let me go back, are you?" I shouted.

Mom whirled. "Mila!" she started, cutting off when she saw me blinking in rapid succession. "Mila," she said, more gently, stepping over the mess and reaching for me.

A trap. Just like everything else.

I scrambled out of reach. "Why? Why even steal me in the first place, if you were never really going to let me live?" I whispered. Just before I turned and bolted for my room.

I slumped on my bed and stared at nothing. When Mom came to check on me an hour later, I rolled onto my left side and refused to look at her.

The mattress creaked and lowered.

"I know you're upset, but will you just talk to me for a minute?"

A head study of a bay horse hung on my wall, right next to the checkered green-and-white curtains. The brushstrokes captured the face so well, I could almost imagine the horse was staring back at me. I wondered how the artist did it, how he breathed the illusion of life into a blank piece of paper. The paper horse stared, and I closed my eyes.

Ultimately, that's all it was. An illusion.

The bed creaked again as Mom shifted her weight, trying to find a comfortable position. Good luck with that—under these crazy circumstances, I seriously doubted one existed.

At least ten seconds ticked by before I blurted, "Why even risk letting me go to school in the first place? Why take a stupid job? Why not just hide out in a cave or something?"

When Mom answered, her voice was thick. "Because I do want you to live, Mila. I want you to have everything this time. And if that means hiding you in plain sight, so be it."

I shook my head. "That doesn't even make sense! This time? What this time? What else are you hiding from me?"

I felt the soft stroke of her fingers, down, down, down my hair. Slowly, like she was savoring every inch. The strangest image flashed into my head. A little girl with long brown hair, squirming through a haircut while a younger version of Mom stood behind her, wielding a pair of scissors in one hand and a lollipop in the other.

But this memory was blurry, fragmented. Nothing at all like the crystal-clear ones of Dad. Maybe some of them were starting to go bad. Maybe, one by one, they'd all bleed away, until I had nothing left to remind me of my fake family.

I curled into a tighter ball.

"I think you've had enough revelations for now." The bed creaked again. "I came in here to tell you that I have to go out on a call—Mr. Danning's gelding just went lame. Stay inside the house or barn, but no rides today. I'll be back as soon as I can."

When I didn't respond, she stood with a heavy sigh, closing the door softly behind her.

The second I heard her car reverse down the gravel driveway, I was up. I couldn't live like this, trapped like an animal in a cage. Going to school couldn't hurt. I'd prove it to her.

Bolstered by the image of Hunter's warm blue eyes, I gathered my backpack and set off on foot for Clearwater High.

Strike number one—I was late to homeroom.

Thanks to a squeaky door, my arrival drew curious looks from the majority of my classmates. I hesitated just inside, tempted to bolt but curbing the impulse. I wanted this, I reminded myself. To go to school, to be normal. Still, their stares felt like an accusation during my walk down the middle row to hand Mrs. Stegmeyer my yellow tardy slip. Like they knew something about me was different, and they were trying to pinpoint what it was.

I'd never enjoyed being the center of attention before, but now it seemed downright dangerous.

Strike number two—the desk under the window was empty. No Hunter.

Strike number three—I couldn't even sit in my own seat.

Leslie, a girl I'd never seen Kaylee exchange more than a few brief greetings with, lounged in my spot, looking far too comfortable with her red head tilted toward Kaylee's. A girl who always reeked a little of the nail polish that she was constantly using to decorate her notebooks—a habit that usually had Kaylee rolling her eyes.

When I made eye contact with Kaylee, she gave me a small, no-teeth smile. Her fake smile.

That couldn't be good. Especially not when combined with the conspicuous shortage of texts.

Or maybe that was just paranoia talking. Mom's stress, crawling under my skin and writhing there until I was just as jumpy as her.

Writhing under my bioengineered skin among wires and plastic and everything else that wasn't human.

Stop it.

I forced a smile that was way more cheerful than I felt and headed for the far back corner where Leslie usually sat, sneaking texts to her friends and defacing her notebooks. And the desk, it looked like, from the bright splash of purple along the inner edge.

Leslie glanced my way. But it wasn't her overly bright smile that made the paranoia swamp me again. It was the focal point of her attention. My arm. The same one I'd injured yesterday.

I shoved my arm under my desk and slouched into my chair, trying to act engrossed in my English lit book. I tried to tune everyone else out, convince myself that it was just my imagination. That Kaylee wouldn't, couldn't, have said anything.

Then I caught the whisper. Super low, but not low enough. At least, not for my ears.

"Can you tell?" Kaylee asked.

They could be talking about anything, I told myself.

But I didn't really believe it.

When the bell finally rang, I was ready. I bolted out of my chair and hurried over to Kaylee, who still managed to beat me out the door, Leslie in tow. "Kaylee, wait!"

She didn't stop, just fluttered aqua-blue fingernails over her shoulder. "Sorry, gotta run . . . later!"

As I watched her scurry away, the niggle of doubt exploded into a full-blown spasm, one that grew in intensity as every class ended with no sign of Kaylee. Plus in physics, the girl across the aisle poked her partner and then jerked her head toward me.

When the lunch bell rang, still no Kaylee. Or Hunter. I wove my way to my locker, fighting off the ever-present trapped sensation as a noxious blend of voices and smells and footsteps flooded the hallway around me. Every time someone glanced my way, my hands curled and my legs tensed, preparing me to bolt. Ridiculous, I knew that, and yet I couldn't stop the fear from spreading. All it would take was one student, just one, to discover what I was, and my life was over.

I reached my locker, and no Kaylee there, either. After shoving my book inside, I clung to the door, focusing on the cool, slick feel of metal in an effort to generate calm. Okay, so Kaylee was a little shocked and yes, maybe angry, about finding out about my arm that way. She'd obviously expected me to tell her about the prosthesis long ago. I got that.

I closed my eyes. Of course, if I really had a prosthesis to tell her about, I wouldn't be panicking right about now. Still . . . all I had to do was talk to her. Explain about my prosthesis in person and make sure she knew I wanted it kept a secret. An easy fix.

I'd just about convinced myself when Jim Dyson, a starter on the football team with a locker next to mine, bumped me with his shoulder. "Hey, did you really try to chop off your own arm and send it to your ex-boyfriend when he broke up with you?"

He leaned against his locker and stared down at me expectantly, his thick brown eyebrows almost merging into a single line across his potato-shaped face, his off-center nose suggesting more than one break.

My fingers tightened their grip on the metal. "What?"

He slapped one beefy hand on his thigh and ignored

my question. "That's warped, man. Warped. Do you have photos?"

This couldn't be happening. "You're joking, right?"

He leaned closer, bringing the smell of sour orange juice and deodorant with him. "Seriously, I won't tell anyone. Just show me, okay?"

That's when I realized that no, he wasn't joking. Yes, he really believed I'd cut off my arm, and yes, he really wanted pictures.

I clenched the green door harder . . . and felt the metal give under my grip. I jerked back like the locker had stung my hand and slammed the door before I could see the damage. Before he could see the damage. I slipped under his meaty arm, fleeing both the locker and his hopeful stare.

Meanwhile, my heart—my something, whatever it was—pounded out a spastic beat. I had to find Kaylee and stop this before it went any further. Before she ruined any chance of me ever coming back to Clearwater High.

I zigzagged through the clusters of students blocking my path and headed straight for the cafeteria.

"Excuse me," I said, cutting in front of a meandering, hand-in-hand couple. I repeated the words after darting through a narrow opening in a crowd of five varsity-jacketed guys, who were much too engrossed in rehashing a practice to walk at a decent speed.

"Watch it," one grumbled, while another yelled, "Hey,

you can jump out of my truck anytime!" Howls of laughter rang out, along with the smack of a high five, and I knew they were staring. I felt a burst of heat across the back of my neck.

Oh, god. This was worse, way worse than I'd thought. How many people had heard the rumors? What exactly were the rumors? Kaylee had to fix this. She had to.

The only thing keeping me from sprinting into the cafeteria was the knowledge that it would draw even more attention.

I made the sharp right that led to the gaping doorway of the cafeteria. Scores of kids already clustered around tables, pulling water bottles out of lunch bags, making faces at apples, peeling back foil and biodegradable wrappers to peer at their mystery sandwiches. I watched them talk and laugh and eat with friends, smelled the intermingled scent of teen sweat and hamburger meat sizzling on the kitchen grill, and it registered that maybe I should just take Mom's advice. Go home, stay away from school.

Hide like a trapped animal. Away from everyone. Away from Hunter.

Away from life.

No.

I pushed into the room, past the six long rows of tables to the one by the back window where Kaylee sat, flanked by Ella and Parker. Our table. Except today, my seat was once again occupied by Leslie from homeroom.

Kaylee's face was averted toward Ella, so I focused on her hair as I took the last few steps. Finding and counting the flyaway strands helped soothe my nerves. This morning when she got up to brush it, I bet she'd stuck out her tongue at her reflection, the same way she did every time she caught a glimpse of those unruly pieces in a mirror. Still the same Kaylee hair, which gave me hope that it was still the same Kaylee underneath.

The Kaylee who'd been generous and kind to the new girl in town. Not the one who'd forced her into the back of a pickup.

After a sudden squeal of laughter, Parker glanced over her shoulder, saw me, and froze with a carrot stick halfway to her mouth. She dropped it and nudged Kaylee. Not to be deterred, I rested my hands on the plastic table and waited.

I didn't wait long. The other two girls ceased their chatter the second Kaylee twisted my way. Her thin, teeth-covering smile didn't reach her eyes. "What?"

The distant tone in her voice sent a stab of fear into my gut. "Can I talk to you for a minute?"

"We're kind of busy here."

I looked around the table, to where Parker spun her Diet Coke and Ella inspected her nails and Leslie swirled a french fry in ketchup. Busy. Uh-huh. Why was she acting like this? Beneath the fear of all the attention, of having my secret discovered, another feeling sparked to life. Something hot and dangerous. "It won't take long," I said, curling my fingers to keep from shaking her.

Her long-suffering sigh was so obvious. "Fine. I didn't want to say this, but . . . Mila, you have . . . *issues* . . . and I'd just rather not be around you anymore."

I—what? "Issues? I have issues? Why, because I told you I didn't want to sit in the back of the truck, but you insisted? Just so you could have some alone time with Hunter?"

Kaylee's surprised brown eyes finally met mine—she obviously hadn't expected to be called on that—while the other girls squirmed.

"Uh, we're going to get some drinks. Do you want anything, Kayls?" Ella asked, her narrow face even more pinched than usual from worry.

"No thanks."

I waited until they left before sliding into Parker's empty chair. Keeping my voice low, I said, "Kaylee, why are you doing this to me? I thought we were friends."

The left side of her lip curled. "You and Hunter looked cozy enough last night on the way to your house—I bet he'd be more than happy to be your friend."

I reeled back. "Are you kidding me? I could have died, Kaylee, and all you're worried about is that Hunter was nice to me?"

Where was the Kaylee I'd met when I'd first moved

here, the one who'd welcomed the awkward new girl into her circle of friends? Because this version of her felt like a stranger.

Kaylee's chair screeched back as she tottered to her feet. "Whatever. Parker told me not to trust you. I should have listened."

Her high-pitched voice, attention grabbing to begin with, doubled in volume by the time she finished. It carried. Conversations muted; heads from four, five, six tables away turned to see what the commotion was all about.

"Lower your voice," I hissed.

I realized my mistake when I saw her eyes narrow, saw the mutinous pucker of her lips. I tried to backpedal. "Kaylee, please—"

"Why?" Her shout drowned out my last-ditch attempt at curtailing drama. In a sweep of voluminous purple sleeves, she spread her arms wide. "It's not like they won't find out sooner or later," she continued, at that same desperately loud volume. So loud that I wanted to shove my hand over her mouth and drag her out of the cafeteria. But that would only draw more attention. I had to act, though. Before she—

"Why not just tell them you're a fr—"

My foot moved fast. In a blur of motion, I hooked her ankle, sweeping her legs out from under her. Her scream rang out as her head flew back. Her hands flailed wildly, and she smacked her cup on the way down, splashing Coke all over her lavender shirt. She hit the faux-wood floor butt first.

The stunned silence and gasps only lasted a second before the laughter started. A table of boys catcalled, and I heard a girl shout, "Good going, Grace!"

Dazed, Kaylee blinked up at me. Probably trying to figure out exactly what had happened. That made two of us.

The sight of her, sprawled across the dirty floor, in between chair legs with her shirt drenched in brown liquid, tore at my stomach. I'd done that. Without any intention, without any thought beyond making her stop. But how?

I shoved aside my disbelief and stepped forward. The least I could do was help her up. But as I moved, something flashed behind my eyes. Not a memory, not this time. Words. Luminous red words. They flickered, appeared only for a millisecond before vanishing, but oh, god, even that was a millisecond too long.

Target: Down.

The horror clenched my chest like a vise, squeezing until I only had one thought left.

Run.

And that's exactly what I did. While Kaylee struggled to her feet, I turned and ran. Fled the room, my actions . . . and those flashing red words that I hoped with every fiber of my being were a stress-induced hallucination. Or a fluke.

The likes of which I'd never, ever see again.

As the sound of my feet smacking linoleum echoed through the halls, I realized Mom had been right.

I never should have come back to school.

TWELVE

Despite my mad dash back to Greenwood Ranch, when I arrived, our Tahoe sat in the driveway like a big green warning.

Great.

I considered hiding on the grounds for a while, avoiding the lecture of badness that awaited, but that was just delaying the inevitable and, worse, potentially sending Mom into a panic when she couldn't track me down. I might as well face the somber, guilt-trippy music and get it over with.

I stuffed my hands into my pockets and climbed onto the porch. The door whipped open to reveal Mom, her blue eyes raking over my outfit before narrowing on the backpack slung over my shoulders.

"I was just going to check for you in the stables . . . but

I see that won't be necessary." Her voice didn't rise, and the way she opened the door wider in invitation seemed calm enough, but the white knuckles on the doorknob didn't bode well.

Sure enough, once the door closed and sealed us in, she whirled, wiry arms crossed against her gray sweatshirt, feet shoulder-width apart and firmly planted. "Don't make me put a tracking device on you."

As she drew in a breath to berate me even more, I held up a hand. "I've got it, okay? Going to school was a stupid thing to do. Don't worry. It won't happen again."

With her startled expression giving her an owlish look behind her glasses, I ran for my bedroom and slammed the door.

I threw myself on the fluffy comforter. Nothing could persuade me to leave this house ever, ever again. I'd eat, sleep, and take up soap opera watching to pass the time. Maybe ride a horse or two, and act out pretend conversations with my imaginary friends.

And then Hunter's text at three thirty-two p.m. changed everything.

Want to go out tonight?

I stared at the five words. Stared, and waited for my logic to laugh, no, *guffaw*, at the idea of meeting him after today's fiasco. Even if I wanted to go, escaping this house would mean a huge operation in subterfuge. In fact, after today,

I could see Mom carting me with her everywhere, on the tiniest, most boredom-inspiring errand, maybe even snapping a horse lead on me, just to ensure I didn't pull another unauthorized school visit.

I waited for the logic, but instead got his sweet smell, the way his mouth curved slightly higher on one side than the other. The tiny mole that doubled as a dimple. And, most importantly, the way he made me feel so real.

The exact opposite of the way I'd felt today in the cafeteria.

Target: Down.

I pulled the comforter over my head but couldn't block out the memory. Was this what I had to expect from here on out? I shivered, despite the warmth of the thick down fabric.

If so, then I had to see Hunter. I had to.

He was the only thing that could keep me from turning into a monster.

Under the safety of the covers, I texted him back.

Sure. Meet me @ the end of the driveway @ 7:30

His return text brought a smile to my face. A facial movement that, after the cafeteria fiasco, I'd been sure would disappear from my repertoire forever.

Then I closed my eyes and planned my escape.

THIRTEEN

By seven twenty-five, doubt had started to set in. I was halfway down the driveway, crouching by a tree and shoving my feet into my tennis shoes. I'd slung them over my neck and crept out the front door barefoot to avoid detection. With sunset hitting earlier and earlier the closer we edged to October, the sky was already pretty dark. Still, I worried that any second, Mom would look out the kitchen window and spot me.

Once my shoes were on, I hesitated, the full force of my actions slamming me like a brick wall. What if I was making another terrible mistake? What if this date blew up as badly as school had today? I looked over my shoulder, at the safety of the guesthouse, then stabbed a button on my phone to make it light up. Hunter's last text appeared a moment later.

Can't wait

The same warmth as before spiraled through me, over-powering any lingering doubts. No, this was the right choice. I crossed the remainder of the distance to the street, determined to revel in the slap of chilly air on my cheeks, the crunch of gravel beneath my feet, and the Hunter-filled night ahead of me.

I slowed to a walk just before I reached the dirt road. Headlights arched in a quarter turn onto our street, and within fifteen seconds, a Jeep rumbled to a stop beside me.

The window slid open, and Hunter's head popped out. "Sneaking out?" He smiled, that amazing, silly, blue-eyed smile that melted away any second thoughts. Now we just needed to get out of here. Before Mom found out.

"Something like that." I hurried over to the passenger door and slid inside, closing my door and snapping my seatbelt as swiftly as possible. "Okay, let's go," I said, silently urging Hunter's right foot to push down on the gas.

He shot me a bemused glance but shoved the gear into first. A moment later, we were on our way.

The Jeep smelled like a mix of the cinnamon air-freshener strip and something sweeter. I counted five wrapped squares inside the center console—three pink, two yellow—atop $1.08 in spare change. A few empty wrappers brightened the backseat floorboards, along with three discarded Monster soda cans.

"Candy and caffeine?" I said.

He reached behind his seat blindly, felt one of the cans, and winced. "Meant to clean the car." Then he plucked a pink square from the console. "Want one?"

I eyed the tiny square labeled Starburst and wondered if I'd ever had one. "Sure."

As we drove down the street and the chewy sweetness unfurled in my mouth—just one more thing I had to thank Hunter for—I stole a glance at him. Perfect. He was just so unbelievably perfect, in a totally nonobvious way. His untucked maroon buttondown brought out the blue of his eyes, while the khakis made him look like he'd stepped out of a trendy clothing catalog.

When he shifted to stop, his fingers grazed my arm, the one I'd "injured" yesterday. I flinched, mentally cursed my idiocy, then overcorrected by sitting very, very still.

Please don't notice. Please don't notice.

He noticed.

His sideways glance burned right through my arm, intensifying the no-oxygen squeeze in my chest. Right then I realized I'd made a mistake. A huge one. His eyes would peel back my skin, layer by layer, and expose the obscene, repulsive monster underneath. He'd see the fiber optics and neuromatrices, the phantom sensations. See the irony of me craving oxygen I didn't need, see the ugliness that made me ill just to think about. All the things iPod Man had waxed on about in that southern drawl would be revealed, plunging Mom and me into danger.

I stared straight ahead and summoned all of my willpower to keep from grabbing for the passenger door handle.

Deep breath in—of course he couldn't see through my skin. That was impossible.

Deep breath out—a few days ago, I would have thought being an android was impossible.

Deep breath in—maybe I still did.

Deep breath out—if not, at least I could pretend.

By the time Hunter pulled onto the highway, I'd grabbed the reins of my control and yanked them tight. "Your mom—she overprotective or something?" he asked.

You have no idea. "What, the sneaking out gave me away?" I said, followed by a breezy laugh that sounded remarkably authentic. A light, steady stream of headlights glared through the windshield, heading the opposite way. Back toward the ranch, where I'd left Mom behind.

Mom. She was all alone at the ranch, under the false belief that I was there. Something coiled deep in my stomach. Or where my stomach should be.

Through the passenger window I stared out into the vast nothing that was rural Minnesota at night, balling my fists in my lap. I had to stop this, this crazy self-assessment every time I felt something human. Questioning my sensations, my organs, all the little details that went on under my skin—it only made things a thousand times worse.

"The sneaking, and the no-computer thing," Hunter said.

The computer thing. Right.

"What about your parents? Are they strict?" I said, desperate to steer the conversation into safer territory.

He shifted in his seat, rubbed his jaw with one hand. "Uh . . . no. They aren't around much."

My concern must have registered on my face, because he laughed. "It's no big deal. My dad travels a lot, and Mom likes to go with him."

"Oh." I didn't know what else to say. Sorry your parents are gone a lot? I'm glad you don't care? At least your parents exist outside of your programmed memories?

Silence ticked away for a few more minutes, until he asked, "Bad day?"

Bad day. If only it were as simple as that. Bad day implied something finite—that after a good night's sleep, you'd wake to a new morning full of possibility. To a fresh start.

What it didn't imply was that you'd wake up every day from here to eternity, only to realize you were trapped in the same nightmare.

"If I lied and said I was having the best day ever, would you believe me?"

"Let's see," he said, followed immediately by "No." Then, "Is it your mom? School?"

He tilted his head slightly to the side, in what I'd gathered was an unconscious effort to enlist gravity's assistance in removing the hair from his left eye.

At this point, I felt like I had to give him something. And he'd undoubtedly hear about the cafeteria scuffle tomorrow anyway. In the scheme of things, it was the safest to reveal, and yet . . . what could possibly be more embarrassing than admitting Kaylee and I had fought over him?

I toyed with the edge of my shirt.

"Promise you won't think I'm really lame?"

His eyebrows rose, but he nodded. "Promise."

I cleared my throat. "Well . . . Kaylee and I got in this huge fight. Over . . . you."

After I said it, I squeezed my eyes shut, like blocking out his expression would magically repel any trace of embarrassment.

"Huh."

Too noncommittal to make me open them yet, though I did detect a hint of levity wrapped around that one syllable.

"Mind if I ask who won?"

Oh, he was definitely smiling now; I could hear the laughter lurking. Sure enough, when I mustered up the courage to look, his grin was lopsided, hampered even more than usual by the way he bit the inside of his left cheek.

What did I possibly have to lose at this point? "Me," I said. Firmly.

His grin widened. "Excellent. You know what this means, right?"

That I have inhumanly fast reflexes, all the better to send my opponent flying across the floor? "That girls are silly?" I substituted instead.

"That. Also, since you won me fair and square, I owe you a prize."

A prize? "Seriously?"

"I never joke about prizes," he deadpanned.

"O-kay. But where . . ." And then I saw them. The blaze of lights in the distance, their whimsical glimmer banishing the darkness and transforming a patch of boring countryside into something far more magical.

Like something right out of a fairy tale.

I sat upright, fast enough to make the seat belt snap across my chest. "The carnival? You're taking me to the carnival?" I didn't even try to hide my quiver of excitement.

Kids at Clearwater High had been talking about it all week, even Kaylee and Parker. But, like with all destinations that weren't school, Dairy Queen, or the tack and feed store, Mom had shot down any talk of an outing.

"I take it you like them?" Hunter said.

"I . . ."

. . . actually had no idea, but I was dying to find out. *Careful, Mila.* "Doesn't everyone?" I hedged.

After a sideways glance that seemed too knowing for

comfort, he shrugged. "Sure."

I sank back into the seat, welcoming the airy feeling of possibility that unweighted my limbs. The early part of the day might have been a disaster, but this night . . . this night was going to be perfect. It had to be.

When we got to the carnival, Hunter led me past a string of people waiting for Real Bungee Jump Experience!, a ride called Twister that spun in circles, and some game where a guy was wielding a sledgehammer and slamming it into a metal disk. Finally we stopped in front of a shooting game. "Here we go."

Under the booth's drooping red canopy stretched a lineup of yellow star-shaped targets. Thirty in total. They were flanked on both sides by an array of stuffed animals—mainly unicorns and donkeys. The gray-haired, scruffy attendant waved a rifle-style BB gun at passersby and called out in a singsong voice. "Come on over, try your luck at Star Shootout! Just hit the inside of the star, nothing to it, and win yourself a fine prize! Three chances for two dollars, nine chances for five."

Of course, the two college-aged guys who pushed away from the booth all grumbles and stuffed-donkey-free didn't appear to agree.

Hunter shrugged, handed the guy a five-dollar bill, and accepted the gun. "Promise me you won't run if I come away empty-handed?" he said, flashing a grin at me.

I laughed. "Promise. But I'm sure you'll be fine. It doesn't look that hard."

"No pressure there," he teased. But I noticed that as soon as he hefted the rifle up to his shoulder, he tensed. A transformation came over his face—no smiles, just a determined look in his eyes and complete focus on the target.

He even bit the corner of his mouth in this completely adorable way, just before shooting. And missing the first star by a good two inches.

Oops.

He went through shot after shot, some way off, others just outside the star. The last one landed right on the line, but the carny shook his head. "Sorry, it's gotta be all the way inside. Wanna go again?"

Hunter sighed, shot me a rueful look. "Pretty sure I'd just be throwing my money down the drain."

"What about your girlie there, she want to try? Or she one of those types who needs a man to handle the gun?" he said with a wink at Hunter.

Ew.

"You game?" Hunter asked with a lift of his eyebrows, already digging into his wallet for another five. If I hadn't been before, I sure as heck was now, I thought, shooting the attendant a disgusted look and ready to take down some stars. But when Hunter handed me the gun, it was still warm from his grip, and he stood so close, I could barely think, let alone aim.

No, not distracting at all. Between his proximity and having zero experience shooting guns, we'd most likely have to purchase a stuffed animal if we wanted one.

Except . . . that didn't happen.

Because when I finally lifted the gun, I didn't even have to think about how to use it. The thing just became an extension of my arm, fitted perfectly in my hands. And when I aimed, something crazy happened. As I stared at the star, something red flickered behind my eyes.

I almost dropped the gun. *No. Not again.*

"Are you okay?" Hunter asked, still breath-defyingly close.

I shook my head, dazed, clutching the lowered gun like my life depended on it. The red light disappeared.

"Aw, sugar, don't get cold feet now. Your boy there will still like you, even if you don't come within five hogs of making that shot."

I was still shaken, but the carny's words rekindled my anger. Before I knew it, the gun was lifted and aimed. I took a deep breath, and—

Target: 10 ft.

—swayed when the red words flashed, fully formed this time, but only just. I couldn't drop the gun again. Hunter would think I was crazy, and the carny . . . well, he'd believe whatever wackadoo story he'd concocted in his head.

Meanwhile I commanded, *Get out of my head. Out. OUT.*

And then, like my brain took on a life of its own, the star enlarged before my eyes, allowing me to zoom in on the exact center.

Target: In view.

I knew before I pulled the trigger that I'd hit the star, dead-on. And while my legs weakened from the flashing red words, while my hands clamped down on the gun as I tried to shove them out, the actual shooting felt good. It felt so good that I went ahead and shot out the next one. And the next one. And the next.

Until I noticed the crowd gathered around me. The whistles. The carny's yell of "Sweet cartwheelin' Jesus!" Hunter's startled, laughing exclamation: "Admit it, you're a ringer. I bet you shot guns for kicks back in Philly."

But when the crowd started applauding, that's when my stupidity really hit home. Way to stay under the radar. Of course I could shoot a BB into the middle of a teensy-tiny target—and it wasn't because of years of practice.

I set the gun down, forced a smile at the now frowning carny, who scratched his stubbly chin and stared at the hole-laden targets like he'd never seen them before. "Did we win something?"

We escaped the tent less than a minute later—one medium-sized stuffed donkey richer. And with me vowing to suck at any other game we tried. Luckily, the next booth we hit sold cotton candy.

As we strolled under the lights and listened to the music, I sighed, letting the sugary concoction melt in my mouth. Barring the shooting mishap, this was as close to perfect as it could get. I reached up to wipe a tiny speck of pink from Hunter's cheek. "You missed your mouth."

At the word "mouth," his gaze settled on my lips.

Okay, I'd lied. Maybe it could get more perfect. Butterflies in the stomach? Forget it.. This felt nothing short of a flock of delirious blue jays flapping their wings in a group takeoff. The speck of cotton candy slipped from my hand when we stopped walking, right by a huge roller coaster.

He pulled me closer. "I know the good-night kiss is supposed to happen at the end of the date, but I'm having a hard time waiting."

"Kiss?" I repeated, my eyes now glued to his masterpiece of a mouth. I'd read once in Kaylee's copy of *Glamour* that people perceived beauty based on symmetry. What a shame. Because Hunter's slightly lopsided mouth was about the most amazing thing I'd ever seen.

"If that's okay," he said, his free hand gliding into my hair, like he was memorizing the feel of it.

From our left, girls shrieked in terror as the roller coaster took a sudden dive. I tuned them out and nodded mutely in response, saw his mouth draw nearer. My eyes fluttered closed as every bit of my body tensed in nervous anticipation. I was swaying into him—

—and that's when I saw them. The white walls. Only this time, I saw more. A girl with brown hair. Chained to a chair in a large, barren room, her body pummeled by the glare of too many fluorescent lights.

I saw the back of a white lab coat. The back of a man's dark head. He stood in front of the girl while her head whipped back and forth. He lifted his arm high, and in his hand . . . a gun?

Oh, no.

I gasped and lurched backward. Something terrible was going to happen, I knew it. Oh, god, he was going to—

I watched as the man's hand flew down and smashed the gun against the girl's skull. Again. And again. And again.

Somewhere in the distance, outside the room, away from the icy terror crackling through my legs, my arms, my chest, I heard Hunter's voice.

"Mila, are you okay? Mila?"

I heard it, but I couldn't answer. I couldn't yank myself away from the horror playing out in my head.

No, all I could do was stand frozen while more images streamed behind my eyes. Watch the girl thrash against the chains while the man tossed the gun and grabbed a huge power tool off a small metal table. He pressed a button, and a harsh grinding noise filled the room. A drill. *A drill.*

I stumbled again. *No. Please, no.*

But of course my mental pleas were useless to prevent a chain of events that had already occurred. The man raised the drill high . . . before plunging it into her chest.

Her scream drowned out everything else.

I felt Hunter squeeze my arms, call my name again. But the man in the lab coat, he'd pulled the gun back out. He aimed it at the girl, the girl whose brown hair was so familiar, and pressed the end of the barrel to her forehead. Unsatisfied, he slid the gun around until it was shoved directly against her scalp.

From my viewing angle, I couldn't see the girl's face. But she must have said something. Mouthed something. Because while she didn't make a move to defend herself, the man's shoulders jerked back like she'd struck him. He shook his head in disgust.

Her hair. Nut brown and waterfall straight, with just the tiniest hint of wave. It was—

The sharp blast of a gunshot and realization roared through my head simultaneously. Her hair. I saw it in the mirror every morning.

It was just like mine.

My eyes jerked open. The girl vanished, even though, in the distance, I still heard screams. I was still shaking. Something . . . no, someone was shaking me.

"Mila, what's wrong?"

"I'm not—I don't—" I blinked as the merry lights and bustling crowd of the carnival came into focus, as I became aware of Hunter's concerned face blotting out the sky and the pressure of his grip digging into my arms.

Safe, I was safe. There was no gun, no man in a lab coat. The screams were from the roller coaster.

I was safe. Now. But at one time, I hadn't been.

A shudder ripped through my body, and I realized my cheeks were damp and cold under the breeze. Tears for a me I couldn't even remember.

At my shiver, Hunter dropped his hands and stepped back. "What's wrong?"

"I don't feel well," I managed from between numb lips. Not a lie. "Can you take me home?"

His shoulders rounded, whether in disappointment or relief, I couldn't tell. "Sure," he said after a brief hesitation.

His gentle palm on my back guided me through the crowd, out the gates, and toward the Jeep. But for once, his touch couldn't override the cold that circulated under my skin or the goose bumps I felt racing along its surface. And it was like every trace of magic had leached from the carnival. Instead of a fairy tale, now all I saw was a sad cluster of beat-up rides squatting in an unwanted field. A kiss? Had I really expected it to be that easy? That something so stupid as touching Hunter's lips to mine would solve all my problems, *ta-da!* Banish the truth of who, of what, I was? Banish whatever horrors lurked in my past? How could it, when I didn't even know the complete truth myself?

Only the radio and street noise broke the silence on the way back to the ranch. I knew Hunter kept sneaking looks at me, but I just stared straight ahead. I couldn't talk right now, not when my pretense at being normal slipped further and further from my grasp.

Without any prompting, Hunter cut the lights on the Jeep when we turned onto my street and then eased the car into neutral a good ten feet from the driveway, where the thick cluster of trees would hide the car from view. He reached across the discarded Starbursts to layer his hand over mine. "Maybe we can do this again sometime, when you're feeling better?"

His tilted head and wide eyes gave his expression such soulful confusion that some of the icy chains finally slipped from my chest. My lips even lifted into a smile, tiny but genuine. "I was hoping you'd say that."

Then, in a burst of bravery I didn't see coming, I leaned forward and pressed my mouth briefly to his stubble-roughened cheek. I pulled away before he could react, yanking on the passenger door handle and jumping out into the night.

FOURTEEN

The living room window was dark when I snuck up to the front door, making me hopeful not only that my absence had gone unnoticed, but that Mom had decided on an early night. I checked my cell phone. No missed calls, an excellent sign.

Relieved that I wouldn't have to tack another fight with Mom to my growing list of the day's horrors, I dug my key out of my pocket. Tomorrow, I could ask her about the memory—once I had bolstered up enough courage.

But when I reached for the door, I heard something. A muffled moan, male voices.

I froze with the key barely grazing the lock. The TV? Maybe. But it was unlike Mom to watch the one in her bedroom, and the living room lacked the telltale flicker of lights.

Then I inserted the key into the lock, and the door moved. The door—it was already open. Nothing short of a catastrophe or a stroke would make Mom forget to shut the door. Carefully I inched the door open so I could peer inside. Nothing. Quiet.

I crept inside the darkened room . . . and almost fell flat on my face.

My toe, it had caught on something.

Only that patch of floor should be bare.

Keeping my hands steady against the deepening stirrings of fear, I pressed a button on my cell phone. The light was faint, but it was enough to make the fear explode. The thing I'd tripped on was a green plaid pillow, from the couch. A pillow that had been ripped to shreds.

As I raised the phone, the rest of the room came into view. The couch was overturned, the gaping wounds in the green-and-tan plaid fabric spilling puffy white cotton guts. Wooden drawers from the bureau littered the old hardwood floor. And papers . . . papers everywhere.

And then I realized: the room . . . it was way brighter than it should have been, based solely on my tiny cell-phone light.

Visual scan activated.

The red words shimmered behind my eyes.

Without my permission, my vision zoomed around the room, focusing in on tiny details I never should have been able to see, not this up close and personal.

Night vision activated.

As if the red words weren't bad enough, this time an impersonal female voice echoed in my head, repeating them. A familiar voice.

My voice, I realized as my knees started to shake. Only a smooth, heartless, digitized version.

I reached for the wall to stay upright as terror crashed over me. I fought the words, strained to silence the voice. At the same time, I heard something stir in the hallway. The faintest wisp of a breath.

Reality pounded me from all directions.

Someone had found us.

Mom.

I vaulted over the cushion and flew past the couch. Just as a lean, tall figure emerged from the hallway.

Not Mom. A man.

With my enhanced vision, I saw him open his mouth to shout, and knew I had to silence him before any of his companions discovered me.

I surged forward while simultaneously pulling back my arm. So fast he didn't even have time to vocalize. And then my fist smashed him in the throat. No thinking involved. Just my left hand, knowing exactly what to do, like I'd performed the maneuver a million times before, slamming into his neck with the velocity of a baseball.

His eyes widened, and a sleek device slipped from his grasp when he futilely grabbed at his throat. I caught the Taser with one hand and snagged his wrist with the other to keep him from hitting the ground. When he fell backward, there was a sickening but soft snap as his arm fully extended and hit resistance. I winced. Shoulder dislocation, at the very least.

I eased him to the floor, and that's when the red lights, the voice, forced their way into my head again.

Target: Immobilized.

I steadied myself, then crept down the hallway, peering into my bedroom on the right. More chaos in here, much more. My clothes, my papers, they covered the floor like trash, so much that I could catch only glimpses of the red-and-gold rug. Half of my mattress was off the box spring, propped up against it like an indoor slide, a huge slash traveling down the center.

My eyes flew to my nightstand, knowing what I would find. Sure enough, the bronze picture frame was empty. All that showed behind the shattered glass was a brown piece of cardboard. My picture of Dad . . . gone.

I curled my hands into fists, trying to dampen the pain by telling myself they'd stolen a stranger. Dad didn't exist. Everything Mom had told me—it was all true.

Another strange sound escaped from the back of the hallway. The garage. Mom.

I sprinted down the hall and shoved open the door.

I took in the scene in the blink of an eye. Three men up by the big door—two tall, one short with a wide nose—rummaging through boxes. Mom, tied to the furnace with thin, wiry rope, a splash of gray duct tape over her mouth, staring stoically ahead. And a fourth man in a Windbreaker, standing beside her—smacking a wrench against his palm.

The whites around Mom's blue eyes showed. The tape turned her words into muffled noises, but I was pretty sure she was trying to say, "Mila, run!" as the guy with the wrench rushed at me, swift and sure.

But not as swift and sure as me. I ran, just like Mom wanted.

Right in her direction.

I reached the Windbreaker guy at the same time he lifted the wrench. Despite having her arms tethered, Mom kicked for his knee, right when my hand lashed out at his nose. Our combined forces knocked him back a step. He crashed into boxes, and all of them toppled to the ground.

Rough arms grabbed me from behind. My head whipped back, and *bam!* I heard a sharp crackle of cartilage crumpling under my skull. His harsh cry didn't stop me. I spun—and rammed an elbow into the short man's left kidney, making him stagger. All it took was one swift kick to the same spot to send him crashing onto a pile of discarded garden tools. His shriek rang out when his head smashed the back of a shovel.

I raced to Mom before the last two guys could reach me, freeing her from the rope and tape with two powerful yanks of my hand.

Mom lashed out, her elbow catching a nose. She ducked away, but he didn't try to grab her. No, both men were now completely focused on me.

They came at once. One lifted a sleek metal Taser and took aim. And it was like someone flipped a switch inside me, triggering me into total fight mode.

The moves flew through my head first, and I executed with perfect synchronicity.

Drop to ground, foot sweep to target's ankles.

The Taser's prongs flashed and ripped through the air, hitting the ceiling as the man stumbled back.

Target: Vulnerable.

Spin.

One hand to his wrist, other on his Taser. Snap backward. Ignore crunch and scream, continue to incapacitate.

Block target's attack with right arm.

Left hand, slice to crichoid cartilage. Right knee to left kidney. A final chop, to back of target's neck.

Target: Immobilized.

"Mila, behind you!" Mom yelled.

But I was already on it. Like I was performing a carefully choreographed dance, I swooped down, scooped up the discarded Taser, and whirled, all in one continuous motion. I aimed just as the fourth man was reaching for his holster. One flick of the switch, and the white light shot out like an electrical tongue. His entire body convulsed, the coppery smell of burned metal searing the air.

Target: Immobilized.

I turned to do a quick inventory. Four men down. And I wasn't even winded. Maybe it was impossible for me to be winded. It was like I was a fighting machine.

Reality crashed over me. A fighting *machine*.

"Mila?"

I looked over to see Mom still staring at the fourth target, the one I'd stunned. He hadn't moved. I knew what she was asking, and the truth was . . . I didn't know. I didn't know, and I was afraid of the answer. Because the Taser hadn't been set to bring down a human; it'd been set much higher. It'd been set to bring me down.

She shook her head as if to clear it. And that was all it took to spring her back into action. "The car!"

I staggered back, horrified at the damage I might have done, but Mom grabbed my arm and dragged me toward the door. "Let's go. Now."

I stumbled along in her wake, in a daze.

Mom didn't stop once, just vaulted boxes, pulling me along until we'd made it outside and were rushing for the SUV.

I slowed before we jumped off the porch. "Wait, what

about our stuff? The iPod?"

She yanked. "Out here." Before we made it to the end of the dirt path, she swerved, toward the line of stepping-stones that ran along the side of the house and the driveway. She squatted down and, with a strain of her shoulders, pushed the third one to the side. Underneath wasn't dirt, like you'd expect, but a hole. And inside that hole was a small metal lockbox.

She grabbed it and started for the SUV once more. "Suitcase is in the car."

And with a stab of realization, I understood. The dark-blue suitcase that was always in the back of the SUV, it wasn't part of some weird grieving process for Dad. How could it be, when that person didn't exist? No, all along, Mom had been ready for this moment.

And now it was here.

Mom wrenched open the door and vaulted into the driver's seat, jamming the keys into the ignition.

"Move over." I jumped into the car after she scrambled over to the passenger side. I pulled the door closed and gunned the gas pedal into reverse. The SUV shot out of the driveway backward.

As the familiar sight of Greenwood Ranch faded in the rearview mirror, the same thought whirled through my head, around and around like the tires below us.

A fighting machine.

The voice on the recording, my mom's outlandish story—all of it was real.

My fingers squeezed the wheel, so tightly that I felt the metal underneath the padding start to yield. No matter what, I wouldn't let anyone change me. I wouldn't let them strip away whatever tiny parts of me were human.

. . . a fighting machine . . .

Assuming I had any humanity to lose.

It wasn't until we'd driven through the residential streets and onto eastbound 94 that I realized I hadn't turned on the headlights. No headlights to pierce the streetlamp-devoid Clearwater country roads, and yet I could still see perfectly. I'd noticed every slight curve of the road, every leaf on the trees swaying lightly in the breeze, even the license plate numbers on the old trucks and cars parked at the far ends of long driveways. I could see all of it, clear as day.

I shook my head as I snapped on the lights so we wouldn't get pulled over. I'd been out at night before but had stumbled in the dark just like anyone else.

Up until yesterday.

Something suctioned at my stomach, leaving a strange emptiness to creep into its place. Night vision wasn't the only thing I'd acquired over the last twenty-four hours. There was also the way I'd calculated the precise distance to the targets at the carnival and shot them without a single deviation. How I'd taken down five armed men with minimal exertion. The "Target: Down" and "Target: Immobilized." Glowing red evidence behind my eyes.

I drove on, trying to push the thoughts away, trying to erase the dawning, awful certainty of what must have happened. I'd always been different, part of me argued—the part that still desperately needed to believe in the woman sitting beside me, despite everything that had happened. After all, I'd heard Hunter speak all the way across the Dairy Queen, picked up the thump of Maisey's bucket from an impossible distance. I'd hurt Kaylee when I could have sworn I barely touched her. All those things had occurred before the accident.

But the bigger part of me, the more certain part, rejected that rationale as bogus. Those things were minor. Too minor, when compared to combat fighting and gun handling. It was almost like . . .

My throat constricted as I allowed the realization to fully surface.

. . . like someone had switched me into a different mode.

I remembered Mom, back at the house after the accident. Tinkering with my arm, my neck, all while a stranger chipped away pieces of my life with every brutal word.

Tinkering with my neck. When my arm had been the only part damaged.

The crunch of plastic under my hands alerted me to how hard I clutched the steering wheel. I relaxed my grip. I needed the truth before I permanently maimed the car.

"What did you do to me? Press some kind of activation switch after you stitched me up?"

I felt that same tiny flare of hope from before, when I'd first shown her my arm. That same rise of breathless anticipation that maybe, just maybe, I'd come to the wrong conclusion, even though I knew better.

"I'm sorry, Mila."

Three words, I realized with a choked sob. That's all it took for hope to die.

When her hand settled on my shoulder, I shook it off, making the Tahoe swerve. "Don't," I said. "Just tell me what you did."

Despite my resolve to stay focused on the twin glow of taillights ahead, I caught the way she deflated against the seat and the weary drag of her hand down the back of her neck. "I kept your hardwired defense system inactivated until you injured your arm . . . at which time I worried we'd find ourselves in a situation exactly like this."

I flinched, repulsed by what I knew was coming next but still needing to hear her admit to the details. "So, what? You turned me into some kind of psycho killer without telling me? And I'm supposed to be okay with it?"

"No."

At that unexpected reply, my head whipped toward her. "No, what?"

"No, you're not a psycho killer, and I didn't expect you to be okay with it. But I did reactivate your defense mode. You should be fully functional after forty-eight hours."

So there it was, plain as day. Another betrayal in a whole string of them. One thing became blindingly, painfully clear: there was no one I could trust.

A single tear slid down my cheek. I dashed it away, angered by my weakness.

Mom sighed. "I know you're upset, but I was trying to keep you safe. You have to realize: that wasn't the regular military after us—that isn't their MO. They would have come after us en masse, guns blazing, no sneaking in the middle of the night. No, this reeks of Andrew Holland."

"Who?"

"General Holland, the cocreator of the MILA project— the man you heard on the iPod. He's in charge of SMART Ops."

"SMART Ops?"

"Secure Military Android Research and Testing, a clandestine military operation run by Holland. And there's a reason for that. The man is a coldhearted megalomaniac. I didn't see it at first, but—"

"Stop!" A general? SMART Ops? A clandestine military operation? Was this all for real? I shook my head before another question could tumble out. "I don't want to know."

"But—"

"I mean it!" I flung my open palm at Mom, hoping the visual cue might silence her if words couldn't. "I can't take any more, not tonight."

I felt her gaze search my face but refused to acknowledge it. I couldn't. I was too afraid that even a single trace of concern would push me over the edge. Turn me into either a screaming lunatic or a bawling wreck.

Besides, as far as I was concerned, this was all her fault. Nothing she could tell me about this mysterious SMART Ops would change anything. Not our course of action, or our inability to turn around and return to our old life in Clearwater. Return to Hunter. It wouldn't magically enable the man stored in my memory to really become my father.

It wouldn't make me real.

Beside me, Mom's blond head bowed over her hands.

"Where are we headed?" I snapped.

"Toronto," she said. "Pearson Airport. Holland will have us flagged at every U.S. airport. Our chances are much better in Canada, and from there, we'll head abroad."

I heard her explanation, but all I could think was *Canada*. We were going to Canada, and then boarding an airplane to some other foreign country. At this point, it didn't really matter where. All that mattered was that Clearwater, even the U.S., would be out of reach for good.

Loss clawed at my chest as an image of Hunter's blue eyes flashed before me. His quirky smile. I'd known we were leaving the state, but another country? That seemed so final. Now I'd never have another chance to make the fairy tale real.

Desperately needing the distraction, I reached over to plug the information into the Tahoe's GPS system. Mom stopped me.

"Wait, they might be able to track the car's GPS system. But—" She broke off and turned toward the passenger window. The struggle back at the house had caused blond strands to escape her ponytail and hang haphazardly down her neck, ruining her usual illusion of perfection.

"But what?"

After a large sigh and one more glance at the dead night streets of rural Minnesota, she swung back around to face me. "You have built-in GPS. And yours has stealth mode."

My lips parted, but no words came out, just a strangled gasp. Compliments of the rocklike lump stuck in my throat. GPS. Stealth mode.

Just when I thought things couldn't get worse, Mom shattered any chances I had of being human. Over and over again.

"Mila—"

I flashed her my palm again. "Later. Please," I whispered.

The ache in my chest expanded, stretched, until I was sure it would distort my skin beyond repair.

I'd lost Hunter, I'd lost my family, and now, with every new ability that revealed itself, I was losing me.

PART TWO

FIFTEEN

t wasn't until we'd left Minneapolis far behind that I was ready to broach the topic again. "So how do I make the GPS work?"

Mom shifted in the seat, her eyes never moving from the rearview window. She must have been really stressed, if even the idea of explaining my GPS feature didn't perk her up.

My hands tensed.

"Now that I reinitialized all your functions, it will update wirelessly, so you're always current. As far as activating it . . . you just issue the GPS command."

The GPS command. Right. I liked how she made it sound so everyday, like toast and orange juice in the morning.

Feeling like the biggest fool in Minnesota, I muttered, "GPS."

"Not out loud. In your head," she said, with a hint of a smile in her voice this time.

Her amusement made me grit my teeth. I unclenched my jaw while passing a slow-moving Buick on my left, then concentrated.

GPS.

Deep down, I didn't really expect it to work—okay, maybe a little piece of me hoped it wouldn't work—so I jerked in my seat when the word blinked red behind my eyes.

Like magic, a glowing green map unfurled before me, unleashing a detailed schematic of Minnesota. And there we were, a tiny, blinking orange dot.

I waited, waited for the world to quit swaying under our car, for my mind to quit fighting itself. It was disconcerting, because half of my brain was trying to spit the image out like it was a sour swig of milk, while the other half held on tightly, refusing to budge. And despite my very human desire to get rid of the monstrosity, the thing that marked me as different, the android side was winning. Hard as I tried, I couldn't make the map disappear.

"Turn it off. How do I turn it off?"

My voice sounded weak, faint, even to my own ears. I felt rather than saw Mom's concern as she turned toward me. My hands clenched the wheel to keep the Tahoe from swerving.

"GPS off."

I latched onto the phrase with a gulp of desperation.

 GPS off.

The war in my head ended the instant the map vanished.

"What's wrong? Are you okay?"

If you could be okay with a throbbing brain, then sure. I was fine. "I just . . . don't want to look at it right now."

"Okay."

Silence stretched between us, awkward, heavy. Full of lies and betrayals. But underneath all the anger, the hurt, I had to admit I was grateful for her presence. And despite wanting to call her, to think of her as, Nicole, I couldn't quite overcome the programming in my brain that made me think of her as Mom.

I stared glumly ahead. I had a long trip to work on that, though.

Once again I felt her focus on me. A moment later she said, "I think we should pull over for the night soon. It's a little risky, but I need to be fresh for tomorrow, at the airport. One mistake, and . . ."

She didn't finish, and I didn't ask.

"Anyway, we need to change our appearances, too. To match our new passports."

New passports?

Digging into her purse, she pulled out two blue laminated folders and handed one to me.

Two laminated folders that held brand-new futures—futures I wasn't sure I wanted. I flipped open the passport and gave the information a cursory glance.

Just yesterday, I'd discovered I wasn't Mila the girl, but Mila the android. Now I no longer got to be Mila at all. My new persona was Stephanie, a Photoshopped image of me with short, jagged black hair.

At the rate I was going, I'd never figure out my true identity.

"You didn't even ask," I muttered under my breath. It was a tiny thing, given the events that had transpired. So tiny. Yet, just for once, I would have liked some input into my own future, even if that only meant picking out a phony name and hairstyle.

"What?"

"Nothing. Where should I pull off?"

Mom drummed her fingers against her leg, apparently lost in thought. Finally she said, "Doesn't matter. Anywhere between here and Chicago. We'll try to find a motel that looks a little run-down, where they're more likely to let us have a room without asking for ID."

A run-down motel, a run for the border. I'd appreciate it if sometime soon, things would start looking up.

At the next decently sized exit that advertised gas-food-lodging, I pulled off the freeway. A couple of nicer-looking chain motels hovered near the off ramp, but Mom shooed me past them. I drove farther down the street until we came to one that satisfied her, one with only three cars in the parking lot, a beaten-down two-story with a neon sign advertising VACANCY.

After accepting the key card from the sleepy old woman behind the desk, we drove around to our motel room. The fresh coat of tan paint on the door looked hopeful, as did the shiny brass 33 centered just above a tiny peephole. But the inside didn't follow through. The door swung open, revealing two dated and dingy double beds with orange-and-brown comforters, tan carpet that had seen better days, and an old-fashioned big square TV bolted to a table. As if anyone would want to steal that dinosaur. Pine-scented air freshener couldn't mask the musty reek of mold, nor could the plaid pattern on the comforters hide the five dark stains scattered between them. I didn't even want to think about what had caused them.

I tossed the suitcase on the squat chair in the corner—the cleanest-looking spot in the room—and carefully perched on a stain-free edge of the bed. Despite the fatigue tugging at her eyes, Mom completed an efficient sweep of the room, checking under beds and the bathroom before returning to hover by the door, purse in hand.

"I need to head back out to the drugstore and grab some supplies."

I stood back up. "I'll go with you."

Mom gave a firm shake of her head. "No, you stay here. There's something I need you to look at." She rummaged through her purse, pulling out a clear plastic square case, less than two inches long per side. Inside was a flat blue square with a gold computer chip embedded inside.

She popped the top and then upended the card into her palm, the contrast between the deep blue and her pale skin startling. I noticed the mishmash of tiny lines in her skin, threading out from the longer indents. Signs of aging. Something my palm would never do.

"I know you weren't ready to listen in the car, but it's crucial you know who we're running from. I managed to accrue some information before I left, and it's on this memory card."

I stared at the square as the back of my neck prickled. Why would she give me that when we didn't have a computer? That didn't make any sense, and yet, in a terrifying glimmer of realization, I was afraid it did. "Please tell me you stashed a laptop in the suitcase that I don't know about."

Mom's teeth sank into her bottom lip while her fingers worried the nosepiece of her glasses. "Mila," she said quietly. Nothing else, but her tone told me all I needed to know.

The laugh I tried to force came out garbled, and I felt cold, so cold, like that memory card had banished every bit of warmth from the room. "Right. I'm the computer." Not only that, but somewhere on—no, in. *In!*—my body, I had a slot for that card. An electrical portal.

How was that even possible? How could you have a port for a memory card in your body and not know about it?

I couldn't look at Mom, couldn't bear to see the phony sympathy on her face. And it had to be phony, corrupt, because after all, she was the one who'd created me. She didn't get to make such a repulsive freak of nature and then feel bad about it afterward; that wasn't how it worked. So I focused on the blue card and asked the question burning through my mind instead.

"Where is it?"

She reached forward and clasped my right hand between her slender fingers. The urge to yank my arm out of her grasp was strong, but I resisted, let her tug until it stretched between us like an unwilling bridge. Then she rotated my wrist until my palm faced the ceiling.

She slid a finger along the crease of my wrist. "Here, where it's hidden from view."

Even after she pointed it out, I couldn't see it at first. My finger traced her path and found only skin.

"Pull the skin toward your elbow."

Sure enough, when my thumb pressed the skin the way she'd instructed, it appeared. A perfect straight line, like a paper cut. A thin slot. Just the right size for the card.

I stared at the slot, my wrist, my entire arm, like they belonged to someone else. Like they were completely alien entities.

Mom had forbidden computers while, all this time, I'd been walking around Clearwater with a memory card slot. In. My. Wrist.

When Mom released my hand, I didn't move. I held my hand in that same outstretched position, as far away from me as possible.

Regrettably, she took that as a sign of interest. "There are two ways to assimilate the card's data. The fastest way is internally—inside your head. But we also created a feature where you could project the data into the environment. Mainly for our benefit, so it'd be easily accessible in the field. I think that's also going to be the best way for you."

"Why?" I couldn't help it. I didn't want to know, and yet, in a sick way, I did. After all, this was my wrist we were talking about. That, and my ability to project data out into the atmosphere.

Whatever that meant.

"Because you've become accustomed to processing things more like a human, so analyzing that type of data internally might be overwhelming. For now, anyway."

She extended the blue square to me. "Would you like to try?"

Funny how the sight of an inanimate object could trigger

such revulsion. I wanted to smash the chip under my heel and flush the remnants down the toilet until they were long gone, too far away to hurt me.

But that wouldn't change anything.

Besides, Mom was right: I needed to learn about this SMART Ops, which I could do in one of two ways. And even though the idea of inserting a memory card into my arm terrified me, it seemed less risky than listening to Mom and chancing another one of her bombshells.

"Not until you leave."

A flicker of hurt crossed her face, which led to a corresponding pang in my own chest, followed by a spark of anger. "Would you drop the mom act already? We both know it's fake."

She exhaled sharply. "You don't . . ." She closed her eyes and stepped away. When she opened them again, her expression was carefully composed. "Fine. Just . . . the command to view the data externally is 'Project.'"

"What, so I just say that word and presto, data comes flying out?" I was having a hard time picturing any of this. I didn't want to picture any of this. Right now, all I wanted to do was dive under that dirty comforter, scrunch into a ball, and hide until all of the crazy reality that was my life went away. Major android fail, that's what Kaylee would say.

If Kaylee weren't hundreds of miles away and didn't hate me right now.

Oh, and if she knew I was an android.

Mom held out the card, which I accepted with a steady hand, fighting off a shudder at its sleek, plastic, lifeless feel. The last thing I needed was for Mom to change her mind and insist on staying.

I must have faked it pretty well, because she shouldered her purse and headed for the door. "Just remember—try not to fight it, and if the card is overloading you somehow, eject. And don't leave this room. Understand?"

She hesitated with one hand on the doorknob, as if giving me a chance to change my mind and invite her to stay. But I couldn't. I couldn't even look at her, the sight of that familiar heart-shaped face, those pale-blue eyes, made me long for a life I could never have.

The gentle click of the door closing signaled her defeat.

I waited. Stared at the card and waited until I heard the rumble of the Tahoe's engine fade. I pinched the card between my left thumb and ring finger, stifling the urge to fling it across the room. I held my breath and brought the blue square closer and closer to my wrist, until it was only a whisper away from touching, then almost choked on a burst of panic. How could I do this? How could I force this tiny slip of plastic into my flesh, when everything inside me screamed in revulsion?

I closed my eyes, steeled myself. I opened them a false heartbeat later and, before I could chicken out, bent my wrist back, exposed the tiny slot, and pushed.

The card slid inside smoothly, without a hint of resistance. Like my own body had betrayed me.

At first, all I felt was a light pressure, under the crease of my wrist.

Input: Accepted.

Then, in a lightninglike snap, the pressure erupted into a jolt that crackled up my arm.

When it reached my neck, I panicked. This couldn't be happening.

The energy rushed my head like a swarm of glowing bees, and I pushed against it, desperate not to let the glowing mass in. The effort was dizzying, draining, and a second later, my legs buckled. I collapsed onto the bed, and that tiny distraction weakened my defenses just enough. With a final push, the energy buzzed into my brain.

I felt something give, felt a portal open. And then the data began flowing in.

Virus scan complete.

Copying data.

Scan metadata.

The words blinked behind my eyes, their eerie red flash echoed by my own dispassionate voice. The room swayed, and my fingers dug into the scratchy comforter as if that could stop the horror from unraveling inside my skull. But of course it didn't work. Data continued streaming in as unstructured strands of letters and symbols, none of which made any sense.

All of this took place in a flash, but I could see every detail. One by one, the nonsensical patterns rearranged themselves into sentences. Images. Information I could finally comprehend.

> *ATTN: General Holland*
> *CLASSIFIED*
> *Re: MILA PROJECT*
> *Your request for more funds has been approved. As usual, all details of this transaction and the MILA project are to remain top secret, available to SMART Ops only. We're both aware that some of the higher-ups are far too shortsighted to support this research, and I doubt the American public is ready either.*
> *In the future, I expect you to clear any failures with me before terminating them. I'm being generous with diverting funds, but that won't last forever.*
> *Signed,*

My head. I was opening documents in my head. The me I knew, the human me, couldn't quite comprehend that these events were unfolding, but that obviously didn't matter. Mom might have erased the memories of my true nature, but that didn't mean my true nature stopped existing. My true android nature.

My horror mingled with a sick fascination, just as the information pulsed into my head at a higher speed. And then chaos erupted.

Suddenly, everything streamed ten, twenty times faster, blurring past in an unintelligible rush. Endless amounts of data, simultaneously demanding to be copied, scanned, analyzed, sequenced.

The faster the strands streamed, the more they jumbled together—photos spliced with random symbols, diagrams melding into meaningless arrangements of letters, all entwining into a giant mess. Like a ball of tangled yarn that kept growing and growing and growing, filling my head until I couldn't see, couldn't focus, until my consciousness dwindled to a single, panicked thought:

Get it out.

I dropped my head into my hands, trying to stop the irregular pulsing rhythm, the skull-cracking pressure of the expanding data web.

Overload.

The word glared like a big red confirmation. My human and android parts, in agreement for once.

I had to get this mess out somehow, force the information someplace else. Someplace where I could *see* it correctly.

The command to view the data externally is "Project."

I spoke the word inside my head.

Project.

The word fizzled and vanished while the pulsing grew stronger.

PROJECT!

This time, the word didn't vanish. Instinctively I reached out to grasp it, fumbling my way through data streams and feeling unbelievably awkward. Right when I thought it was going to slip away, I wrapped my mind around it.

PROJECT.

Current sizzled. I felt a swoosh as data rushed in the opposite direction. In rapid succession, four green walls flickered into existence around me, enclosing me in a glowing square that sliced right through the bed and motel carpet.

Tiny blinking green icons filled them.

I shook my head but nothing changed. The green box remained, shimmering, its effervescence an unnerving contrast to the motel room's dingy orange and brown. The icons remained in place as well.

Too much. After everything else tonight, this was just too much.

I jumped off the bed with a crash of battered springs, backed away from the surreal glow. The blinking green icons followed.

I fought off the image, willed it away. Tried to deny what my own eyes were showing me, an effort that weakened me, made my legs quiver as they threatened to collapse once more.

No escape. There was no escape. No escape except . . .

Eject.

At the same time I thought the word, I pushed hard on the slot beneath my wrist.

One blink, and my whole environment cleared: my mind, the room, everything.

Everything except my wrist. The upper half of the card poked through my skin like a chunk of blue shrapnel. I shuddered at the visual, yanked it out, and chucked the thing at the dresser. Mom would have to tell me about SMART Ops if she wanted me to know more, because I was never sticking that thing in my arm again.

I paced the room in a futile attempt to settle. But when I looked at my arms, my hands, my legs, I no longer saw the limbs of a normal teenager. All I pictured was a human-shaped container. A machine, built for holding sequences of raw data.

I brought my fist to my mouth. I couldn't get caught up in this way of thinking. If I did, I'd lose whatever tenuous claim on humanity I had left. A teenager; I needed to believe that part of me was that normal teenager still. But how?

If only Hunter were here, with his lopsided bangs and lopsided smile and his flutter-inducing touch that said there was more to me than what they'd created in the lab. But he was back in Clearwater, and I was here. Still, his voice. If I could just hear his voice.

My gaze fell on the white rectangle Mom had dropped on the dresser. A moment later, the room key was clenched in my hand, and I was out the door.

SIXTEEN

made sure the lock engaged before heading toward the pitted parking lot. Across the street, the twenty-four-hour sign on the All Nite mini-mart attached to the gas station blinked. The parking lot and streets were quiet, except for the freeway noise from three-quarters of a mile away. Still, I wondered if I was making a mistake. What if the men from SMART Ops had somehow found us again and were out here, watching me?

I hesitated, just as red words flared in my head.

Visual scan: Activated.

I froze next to a maroon sedan, trying to push away the images that zoomed through my mind. The models, makes, and colors of all the cars in the parking lot. Their license-plate numbers. Close-ups of the bedraggled garlic bushes that surrounded the perimeter, the lone oak tree. The viscous spill of brown liquid on the asphalt to the left of our room.

No human threat detected.

My hands shook, so I shoved them into my pockets and fought back the dizzying swell of disgust. I could hate the functions all I wanted, but I couldn't argue that this one was useful. It would be a waste not to make the most of it.

But as I hurried across the parking lot and into the street, I realized I missed the darkness. While night vision was handy, having the dark ripped away from me without choice felt like just another piece of humanity had been stolen.

The red twenty-four-hour sign on the door blinked and emitted an intermittent buzz. I kept my head low while walking through the door but took in everything. Despite the ratty exterior, the inside of the store was spotless. Five aisles of snacks and sundries were neatly arranged in the middle of the small enclosure, with a gleaming silver soft-drink dispenser in the back left corner and a refrigerated section on the right. But I wasn't here for food.

A middle-aged woman—DANA, her name tag read— flashed me a lipstick-stained smile before returning to a gossip magazine behind the counter. She didn't seem especially interested in me. Unfortunately, the young male security guard filling his coffee cup in the back did. He smiled and waved a friendly greeting, but all I could think about was whether or not the gun I saw strapped to his waist was loaded.

Before I knew it, my eyes zeroed in on the weapon. Inside my head, a beep sounded. Then the image enlarged behind my eyes, rotated in a three-hundred-sixty-degree turn.

While the gun twirled, the red words declared:

Sig Sauer P229, 9mm.

I whirled from the guard, averting my face, pretending to inspect the candy section while grasping the shelf to steady myself.

My panicked gaze fell on a package of Starbursts. The sight reminded me of Hunter's Jeep, of how he made me feel so very real and vulnerable. The simple memory of his hand, reached across the scattered candy to curve around mine, was enough. No matter how silly it sounded, those feelings I experienced with Hunter made me feel like anything was possible, like I didn't have to turn into a machine.

Overcoming my inertia, I grabbed the candy and carried it to the counter. I could sense the security guard's stare but didn't look his way.

No need to worry yet. More than likely, they'd had a high rate of crime in the area, and this was all just an exercise to prevent any shoplifting. But I didn't know enough about the SMART Ops and how they operated to be one hundred percent comfortable with that assessment. Plus any attention at this point was bad.

I caught the slightest sounds he made, even over the pop song that played a way-too-jaunty tune. The slight creak of his knee when he shifted his weight. A raspy noise, like he was scratching the stubble on his chin.

I needed to get out of here. Now.

"Can I have one of those precharged disposable cell phones, too?" I said in a low voice, pointing to the display behind the cashier's bushy brown hair.

The woman clicked her tongue. "Oh, no, hon, did your smartphone die? Everyone thinks they're so amazing, but give me something basic and reliable any day."

I let my hair shield my face and gave a small smile, but didn't comment. The less memorable our interaction, the better. The register beeped. After I paid, I thanked her and scooped up the plastic bag to leave. The security guard's gaze rested on me from ten feet away.

As I walked toward the door, I just knew the security guard would follow.

I entered the deserted night, the distant rush of cars and the hum of the neon sign the only noise. The word VACANCY across the street glowed like a beacon, but I ignored it and made a right turn instead. Toward the empty stretch of road ahead. If this guy wanted to follow me, I wasn't about to lead him to Mom.

One, two, three more steps down the cracked sidewalk. He followed. Maybe he was just coming outside for a smoke. Maybe—

I whirled just as his hand reached to tap me on the shoulder.

"Oh!" he said, jumping back. "I'm sorry, I didn't mean to frighten you. I was—I was just wondering . . ."

My fingers tightened on the plastic bag reflexively.

". . . if you're from around here, maybe you'd like to go grab a cup of coffee sometime?"

I blinked. A cup of coffee? This guy was asking me on a date? My fingers relaxed at the same time I felt warmth spread through my cheeks.

Fake warmth that felt so amazingly real.

"Um, thanks, but I don't think my mom would approve." On so many levels.

His tentative smile vanished. "Your mom? How old are you?"

"Sixteen."

Now his cheeks were the ones blotchy with embarrassment. He lurched several hasty steps back and held his hands out in front of him, as if they could protect him from his own disastrous thoughts. "Oh . . . ah . . . I had no idea. I figured, with you walking by yourself at night . . ." He kept glancing back over his shoulder at the mini-mart, like the cashier might dash out and save him.

"Just grabbing a snack and heading back to the hotel room," I said, shaking my bag and biting back a smile. "Have a good night."

Once he slouched his way back into the mini-mart, I scurried across the street for Room 33.

I immediately crossed to the bed and sat, digging the phone out of the plastic bag so I could activate it and begin punching in his number.

Security mode: On.

The voice command startled me so much, I almost dropped the phone. Security mode, what did that even mean? Was I going to be tracing this call somehow, or even recording it? Hastily I hit the disconnect button.

I stared at the way my fingers tightened around the phone. All I'd wanted to do was hear Hunter's voice, just for a few minutes, and now even that had been taken from me. But I couldn't risk his safety, or Mom finding out.

I turned off the phone to preserve the battery and shoved it into my bag while cold seeped into the ever-widening void inside me. Then I slumped onto my back on the bed and stared at the small black beetle that crawled across the yellowing ceiling with no apparent urgency or concern, wondering if emotions were a little overrated.

Forty minutes later, I sat in a stiff-backed chair in front of the wobbly motel mirror. With one hand, Mom deftly pulled a comb through my hair, stopping about halfway down.

"Shorter," I said.

Blue eyes met my green ones in the mirror. "Are you sure?"

No. "Yes. Besides, it's shorter in the passport photo."

A pause. "You realize it won't grow back."

I froze, transfixed by the chin-length strands in the mirror. Actually, I hadn't realized, but it made sense. Of course my hair couldn't grow. Why would it? Hair growth implied human hair follicles. Live ones. Such a stupid little thing, and yet as my gaze swept the discarded, curling strands that littered the brown carpet, my eyes burned.

"Shorter," I repeated stubbornly. "Anyway, why do you care so much about my hair? It's not like it matters."

In fact, Mom hadn't been thrilled with this whole experience. She'd immediately turned away when I'd first emerged from the bathroom with my hair jet-black, as if she couldn't bear to look at me, and the first snip had been especially hard for her, based on the way her fingers trembled while holding the scissors.

She tugged the comb back through, stopping just below my ears this time. She lifted the scissors.

Snip, snip.

Pieces of black hair scattered onto the white towel wrapped around my neck and onto the floor, triggering a memory of a different mirror, a different haircut. That same little girl I'd remembered before, sitting in front of Mom with a towel blanketing her, holding out a hand for a lollipop while Mom snipped away.

I frowned. The memory was still fuzzy, vague. The little girl's face was impossible to see.

I pushed to retrieve the image, to focus in, but the

memory disintegrated into nothingness, leaving behind a residue of longing that I didn't understand.

That longing vanished as another memory surfaced.

White walls, white lights. The smell of bleach. A man in a lab coat, powering a drill to life . . .

I shook my head and, ignoring Mom's sound of protest, bolted out of the chair. No. I didn't want to experience that, not again. I raised my hands to my cheeks and focused on the mirror. I saw a girl with short, choppy black hair, a girl who looked dangerous and edgy. Much more fitting than the innocent schoolgirl look the U.S. military had chosen for me.

Much less like the version of me from that awful memory.

"Are you okay?"

I caught Mom's gaze in the reflection again, saw the way her hand hovered halfway to my arm, like she wanted to comfort me but realized her touch wouldn't be welcome. I sidled away out of reach, in case she overcame her reservations.

Should I ask her about the memory? Demand an explanation? Or was it another one of the things I'd be happier not knowing?

I chose the latter and instead asked a different question that had just occurred to me. "Who chose how I look?" I asked, turning to face Mom in time to watch her fumble the scissors in an uncharacteristically clumsy act. She stooped to the ground, pausing there for a few heartbeats longer than necessary. I wondered if something in my question had upset her, but by the time she rose, her face was a poised mask. Still, something tight grabbed at her mouth, thinned it.

"Not me" was all she said, before turning and disappearing into the bathroom.

When she reemerged later, her hair fell to the same spot inches past her shoulders, but the familiar blond color was gone, replaced by a reddish brown to match her phony passport photo. This was not the Mom from Clearwater, from my programmed memories, and just like that, I felt another tether to my past tear free.

My hair was still scattered across the stained carpet like the dandelion seeds I'd seen a toddler blow back in Clearwater, walking with his mom down our street. I leaned over and rescued a few silky strands, only to let them slip between my fingers, to watch them float back to the floor. Hair, weeds, life—all of them transient.

Shaking off the melancholy, I started picking up the hair in earnest.

"Here, let me help." Mom squatted down to scoop up pieces, too.

"No, thanks, I've got it."

She remained in a squat, balancing her hands on her thighs. "Mila, I realize that you're angry, but we have to be able to work together."

The darker hair gave her skin a porcelain glow, adding a

hint of fragility to her face. But I knew it was just an illusion, in much the same way that my appearance was. No one would look at her long-legged, slender beauty and suspect the mental and physical strength that lurked beneath. Just like no one would look at me and suspect I was anything other than a normal teenage girl.

It made me wonder how many other people out there hid behind their outer shells.

"Fine. But only if you drop the Mom act completely, and treat me like an equal. Deal?"

She stared at me for several long seconds, her eyes roving over my face almost as if she were memorizing the contours, while her hand clutched the phony birthstone charm. For a moment I thought she might argue. Beg me to believe that, despite everything, she felt like a real mom, that she hadn't faked that part. And before I could help it, that same crazy hope spiraled through me.

It died a second later, when she agreed, in an oh-so-soft voice: "Deal."

I immediately went back to collecting hair off the floor, all the while trying to convince myself that that's exactly what I'd wanted her to say.

SEVENTEEN

The room was dark and still except for the soft rhythmic sound of Mom's breathing when I bolted upright into alertness. The bedsprings squeaked loudly in the quiet room. I glanced at the digital clock bolted to the nightstand. Three twenty-five a.m.

A strange scuffling noise had roused me from sleep, or my resting state, or whatever the hell I did when I lay in bed. Not a topic to investigate now, not when I heard the sound again, like a shoe scraping concrete.

Someone was outside.

I slid to the floor and leaned over Mom's sleeping form, jumping back when her eyes flew open and she sat up abruptly.

It shouldn't have surprised me. Nothing Mom did should

surprise me anymore.

"Is someone here?" she mouthed. I nodded and jerked my head toward the door.

Mom slid out of bed, fully clothed, like me. She snagged her glasses off the nightstand and fixed her gaze on the door.

A knock. "Maintenance," a gruff male voice called.

I took a step forward, but Mom's outstretched arm held me back. "Wait here," she whispered. She crept toward the door and looked out the peephole. "What do you need?"

"Sorry for the inconvenience, ma'am, but there's been some complaints of power outages in some of the rooms and the front office. Unfortunately, the fuse box is in there. We just need to come in to check it out." His voice was just loud enough to be heard through the door.

Fuse box? In our room? Mom's gaze sought mine in the dark, and I could tell we shared the same thought.

Not very probable.

"Just a minute while I put on some clothes."

She hurried back over, pushing her mouth close to my ear. "Run a scan. Find the precise location of any nearby electrical circuits."

"But I don't know how—"

Her fingers dug into my shoulders. "You do know how. You just don't know you do—just like the GPS. Focus, and turn a slow circle. The current is detected through a sensor behind your eyes."

My hands flew to the sides of my face. Like maybe I could somehow feel the sensor there.

"Hurry, Mila," she whispered. "We need to know if there's anything near this room."

It was the "hurry" that did it. Though my stomach churned and my fists balled, I turned a slow circle and issued the mental command.

Circuits.

As if by magic, a digital green map blossomed in front of me. It fizzled into tiny dots of static an instant later.

Circuits scan: Blocked.

An icy-cold sensation trickled down my back. "It's blocked."

Mom blanched. "If they knew to bring an interference device, it must be Holland's men. They've found us."

They'd found us, and we were trapped.

Mom burst into motion. She swept into the bathroom and turned on the light. The sound of the shower beating against the wall followed. She closed the door before hurrying back. "We only have one chance at this. We need to get them inside, close the door, and subdue them before anyone else notices. You ready?"

Something metal scraped against the deadbolt while I stood frozen.

Mom must have sensed my fear, because she squeezed

my shoulders and whispered, "A team, remember? I can't do this without you."

The chill spread from my back to the rest of my body. She wanted me to help take these guys down, like I had back at the ranch. She wanted me to be an android, when right now all I wanted was for her to protect me, like I was an actual daughter and she was an actual mom.

But I was the one who'd asked for it. I was the one who'd said "team." I couldn't back out now.

I scanned the room, searching for a potential weapon. My gaze returned to the dresser. I hesitated over the scissors before shoving them in my pocket, the man back in Clearwater still too fresh in my mind. Team or no team, android or human, I wouldn't let anyone turn me into a killer. Instead, I grabbed the hair dryer and the heavy round hairbrush.

"Ready."

I vaulted the bed and dropped to all fours behind the fabric chair near the window, from where I'd have a direct line to the door. Up close, the chair smelled like spoiled milk, and dust erupted when I brushed it with my forehead.

As Mom clicked the deadbolt, every bit of my focus switched to her. We'd only have one shot. If they held a gun to Mom's head before I could get to them, it was all over. I couldn't risk her getting hurt.

Mom opened the door, feigning a yawn. "Are you sure

you can't wait until morning?"

A sturdy dark-haired man I didn't recognize shoved his way into the room, followed by a shorter man with a navy-blue hat. He ducked his head, but I could still see the swollen nose and purpling eye. He was one of the men I'd taken down in the Greenwood Ranch driveway.

Mom stepped back, continuing with the charade. "Okay . . . but if the fuses are in the bathroom, you'll have to wait a few minutes. My daughter was in the shower when you knocked."

Both men's gazes swept the empty beds before focusing on the bathroom door. My hands clenched on the hair dryer and brush. Wait. *Wait*. Too soon could bring unwanted attention. Too late could bring much, much worse.

And then the second man walked all the way into the room, carrying a silver toolbox. As the door clattered shut, everything happened at once. Mom's foot whipped out, slamming into the back of the second man's knees. The dark-haired man reached into the toolbox, pulling out a black gun.

And I leaped up from behind the chair, took aim, and threw.

The hairbrush cracked the dark-haired man in the wrist, making his gun clunk to the floor. Mom kicked it toward the bathroom before turning back to the man from Clearwater, who'd pitched forward onto his hands and knees. His hat catapulted off his head.

The dark-haired man recovered more quickly than I'd anticipated. He dived for the floor, for the gun. He was going to reach it before me.

Incapacitate gun hand.

The command drove me into action. I launched myself after him while, right before my eyes, his arm turned into a 3-D graph of internal anatomy. Pulsing green lights accentuated the most vulnerable points.

Accessible targets.

Midair, I yanked the plug away from the hair dryer. He'd already grabbed the gun with his right hand and was rolling onto his side, sweeping the weapon in an arc that would reach Mom.

Now.

I landed beside him, hip first, taking aim as I slid across the carpet. Then I shoved the plug into the mass of nerves in his armpit, the brachial plexus.

Target: Immobilized.

The unreality of the situation flashed through me as the metal prongs sank deep into his flesh, but I had to stay focused. Until I was sure I had him subdued.

His entire arm went slack and his scream pierced the room before I stifled it by clamping my hand over his mouth. A quick jab to the trachea would silence him, but I didn't want to hit him again, not unless absolutely necessary.

Suitcase. On the dresser.

Keeping my left hand over his mouth, I used my right to rummage through the unzipped bag. I grabbed the first wad of soft cotton my fingers touched. A few seconds later, the man was sporting one of Mom's favorite gray tank tops in a way the manufacturer had never intended. Now I just needed something to secure his hands.

And then I paused. I'd just stabbed some guy, an utter and complete stranger, in the armpit with a hair-dryer plug.

And I'd done it well.

Unreal. "You okay?" I asked, glancing Mom's way. The other man was stomach down on the floor and unmoving, and from the slackened look of his jaw, out cold. Still, Mom had one knee lodged against his spine, just in case.

"Got anything to tie him up with?"

Her free hand reached into her pocket and pulled out a handful of multicolored zip ties. I caught the two she tossed at me. "Use these." Her voice sounded as capable and calm as ever, even with a large red spot on her left cheek. Obviously her captive had gotten in a punch before she'd taken him down.

I went to grab my guy to flip him onto his stomach but hesitated with my hand on his shoulder. His eyes were glazed with pain, and his good hand wrapped protectively around his injured arm. A sharp pang hit me.

I'd known right where to strike and had done so without

conscious thought. Without even bothering to consider if I'd do any permanent damage.

. . . a fighting machine.

"Mila, it's okay," Mom said, summing up my predicament with one quick glance. "I know how you're feeling, but remember—he would have had no problem shooting me. And what he has planned for you . . . it's much worse than what you did to him."

Maybe so, but I didn't want to be this Mila, the one they'd created in the lab, who maimed and hurt and one day, possibly, even killed people.

But for now, I had to forget all that and tie this man up.

I moved efficiently. When I rolled the man onto his stomach, he groaned but didn't protest or open his eyes. He was barely conscious. Hopefully that meant this would hurt less. Still, I kept my hands gentle when I bound his wrists with the pink zip tie. The green one I used on his ankles.

Mom's guy was similarly bound, with a pair of socks stuffed into his mouth. She rose, taking two steps over to the bed before sinking onto the edge. The only indication of nerves was the way she fiddled with the nosepiece of her glasses.

"Now what?" I asked, looking at the two prone men, the tightness building in my chest. I tried to will it away by reminding myself it wasn't real, that according to Mom, the tightness was merely a re-creation of someone else's emotional reactions. Like an emotional residue.

Mom eyed the two men, who were just starting to stir. "Get our stuff out of the bathroom and wipe the room down for prints. By the time you're done, they should be able to answer a few questions."

I grabbed our suitcase, carried it into the bathroom. I shoved everything off the counter into the bag, then did a sweep of the rest of the room. In the trash can I spotted our empty boxes of hair color, and I fished them out to throw away in a more secure location.

Fingerprints. I yanked down a towel, dampened it under the faucet, and wiped everything we might have touched clean.

When I walked out, the two men were still on the ground, but the one closest to Mom had started struggling against his restraints.

Mom glanced up at me, her lips thin and determined. "Ready?"

Before I could answer, she dropped next to the man and rolled him over, onto his bound hands. Then she pressed the gun against his temple.

"We already know you're working for General Holland. Tell us how much he knows."

He didn't attempt to make a sound against his impromptu gag, and even though Mom held the gun, his glaring eyes stayed glued to me. I saw her hand tremble slightly before she whipped the gun down and cracked it against his knee.

The socks stuffed into his mouth absorbed his scream.

I staggered back a step. "You said question them, not beat them," I said, my eyes accusing.

Mom dragged a weary hand down her cheek. "It's the only way to get them to talk. You can wait in the bathroom, if you want. I can handle this."

I almost did it—fled to the bathroom, turned on the shower and sink full blast to block out any noises. But that wouldn't be fair to Mom.

Like it or not, we were a team. And our survival depended on us acting like it.

"Now tell me what you know," Mom said to the balding man, yanking the socks from his mouth.

He hacked, turned his head, and spit on the floor. "Holland? We don't work for Holland." His focus returned to me and his mouth slackened. I could almost feel the path his eyes took as they crawled over every inch of my body.

Mom's fingers tightened on the gun. "Quit lying. And look at me, not her."

At her command, the prisoner shifted his attention to Mom, but a few seconds later, his eyes were back on me.

"Do I look like a military wannabe to you? All we want to do is get a good look," he said, nodding at me. "Hand her over and we'll pay you, enough that you can disappear anywhere."

He raked me over from head to toe again and whistled softly. "Damn, now I can see why they're so gung ho to grab you. If I didn't know better, I'd say you were the real thing, and not just the military's latest toy."

Toy. He'd just called me a toy. I clenched my teeth against the burst of pain, against the traitorous thought that his assessment wasn't that far off. Mom's breath hissed between her own teeth, before she grabbed him by the chin. "Quit wasting my time. Now tell me—have you reported back to SMART Ops yet? Does Holland know you found us?"

His lip curled into a sneer. "I'm telling you the truth. It's not my problem if you're too stupid to believe me."

Mom moved the gun to point at his thigh. "Maybe I won't shoot you in the head. But the leg . . ." A click signaled the gun was cocked.

The sound sent nausea barreling up my throat. I didn't think Mom would really shoot a helpless man, but even the possibility made me sick. All I could picture was the other girl, the drill, the gun at her head. . . .

Somehow I had to convince him to talk without Mom shooting him. Even if I had to bluff my way through it.

I flung my body down to the floor on his other side and grabbed him by the hair. "Forget the gun—I have access to hundreds of ways to torture the information out of you. Ask your friend over there. He's going to be fine, but I can't really say the same for his arm."

The smile fell from his face. His dark eyes flickered to his moaning companion while, under my fingertips, I felt his pulse throb through his scalp.

I fought off my urge to let him go and forced my other hand to cup his cheek. If my threats terrified him into talking without the use of violence, then it was worth it.

"I could start with something simple, like jamming my finger into your ear—hard enough to make your eardrum burst. I'd just have to be careful not to poke my way into your brain. Oh, and . . . I'll know if you're lying."

I honestly had no idea if I'd know or not, but it sounded good.

His dark eyes stared into my green ones, and his Adam's apple bobbed as he swallowed. Hard. My fingers dampened from the sweat leaking from his scalp. Then he started talking.

"It's just us so far, the group from your house. The others are scouring all routes heading out of Clearwater. We got a late start, but we caught up to the signal on your car—we'd bugged you."

"Bugged us? Then there are more of you coming?" Mom broke in, a hint of the panic she'd been so carefully repressing evident in the rising pitch of her voice.

"No, not yet. They weren't sure if it was a decoy, if you'd found the bug and planted it on someone else."

"Have you reported back yet?" A hesitation, so I forced

my hand to graze his ear, as a reminder, while Mom jumped to her feet.

He flinched. "No, we haven't reported back. We were supposed to once we confirmed your identity one way or the other."

Mom rushed around the room, wiping for traces of fingerprints and shoving any remaining items into our suitcase. Then she walked back into the bathroom, emerging with two washcloths. A moment later, both men were effectively gagged and her tank top and socks rescued, albeit a little damper than she prefered.

"When your friends find you, pass this along. The next one who comes after us will sample those torture techniques Mila was talking about. Understand?"

His eyes widened and he gave a jerky nod.

"Good." Mom knelt to dig through the gunman's pockets and withdrew a black walkie-talkie-looking device. I watched her frown at it as I followed suit. No identification, but I did find a key ring to a rental car.

"What's wrong?" I asked as she stood, the crease deepening over her nose.

"This is what they used to jam your reception, but I don't recognize it. Holland never showed us anything like this before." She stared at the device like it was toxic before punching two buttons. The green light blinked off. Afterward, the way she slowly raised her head made me suspect the worst. "I think they were telling the truth—they're not working for the military."

We rushed to the door and slipped into the chilly night with those words repeating in my ears. As if things weren't bad enough, now we had two groups hunting us down.

Outside, nothing stirred. Not a noise except the never-ending trek of cars racing by on the highway. A quick perusal of the parking lot revealed that in addition to the three cars I'd noticed when we'd first pulled in, a fourth one was parked on the north side of the lot—a black Ford Explorer with tinted windows.

Red shimmered behind my eyes. "No," I hissed, clenching my jaw and willing it out of my head. No scans. We'd manage just fine without any unwanted help from my robotic voice.

Visual scan: Activated.

Human threat detected.

I stopped fighting and froze. "Someone's here."

Mom stopped. "Where?"

"There." I pointed. Off to our left, on the sidewalk in front of the motel, my visual field highlighted the figure in green light. I focused on his face and groaned. The stupid security guard, from the convenience store. He was heading our way. "What do we do now?"

"Act like you're searching for something in the back of the car."

Mom hit the remote to unlock the doors, so I shoved the suitcase inside, then leaned halfway in and pretended to rifle through the driver's seat-back pocket.

Mom scooted around to the passenger side and rummaged near the floorboard.

Meanwhile I held my breath, listening as the guard's whistling alerted us to his approach. He was getting closer. And closer.

I didn't dare look up from the tan leather, but I could hear his boots crunch loose gravel, hear their path lead him straight to Mom. "Everything okay? Motel owner's a friend of mine, and he asked me to check out some noise disturbances."

Noise disturbances—that had to be us. I gripped the leather pocket hard while Mom straightened.

When she spoke, she sounded pissed. "Why do you think we're leaving in the middle of the night? It's impossible to sleep with those morons in thirty-five making all that racket. They finally shut up about fifteen minutes ago, but since we were awake and have a long trip ahead of us, we decided to get an early start."

Thirty-five. The room two doors down.

"Racket? What kind of racket? Did it sound like anyone was injured?" Through the window, I watched him search out the room in question. Crap. If he went to question them, we'd be in serious trouble.

Mom must have realized that at the same time, because she scoffed. "Oh, not that kind of racket. You know. The other kind," she said, with an eyebrow lift and a hush-hush head jerk in my direction.

Even though the couple and their boisterous nighttime activities were imaginary, my cheeks burned. Especially considering how the guard had hit on me not too long ago. Which gave me a great, yet mortifying, idea of how to scare him away.

I straightened, hoping my flaming cheeks weren't super noticeable in the dim light.

"Hi there!" I waved over the top of the car. It took a few seconds for him to make the connection, but when he did, it was almost comical.

He gasped, then backed away from the Tahoe like it might shock him, tripping over his own feet. "Hello," he said in a gruff voice that sounded obviously fake, his hand flying up to tug at his collar. He couldn't turn back to Mom fast enough. "Thanks for clearing that up. I'll go let the owner know. Have a good evening."

Then he ducked his head and darted for the office, careful to keep his eyes focused straight ahead.

I would have laughed, but Mom cut me off. "We need to disable their car before he gets back," she said, watching his retreat.

"I'll take care of it while you look for the tracking device."

I darted silently for the Explorer. No one inside, good.

My fingers dug into my pocket, found the scissors I'd stashed there in hopes of not accidentally hurting anyone too much. After peering over my shoulder to ensure the guard was still safely inside the office, I started with the driver's side. I aimed at the tire and used a quick, forceful jab to puncture the rubber. The scissors sliced through the outer layers more easily than I anticipated, the tire sheathing them so far, my hand touched rubber.

The act reminded me of a similar one I'd performed just minutes ago, only that time I'd sunk metal into human flesh. I forced the thought out of my mind and continued to the next tire.

In under two minutes, all four tires were sporting brand-new scissor-sized holes. Even if our hunters somehow managed to free themselves, they wouldn't get far.

I jogged over to where our SUV was parked. Time to get on the road, the quicker the better. Though that task proved more challenging than anticipated when I found Mom half-way underneath the vehicle. Only her long legs stuck out.

"Didn't find it yet?"

From around the corner came the creak of the office door. The guard. "Hurry up!"

"Just a second." The soft glow that followed her as she scooted around to the back driver's wheel told me she'd grabbed our emergency flashlight. The guard stood with his back to us and the door partially open, but the moment he turned around, he'd see the light too, and wonder what the hell we were doing. She slid back out, greasy fingered but triumphant. "Here it is," she said, holding aloft a blinking red piece of metal, encased in what appeared to be some type of clear siliconelike substance.

The second Mom pushed to her feet, the door clanged shut. After a cursory glance our way and a lackluster wave, the guard hurried toward the street.

I sighed in relief while Mom launched into an excited whisper. "This isn't a regular military tracking device. You're programmed to sense the signals they emit. But the synthetic this thing is encased in must have somehow blocked your ability while still allowing the signal to go out. Ingenious, really." She gingerly turned the device over in her hands, like it was precious.

Ever the scientist, even now, under dangerous circumstances. I threw open the passenger door. "Great, Mom, but can you get excited about the device that nearly killed us after we're in the car?"

A sheepish smile erupted across her formerly fascinated face. "Right—sorry!"

Her smile broadened as she climbed into the driver's seat and gunned the engine. "Why do you do that?" I said while we reversed out of our parking spot.

"Do what?"

"Smile whenever I say something particularly obnoxious."

This wasn't the first time it had happened, but it definitely ranked up there as the oddest.

She braked hard as the light in front of us turned yellow. "Because it's proof that you're more human than you—than anyone—thinks."

"Is that supposed to make sense?"

She beamed at me, lifting her hand to smooth back my hair. "Oh, it's perfectly logical. Think, Mila. The government didn't really program you to have a subversive sense of humor. Neither did I, not even when I implanted the memories and uploaded the teen-speak programs. That's all you. It means you're growing, evolving . . . just like a human would."

I considered her words, and as I did, a feeling of warmth—hope—blossomed inside me. In the grand scheme of things, yes, this was all relatively minor. It didn't change the fact that I was full of engineered parts to mimic being a human so I could blend in as a spy. But it was something. A spark of promise for what might be, for how I could change.

For how I could change, if we lived long enough for that change to occur, and if somehow, some way, I could find the path back to Hunter.

And then we were back on the highway, back on the run to a whole new life.

EIGHTEEN

Directly ahead of us was a bridge, its supports arching above the three-laned street in a crisscross of white. Once we passed over the blue water, we'd be out of the United States. Probably forever.

The possibility of a new life that had buoyed me just hours ago drained away, leaving me empty and filled with a silent longing.

Hunter.

Once we crossed into foreign territory, he'd be that much harder to reach.

I bit my lip and stared out the window.

Digital signs directed us to the appropriate lane. We pulled up behind a long line of cars.

We bumped forward, one vehicle at a time.

"Almost there," Mom said when another car moved. Her hands tightened on the wheel. "Let's just hope they aren't expecting us."

I peered over my shoulder, at cars boxing us in from behind, and then ahead, at the six uniformed, armed workers in the kiosks and the line of official cars in front of the small building to the left. I rubbed my fingers up and down my seatbelt to calm my nerves. I was afraid that if they were expecting us, then we didn't stand a chance.

Finally we approached the blue-topped enclosures that housed Canadian border patrol. We were only two cars back now in lane seven, not far from the red sign proclaiming STOP/ARRÊT.

Over in lane number six, I watched as the uniformed worker shook his head at something the driver said through the open window—even I couldn't hear over all the idling engines—and gestured a tall male coworker over. After he issued a command to the driver, the trunk popped open and the second worker started tearing through the contents, while the first one opened the back door and peered inside.

When they finished, the two guards conversed, shaking their heads. One held up a laptop and gestured to it. Then they directed the driver over to the left, where a green sign proclaimed EXAMINATIONS/CUSTOMS.

From the way Mom clenched the steering wheel even harder, her knuckles whitening under the skin like little curved stones, I knew she'd noticed the commotion, too.

The green Camry with a Canadian license plate in front of us pulled forward. We were next.

"Are we going to be okay?" I asked, lacing my hands tightly together in my lap and squeezing.

"I hope so," she said softly. "But we have to do everything possible not to get pulled out for inspection."

Pulled out. I looked at where the gray Oldsmobile had parked as directed in front of the examinations building, watched as the driver was escorted inside. Pulled out like that guy.

Judging by our border patrolman's surly frown, I could only guess his pullout quota was higher than average.

"Remember, let me do all the talking."

I flipped open my passport and stared at the photo inside. Stephanie Prescott, born November 18, age sixteen.

It looked good, but good enough to hold up under inspection, along with the SUV's phony registration to Mom's fake name? Good enough to escape the notice of the military? And what about the mysterious group from the motel with all their technology—were they somehow monitoring the checkpoint too?

Too many unknowns to loosen the sensation of steel bands gripping my chest. Too many ways to get caught.

And beneath the fear, the traitorous thought underlying everything. The thought that if we were rejected, we'd be returned to U.S. soil. Which would put me that much closer to Hunter.

The Camry pulled away from the checkpoint, and the uniformed guard waved us forward. Showtime.

I rolled down the window as Mom pulled forward, hoping the fresh air would drive away the panic that clutched at me with sharp claws. My toes curled into the soles of my shoes. Mom turned her head and shot the border patrolman a strained smile, while I prepared for the worst-case scenario.

The short, jowly man didn't give so much as a hint of a return smile as Mom handed over the requested passports and car registration.

He glanced at our passports and frowned.

Typical frown, or did it mean something?

"Where's your final destination in Canada?" he asked.

"London, Ontario."

"Reason?"

"Funeral, unfortunately," Mom said, making her voice crack a little on the last syllable.

He didn't say anything else, just studied Mom's passport picture, then stared at Mom. Looked down again, looked up. His frown deepened.

My panic swelled, surging through my arms, my throat. He knew something. He was going to pull us out.

"Well," he started, scrutinizing Mom's face.

I grabbed the center console to steady myself. This was it. This was when he sent us to the customs building. From there, they'd figure out our passports were false, call the U.S. government, and we'd be toast.

". . . you don't have that black eye in your passport picture."

What?

I bit my cheek and stared at my lap, holding back a nervous giggle. The driver's seat creaked when Mom shifted her weight, and her hand flew to her cheekbone.

"No. No, I don't. I only bring it out for special occasions." She topped off that whopper by leaning closer to the window and gazing up at him from beneath her lashes. "If you must know, I lost a fight with our dog's nose." She flashed a bright smile, the likes of which I'd never seen, and suddenly I wanted to crawl into the backseat. Was Mom actually flirting with this guy?

If so, it was working, because his sour expression melted into a return smile. "Big dog?"

She nodded. "Rhodesian ridgeback, a ninety-five pound baby."

I didn't even know what a Rhodesian ridgeback looked like, but it didn't matter. Her charm was working wonders.

He handed the passports back to her. "Well, when you get back, take that dog to obedience class. Have a nice visit."

He said the magic words and waved us on, and just like that, we were in Canada.

Being on foreign soil must have soothed Mom, because she fell asleep twenty minutes after we passed through the checkpoint and switched roles, her light snores discernible over the persistent hum of the tires. Her cheek was curled into her hand. Sleep softened the worry lines around her eyes and mouth and made her appear younger, more relaxed than usual. I'd always attributed her tension back at the ranch, her overprotectiveness, to losing Dad. In retrospect, I realized she'd probably been on edge almost every second. Anticipating the day when we'd have to toss our belongings into the car and do exactly this: flee.

Why, though? Why had she taken such chances, put her life in this type of danger? Despite the doubts the man at the motel had raised, I had to believe what Mom had told me was true. That she realized they'd created something beyond their expectations and that I deserved a chance at a real life. People didn't subject themselves to these types of risks on a whim.

Uneasiness stirred in my gut. At least, I hoped they didn't.

We reached the Toronto airport without any further drama. I followed the signs and headed for long-term parking, taking the ticket and tucking the SUV into an open space in the middle of a huge cluster of cars. Hiding in plain sight, so to speak.

"You ready, Stephanie Prescott?" Mom rechecked the interior pocket of her purse for our passports before turning to give me a once-over. Time ticked on, and her once-over turned into a twice-over, and a thrice-over, until a chill feathered over me.

"What?"

Without warning, her hands whipped out to cup my cheeks, and the unexpected intimacy of her touch floored me. "If anything happens, you need to forget about me and go to Germany alone."

Despite her warmth, the cold spread, like someone was rubbing my skin with pure ice. I closed my eyes and pushed the anxiety away. "Okay."

One quick squeeze before she sagged against the head-rest. "Thank you, Mila."

At her heartfelt thanks, guilt pinched my chest. I'd only agreed to reassure her.

We grabbed our suitcase, locked the car, and followed the signs toward the stairwell, going downstairs until we got to street level.

The airport's exterior resembled a giant roller coaster, with its elegantly curving rooftop and white metal strips crisscrossing the endless stream of windows.

A roller coaster, or a sleek, giant prison.

Six other travelers surrounded us as we crossed the street:

a middle-aged mom and dad with two young daughters, and a pair of businessmen in suits and ties, rolling leather briefcases behind them. I searched the sidewalk ahead of us and spotted three more single passengers, two older women and one lone man in a Windbreaker, lounging against the wall as he smoked a cigarette, his eyes taking in all of us.

His scrutiny made me want to speed up, but I forced my feet to maintain a leisurely pace. In the back of my mind, though, I wondered if he could be connected to the men from the motel, or the military. If he had a Taser or, worse, a gun.

Electricity stirred in my head. My hands fisted when the glowing words appeared. When my smooth, mechanical voice spoke.

No weapons detected.

As we walked toward the glass doors that opened up into Terminal 3, I found my gaze kept sliding over the other travelers. Wondering how we would even know in time if someone was following us.

Our suitcase clanked over the sill of the sliding glass doors that led inside the airport. The wide-open interior enveloped us, its soaring, curved ceilings making me feel overexposed. The starkness of it all—the white floors and gleaming metal—while aesthetically pleasing, reminded me once more of the girl in the room.

I shuddered at the memory, realizing I'd never asked Mom about it. Now certainly wasn't the time, though.

Instead, I focused on Hunter. On the husky rasp of his laugh, his clean, sandalwoody smell. His unconditional support after I'd been thrown from Kaylee's truck. The flutters he ignited when his skin touched mine. And again when his eyelashes swept down before our almost-kiss.

Once we got on the plane, Hunter would be out of reach for good.

I followed Mom to the second level, up to ropes that marked the entrance of the Finnair ticket counter. Only three passengers stood in line ahead of us—two women and one little boy—so we waited quietly. As a group, they strode up to an available agent at the ticket counter, leaving us at the front of the line. Praying that our passports would hold up one more time.

"Next in line, please."

A harried-looking woman, middle-aged with tight brown curls, greeted us. Mom asked her about the next available flight to Berlin—there'd been no way to book it safely in advance without potentially alerting the military—and the woman's fingers clicked over the keyboard.

"You're in luck. We have seats available on the next flight, leaving in three hours. But since this is last-minute, the tickets are $3,339 each."

"We'll take them."

"Passports and credit card, please."

Mom dug in her purse and produced the phony passports

and the credit card issued to the fake name. She handed them over with a steady hand, even though I was sure she was as tense as I was. If the credit card and passports were rejected, we could kiss our escape plan good-bye.

The woman barely glanced at the photos, simply typing in our names. Mom relaxed next to me. So close. Then the woman swiped the credit card.

A harsh beep sounded, one that radiated straight into my chest, freezing it. The woman frowned down at the screen. When she looked up, her features were arranged into a polite mask. "I'm sorry, your credit card has been declined. Do you have another form of payment?"

Mom's fingers tightened reflexively on her purse. I could sense the swelling panic inside her. Or maybe that was just me, projecting my own fear.

Mom's laugh rang high-pitched and false. "There must be some mistake. Can you please try it again?"

With a weary sigh that spoke of annoyance, the woman managed to cling to her fake smile as she went to swipe the card again.

I curled my hand around Mom's rigid arm. Trying to will her into a confidence I didn't possess. The card had to work. It had to. If only there were a way to force the machine to work. . . .

This time, when the red shimmered behind my eyes, I didn't fight it.

Locating signal . . .

The ticket agent shook her head. "You know, if they don't work the first time, they almost never—" She broke off with an arch of penciled-in brows. "Never mind. It went through."

With my hand on her sleeve, Mom's tiny shudder was unmistakable.

"There aren't any window seats left, but we do have an aisle seat toward the back of the plane with an empty seat next to it, if you like."

"Perfect, thank you."

Under the counter, Mom's hand, clammy with sweat, found mine. We were almost there. We checked our suitcase and headed toward the hall the agent had pointed out, toward airport security.

Only one hurdle to freedom left.

NINETEEN

We didn't get very far before Mom stopped outside a newsstand.

"We have a long flight ahead of us, so I'm going to grab a few books. Do you want anything?" she asked as she bent over to tie her blue shoelace.

I looked inside the newsstand-slash-bookstore while other passengers veered around us to continue down the hallway. Despite its cramped size, every available surface was covered with magazines and books. A tall, twenty-something girl thumbed through an *InStyle* next to her parked suitcase, while her boyfriend draped his arms casually around her neck and peered over her shoulder.

There was something I wanted. But I couldn't buy it in that store.

"Sure, grab me something. I have this inexplicable craving for an espionage story." Mom frowned and I held up my hands. "Okay, okay, just joking. Remember, joking is good?"

That produced a slight smile.

"I'll take anything. Oh, and maybe some teen magazines," I said, eyeing the woman as she toted her *InStyle* to the cashier. "You know, just to blend."

Mom snorted delicately, reaching out to rumple my hair. "Right. Just to blend."

"I'll wait right here," I said.

As soon as I saw her head bent over a paperback she'd picked up—*The Help*—I ducked down and dug the disposable cell phone out of my bag. Mom had ditched our old cells before we'd left Clearwater, worrying that SMART Ops or the men from the motel could use them to track us. Even so, I knew she wouldn't want me calling anyone, and logically I realized that was the safest course of action.

If I wanted to hear Hunter even one more time, it had to be now. Before we arrived at our real destination.

With fingers that felt like they should be shaking but were surprisingly steady, I punched in his number. He answered on the second ring.

"Hello?"

His voice unleashed a river of warmth. I reached out to grab the wall for support. "It's Mila."

"Mila?" A shocked pause. And then, "Are you okay? I've been trying to call you! I even stopped by this morning—"

"I'm fine." I cut him off, even though I could bathe in the concern spilling from the phone forever. The mere sound of his voice soothed me, made everything feel a little less surreal.

"I'm glad. After last night ended kind of weird, I worried. I even went by the Dairy Queen to see if you were there."

The sudden rush of pleasure I felt over the fact that he'd obviously been trying hard to find me waned just as quickly as it flared. Dairy Queen. Studying with Kaylee and eating Blizzards. Kaylee might not have turned out to be a true friend, but those memories were real. For those brief few weeks, everything had been much simpler.

"So what are you doing now?" I asked, determined not to wallow. Hunter was the only person in the entire world who made me feel normal. No squandering these final moments with him on self-pity.

"Nothing much. When can I see you again? I missed you today."

I missed you.

I let my head fall back against the wall and stared blankly as other travelers rushed by. So many of them were on their way to visit family or loved ones . . . or returning home to be reunited again.

The emptiness inside me opened up, threatening to hollow me out until there was nothing left. At that precise moment, I hated the scientists—even Mom—for subjecting me to this. For making me *feel*.

I shouldn't have called him. This was only making things worse. "Listen, I'm just calling to say . . . good-bye. Mom and I, we have to leave."

"Wait—you're leaving Clearwater? You mean, moving?"

"Yes."

"Wow," he said, drawing the word out. Probably trying to make sense of what had to sound like insanity. "Somewhere close?"

"No, not close. We're leaving the country."

Stunned silence ticked away the next few seconds. "That's . . . sudden. Is everything okay?"

I almost laughed. No, everything was not okay, not by a long shot. Of course, any discussion about our current predicament would involve me informing Hunter of my true origins.

Oh, by the way, I'm not exactly human. You know that night you took me on a date? You almost kissed an android.

"Mila?"

I shoved away from the wall to check up on Mom's progress. She was now in line to pay behind just one other person, clutching two books and several magazines in her hands. Not much time left. "I'm really going to miss you."

I dug my fingers into the phone when I realized how inadequate that sounded. There was more, so much more . . . but how did you tell someone he, and he alone, made you feel human? I tried again before he could interrupt. "Thank you . . . for everything," I said, my voice faltering. "You have no idea how much I owe you."

I pressed my palms to my eyes. Just to alleviate the pressure for an instant. The customer in front of Mom slipped away, and Mom handed the cashier her books. "I've got to go."

"Wait! At least—promise you'll call when you get to wherever you're going."

The cashier handed Mom her change. Out of time. What harm could it do to lie, to agree? "Deal. See ya."

I ended the call and slipped the phone out of sight just as Mom turned my way, plastic bag in hand.

"Ready?" she asked.

I pretended to fumble with my bag so she couldn't see my face. "Ready," I mumbled. Willing myself not to cry.

Another person gone from my life. Only one left now.

"So I got you *InStyle*, *Seventeen*, and *People*. Oh, and I looked at some books, but I had such a hard time choosing. I wasn't sure which would be better—one of those fantasy novels everyone's always talking about, or something more down-to-earth. So I got you a couple."

Throughout the small talk, Mom's attention remained

focused on the security official ahead, who waited to wave us through to the widened area that housed scanners. A ruse, I determined. The chatter was a ruse to make us look like a normal Mom–and–daughter duo, when nothing could be further from the truth.

"Okay, thanks."

"Hopefully the weather will be nice in Germany. Typical temperatures this time of year are lower than ours, but I heard they're having an unseasonably warm spell right now."

"Great. I can wear my new minidress. The one that barely covers my butt."

Her gaze shifted sharply to me, and I shrugged. Question answered: she could study security and listen to me at the same time.

I glanced around, and I knew, I just somehow knew, that my android features would choose this special moment to kick in.

Environmental scan: 22 potential human threats within 20-ft. radius.
Weapons detected: 9 within 20-ft. radius.

That made sense. One security agent was checking IDs before the line broke into the three lines next to conveyor belts, leading to the scans. Three security agents worked the left line—two women, one man—two guards at the middle one, both men, and three more guards on the far right line.

And there were even more guards beyond them, loitering just past the scanners. If something went wrong, well . . . let's just hope that didn't happen.

The line inched forward under the bright lights, a few passengers at a time. Mom had assured me that once we were past the ID checker, we'd be fine. Apparently, any metal inside me was untraceable via scanners—the military had made sure of that. Even if I walked through a full body scan, the computer in my brain would falsify the information, resulting in a normal, nonmetal body being displayed on the screen.

As I watched Mom calmly take in the surroundings, I realized this wasn't new for her, like it was for me. She'd been on guard for a long time now, knowing that she and she alone would be the one to keep us safe. That kind of pressure would have broken a lesser woman, but not her. Not even when the reason she was on the run had been acting like a giant, ungrateful brat.

I could only imagine how lonely this past month had been for her, what a mental and emotional toll this whole ordeal had taken.

While I still wasn't happy about being lied to, my anger from the past two days faded, leaving behind only a fierce determination that we would get through this, together. I stared at the familiar graceful lines of her profile, and it hit me. I couldn't think of anyone else I'd rather have on my side.

I should tell her.

"Mom," I started, but then we were moving forward again. Only two families between us and the security guard now. Then one. Before I realized what I was doing, my hand was on her arm, squeezing.

Then it was our turn.

The bored-looking guard lowered his head to glance at our IDs. His gaze jerked back up to our faces. I tensed. Forced a smile while I reached for Mom's hand, preparing to run.

Then he shrugged and waved us through.

Mom steered us for the middle line—one less security agent meant they had less time to be attentive—and we took off our shoes and placed them in one of the gray plastic bins. Mom's purse went on the conveyor belt next.

"Make sure to empty out your pockets, please—no change, keys, even paper. The new scanners will find everything," the security guard called out from the next line over.

I fumbled through my pockets—empty—while staring at the carefully crafted scanner. With technology changing all the time, how could Mom be sure I'd fool it?

As we shuffled forward, waiting for the burly man in front of us to empty his pockets of change, that scanner consumed my attention. The entire area smelled of a mixture of antiseptic and faint human sweat.

Just as the man stepped through, the alarm blared. I froze.

"Sir, step back through and make sure you completely empty your pockets."

The man backtracked under the frame, his face flushed. He blocked our path while he dug through his pockets and produced a wadded-up gum wrapper. "Oops, didn't know this was in there."

When he walked through the next time, I could see the tension in the way he carried himself so stiffly, like he was convinced he'd set the alarm off again.

It stayed silent this time.

And then it was our turn.

I stepped in front of Mom. That way, if anything happened to me, she might still have a chance to turn around and run.

As I walked up to the rectangle that resembled an empty doorframe, I forced myself to smile and make eye contact with the young, broad-chested security agent waiting on the opposite side.

This was it—a test to see if the military had really pulled it off.

Inhaling a deep breath I didn't need, I strode through the scanner, trying not to anticipate the sound of a siren and failing miserably.

I burst through to the other side, and . . . nothing. Just amazing, blissful silence.

I squeezed my eyes shut, just for a moment. Mom and I were going to make it. I crossed over to the conveyor belt to grab my shoes, which I slipped back on my feet. The grin I threw over my shoulder at Mom was wide as she passed through the doorway behind me. Home free.

I was jerked back around by an unexpected explosion of noise, harsh and frenzied. Not a siren.

Barking.

The German shepherd lunged to the end of its leash, dragging a male guard behind it while a uniformed woman stepped forward. Its mouth opened, white canines gleaming as it snarled and snapped at my leg. Only my quick reflexes saved me. I leaped back just as the dog's powerful jaws snapped shut, right where my thigh had been less than a second ago. I stared at the crazed animal in horror.

Why, why was it barking at me? Did it sense something the scanner couldn't? What if I didn't smell right? If so, the guards couldn't know. They had to think there was a logical explanation.

"Please get it away from me," I said, shrinking. "I don't want to get bitten."

The young guard holding the leash yanked the dog back, snapped out a sharp command. The dog ignored him. Those glistening brown eyes refused to leave me, and the second the handler gave it slack, it lunged again, assaulting me with that rapid-fire bark and a dose of musty dog breath.

Drool flew from its black lips, and its teeth snapped as it lunged a second time. All I could think was *It knows. Somehow this dog knows I'm not real.*

I stumbled back even farther as its claws scratched at the slick floor in a frenzied effort to reach me. Deep barks echoed through the building. And I saw when everything began to change. The stiffening of the female guard's posture, the minute narrowing of her eyes. The flutter of her fingers toward the walkie-talkie on her hip. The hiss of Mom's sharp inhalation.

Nine guards within a twenty-foot radius, two of them and a dog right in front of me. Fear pumped through my chest. Maybe I could make it back to the front exit, given the crowd cover and the fact that it was doubtful their weapons could stop me anyway.

Maybe I could make it, but Mom never would.

Her words tumbled through my head. *Promise me, Mila.*

I'd promised. But it was a promise I'd never intended to keep.

"You're both going to need to come with me. Leave your bags, but keep your identification and boarding passes with you."

"Can't you just scan her here? We're going to miss our plane." Mom thrust her hands on her hips and said everything with a hint of a whine. A total act, because Mom never whined. "Dogs never like her . . . they can sense her fear."

The male guard backed the dog away while the woman shook her head. "Ma'am, this animal is highly trained and we have policy to follow. Now let's go." Her voice wasn't unsympathetic, but she wasn't going to budge, either.

Mom rested her hand on my shoulder and slanted me a sideways glance. "You ready, Stephanie?"

When she uttered "ready," she rubbed her nose. It was subtle—I never would have caught it if I hadn't been expecting it—but her finger pointed briefly past security, toward the narrow passageway that led to the gates. And she mouthed a word.

"Map."

I smiled, nodded, murmured a low "Okay." I watched as the woman turned to lead us back the way we'd come, past the security lines and toward the check-in area, while I concentrated: *GPS*.

I waited as Mom pretended to stumble into her, deftly using her foot to whip the woman's ankle out from under her, while a green schematic of the airport burst into my visual field.

And then I grabbed Mom's hand and we were running.

The map self-adjusted as we sprinted down the passageway, showed us closing in on the thin finger housing C gates 27 through 41. We burst into the concourse before security knew what had happened. As we passed a frozen yogurt shop on the right, I yanked two cups out of a startled pedestrian's hands, throwing them down on the floor behind us, hoping the slickness would slow our pursuers. Security's shouts followed us past Starbucks and Beaches Boardwalk while we navigated through clumps of travelers, bumping coffee cups and purses along the way. Each and every foot strike pounded more terror through my legs and urged me to run faster. Only a huge force of will made me keep pace with Mom.

Ahead, a group of businessmen looked back over their suited shoulders. They darted out of our path with a screech of suitcase wheels, while the map highlighted a simple truth: the concourse ended soon, which left us only one way out.

The unattended gates.

More footsteps behind us now, more shouts.

"This way," I yelled, veering right after Gate 29 and pointing at the door to Gate 30.

Through the panel of huge windows, I could see that Gate 30 had a Jetway but no plane.

I sprinted for the door, a pack of security guards behind us and the unknown ahead of us.

We ignored the startled cries of waiting passengers. A blue-skirted airline attendant dashed out from behind the counter and made a grab for my sleeve. "Hey, you can't—"

I shoved her off and yanked open the door. Her protest followed us as our shoes thudded down the narrow corridor.

We hit the sharp turn to the left running. Ten feet ahead,

a big square opened up directly to the outside, giving us a clear view of the tarmac, the wing of the plane the next gate over, and the runway beyond it. Empty space awaited. That, and a huge drop onto hard, hard ground.

I looked over the edge, and the red lights shimmered.

Distance: 9.1 ft.

Impact acceptable.

I could make it—but Mom's human body might not.

"Go," Mom panted, pulling up to a stop just before the edge. "It's not that high, a straight drop, no sheer or sharp objects like with Kaylee's truck. You'll be fine."

In a split second I realized she wasn't joking. She expected me to jump onto the hard, dirty, uninviting tarmac—and leave her behind.

Mom grabbed my shoulders. Hard. "Go! *GO!*"

The Jetway vibrated. Out of time—the guards were here. As Mom spun to see the first one's face pop around the corner, I yanked her toward me, wrapping my arms around her waist and forcing her against my chest.

And then I leaned back into empty space, pulling us both down, down, down.

"No! Stop!" the lead guard yelled, throwing his hand out as if to grab us. But he was too far away.

Air whooshed by as we free fell to the tarmac.

My back hit the ground with a loud smack, followed by my skull. The stun of impact, the pressure of absorbing

Mom's fall—they stilled me for an instant, my vision full of reddish-brown hair and blue sky. An airplane roared in the distance while Mom lay unmoving on top of me.

Was I okay?

Internal scan: No damage.

Relief rushed through me, until I realized:

Mom wasn't moving.

The growing commotion above us echoed the growing rigidity in my limbs, the tightening grip on my throat. I gently rolled her to her back, got on my knees beside her.

"Are you all right?" I said, searching for some sign of injury while begging, *Please be okay, please, please, please.*

A second later, her pale blue eyes flew open and immediately narrowed on my face. "You *promised* me."

The rigidity vanished and I sprang to my feet. "You can ground me later." I pulled her to a stand, combating the urge to yank her into a huge hug, just in case she was sore.

While I made sure she could support her own weight, the security guards above crammed closer to the edge of the dropoff.

One grabbed his buddy by the shoulder. "Jesus Christ, did you see that? They've got to be high on something. . . ."

Another shouted into a walkie-talkie. "Suspects on tarmac outside C Gate Thirty, Terminal Three. Send units to apprehend."

We needed to get out of there.

As I urged Mom into motion, my gaze fell on the red-and-blue insignia of the British Airways plane idling at the next gate over . . . and the half-full luggage truck idling beside it.

"Come on!" I grabbed Mom's forearm and pulled her into a run.

The loud hum of the plane's engine must have covered all of our commotion from the two busy luggage workers, but our run alerted them. As one of them turned from shoving a bag onto the upward conveyor belt, he saw us. He motioned to his coworker, who turned our way too. They just stood there, watching us run at them with puzzled expressions. Wondering, maybe, if there'd been a luggage screwup of epic proportions.

Somewhere behind us, I heard the shouts of security guards. Ground-level shouts.

Human threat detected.

Mom stumbled a few times as we raced for the truck's open cab, but I caught her. Kept propelling her forward. When we were ten feet away, the worker pointed at something behind us.

The guards.

A glance over my shoulder confirmed it. On foot, but gaining.

Distance to threat: 42 ft.

"You first," I shouted at Mom as we finally reached the truck. I boosted her into the cab and jumped into the driver's seat behind her.

Just then, the worker darted forward. Before I could pull away, he had one foot on the passenger floorboard and one hand on Mom's arm, trying to force her out.

With my right hand latching onto Mom's other arm, I floored the gas, then spun the wheel to the left. At the same time, I saw Mom lift her outside foot and shove hard on his chest. The guy stumbled back onto the tarmac.

My elation was short-lived. Midway through our turn, I saw the group of guards on foot, but they still weren't close enough to catch us.

No, it was what I saw when I pulled around the tail of the British Airways plane that drained the relief from my body. Two security cars. Blocking me from the path I'd planned on taking to get us back to the street, and worse— headed right toward us.

Distance to threat: 35 ft.

Engage?

"No!" I said, gritting my teeth and trying to banish the ridiculous red question from my head. Engage, right. A guarantee that someone would get hurt.

I whipped the wheel to the right, seeking another escape route. Tarmac surrounded us, with its Jetways and luggage trucks and waiting planes, split between the spokes of

Terminal 1 and Terminal 3. Beyond it lay long runways and patches of grass.

Shrill sirens cut through the airplane noise, getting closer and closer by the second.

I backtracked toward Terminal 1. Our truck sped across the tarmac, while an Air Canada plane slowly rolled out of the gate to our left. If the plane continued its trajectory at that speed until it hit the runway, would we make it past?

The calculation buzzed in my head, incredibly fast.

Current speed: 45 mph.

Approximate speed of vehicle ahead: 30 mph.

Clearance possible.

I inhaled deeply. We'd never outrun the cars behind us in this poky thing, which meant we'd have to outmaneuver them.

Mom's hand shot out to clutch my knee with surprising strength. When I glanced at her, her expression was tight, her eyebrows lowered to give her that fierce expression.

She must be feeling better.

"Can you drive?"

Her gaze shifted, to where the plane kept rolling. "Right in front of that plane?" she said.

"That's the plan."

"You got it. On the count of three? One—"

Mom's left hand clutched the steering wheel.

"Two—"

I scooted toward her, to the right, while she rose into a half stand.

"Three!"

I released the wheel and lunged for the passenger side, while Mom vaulted across my lap. The truck jerked left and slowed, until Mom regained control of the wheel and smacked her foot to the gas.

"Keep going!" I yelled, standing up and facing backward. Gripping the seat tightly, I stepped up onto the small ledge.

"Mila! What are you—"

I'd launched myself across the two-foot gap and into the first luggage trailer before Mom could finish her sentence.

"Keep going!" I repeated, staring behind me.

Distance to threat: 20 ft.

They were so close. As I stared into the approaching windshields, fear locked my legs in place. *Move, Mila. Now!* I scrambled past the remaining suitcases in my trailer, shoving a few of them out until they smacked the pavement. Then I made my way to the end of the trailer and jumped into the second one.

The car on the left veered sharply to avoid a suitcase. The car on the right hit a big one with its inside tire. Brakes squealed as the front tire bounced over the case, then the rear. I grabbed the heaviest suitcase I could find and pushed to the end of the trailer. Readying myself.

From the opposite direction, the plane's engine rumbled its approach.

"Mila!"

I looked over my shoulder, and my heart seized. Oh, god, the plane was too close. My analysis had malfunctioned. We were going to crash.

And then we were crossing. On my left, the giant nose of a jet barreled right for us, its roaring engine sounding like it could devour us. I bet the pilots never dreamed anyone would be stupid enough to try to cut them off.

Hopefully, we weren't being stupid.

With all the force I could muster, I turned back to the security cars and swung my arm forward. The suitcase flew.

It smashed the windshield of the lead car. The car wrenched left and braked.

When we'd cleared the plane and the other car was directly in its path, I threw a second suitcase. And a third.

One hit the driver's side windshield, while the other skidded under the hood. The car jerked, slid to the right.

And ran right into the plane's front left wheel. A hideous screech filled the air as the plane forced the car forward.

I turned away and hurried back to Mom, leaping both trailer gaps until I was back in the passenger seat.

We'd barely raced past the end of Terminal 2 when more sirens blared, the sound paralyzing me.

Threat detected.

I watched three more cars zoom at us head-on from an extension of Terminal 1.

With a shaky breath and a lead ball in my stomach, I turned my head to the right.

Threat detected.

Two more from that way.

Peered over my shoulder.

Threat detected.

Three more. At this point, I didn't have the strength to fight off the red words, the voice. It didn't matter. We'd lost.

Mom glanced toward the runways, but I shook my head. "There's no way. Not with that many cars. We'd never make it—they're too fast."

Besides, there was a new development. Though the windshield of one of the cars behind me, I'd seen glints of metal in the sun. Both guards were holding guns.

"We need to stop the truck and surrender."

At first I thought Mom would listen. Though her shoulders remained rigid, her jaw tense, she eased her foot off the pedal, letting the truck slow. The cars in front of us slowed, too.

And then she gunned it and yanked hard on the wheel to the left. Toward the runway.

"What are you doing?" I shouted, watching with dizzying

dread as the security cars followed.

"You're going to jump out up here, and I'm going to keep going. Most of them will follow me since I'm heading for the airplanes. You just need to overpower one guard, grab one car."

"And just leave you behind? No!"

"Mila, please."

I shook my head. No way.

Mom smacked the wheel as the cars closed in behind us. "Damn it, Mila, you promised."

The guilt pinched again, but all I could think was how much worse it would be if I abandoned Mom now. "I lied. Please, stop the car, before you get hurt."

Her foot pushed harder on the gas. "Then you need to promise me something else. If we get taken back to the compound, whatever you do, don't show your emotions, don't lose control. Your feelings are a detriment there. Do you understand?"

"Yes! Now please, stop!"

She hit the brakes, and the truck jerked to a halt. She stood and lifted her hands over her head, and I did the same.

Then all we could do was wait while the cars pulled up. While security piled out, guns pointed, yelling at us to slowly exit the truck, keeping our hands up and visible at all times. While they told us to kneel on the tarmac and they gradually approached, guns trained on our heads.

While they cuffed us and loaded us into separate cars, returning us right back to the situation we'd been desperate to escape.

TWENTY

Ten minutes later, five guards marched us down a brightly lit hallway that smelled faintly of cigarettes. The leader stopped outside a room labeled DETAIN-MENT and unlocked it with a key card he produced from his pocket.

"Inside," he said gruffly, shoving open the door. The guard holding my elbow steered me none too gently inside, and Mom followed.

The room was a small square of hopelessness.

A flash of red. And then:

Dimensions: 10 ft. by 9 ft.

I swallowed a horrified giggle. Perfect. And now I knew the exact measurements of hopelessness.

The flimsy folding metal table sitting in the middle bore

the jagged scars of a knife or key or other sharp instrument across the top and was accompanied by four plastic chairs better suited for a patio, two on either side. A video camera angled down from the ceiling in the back left corner, its blinking red light confirming its functionality. No desk, no decorations, nothing that carried enough heft to be used as a weapon.

"Sit," the leader barked.

Our guards escorted us around opposite ends of the table and slid the two chairs back, the scraping sound making my guard wince. I sank into my chair, watched Mom do the same in hers.

They didn't even uncuff us to take our fingerprints. A guard just came up behind us and ran our fingers over some handheld scanner.

Absently I pushed against the cold metal that caged my wrists, feeling the chain tauten between them.

Tensile strength: 495 lbs.

Instead of reassuring me, the information only intensified the uneasiness gnawing at my stomach. Any escape attempts would put Mom in danger. I couldn't chance it.

One guard left, while two guards remained in the room, with four more outside. The longer we went unquestioned, the harder the pounding in my ears. Not even bothering to talk to us had to be a very, very bad sign.

With the two guards there, we risked only minimal, bland

conversation over the next few hours. Waiting. And waiting. Finally the door opened. One look at the dark-suited man who cautiously rounded the corner, his gaze sweeping over our positions and the room methodically, told me we were in trouble. This guy acted like a professional, much more so than the airport security. But who was he?

Target: Located.

I clenched my hands behind my chair. *Stop it. Stop, stop, stop.*

Mom's entire body stiffened as the man pulled a CIA badge out of his suit pocket. Then her head fell forward. I turned to comfort her at the same time as the man said, "Hello, Nicole. We've missed you."

We've missed you.

My head jerked back to the man, while my balled hands started to tremble. Mom . . . Mom knew this man. Which could only mean one thing.

The government had found us.

The man's brown eyes swept from Mom to me, and our already slim odds of escape shrank to almost nothing.

"Nicole Laurent, you are wanted on the grounds of espionage and theft of military property. You and the MILA are to board a plane back to U.S. soil, effective immediately."

Mom slowly lifted her head. Her lips tightened, but she didn't say anything. She just stared straight ahead.

He smoothed his fingers down his navy tie. "Did you really think you'd get away with it? You're a scientist,

Nicole, not an agent. Too much lab time, I guess." His gaze shifted back to me, and he shook his head. "If you were having difficulties with the project, you should have asked to be reassigned."

Mom's laugh rang hollow. "Right, Frank. Like General Holland would have allowed it. Besides, it wouldn't have fixed anything. What we're doing—what *you're* doing—is wrong. Look at her. Look. Tell me what you see? A machine, or a scared teenage girl?"

The discomfort caused by Frank's thorough inspection made me squirm. I wanted to cross my arms over my chest, but the handcuffs prevented me.

"It doesn't matter what I see, you know that. It's not my decision either way. Just like it's not yours."

"You realize how illegal this is, Frank? We're not on U.S. soil," Mom said.

He shook his head and retreated to the door. Just before he opened it, he turned back to Mom. "I'm sorry it had to go down this way, Nicole."

When the door shut, the lock clicking behind it, Mom glanced at me. "Remember what I said," she whispered. "When we get to the compound, no emotions."

I looked away, at the plain white wall to my left. Otherwise, the tears welling in my eyes would have revealed the truth: we weren't at the compound yet, and here I was. Already failing.

TWENTY-ONE

The CIA agent had been gone for one hour. Mom had wanted to talk, but I shook my head, nodded at the camera. Even though, statistically speaking, our chances of escape continued to plummet with every minute ticking by, even a slim chance was worth keeping silent.

We'd had no bathroom breaks, no offers of food or water. Artificial thirst stirred in my throat. I was fine, but I calculated that Mom had to be uncomfortable by now. Undoubtedly intentional on the part of our captors.

My thoughts drifted to Hunter, and the excitement in his voice when we'd talked on the phone. He had felt the same as me, but ultimately it didn't matter.

"Promise you'll call when you get to wherever you're going."

My breath hitched. Call him . . . if only that were a possibility. Where we were going, I was pretty sure I'd need all the reminders of my human side that I could get.

An echo of footsteps drew my eyes to the door. The precision, the uniformity.

"They're coming," I said.

The footsteps pounded out an ever-closer rhythm. Five feet away. Then one.

The door burst open, followed by six swiftly moving men in military camo fatigues, their guns drawn.

Frank was absent. In his place was a tall, narrow-faced man with copious acne scars. His voice was deep and clipped. A voice accustomed to giving orders and having them obeyed. "Resistance will not be tolerated," he said, drilling me with his unwavering gray stare. "Davis, Rogers!"

The commander nodded at the two impassive-looking young men up front. As a unit, they surged forward, one clasping my arm, the other Mom's, their hands cold and dry. The leader jerked his head toward the door.

And despite how much the waiting had worn on me, despite how much I hated the tiny, empty room, suddenly I wanted to stay put. At least this room was a known entity. Whereas wherever they were leading us . . . the compound . . . based on Mom's aversion, I could only imagine the worst. A place where terrible things happened.

A place where they tortured "girls" like me.

I shuddered just as the soldiers jerked us roughly to a stand. And then we were moving.

The cuffs, the men with guns, the narrow hallway—it all combined to crush me with that trapped feeling from Clearwater High, except one hundred times worse. Only Mom's presence kept my feet moving. As long as we were together, I could handle this. As long as they didn't take her away. Over and over again, I craned my head just to double check that she was still back there.

Moving swiftly, we headed the opposite way down the hall than we had come, through a labyrinth of uninhabited, narrow corridors, our footsteps echoing around us.

GPS.

The green map in my head pointed out which direction we switched to every time—east, south, east, north—but that was relatively useless information in the scheme of things.

We arrived at a heavy, white metal door and burst into the brisk outside air, the roar of an airplane in early takeoff vibrating just ahead. The thick odor of burned gas drifted our way.

Four more soldiers stood at attention, forming two lines of two on either side of the door. Just beyond them three plain white vans awaited, engines whirring as they idled.

I wondered briefly what lies the military had concocted

to explain us and their presence. I'd probably never know.

With a roar of its powerful V-8, our van took off the second we were shoved inside, and it headed onto a narrow, empty strip of a road that led away from the main terminal. Five minutes later, we'd reached a guarded gate, which opened and admitted us to a separate runway, where a few long, squat buildings sprawled on the left side. A private terminal, surrounded by open stretches of asphalt and grass.

Nowhere to run, even if I could possibly escape without endangering Mom. I stared out the window, took one last long look at Canada. My halfhearted wish from the border crossing came back to haunt me, and even though I knew it was illogical, I couldn't quell the feeling that I'd brought this upon us.

That somehow my qualms about leaving the United States and Hunter had backfired and landed us in this horrible mess.

TWENTY-TWO

Less than three hours later, Mom and I sat next to each other on a plane after all. But not one bound for Germany. The soldiers wouldn't release a single detail, but I was relatively certain that Mom, who placed one shaking palm on the window and stared into the clouds, had a good inkling as to our ultimate destination.

Mom shifted away from the window to lean close to my ear. "Mila, don't give up," she whispered. "I'll figure something—"

The guards behind us kicked our seats forward. "No talking!"

I focused on the cockpit. I couldn't look at her. Not right now. Not with guilt twisting me into a knot. Because not even the terror of the girl and the drill could suppress the traitorous curiosity that snaked through me. Somewhere, beyond the blue sky and patches of white, was the place I'd been created. A place that would still exist in my memory if Mom hadn't wiped that portion clean.

Right or wrong, a part of me desperately wanted to recover that lost information about my past. Real information, not implanted lies.

Maybe once there, I could find something that would help mesh the two parts of me into a whole—a challenge. I was constantly failing that challenge on my own.

The plane angled down for its descent. The soldier across from us sat up straighter, gripping his hands tightly in his lap, while the others shifted in their seats.

I sat up straighter, too. Where were we?

GPS.

This time, when the green map materialized before me, I almost welcomed it. A replica of the U.S. unfolded, with our plane as the tiny, blinking dot somewhere in the east.

The barest hint of a desire to get a closeup crossed my mind, and instantly the map stretched out in front of my eyes. States elongated as I zoomed in on our exact location. West Virginia. We were flying over Martinsburg, West Virginia.

Our dot was headed right for D.C.

I gaped, saw the soldier across the way nudging his

partner and pointing at me, and snapped my mouth shut. Were we landing at Dulles?

The D.C. area enlarged, showing me a private CIA airport in Langley and another called Davison Army Airfield.

Current trajectory: Manassas. Whitman Strip.

A tiny private airport.

The logic behind the choice hit me immediately.

Private.

Of course it was. This was a secret group, after all. A private airstrip assisted with deniability if something major went wrong.

That thought sucked away all my curiosity in an instant and sent an uncontrollable chill through me. Mom pressed her shoulder up against mine to reassure me. *"It's okay,"* she mouthed.

I really, really wanted to believe her.

Around us, the soldiers buckled into their seats, finally settling in for the landing.

The plane bumped down onto the narrow landing strip, smacking the ground three times before rolling. Around us, nothing but grass and a cluster of trees. I saw streets off in the distance, what looked like open space, and beyond that, buildings.

The airport itself appeared deserted.

While we were still rolling, the soldiers across from us jumped out of their seats. They formed a line in the walkway toward the cockpit. The solider who'd shushed us from behind—a short, stocky brute of a guy—and Davis from the detainment room stopped right in front of our seat, blocking us in with thick, khaki-clad thighs. After the flight with so many men, the airplane had started to smell, a really unfortunate blend of sweat, dirty socks, and spicy deodorant. Lungs or not, I was more than ready to get some fresh air.

The leader, the narrow-faced man who'd spoken to us back in Toronto, stood at the front. He turned to watch us just as the plane shuddered to a stop, legs shoulder-width apart, body tense. Definitely not at ease. "We're opening the door. Follow directions, and we'll get along just fine."

Two men grabbed my forearms and guided me down the steps while three more soldiers fell in several yards behind us.

We were ushered at a brisk pace down the runway, toward stretches of grass and a tiny parking lot. The air was heavy with unseasonal humidity, bringing a sheen of sweat to the leader's neck, a dampness to my captors' hands that made me feel slimy and in desperate need of a shower. Plenty of lush green trees, but not an outsider in sight—just three dark Suburbans.

The leader stopped ten feet away from the middle Suburban, and we jerked to a halt behind him. He executed a neat about-face, pulling his hands apart and pointing at the first and last Suburban. "Load the SUVs."

Tension gathered in my limbs. Surely they didn't mean to—

Behind me, I heard Mom being dragged in one direction, while my captors tugged me the opposite way. No. No, no, no. They couldn't separate us.

While my escorts pulled, I craned my head over my shoulder, frantically seeking out Mom's tall, sleek figure. What I saw made my entire body go rigid. Two guards were already ushering her toward the first Suburban.

"Mom!" If they separated us now, would I ever see her again? What if they took her to an entirely different location?

What if they killed her?

Human threat detected. Engage?

Yes.

A quick jerk up and back released my arms. My left elbow whipped behind me, delivering a brutal jab to that soldier's throat. I let momentum spin me around, and when the other soldier lunged, my left foot rammed him hard in the gut.

Before he even hit the pavement, I was up and running. Preparing to take on the next closest soldier. And the next. And the next.

"Mila, stop! You're only making it worse!"

I didn't even hesitate at Mom's frantic words, not with this power surging through every limb, every cell. I didn't care how many men I had to fight. I'd litter this entire parking lot with bodies if I had to—whatever it took to reach her.

"Fall back with Laurent! Fall back!" The leader screamed commands from somewhere behind me. Right as my fist lashed out and caught the closest soldier in the nose with a crunch of buckling cartilage.

Blood spurted as he flew backward, while two more rushed me from both sides. I sent them both crashing to the ground with minimal effort. My gaze swept past the remaining men and locked onto Mom, whose newly dark hair whipped side to side. "Mila, no!"

I hesitated. Then I advanced another step.

"Don't even think about it," the soldier holding Mom warned, but his voice wavered as he took in his fallen partners. Camo-decked bodies sprawled out around me, some groaning, some out cold. It looked like a bomb had gone off. And now only one man was keeping me from Mom. Once I took him down, I'd grab her. We'd steal one of the Suburbans and—

Just as I went to swoop in and grab him, I heard a click of metal that made my phantom heart stop cold.

The leader stood behind me. And his gun was pointed at Mom's head. "You move again, she's dead."

His steely voice, his steady stance. I didn't doubt him for a second.

I didn't resist after that. Not when Mom craned her neck over her shoulder and yelled, "Don't trust anyone," or when they loaded her into the first Suburban, even though it felt my entire life ended on the spot when she left without me. Not when they put a bag over my head, blinding me.

Not even when they shoved me into the last Suburban and the pock-faced man laughed and said, "Forget about your GPS—it won't work in here."

No, the realization that my impulsive attack could have cost Mom her life drained every last bit of resistance out of me.

Not to mention the second realization that was shredding my phantom heart with iron claws—I'd never told Mom I'd forgiven her.

I knew from their occasional throat clearing, fidgeting, and coughing that three soldiers accompanied me in the SUV—two up front, one in the third seat behind me. They remained silent. No music, no talking. Nothing except the drone of the wheels against the road. Their silence felt more ominous to me than anything.

Where were they taking me? And was Mom going there too?

After traveling on highways and then in stop-and-go traffic, we made a turn and went over a bump before heading down. Our wheels echoed now, making me think we'd entered an enclosed building of some kind.

"You can pull her cover off now. She'll be clueless anyway."

Behind me, a rough hand yanked the cover off my head. Just in time for me to see a sign that said NO ENTRY: CONSTRUCTION WORKERS FOR MALLORCA UNDERGROUND MALL COMPLEX ONLY.

The driver rolled down his window and stuck out a badge. The security guard scanned it, then waved him through, the outline of a gun showing under his untucked shirt. Overhead, two video cameras recorded everything.

As we passed through, the soldier in the passenger seat said, "Why do you keep calling it a her? You know that's not a real girl, right, Jennings? I know you've been hurting for dates lately, but this one's strictly prohibited."

The guy behind me guffawed, then leaned forward, so close I felt his breath on my ear. It smelled like the bottom of the coffeepot after Mom left it out overnight.

"She looks pretty girl-like to me," he said before reaching over the seat to trail his fingers down my cheek. "Damn, she feels girl-like, too. All soft and stuff."

His thick fingers squeezed my skin. I went very, very still, keeping focused on the tan headrest in front of me to fight off the revulsion. Everything unmoving except my own fingers, which curled together in my lap. Where they were safe from temptation.

I couldn't give them any excuse to say I'd caused a

problem, not when they had Mom.

If it weren't for that, I'd turn around and see how much he liked being touched without permission.

"Jennings! Sit back and keep your hands to yourself. That machine's worth way more than your entire life's salary."

I never thought I'd be so happy to hear the leader's curt voice. Or to be referred to as a machine.

Down we went, making a left and then following dim lights into a cavern of concrete. Another left led us behind a wall, to a parking bay with six other cars. The driver turned off the gas, jumped out the door, and immediately yanked mine open. I hopped out, searching behind me for even a hint of the other SUV that carried Mom. No sign of it anywhere.

My escort grabbed me with a viselike grip, leading me away to a plain metal door. When we reached it, I shot one last look into the garage, even though I knew what I'd find. Empty. She still wasn't there.

The soldier entered a pass code, and a moment later the door slid open—revealing yet another pass-code-protected door. Someone was obviously serious about security.

"Holland won't give the word to bring her in until he sees you. So no stalling," my escort said.

I was led down a narrow cement-floored hallway, past a small open room featuring only eight cubicles. Four men and two women typed on computers.

We rounded a corner, where the hallway dead-ended in a large door.

Another plain metal door, the sight of which made my entire body balk. I knew that door. I knew it.

The man yanked on my arm, forcing me to follow him inside, into a stark white room, the floors reflecting a glare from the forty-two unnaturally bright lights crisscrossing the ceiling. Yet for all the illumination, the room felt sterile and cold. Embedded computer screens glowed from the back wall, and high above them sprawled a huge window, framing a group of six men.

Spectators, I realized.

Their heavy stares sent a shiver through me. I'd been here before. This exact room.

I scanned the enclosure again, this time focusing on the left wall, where a low-backed chair was tucked under a massive steel worktable. Twelve toolboxes were stacked on top in two identical rows of six. The toolboxes whispered of something ominous, but it was what I saw behind them that made my legs go still. A pile of thick metal chains on the floor, gleaming under the artificial lighting.

Chains . . .

The memory rushed up on me. Being chained in this room. My hair whipping side to side as the lab-coated man smashed my face with the gun.

The harsh rasp of the drill, raised high over my head.

My scream, pinging through the room. Like it was clawing at the walls to escape.

My head . . . jerking back, as if dancing to the deafening gunshot.

I staggered backward and gasped in a compulsive bid for air, an action that couldn't possibly dim my horror because my body didn't require oxygen in the first place. Only one thought blazed through my head.

Get out. Get out now.

I whirled for the door, desperate to escape, ready to mow down whoever stood in my way regardless of the consequences. Terrible things happened in this room, and I wasn't about to stick around and wait for them to happen again.

Only . . . the door had just closed. Closed, sealing in a tall, steely-eyed man with silver threaded through his dark hair. A man whose broad face might have been pleasant if it hadn't been for the harsh mouth, or the possessive gleam in his gray eyes as they pored over me.

"Welcome back, Mila."

I couldn't move, couldn't think of running now, because I recognized that Southern drawl instantly from the iPod.

Finally I was face-to-face with my other creator.

General Holland.

TWENTY-THREE

waited, still as a rock as Holland approached, absorbing every aspect of his appearance and trying to find a match in my memory. Nothing. His long-legged gait flowed smoothly, leisurely, and his boots were quiet when they touched the floor. It was the walk of a man in a control; a leader unconcerned by making others wait.

His mouth curved upward into a smile that didn't crease the skin near his eyes. He pulled up in front of me, itemizing me. He inspected me the way Kaylee used to inspect her favorite boots—the way you inspected something you owned. And then he was actually circling me, like I was a horse for sale and he was a potential buyer.

Control yourself. Don't move.

I felt his warm, wet breath near my neck, and then, oh,

god, he was touching me with thick, firm fingers. They prodded my scalp, ran along the back of my neck, lifting my shirt, and when he reached my right arm, they probed at my wrist, feeling the slick line of my memory card port. I didn't think I could bear it, and yet I did, even though his touch felt like it killed something inside me. It wasn't perverted but clinical, and yet that was almost worse. Because to him, it was clear I was nothing more than an inanimate object. A car in a showroom. As good as dead.

With every slow, booted step he took, the basement walls felt more and more impenetrable, and despite the lack of desire in his hands, I wanted to scrub an imaginary layer of dirt from my skin.

"You've caused me one hell of a headache, you know that?" he said when he finally finished his exam, in that booming drawl of his. Tall, broad across the shoulders, and fit, he exuded an initial impression of youthfulness that faded the closer he got. His thick hair was liberally streaked with gray, and the sagging skin beneath his chin was fighting a losing battle with gravity. His black shirt had no traces of lint, and the perfect crease down the front of his tan cargo pants made me aware of how unbelievably rumpled I was in my day-old outfit.

He brought an unexpected sharp odor with him. Rubbing alcohol mixed with peppermint, both astringent and sweet, a combination that gave me a strange sense of déjà vu.

The scent dredged up a deep uneasiness that made me desperate to retreat, but instinct told me that was the wrong move. That I should never show this man a sign of intimidation. "General Holland," I said with forced ease.

After a rise of his bushy eyebrows, the fake smile widened. "Well, I almost think I should be insulted. Since you've been calling Nicole 'Mom,' surely that makes me Dad?"

My desire to scrub intensified. Dad. Coming out of his mouth, the word sounded all kinds of wrong.

His jaw continued moving in between words, and I caught a glimpse of green between his teeth. Gum. That explained the peppermint. "Hell, I searched harder for you than most parents search for their runaway brats."

A perfect clip of the man I'd thought was my dad, the man in Philly, played through my head. A Christmas memory. Opening presents and roasting marshmallows, building a snowman in the front yard and getting in trouble for decorating it with Mom's favorite silk scarf. Dad's boisterous laughter as we pegged him with snowballs, and leaving cookies out for Santa.

Lies, all lies, I knew that now. Like it or not, Holland was right. He had more claim on the title of father than the programmed version who didn't exist.

Holland continued his inspection, and I wished I could lash out. Punch that expression right off his face.

But Mom's warning was clear.

I settled on words instead. "That doesn't make you my dad, it makes you my keeper," I said, careful to keep an even tone. "All I am to you is a liability—don't pretend otherwise."

Holland frowned. "Mila, you are the result of years and years of research, of hundreds of millions of dollars. Of course you're not just a liability. You're an important part of the U.S. military's defense system. A masterpiece, really."

Quick as a snake, his long, thick fingers whipped out to touch my bare arm. His skin barely grazed mine, but this time, I was unprepared. I jerked away in revulsion, causing his mouth to sag even more.

"Now, there's no need for that." From his right pants pocket, he produced a damp square of paper. A sharp scent wafted toward me as he wiped off each finger on both hands before replacing it.

I guess that explained the rubbing alcohol I'd smelled.

"Now then. Let's get a good look at you."

He crossed his arms, bringing one finger up to tap his clean-shaven jaw. "Mind you, it's not that I'm unsympathetic to the . . . situation. But Nicole took unconscionable risks. Can you imagine the damage you might have caused if one of our enemies had found you?" His eyes narrowed. "We have a duty here, Mila—one that Nicole should understand. And the honest-to-god truth is, no matter what she told you—you're not human. You never will be."

His voice wasn't harsh, or cruel, or even angry. Just matter-of-fact, like he was discussing the components of the lights above us. Which made what he was saying so much worse.

Not human. Not human. Not human. It was like his words tried to burrow under my expertly manufactured skin, tried to wrap around my very core and extinguish any remaining spark of hope that I had left. Darkness swamped me, and I pulled up the one image I knew could help.

Hunter's pale blue eyes, his lopsided smile, blazed to life in my mind, photograph perfect and so, so real, it almost felt as if I should be able to conjure him into the room with us. The warmth stirred in my chest, the floating, slightly light-headed sensation I experienced when he touched my hand or leaned close, and I let it soak in, surround me, rekindle the hope Holland had tried to crush.

He wouldn't win. Not that easily.

I lifted my chin and glared. "You don't know anything about me. Not anymore."

Holland's thick lips tightened briefly and then relaxed, allowing a raspy chuckle to escape. Clasping his hands behind him, he strode even closer. "Still feisty, I see. But did you really think that Nicole could make you human, just by tampering with your memory banks and enrolling you in high school?" He shook his head before continuing.

"She did you a disservice. It's cruel, really—giving you false hope, making you believe things that just aren't true."

He squatted a little so he could meet my shorter frame at eye level. "It doesn't do you any good to cling to these illusions. Unlike Nicole, I would never lie to you. You have my word on that."

At my mutinous expression, he sighed and rose, shaking his head. "Either way, it doesn't matter. Now that we've got you back, we'll make the best possible use of you—or parts of you—that we can."

Parts of me? An image of me, screaming while Holland sawed a giant seam down the middle of my body, then tore pieces from deep inside and dropped them into the out-stretched hands of waiting soldiers, filled my head. I fought back a shudder as I studied the narrowed, cool gray eyes that were now completely devoid of humor. How had Mom ended up working with this man? Sure, she'd lied to me, but out of kindness and concern. Whereas Andrew Holland . . . well, figuratively speaking, he had less heart than I did.

Mom. If only I could talk to her, see her, just for a minute. Just to make sure she was okay.

"Can I see my mom? Please?" I said through gritted teeth, while the urge to lash out grew stronger. In an attempt to curb it, my fingers clenched into fists, tighter and tighter.

Maximum force: 300 lbs. per square inch.

The red words in my head startled me, and I loosened my

hands instantly, shaking them out like I could shake away the reality of the words, the voice. That amount of pressure could be deadly.

Holland shook his head, his slight smile lingering. "I'm afraid that's not possible at the moment."

"Why not? What have you done with her?" Terrible thoughts attacked me—images of Mom unconscious in a dark cell somewhere in the depths of this place, blood trickling onto the floor from where they'd tortured her for information.

"Nothing. I assure you, Nicole is just fine. Do you really think I'd do anything to harm her? Especially when I know she's the best way of ensuring your cooperation."

His words sounded innocuous enough, but I detected their hidden meaning. So long as I did whatever Holland asked, Mom would be safe. But if not . . .

"When, then? When will it be possible?" My complete lack of power, Mom's absence, they both hit me at once. Whether or not I ever saw Mom again was completely dependent on this cold, hard man's whim, and despite my efforts to push them away, that realization made my eyes flood with helpless tears.

Holland heaved a deep sigh and shook his head. "Damn," he said softly. Out came the wipe again, the pungent bite of alcohol, while he carefully cleaned his hands. "I'd prayed that your emotional responses had neutralized during your time away, but I can see that's not the case. Still, that's exactly why we made sure to have an alternate—and improved—version."

An alternate version. Words that even my superbrain needed a split second longer to process.

"What do you mean?" But I was very, very afraid I knew exactly what he meant.

"We didn't just trunk all our research because of a few glitches. We created another MILA." Holland slid the wipe back into his pocket before smiling, the first genuine smile I'd seen from him.

A smile that seemed to suck all the warmth from my body. "Are you saying there's another version of . . . of me?" My voice fell into a whisper.

Holland's smile grew broader, balling up his beefy cheeks and deepening the four creases that branched out from his eyes to his temples. "Exactly. Want to meet her? A version without your overreactive emotional garbage."

He glanced up at the rectangular spectator window and gave a nod. Then he turned to face the door I'd originally entered.

I stared at it, still fumbling to grasp the implications of what he'd just said. In a few moments, something was going to walk through that door. Another MILA.

Another girl formed using the exact same research that had created me.

Well, not exactly the same. This MILA wouldn't have my "overreactive emotional garbage," as Holland had so tactfully put it.

My simulated heart accelerated, pounding frantically, like it was trying to escape my body. I lifted a hand to my chest, trying to take comfort in the very human thumping while fighting off the feeling that everything about it was a mockery. Muffled footsteps came from outside the door, followed by the beep that signaled a code had been entered successfully. Then the metallic click of the locking mechanism disengaging.

Finally the door slid open, and a girl entered.

Her attire was normal enough—charcoal-gray sweatpants and a long-sleeved white tee. Okay, so maybe her gait was a little too fluid. So graceful, her sneakered footsteps barely made a sound on the concrete floor.

But that wasn't what filled me with mounting horror. It was her mouth, with the extra-wide lower lip. Her strong build—more quarter horse than thoroughbred. The precise, round shape of her large eyes, the same green as mine. Holland had said "an alternate version," when apparently what he really meant was "identical twin."

I stood frozen, unable to run, to turn away, even though part of me pleaded to do just that. I couldn't even swallow as she sauntered toward us. I searched for some distinguishing mark, characteristic, anything that might tell us apart. She couldn't be exactly the same as me. She couldn't.

Except she was. In every way that I could see, barring her hair. Mine was still all choppy and black and punker wannabe from my futile disguise attempt. My fingers crept to my neck, suddenly even more fiercely attached to my new look. At least it kept me from being a complete clone. I forced my attention back to Other Mila. There had to be something there, something different about her that I could pick out. I just needed to look carefully enough.

After one brief glance at the girl, Holland's cunning gaze remained focused on my face, savoring every nuance of my reaction. "Mila, allow me to introduce you to your sister, if you will. This is MILA 3.0."

Other Mila, my twin, came to life then, with a polite smile and an extended hand. "It's nice to finally meet you," she said in a pleasant tone.

Only it was like I'd said it. Because her voice . . . her voice was mine, too.

I flinched, stumbled a step back from this gruesome thing. Staring at her—it made it that much harder for me to cling to the hope that I was real. If I were, then she never would have been possible. Besides, if we looked exactly the same, who knew what else we shared? I mean, we'd been created in the same lab. Did that mean we shared the same exact thoughts, the same exact way of looking at the world? Was she reading my mind, right now?

Even after discovering the truth of my origins, I'd never

thought to question my individuality. I'd just always known I was unique, original—my own creation, just like any other human being. Now Holland was trying to rip that facade away with his latest handiwork . . . rip away everything that made me believe I was more than just a mass-manufactured machine, no more special than the next one on the assembly line.

She glided a step closer to compensate for my retreat, her overly familiar hand still looming in front of me, waiting for me to shake it. The idea of touching her skin repulsed me. Would it feel like touching *me*?

Cognizant of Holland's watchful eyes, I hesitantly reached out and clasped her fingers in mine. Her skin was smooth, lukewarm, neutral. All that concern, and I felt . . . nothing. No connection, no disgust.

It was just like touching anyone else.

Other Mila didn't act perturbed in the slightest over my appearance. Our appearance. She just stepped back to stand at Holland's side, a slight frown drawing her brows downward as she glanced at her creator. "Why isn't she happy to see me?"

Holland patted her head, the way you might pat a dog. "Don't worry, you did well."

Three's lips—I would not think of her as Other Mila, I couldn't—launched into a bright smile. *My* lips. I stared with a sick fascination. I'd never realized my eyes looked so squinty when I smiled like that.

Her grin vanished an instant later. Three just stood, face placid, arms dangling loosely at her sides. As if awaiting her next command.

My skin felt like tiny insects were crawling on it when Holland patted her again. "Amazing, isn't she? It took three tries, but I think we finally got it right."

Three tries . . . . "There was another version?" I asked. Unsure that I really wanted to know the answer.

Three smiled, bouncing up on her toes in her eagerness to respond. "The first MILA prototype was embedded with one thousand more pain receptors per square inch than the subsequent versions."

Subsequent versions—meaning her and me. I guess that was one way to depersonalize us.

"While the extra receptors ensured that version 1.0 wouldn't be detected via lack of pain response, they also caused her to fail the torture tests."

"Torture tests?"

Three blinked at me, once. "Replications of torture scenarios in the lab to see how easily the participants might give up information if they're captured."

The memory flashed in my head again, and reality crashed over me. Wrong, all wrong. Tests, torture. The drill, the gun. Screaming. But it hadn't been my screaming after all; the girl in the room hadn't been me.

Instead of soothing me somehow, that knowledge made me feel one thousand times worse. Because that girl could experience way more pain, serious pain, and they'd tortured her to test her limits.

Ultimately, the one thing that had made her more human had actually sealed her "death," had led to her being recycled like a bit of aluminum foil, with just as little concern.

If I could puke, I would have done it now. My stomach burned, and the force of the nausea made my head spin. Lucky for me, that seemed to be one biological function they'd skipped.

The last thing I needed to do was let Holland guess my reaction.

"I . . . I was already created by then, wasn't I?"

"Yes. Mostly," Holland said.

So they must have made me watch, that much was clear. But why were my memories of that so uncertain? Why hadn't I been able to recall all of this on my own?

The answer was simple. Mom. To spare me.

"Thankfully, we'd already made adjustments. Fewer pain receptors, just enough to alert you to when a real person would feel pain."

I peeked at Three, to see if she had any response to the implication that she wasn't real. Nothing. Not a flicker of her eyes, not a twitch of her mouth. She just stood there, studying my face silently. And looking so eerily like me.

No, not studied, I decided. Studied implied genuine curiosity. And while her gaze remained focused on my face, behind her eyes lurked a disinterest. Like without a mission from Holland, she didn't really exist.

Well, at least now I had a logical answer for what had happened when I'd been pitched out of Kaylee's truck. The scream, but with hardly any pain behind it. I'd never been able to figure that out before.

"What do you plan to do with me?"

"Originally? We planned to terminate you. I'm assuming that's why Nicole took you. You were supposed to mimic human emotions, not actually experience them, and definitely not so completely. Your system refused every attempt to override them, so we decided to terminate you and try again."

Terminate me. Terminate.

It felt like everything inside me had frozen solid, trapping me in an inadvertent lockdown mode as I stared at Holland's impassive face. He wanted to get rid of me entirely. To erase me from existence like I was nothing more than a flawed computer program. Since he truly believed I was no more or no less alive than that, he'd have no qualms about it. Of that I was sure.

The trapped feeling vanished, replaced by an overpowering compulsion to flee. I had to get out of here. Now. My frantic gaze found the door—the one potential source of freedom—and I was already readying myself for the inevitable battle to get there when reality halted me in my tracks.

Nothing had changed. Holland still had Mom. My mom, who hadn't stolen me from the development site because she worried I was too human to perform as an android. She'd stolen me because she thought I was so human that, to her, the idea of termination Holland tossed so casually around equaled murder.

My murder.

I felt a single tear well up in my right eye, poised to release from my manufactured duct. I commanded it to stay there. To Holland, emotions were a liability. A weakness worth destroying me over.

Holland was angled away from me, making eye contact with the spectators in the window. He nodded at some signal I'd missed, then turned around with another crack of his gum. "I do have some good news for you, Mila. The powers that be want me to test you again, to see if you might have some value we missed. A reprieve of sorts."

"And if I say no?"

I knew the answer before he responded. Mom. He'd use Mom as insurance.

"Pass these tests, and you prove Nicole didn't totally screw up. We'll reconsider both of your outcomes. Don't pass, and she's facing a life sentence. So, instead of goodbye, I'll say . . . good luck." He pushed up his sleeve, glanced at the wide-faced watch nestled in brown arm hair. "Test number two dash one five to commence shortly. Oh, I almost forgot. Don't move this time, Mila." His drawl was laced with warning.

The knowledge of Mom's precarious position was the

only thing keeping me still when his hand shot out. I caught a flash of silver before he grabbed my right ear. He shoved something cold and foreign deep inside, propelled by a thin sticklike object.

I heard a faint click, and then:

Security Chip: Activated.

The probe withdrew, but Holland's chubby finger returned to my ear's outer shell. The feeling of his damp flesh, pressing hard against my cartilage, brought back the horror of the memory from the lab, but no, no, no, I couldn't—I *wouldn't*—flinch.

Wireless Receiver: Activated.

"That ought to do it," he said, releasing me. "Now we won't have to worry about you trying to escape. That chip will send the compound into lockdown mode if you come within ten feet of the entrance."

Holland patted Three on the back and said, "Give her hell, okay?" Then he executed a brisk about-face and strode for the door. It whirred quietly closed behind him. Sealing me in for some kind of test.

My gaze shifted to my look-alike, standing in the same spot where Holland had left her.

Correction—sealing *us* in.

PART THREE

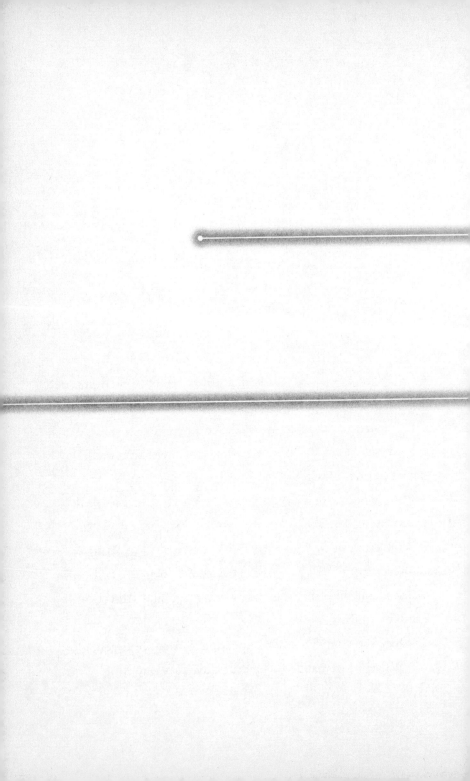

TWENTY-FOUR

ere I was, in this barren room, fluorescent lights glaring overhead and cold concrete floor beneath me, miles away from Clearwater in every sense of the word. Alone for the very first time with the twin I hadn't known existed.

Our identical gazes connected. Well, almost identical. Once again, I noted a striking difference between us: the lack of warmth in Three's green eyes. Instead of the disinterest from before, now Holland's other creation watched me like she was performing a visual dissection. Limb by limb.

Once she completed her inspection, Three shrugged.

"What?" I demanded when she didn't say anything.

"You can't tell by looking at you that you're flawed, that's all," she said, in that voice that was so disconcertingly similar to mine. No, not similar—the same. And, given her casual tone, she might as well have been discussing a new computer program.

Come to think of it, that was more accurate than I cared to admit. "Not that it matters," she continued. "I have my orders." She paused, smiling. "No hard feelings."

No hard feelings. Like it wasn't my life on the line here.

Without any discernible cue, Three's attention shifted to the window above us. My gaze followed, and I felt a jolt. Standing close to the glass was a boy, maybe eighteen or nineteen—he looked way too young to be up there. To be part of . . . this. His dark hair was flat on one side yet bristled up on the other, like he'd slept on it funny and hadn't taken the time to brush it. Rangy and awkward in his wrinkled white collar and loosened tie, his shoulders slumped as if trying to escape the confines of the tight collar. Yet his gaze was anything but casual as it focused unwaveringly on me.

Two . . . can you hear me?

The raspy voice echoed directly inside my head.

What the hell? I lurched backward, my hands flying to my ears, while my eyes darted toward Three. No reaction there. She stood patiently, staring up at the boy like an obedient dog.

The boy. He had to be the one who'd talked.

I shook my head a few times, as if the repeated motion could expel the nuisance. Of course that didn't happen.

I take it by your reaction that I'm coming in loud and clear?

I nodded cautiously.

Good. My name is Lucas Webb, and I'm going to be the proctor for your upcoming tests.

Tests again, just like Holland had mentioned. But what tests? And . . . could this guy hear my thoughts the way I could hear his voice?

I watched him, thinking, *Can you hear me?* in his direction, but there was no change in his expression and no response. At least, not until a slight smile appeared three seconds later.

You have to speak out loud if you want me to hear you. You can only hear me because General Holland activated your wireless receiver.

Okay, so that made Holland wafting his peppermint breath in my face while stuffing a finger down my ear a little less creepy. But only just.

A few feet away, Three finished performing a strange ritual, using her left hand to rotate the joints on her right arm through their complete range of motion.

"What tests?" I said, watching her with growing unease as she switched, now using her right hand to move her left. Each finger was bent and extended, followed by the wrist. If she followed the same pattern as the other side, next would come the elbow, and then the shoulder. Like one of the runners at school, warming up for a competition.

An icy fist squeezed my heart. Just an echo, I reminded myself, in an attempt to shake it off. A phantom sensation. You don't have a heart.

The reminder didn't help.

The tests that will decide your . . . ultimate outcome.

There was a slight hesitation to Lucas's words, though his expression remained neutral.

The tests are designed to showcase your abilities as well as your deficiencies. Once you've completed all three, your actions will be evaluated and scored, and that will determine your future with us.

The voice stopped, but Lucas continued his impassive stare through the glass.

My deficiencies, meaning . . . my emotions? Was this strange, disheveled guy telling me that any show of emotion would be counted against me?

I didn't have long to ponder it, because three seconds later, he uttered his next words:

The first test starts . . . in three minutes.

TWENTY-FIVE

"**A**re you prepared?" I heard my voice ask. Not my voice. *Her* voice. Three watched me, head cocked. "Prepared?"

She nodded. "To test your fighting skills, to ensure Dr. Laurent didn't tamper with them too much when she made unauthorized adjustments. We all get tested on our physical combat prowess."

Fighting skills? Queasiness rolled through my stomach.

I glanced up at the spectators' window, where another six faces pushed close to the glass next to Lucas Webb's, one of them Holland's. I wouldn't be surprised if they started placing bets.

I shook my head and gestured to her. "I don't want to fight. I don't want them to make me into"—I swallowed the "you" at the last second, realizing how awful that might sound—"into something I'm not."

She tilted her head again, brown hair sliding over her right shoulder. If I touched it, would it have the exact same silky texture as mine? "I know what you were going to say," she said, echoing my hand motion in an uncannily identical wave. "You don't want them to make you into me. Don't worry—you're not hurting my feelings. It's a pretty illogical thought, though. You are me, just with more emotions. And our wants are irrelevant here."

You are me. . . .

The idea ripped at the thin fabric holding me together, tried to release every bit of fear I'd been stuffing back, hiding from view. That's what they wanted . . . Holland, this creature, all the curious eyes up in the window. They wanted to turn me into a true clone of the creature standing across from me. For me to give up my feelings and give in. Three had said our wants were irrelevant, but I wouldn't, *couldn't* believe that. No matter what, I wouldn't let them make me into her.

Without warning, Three took a graceful step toward me, and I lurched a corresponding step back. A waltz of sorts. "You should make sure you follow directions while you're here."

"Why? You can't possibly care what happens to me." Or could she? After all, Holland had mentioned fixing my emotional flaws, not getting rid of emotions altogether.

She did that one slow blink again, which I was starting to figure out meant she was puzzled. "We come from the same building materials, share the same technology. If we were human, we'd be sisters. We understand each other."

Sisters.

I wanted to cover my eyes, to turn away, to wish this entire scenario out of existence. This . . . distortion of me actually felt a connection between us. She thought we were the same. Which, if it was true, meant either she was more human than they gave her credit for, or . . . I was less human.

My head whipped back and forth, faster and faster. "No, we don't understand each other. I have feelings. While you . . ."

That slow blink again. "I have feelings. But mine function properly, as behavior guides. Whereas General Holland says you actually experience emotions, similar to a human." She frowned. "Hopefully they can fix that."

Fix that. As if erasing my emotions would be as easy as changing a dead car battery. A shudder tore through me. That couldn't be the case.

Until this moment, I hadn't realized what a service Mom had actually done for me. Even though she'd lied in the process, at least by making me think I was her daughter, that I had a father, she'd taught me how to love, how to experience a full spectrum of feelings, the highs and lows and everything in between. Having that snatched away with a simple procedure . . . surely that wasn't possible?

Before I could freak out completely, Lucas's voice rang in my ears.

The purpose of this first exercise is to test your defense skills. It's crucial that you not be taken down and captured in hand-to-hand combat.

His voice sounded smooth, detached. Like he was talking to a machine instead of a person.

I glanced up at the window again and glared, pouring out every bit of anger and hatred for this place, Holland, the creature next to me who hadn't asked to be created but disgusted me nevertheless because she reminded me how far from human I truly was, and him. The young man who'd administered these tests, who was ordering me to fight without a single thought for how that might affect me.

Through the glass, our gazes connected. The intensity of mine must have startled him, because his lips parted in surprise. After a couple of seconds he broke contact, looking down like my stare was burning a hole right through him. Both hands raked through his hair, mussing it even more. He was suddenly looking extremely uncomfortable up there.

I squashed the pang I felt. After all, he'd administered this test. If he felt bad enough, he was more than welcome to trade places with me.

When he finally straightened and reestablished eye contact, I lifted my hands, palms out, and shrugged my shoulders. *"And?"* I mouthed.

. . . and we really want to compare your capabilities to those of Three.

His tone was softer this time.

Ready?

All the warmth rushed from my body, leaving me cold, so cold. My hand flew to my mouth to mask a panicked giggle. Ready? Hardly.

My fists balled just as I heard Mom's voice.

"Whatever you do, don't lose control. Your feelings are a detriment there."

I drew in a deep breath and relaxed my hands. "Do I have a choice?" I asked in a steady voice.

His thick eyebrows shot up his forehead before his lips twitched. My fists balled again. So glad I could amuse him.

No.

"Then don't ask." At that, I turned away, disgusted.

A brief pause, and then Lucas's voice boomed into the room, this time via a hidden speaker.

"The test will commence in five . . . four . . . three . . . two . . . one."

Three lunged before the "one" could even finish leaving Lucas's lips. I feinted back, placing myself out of reach just in time. She frowned and blinked. Puzzled again.

"You're not scared, are you? Because they'll deduct points for that."

She was right—I knew that. While I might not have any desire to fight, my less emotional sister had a point. Right now, my desires were irrelevant. Especially if I wanted a chance to see Mom again.

Alive.

I nodded, opening my mouth to say "Oka—"

Three's foot whipped into my face with a deafening smack.

Contact made.

Thanks for nothing. That was my dazed mental response to the internal voice as I flew backward and landed hard on my right side, my hip striking the ground first, followed by my cheek. Hard enough that the force of impact reminded me of my fall from Kaylee's truck. I didn't have time to check for potential injuries, though, because Three followed the kick by lunging forward, so quick she was almost a blur. I rolled to the left, missing her pounce by a millisecond.

I barely had time to regain my feet when *crunch!* Her hand caught me in the left shoulder, with even more force than the kick.

I stumbled, went down, once again barely rolling out of the range of the kick that followed. At this rate, I was going to lose within two minutes. They'd terminate me, and who knew what'd happen to Mom.

As I scrambled away, I frantically wondered how I could prevent any of that from happening. Maybe it was because I was out of practice, maybe they'd upgraded Three's training programming, maybe Mom had erased something crucial when she'd hidden my past. Whatever the cause, my twin was kicking my butt and then some. The structure forming my hip felt like it needed an extra-long session with Mom's special toolkit.

If I kept this up for long, there wouldn't be anything left of me *to* dismantle.

Just then, a noise blasted into my ear. Like maybe Lucas had coughed. It shifted my attention back onto Three, but not quite quickly enough. Her foot stomped into the ground, scraping against my ear with enough force to send even my meager pain receptors shrieking.

That would have been my face if it hadn't been for Lucas.

And she was still coming.

I threw myself into one more desperate roll, needing to buy myself even a fraction of a second to regain my feet— before my better-equipped counterpart crushed me like a tin can.

A counterpart who was only two steps away. And who'd be anticipating another roll by now.

Backflip.

I didn't question the voice this time. Didn't stop to consider that I'd never performed a backflip in my entire life—at least, not in my admittedly patchy memory. I just latched onto the idea, and before I could blink, my body flew into action, like it had done this one hundred times before. I slammed my palms into the ground, kicked my feet over my head, and pushed. Hard. For a second I revolved in the air with nothing to anchor me, face rotating toward the ground, and fear punched me in the gut. The next instant, I was grabbing the floor with my toes.

As I landed, a familiar rush swept though my body, like a burst of the adrenaline I didn't have. No time to celebrate the success of my acrobatics, though. I dropped into a defensive stance the instant my feet hit the concrete. Braced myself. I couldn't keep running—I had to hold my ground.

At least this time I was semiprepared when the blow hit.

I swerved, just enough so that her fist glanced off my cheek. Still, the force made me lurch sideways. But I didn't go down. I recovered my balance, ducked her follow-up punch . . . then lashed out with my foot.

She dodged just in time, but finally, *finally*, I'd done something offensive. Rolling around on the floor might have saved my body from damage, but I sincerely doubted it was scoring me any major points with the spectators.

Even now, I felt the weight of their eyes on me. Holland's, and Lucas's. And despite my one nondefensive maneuver, ice prickled down my back. I was still failing.

On the plus side, Three recognized that I'd snapped

out of my initial ineptitude. She pulled back and circled me slowly, those eerily familiar eyes scrutinizing my every move as I circled with her. She was just waiting for me to make a mistake.

I lashed out with my left foot—a decoy. As she feinted to the side, my right jab connected hard in her throat. She stumbled back, three steps, then four.

A human would have been incapacitated by that blow, the fragile trachea closing off momentarily. In fact, I'd used that exact move back at Clearwater. But Three recovered as soon as the backward momentum stopped.

I lashed out with my right hand. With equal swiftness, Three threw up her left forearm to block my move. And so it went as we continued circling. One of us would strike, the other block, keeping us locked in a never-ending stalemate.

But I had to win.

How on earth could I sneak past her defenses? Especially when, most likely, both of us had been uploaded with the exact same training programs, making it impossible not to predict each other's moves?

The answer emerged like a whisper inside my head. Simple. I shouldn't be relying on our similarities. I should be playing up our differences. If I couldn't win on her terms, I'd have to win on *mine*.

"So, do they let you listen to music here?" I asked, with

every sense on full alert, ready to lunge at the faintest sign of motion.

"Your distraction attempts won't work, you know," my counterpart said patiently.

"Who said anything about distraction? I just think we deserve a little music. In the movies, there's always music when people fight." Well, at least in the one action movie I'd ever seen. With Mom . . .

I pushed her image out of my head. The intent was to distract my opponent, not myself. "Here, I'll sing you one of my friend's favorite songs. She played it all the time back in Minnesota." And then I launched into a semituneful rendering of "Brown Eyed Girl." A song that Kaylee had blared every time it came on the classics station she loved.

My voice echoed in the sterile room, accompanied by our footfalls as we continued our circular dance.

I finished the first verse and launched into the chorus. Wishing I could spare a glance for the faces watching us from overhead. They had to be wondering if Nicole Laurent's prize machine had short-circuited. Or been permanently damaged by her tampering. But I didn't dare. The second I took my eyes off my *sister*, even for a second, she'd strike.

"This song isn't even appropriate. Neither of us has brown eyes," Three finally said. But she remained vigilant.

She sidestepped. I sidestepped. And sang. Only five feet separated us.

"We used to sing, sha la la la—"

Left roundhouse kick.

Right uppercut.

A list of potential moves paraded through my head, but I ignored them all for one I knew the android part of me would never consider. Mainly because it was asinine. No experienced fighter in her right mind would try it. The probability of serious injury was way too high.

The move's lack of logic was exactly why it might work.

So I continued belting out the peppy chorus—even as I dived headfirst for her feet.

I realized how truly ridiculous this move was. But it was too late. Ignoring the Abort! flashing behind my eyes, I dug up my failing courage and hoped for the best.

My combatant's reflexes were lightning quick, but that was only because her internal computer processed all the likely attacks and prepared her body to act on them. But she wasn't prepared for this. That gave me the extra tenth of a second I needed.

She recovered fast, her right leg lashing toward me mid-dive. Not fast or forceful enough. As her foot went up, I grabbed her calf, jerking hard as I shifted all my body weight to the right.

I let go and had rolled harmlessly out of the way when she crashed to the ground. An instant later, I leaped onto her waist, pinning her arms to her sides with my hands, her torso with my knees.

"La la te da," I finished softly.

She thrashed, but I held tight. No way was I doing this again. This test was over.

Finally she relaxed. From her supine position, she blinked at me, nose wrinkled. "Next time, can you please sing something else? I find that song . . . annoying."

A small, slightly hysterical giggle burst from my throat. I'd won! I'd won the fight, and I'd done so by using both my android and my human sides.

My flare of elation was cut short by Lucas's voice.

Well, that was . . . interesting.

He still watched me from the window. He wasn't smiling, but this time, his amusement had been clear in the way he drew out "interesting."

The burst of warmth fizzled completely, leaving behind a twisting knot in my gut. One test, that's all I'd finished so far. I still had two more to get through, and I could only imagine they'd be even harder, perhaps impossible. "Can I see my mom now?"

Three sprang to her feet, rocking lightly back and forth from her toes to her heels. "Are we done, or do we have another round?" she asked, glancing up at the window. The eagerness in her voice told me she'd be more than happy to have another go at me.

No, you're done for now.

From the way she cocked her head slightly toward the left, I could tell Lucas was speaking to both of us.

Three, you scored higher on the first portion of the test, by managing to put your opponent on the defensive and landing some substantial blows.

She smiled, the same way as when Holland had patted her head.

But Two ultimately scored higher by realizing that combat techniques wouldn't be enough to win, and using . . . ingenuity . . .

He did smile this time. It was just the faintest upturning of his lips, but even so . . . I balled my fists against the urge to smack the expression right off his face. This was my life, my mom's life, that he found so hilarious.

. . . to outmaneuver an equally skilled opponent and ultimately subdue her.

Three, please wait by the door for your escort. Two, I'll be down in a minute.

Three immediately swiveled but paused to peer at me over her shoulder. "Perhaps General Holland won't terminate you after all," she said, in the pleasant tone of a cashier. Like she was thanking me for my Blizzard order, and not suggesting someone would be tinkering around with my insides.

She sauntered toward the door, which beeped and slid open just as she reached it. A twenty-something soldier, clad in the standard black T-shirt, multipocketed cargo pants uniform they favored in this place, waited on the other side.

The two of them disappeared around the corner. I waited for the door to close.

Instead, another young man appeared in the open frame, this one clad in a rumpled white-collared shirt, loose tie, and gray slacks with a sagging hem on the left.

The boy from the spectator window.

Lucas Webb.

TWENTY-SIX

ucas paused in the open doorway, his hands thrust into his pockets, a picture of total nonchalance as he stared at me. That illusion shattered when the door began sliding closed and banged into his arm. He emitted a startled curse and stumbled into the room.

I allowed myself a tiny smile at his expense. Payback for his earlier behavior.

The red flush that surged into his otherwise pale cheeks suggested embarrassment, but he didn't look away. Instead, he headed toward me, his forehead creased like I was a puzzle that needed solving.

He didn't walk like the soldiers. He landed heavier on his right foot, and his left foot barely cleared the ground.

His boots looked different, too, thicker soled than the rest, and the left one externally rotated just a little, like his foot wasn't on quite straight. Based on that, I couldn't imagine he was a soldier. He'd never make it through basic training.

But he was here, and he was monitoring these tests. To me, that was all that mattered.

As he drew closer, I lifted my chin, bracing myself for a second degrading inspection like Holland had performed. Queasiness churned in my stomach, but I didn't move. I couldn't mess up again, no matter how violated I felt from their prying eyes and hands.

The tightness in my chest relaxed when he stopped a respectful three feet away. "Lucas Webb, your proctor," he announced.

He withdrew his right hand from his pocket, then froze with it extended halfway toward me, as if the movement had been reflexive, and now that he'd remembered I was something less than human, he wasn't quite sure how to proceed. "Uh . . ."

I let my exhale hiss loudly between my teeth before extending my own hand toward his. Mere inches away, but not touching, so ultimately he'd have to choose. "Mila. And I don't bite."

Again, that slight parting of his lips, the minute widening to his eyes. I was about to give up when he reached out and clasped my hand, practically drowning it with his larger one.

I didn't recall forming any expectations, but I must have, because the feel of his skin startled me. It was warm and faintly damp. Rougher than I'd expected. Small, circular abrasions rubbed my own palm like fine sandpaper as he shook my hand with a firm yet careful grip.

Careful. The way you might actually shake a regular human's hand so as not to hurt her.

I discarded that thought the instant it registered. Ridiculous, and under the circumstances, giving Lucas the benefit of the doubt could prove downright dangerous. I couldn't relax my guard around him, not for a second.

"Nice to meet you," he said, releasing me to return his hand to his pocket.

"If you say so," I said, cautious to keep my expression neutral.

Apparently my minuscule stab at defiance startled him, because his eyes widened once more. Hazel. They were a golden hazel, with little flecks of moss green and blue. The kind of eyes that would be challenging to re-create in a lab.

He cleared his throat before responding. "I'm, uh, supposed to take you in for repairs."

I flinched, strangely disappointed that my instinct had proved correct. He didn't think of me as human at all.

"What's wrong?" he said, obviously tracking my reaction, however tiny.

"I'm not a bike," I muttered before clamping my disastrously big mouth shut.

"I . . . do you always talk in metaphors?"

What? That came from so far out of nowhere that my anger dissolved. "I . . . I've never thought about it before," I said slowly. Pondering. "I guess so. Why? Doesn't Three?"

"No." He broke off to inspect me. Fully, this time, a slow head-to-toe perusal that brought warmth rushing to my cheeks, though there was nothing sexual in the appraisal. But he didn't perform it with the same clinical detachment as Holland had, either. It was like before. Like he was searching every inch of me for a visible solution to a problem that only he could see.

The more seconds that ticked by, the more uncomfortable I became, until I finally couldn't restrain the urge to cross my arms.

That gesture must have snapped him out of it, because he blinked and lurched backward. "Sorry, I didn't mean to . . . it's just . . . I was expecting something different."

Something different. Which meant he must be new. Otherwise he'd have known what to expect.

My stomach sank. That meant he probably wouldn't have much useful information for me, even if I could pry anything out of him. I glanced up at the spectator window and shivered. Still, he'd be more likely to talk anywhere but here. "You said something about repairs?" I prodded.

He blinked, making me notice how his dark lashes were tipped in gold. "Repairs, right. This way, please."

I studied him as he led me with that offbeat gait to the door. He was tall—six foot, one inch—and lanky thin, not built at all like the firmly muscled soldiers I'd seen. Or even Hunter, for that matter. But he'd surprised me with the casual strength in his handshake. I wondered if that lean frame of his was equally deceptive.

Lucas took me down a different hallway from the one I'd arrived in, leading me deeper into the building's interior. Quiet and dim, with no one else around but us.

GPS, I commanded. I felt a spark in my head, then . . . nothing.

Must be jammed down here, just like in the car.

After we passed five doors on the right, each one as unmarked and plain silver as the next, he finally veered toward the sixth one.

Another sliding steel door, like the one that led into the first testing room, only bigger—thirteen feet across by nine feet high. Under a large keypad built into the white door-frame on the right side sat a tall, thin silver table. The only items on it were two metal cylinders.

As I watched, Lucas reached into the cylinder on the right and withdrew a Q-tip. Then he opened his mouth and swabbed the inside of his cheek before pressing a small green button at the bottom of the keypad. A narrow tray shot out below it, the top of it covered with a shiny plastic material. He wiped the Q-tip on the plastic, then pressed the button again, and the tray slid back into the wall.

A red light on the keypad blinked to life. "Identity confirmation or denial will occur in ten seconds."

He tossed the Q-tip into the left cylinder as the countdown commenced.

At the end of ten seconds, the red light turned green. "DNA scan verified: Lucas Webb. Please enter your pass code."

He typed in his twelve-digit code, which I memorized, my uneasiness growing. All that extra security, in what was already a secret government facility? It didn't bode well for whatever was on the other side of that door.

The door hitched at first before finally sliding open with a beep.

He frowned down at the track. "When are they going to fix the moisture level in here? It's going to start damaging the equipment soon. The computers . . . ," he muttered, breaking off as if talking to himself.

Huh. This guy had fewer social graces than I did. Which made me bold enough to ask, "What's wrong with your leg?"

He shrugged, seemingly unperturbed by my question. "I was born with a clubfoot. After five surgeries, this is as good as it gets." Not even a trace of bitterness in his voice.

Despite myself, I felt a flicker of admiration at his easy acceptance.

I was expecting a room full of clutter, but when I walked in, the first thing I noticed was how spotless everything was. Four industrial-grade refrigerators lined the left wall; two of them had WARNING: BIOHAZARDOUS MATERIAL INSIDE. To our right was a large desk with a computer monitor on top of it. In the middle of the room were two huge reclining chairs, one that appeared to feature the long, skinny tube of a sophisticated laser on top, the other next to a table holding an enormous toolbox.

But the room's dominating feature was the odd device in the far back corner. It was a large, clear tube—big enough for a human—that stood upright on the floor. The clear surface had a grid of tiny lines covering its entirety, some of which flashed at random moments. The whole thing was attached to a humming machine with a display of computer monitors hanging in midair above it.

Lucas halted in front of one of the elevated gray vinyl-and-metal chairs—sort of like one I'd seen in an ad for a dentist's office. A computer monitor hung suspended above it. Luca made an awkward waving motion at it with his hand. "Please take a seat."

I eyed the chair warily from behind his tall frame. Wires ran underneath the bottom and plugged into a black box on the floor. A computer, I realized. Above where my head would reach, two rectangular compartments protruded on both sides.

"Can't I sit in that one?" I said, pointing to an innocuous-looking rolling stool to the left of the chair.

His lips twitched. "No, that's where I sit."

I sighed. "How about I stand?"

He shook his head. "I wouldn't suggest it. Not unless you want Holland to send some men in to strap you down."

That sent me scurrying forward. "Pass," I said. Trying not to panic as I remembered Mila One, chained to a chair during the so-called torture tests. Thrashing against her restraints while a man took a drill to her chest. That could easily be me, and even though I didn't have the same pain reception as Mila One, the idea of a bit driving through my skin, of a bullet slamming into my skull, filled me with horror all the same.

I hopped up onto the high seat, which put my face level with Lucas's, and took the opportunity to study him. Overall, his appearance would probably rate as rather unremarkable to the girls back in Clearwater—no super-defined cheekbones, no purposely mussed hair, no perfectly symmetrical features that bordered on the feminine. Just a slightly crooked nose and pale skin that didn't look like it tanned easily. Nothing that stood out as unappealing, but nothing noteworthy, either.

Except his eyes. His eyes fell into an entirely different

category. Not only the startling mix of colors, but the way the thick lashes changed from dark brown to gold at the ends.

"Lean back, please."

I complied, fumbling for a way to ease him into conversation, both to distract me from whatever came next and to hopefully get him to share anything helpful. "You seem young to be working here," I finally said, truthfully.

"I'm on sabbatical from MIT."

"Didn't you like it there?"

He stopped tugging at a compartment above the chair long enough to look at me. "Actually, I loved it. It's the first place where I didn't feel weird around people my own age."

So Lucas had felt like an outsider once, too. If he'd been in Clearwater, would we have eventually found each other, the same way Hunter and I had?

Hunter. Up until this moment, he'd been the only boy I'd been alone with like this, one-on-one. Under circumstances so vastly different, I felt torn between laughing and crying.

A fierce wave of longing gripped me, reminding me that I needed information if I ever hoped to escape this place and talk to Hunter again.

Best to start slowly, though. To continue with these casual inquiries so that he didn't question my motives. "If you liked it so much, why are you here?"

His expression went from open to strangely guarded, and I saw the way his shoulders tensed. "I couldn't pass up an opportunity like this, to consult for the military. Especially since I'm the only male in three generations who isn't a full-fledged member." He paused, inhaled, and then a small smile reappeared. "This boot's not made for walking," he joked, with an ease that once again startled me. If only I could accept my difference so readily.

"I wonder if that's why Mom decided to work here," I mused. "Not because she wanted to be in the military, but because the opportunities were so good?"

Lucas had been in the process of reaching over my head for a compartment on the left side of the chair but froze with his hand hovering just in front of a small round circle on the metal when I said "Mom." He shook his head, sending the longish strands on top into a jerky dance.

"What?"

"Nothing. It's just . . . Three never refers to any of the scientists that personally. To be honest, it's a little disconcerting."

I didn't know what to say to that, so I remained silent while he pushed the circle. A lid eased open, exposing a silver plug nestled inside, the size of a USB port but with a different configuration. "And I'm not sure about Dr. Laurent. Sorry."

Disappointment sank like a stone in my stomach, but I

forced a polite response. "It's okay."

He yanked the retractable cord out with a zipping sound, and I knew what was coming next. "Here," I said with a sigh, sticking out my wrist.

Lucas's sandy-colored eyebrows drew closer together as he stared at my hand. "That's for your memory card port. This"—he wiggled the plug—"is our proprietary USB plug-in, which fits behind your right ear. Don't you understand your own functionality?"

Feeling incredibly stupid, I dropped my hand into my lap. "I'm catching up. Even though I hate learning about my capabilities."

"Why?"

"Because the more I learn to use them, the less human—the more ugly—I feel," I blurted. I bit my lip and averted my eyes. Too much, I'd revealed way too much. "Please don't say anything. . . ."

Any second now, he'd tell me how he was obligated to report back to Holland.

I waited, fingers clasped tightly. When I peeked up at him, I caught him staring. He cleared his throat and looked away. "My sole purpose is to oversee your repairs and proctor the tests. No one said anything about monitoring our conversations."

I sagged into the chair, allowed my eyes to flutter closed in relief. Maybe I'd misjudged him when he'd been behind that spectator window. If so, now was a good time—the only time, potentially—to try to elicit information about Mom.

I felt a rustle of air as he reached toward my head, his hand hovering close to my ear. "I'm sorry, I need . . . do you mind if I . . . ?" His half cough, half laugh sounded self-conscious. "Sorry. I'm not this tentative when I work with Three. Like I said before—you're different."

"Don't apologize. If anything, the fact that you think I'm different gives me hope."

"Hope," he repeated, with wide eyes. Then he coughed. "Right. Anyway, if you could just pull your right earlobe forward . . ."

I reached up to grasp my right earlobe, where the skin felt warm and soft and oh so authentic. Then, after a deep breath to fill my nonexistent lungs, I pulled the lobe forward and exposed the port I'd never known existed until a few moments ago.

Compassion had softened Lucas's mouth, erased the frown lines from his forehead. And was now allowing him to maintain eye contact with me for longer than five seconds without doing something awkward. How on earth had this guy ended up here? I wondered again. Nothing about him fitted in, from his untidy appearance to his youth to his evident concern over my feelings. The very same feelings Holland said made me disposable.

He was my one chance to find Mom in this dismal place.

"So do I have a room here? For in between tests?" I said, in what I hoped sounded like a casual tone.

"Yeah." Thankfully, he appeared distracted by smoothing a kink in the cord.

"Is it next door?"

"Down the hall and to the left, where all the cells are. Stupid cord," he muttered.

"Mom's, too?"

He gave an absent half nod. "I—" And then his lashes swept upward, and suddenly, I found myself squirming under his hazel-eyed scrutiny. "You're not trying to get me into trouble, are you?"

His tone had cooled several degrees, and his hands became brusque as he firmly cradled my head with his left one . . . and with his right shoved the plug into the space behind my ear.

Before I could answer, the jolt of the connection snapped my head back. I heard my calm, digitized voice as the red words flashed.

Initiate scan.

Retrieving data.

"The data will show up on the monitor in a second," Lucas said, watching me.

Which sounded innocuous enough. Unless the data in question was being sucked straight out of your head.

I shivered, wrapped my arms around my waist. Strained to feel a foreign presence behind my ear. But apart from that first jolt, I felt nothing. Oh, a faint buzz emitted from the vicinity, and I knew the plug was there—my sensors kept a small image of the port with Connection established in the upper right of my visual field. But it just felt ordinary. Not alien at all, like I'd expected.

I shivered again. The thought that maybe my body was getting used to all this was worse than actually being able to perform the functions in the first place.

"Here we go," Lucas said.

Up on the screen, an image of a human body appeared.

No, not a human body, I realized with mounting horror. My body.

Humanlike in some spots, but with parts that no human possessed. Parts layered underneath the surface that spoke of things that weren't alive; my ugliness, all spelled out and irrefutable.

I was afraid that if I looked at that screen for even one more second, every last shred of hope in me would die.

I turned my head away, digging my chin into my shoulder and squeezing my eyes shut. Maybe if I squeezed tightly enough, I'd permanently damage my optic system and spare myself from seeing the truth so plainly ever again.

"Are you okay?"

The sensation of my throat tightening, phantom or not,

made the word hard to choke out. "No."

I heard his whisper of a sigh, the shuffle of his feet, and then a muttered curse as something jerked my chair, accompanied by the ring of shoe striking metal. Every sound precise and audible, whether I wanted to hear it or not. Compliments of my enhanced hearing. "Sorry. Accidentally kicked the chair base."

No words squeezed out this time. Only warmth behind my eyes. Dampness. And finally, release, as tears trickled from beneath my lashes.

I dragged my arm over my face, shielding it from view. Lucas might seem sympathetic, but I knew how Holland felt about tears. The only person I could trust was Mom.

Mom. Who I'd never see again unless I aced these tests. And all I had to do was be a good little android. Strong. Focused.

Emotion free.

"Mila?"

Under the cover of my sleeve, I rubbed my eyes dry, then commanded them to open. I didn't have the luxury of hiding from my fears like a normal girl.

Becoming more Three-like was the last thing I wanted to do. But she had managed to impart one piece of wisdom: sometimes, our wants were irrelevant. Mom was all that mattered, and nothing could get in the way of her rescue.

Not even me.

I lifted my chin, tilted my head to stare up at the monitor defiantly.

Nothing. Just a flat green screen, not a nightmare image in sight. The monitor was off.

Stunned, my gaze flew to Lucas, whose eyes lingered on my cheeks, making me wonder if I'd missed a trace of my tears. "I turned it off. I downloaded what needs to be fixed on here," he said, waving the small electronic tablet he now held in his hand.

"Why?"

He shrugged. "Thought it would be easier," he said, like it was no big deal.

After everything that had happened over the past few hours, his tiny show of compassion felt monumental and threatened to dampen my eyes once more. "Thank you," I whispered.

That red flush crept over his cheeks again. He shoved his hands into his pockets and studied a point somewhere over my left shoulder.

"So, how bad is the damage?"

"Not bad. Just a loose hip joint and a tweaked wire in your shoulder. Oh, and it looks like you had an old injury, to your arm?"

From the fall from Kaylee's truck. "Yeah, Mom tried to fix it with what she had available."

"Oh, she did a decent enough job, don't get me wrong.

We just have better tools here. A one-stop fix-it machine, if you will."

He ushered me over to the clear, person-sized tube I'd noticed when I'd first walked in. After he tapped in a series of numbers and letters on the attached computer, the tube made a huge whooshing sound before slowly grinding open.

That's when I could see that each half of the clear acrylic inside the tube was shaped to fit half of a human body. And when it closed, it would be exactly my size.

"Step inside, please."

I peered at the large, me-sized opening with more than a little trepidation, my stomach rebelling against inserting my body into that carefully constructed space. But Lucas said the machine could repair me, and I had two more tests to pass—and my success was more likely if I was in perfect condition.

Ignoring the pounding in my chest, I stepped in and turned to face him, placing my feet over the two black foot-marks on the ground. A perfect fit. The moment both feet hit the pad, the whoosh started up again. A burst of suction drew me upward, making me yelp. And then the acrylic sides closed in on me, like I was the middle of sandwich. They pressed against me until they melded to my body in a perfect fit. It felt like someone had smoothed on a brand-new layer of skin.

Too perfect a fit. This machine had to have been made

for me, I realized. For all the Milas.

I froze while my pulse pounded a harsh drumbeat in my ears.

Don't panic. Don't panic, don't panic. Focus on something else.

Up this close, I could see the thin lines of silver threaded within the plastic. Reinforcement, maybe? To make it shatterproof? No way out until Lucas released me.

Lucas pushed a button, then flicked up a switch on the panel beside me, and I immediately felt the air grow warm. Inside, though, a freezing cold twisted its way through my body. Through the clear glass, I met Lucas's eyes and focused on the tiny bits of green and blue, to escape my own head, to escape the feeling of being swallowed alive.

"You'll be out of there in under two minutes."

I swallowed, hard. Illogical or not, two minutes sounded like a lifetime.

"An opaque cover is going to lower now, outside the tube. The laser is built into that. Just stand very still, and everything will be fine. I'll be right here."

That worked. I wasn't sure I could move anyway, with fear locking every joint in place.

Five flecks of blue in the right eye, three flecks in the left one, I counted, somewhat deliriously. And then, in my peripheral vision, I saw a red glow descend from overhead.

"Close your eyes if it makes it easier."

I wanted to, more than anything, to block out whatever this thing was going to do. But I couldn't. That would be falling back into the same weakness I'd shown with the monitor, and I had to be strong. Besides, closing my eyes wouldn't block out the three red words, or my own detached voice.

Laser repair: Initiated.

So I stood and stared at Lucas, watching as the red enclosure first blocked out the top of his unruly hair, then his forehead, and finally his eyes, until I was staring straight at a solid silver wall with a faint glow.

The click came next, which I assumed signified the wall had hit the floor. Over my head, I felt the faint red glow grow stronger.

"Let me out," I said, pleading with Lucas.

"You'll be okay. It won't take long."

And then the grid over my shoulder blazed to life. Millions of light cells, activated. All at once, I felt a surge of warmth in my joints, a steady vibration. Like when Mom had fixed my arm but much, much stronger.

Shoulder joint: Repaired.

At that moment, I wouldn't have been able to move even if it had been a possibility. Because those words, they weren't in my calm, digitized voice. They were alien, unknown.

So how were they in my head?

I gagged as realization hit. The machine. It could

somehow project into me.

Terror sizzled through me, like a live current that jolted me into manic, unthinking action.

"Let me out!" I yelled. *"Please."*

The laser carried on its business unperturbed, the red glow descending to pulse warmth into my arm.

Arm: Repaired.

"No," I whispered, giving up on screaming. I didn't know if Lucas could hear me or not, but it was clear he wasn't letting me out. Meanwhile, I couldn't move, couldn't think, couldn't breathe. I wanted to curl into a ball, but the walls had no give, almost like I'd been entombed with my arms and legs extended. A tomb, that's what it felt like. Like I was locked inside a tomb, and I would never, ever get out again.

While the red glow lowered to my hip, the machine's vibrating invaded my skin, my ears, traveling deeper and deeper until every bit of me quaked and I wasn't sure whether it was from fear or the machine, or if they were one and the same.

"Hip joint: Repaired," the smooth, dispassionate voice declared. But the sound was so unwelcome, so invasive, like a stranger forcing his brain into my head.

I heard Lucas outside. His voice sounded shakier than I remembered. "You're almost done now."

When the glow finally switched off, the cover lifted, and

the whoosh signaled that the acrylic sides were opening, I wasn't even sure my legs would support me. The second the opening widened enough, I squeezed my way out, collapsing onto my knees and doubling over until my head practically touched the floor. I opened my mouth to laugh in relief, but all that emerged was a pathetic, choked whimper.

That sound unleashed an avalanche of reaction somewhere inside me, because immediately afterward, I started shuddering.

A few moments later, a tentative pressure landed on my shoulder. My head jerked up to see Lucas leaning over me, his hair even more mussed, undoubtedly from the way his fingers attacked the strands when he was nervous. His jaw was clenched, and his hand hovered over my shoulder before landing there once more with a feather-light touch.

"Are you okay?"

Get up, Mila. Get up and pretend like everything is fine. Lucas might seem nice, but his loyalty is to Holland.

Holland. That one word was enough to spur me into action.

I pushed myself to my feet. "I'm all right. I was just pretending—I thought it would be funny."

He hovered, his face still ashen, the furrow over his nose still deep. "I see," he said slowly. "So it wasn't because you realized what else that machine does?"

"What do you mean?"

"Besides repairs, this is where we plug in the androids to alter their programming. Or terminate them."

Terminate.

The room spun, and for a second, I thought I might faint, even though my legs remained firmly under me. My lower lip trembled, and I pressed my mouth into a thin line.

Control it, Mila.

And I did. But for the first time, a terrible thought descended. Maybe being an android who felt like a real human wasn't such an advantage after all.

"No, I didn't realize that, but whatever." I shrugged like that information was of no consequence, but I'm not sure Lucas was fooled. His gaze raked me from head to toe, like he was searching for any sign that I was lying.

Finally, to my everlasting relief, he nodded. "Okay." He shoved his hands in his pockets. "Would you like a break?"

A break? A break sounded amazing. But the faster I completed these tests, the quicker I might get to see Mom. If I passed them. "No."

"Then I guess I'll walk you to the—"

The automated voice from the door interrupted him. We both turned, waiting for the series of beeps until the door finally slid open to reveal a burly figure.

Holland.

"So. Is she good to go?" His voice boomed into the room, obscenely loud. Even Lucas flinched a tiny bit.

"Yes, sir, we just finished."

"Perfect timing. Why don't I escort our runaway to the next test while you grab the files we'll need off my desk?"

I wished I had a say, that I could refuse and insist on walking with Lucas. But there was no doubt that Holland was the puppet master, and that as long as he had Mom, I'd dance every time he jerked the strings. At least over such a simple order.

I'd hesitated only a second, but even that seemed to annoy him. He gave a curt jerk of his head toward the hall. "Did my Southern manners confuse you? That wasn't a request." His drawl still sounded amiable, but the tightening at the corners of his eyes indicated his displeasure.

While I crossed the length of the room to obey Holland's command, all I could think was *I bet I'm not going to win test two by singing a song.*

TWENTY-SEVEN

As we stepped into the hallway, Holland clasped his hands behind his back, like this was just a lazy stroll. The pungent alcohol smell of him made my head pound, but I didn't dare move farther away. Any show of intimidation on my part would give this man way too much satisfaction.

We took one step, then two, while I waited for him to speak. I knew he must have wanted me alone for a reason, and I wasn't disappointed.

"Now, I realize that Nicole probably painted me like some kind of monster, and I wanted to set the record straight."

My lips parted, and I spared him a sideways glance. A small frown tugged at his mouth.

Seriously? If this was his master plan—to convince me

he was misunderstood or something—then he should have saved his breath.

And why on earth did he care?

His low, rumbling laugh rebounded all around us, echoing like multiple Hollands walked the hall, surrounding me from all sides.

I stifled a shudder at that horrendous thought and waited for him to speak. "Oh, I know you're thinking I'm full of BS, but honest to god, it's true. Do you know I've got a wife at home, two great kids? Girls, like you."

I tried to picture Holland with a daughter, no, two of them—bouncing them on his knee, playing hide-and-seek. Wiping them down at ten-minute intervals with disinfectant.

A tiny snort escaped me, and just like that, Holland shed his amiable mask and pounced.

His burly hands shot out and grabbed my upper arm, whipping me around to face him. My pulse thundered while my mind cleared.

Human threat: Located.

Engage?

More than anything, I wished I could answer yes. But he'd hidden Mom somewhere in this place, and if I wanted her back, I had to play his stupid game.

So, despite the overpowering urge to grab his arms, squeeze, and see how he liked it, I forced myself to go limp.

To keep my face expressionless as I stared into his sneer.

His grip tightened. "Nicole, busting you out of here—you think she was doing that all for you?" His derisive grunt loosened a sliver of doubt, deep within my core. "Let me tell you something—at least I wouldn't risk letting the Vita Obscura get their hands on you."

I couldn't help but repeat the unfamiliar name. "Vita Obscura?"

His gray eyes gleamed. "That's right, you'd better listen up. You think our plans for you were bad? At least we've got the nation's safety at heart. The Vita Obscura? Why, they're just a bunch of money-hungry thieves—they steal technology and sell it to the highest bidder. And if they got their hands on you, well . . ." He let out a low, peppermint-scented whistle. "Let's just say you'd be thinking this place was a dream come true. But don't worry, you'll find out more soon enough."

Abruptly, he released me and started striding forward again, and I hurried to catch up, my mind whirling.

Vita Obscura. We finally had a name for the men who'd come after us at the ranch and the motel.

I didn't have long to dwell on it, because we were back in front of the original testing room's door. Holland reached out to punch in his code before pausing.

"Want to know a little secret?"

The renewed cheer in his voice was answer enough. *No,*

no thank you. But of course I didn't really have a choice.

Even though there wasn't another soul in the hall, he lowered his voice to a whisper. "I'm a terrible loser, and I hate being wrong even more. But I'm thinking that's not going to be a problem here. No sir, not at all."

Then he finished punching in the code. And while the door slid open, I wondered—Mom should have warned me. Because not only was Holland dangerous, but his mercurial, bizarre moods hinted at something far more disturbing: the man was clearly insane.

We'd barely entered the original testing room when the door slid open behind us, and Lucas walked in.

In his right hand he held a small black box.

"That doesn't look like files."

Lucas smiled weakly, his gaze wavering between the two of us. Holland, then me. Holland, then me. Finally Holland waved his hand. "Go ahead, proceed."

But his mere presence in the room made the tension ratchet up, and I knew Lucas felt it too. I rubbed my palms on my pants. *Steady. Don't look at him.*

Lucas stepped away from me, his casualness from the repair room replaced by a stiffness that jerked his lanky frame upright. "You have exactly ten minutes to analyze the contents of these files."

He released the latch and opened the box, lowering it to reveal a red memory card tucked into an indent in the gold interior. Nothing inherently dangerous in its appearance. Except—my last experience, in the hotel room, hadn't been all that stellar.

Lucas closed his fist, blocking the card from view. "These files contain information on a group of interest to the U.S. military, known as the Vita Obscura. When you study them, don't just memorize and store the facts. Focus on patterns, on any insight into the minds and motivations of this group. As well as on any information that might be missing."

That last line lacked any basic logic. "How can I focus on information that's not there?" I said, acutely aware of Holland watching me.

Holland cleared his throat once again, making Lucas flinch. "I'm not at liberty to answer questions. The timer activates as soon as you insert the card."

I waited for more. There had to be more. "And then what?" I finally asked, desperation swelling into my voice, prompting my hand to reach for his sleeve. I caught myself just before I made contact and forced the hand back to my side, closed my eyes, and drew in a shallow breath. Steady, I had to remain steady.

"And then . . . you start analyzing."

Lucas opened his hand, exposing the small red square, a bright splash of color against his pale palm. An image flashed in my head, the image of my mom holding the iPod out to me back in Clearwater in a very similar fashion. A warning that even the simplest of items could turn out to be devastating.

My hand didn't want to move, didn't want to reach out and touch that hard piece of plastic. Out of nowhere, a deviant thought pulsed through my mind. I could refuse. Refuse to do this test, refuse whatever awful thing awaited me on that card.

Thereby condemning both my mom and myself to whatever the military had in store if I failed.

I licked my lips, surprised when they didn't feel dry. Just another phantom sensation, an illusion like all the rest. A tiny tremor raced over me, so small I didn't think there was any way someone would catch it. But Lucas did. I knew from the quick hiss of his startled inhalation.

I had to be more careful.

His gold-tipped eyelashes swept down as he stared at the square with a clenched jaw, and for a moment, I got the insane impression he was going to chuck it, Holland or not. But of course he didn't; that had just been my inner hope projecting onto him. Me seeing things that weren't there.

Still, when my fingers curled around the card, Lucas's fingers curled around mine.

"I'm sorry," he whispered, so softly that Holland, from his sentry post ten feet away, would never catch it.

While I was still processing that, he released my hand

and retreated for the door.

Seeing me looking, Holland gave a small salute that I could only imagine was some kind of mockery. Then he pivoted and slowed his usually brisk pace to keep abreast of Lucas. The last image I had was of Holland's contemplative expression contrasting with Lucas's pale face as the metal barrier slid between us, Lucas's hazel eyes looking stricken.

And then I was alone. Grateful for Holland's absence, yet inexplicably missing Lucas.

The card was still nestled in my palm, a minuscule .15 ounces that somehow felt heavy enough to anchor me to the floor.

The test, I reminded myself, when my hand refused to cooperate and insert the square into my wrist. I was wasting valuable time preparing for the next test, and if I didn't pass that test, I lost everything.

With that thought spurring me on, I held out my right arm and shoved the card into the crease of my wrist.

Input: Accepted.

A faint buzz of electrical current preceded the data, and my wrist hummed. Warmth raced up my arm, shot through my shoulder, and swept into my head.

Once again, my body tried to rebel, and my legs quivered under me while my upper body tensed in a knee-jerk reaction to force the data out. I concentrated on relaxing my hands, my arms, on opening my mind and accepting the data rush.

An instant later, the information whooshed into my head, file upon file upon file. I was ready this time, though, and now the process didn't feel quite so fish-out-of-water overwhelming. Lucas's warning surfaced.

When you study it, don't just memorize and store the facts.

Which meant I really needed to analyze the data. According to Mom, something that might be more challenging to do from inside my head. I bet Three could assess everything internally, whereas, in human fashion, I still utilized my senses for optimal information processing. Not something Holland was likely to reward.

A quick glance confirmed that Lucas had resumed his sentinel spot behind the spectator window. Solo. Holland had probably realized that watching an android inspect data wouldn't be the most fascinating way to pass the time.

I studied Lucas, debating if I should chance viewing the data outside my head. It might lead to a lower score.

Then again, if viewing the data the wrong way helped me score higher on the actual challenge, it'd be all worthwhile, right?

As I weighed my decision, Lucas's mouth formed a word. *"Project."*

Decision made.

In my head, I repeated him.

Project.

The information rush paused on a heartbeat and, a millisecond later, changed direction and swept the opposite way. I felt the zap of the current shift, and one blink later, the glowing square enveloped me. Each "wall" was two feet away from the midpoint of my body, where small folder icons blinked green in midair. Waiting for my command.

When the square first surrounded me, my first urge was to escape. To eject the card like I had back at the motel and toss it across the floor. But the time for hiding from my abilities was over. This was what I'd been created for. There was no reason for me to be afraid. At least, that was the mantra I whispered to myself in hopes that maybe I'd actually start to believe it.

One thing at a time. Start small.

I focused on the icons. My hands started to lift, until I remembered the spectator window. I shoved them into my jeans instead, determined to manipulate the icons with my mind. I couldn't afford to squander any points.

Concentrating on the folder that said BACKGROUND, I glided through my head to hunt down the command.

The entire process was smoother, less clunky than the first time I'd performed it in the motel. A confirmation that with every computerlike act I performed, I became a more efficient machine.

Open file.

The folder unlocked, unleashing page after page of information, all of it hovering in the air before me.

Before I realized what was happening, that I even knew how to work so fast, pages had shifted to the side, some of them gliding around to the opposite walls of my information enclosure. The thing masquerading as my heart crashed under my ribs as a heady blend of exhilaration and terror radiated through my chest. The first page arranged itself directly in front of my eyes, green words gleaming. And at the very top of the page was a name. One that meant nothing to me.

Trenton Blane.

Aware that seconds were ticking by, I scanned the rest.

White male, born forty-two years ago in Scranton, Pennsylvania. Five feet eight inches tall and 165 pounds, dark-brown hair, and no known scars.

Father: Harvey Blane, deceased from neurological trauma and cancer consistent with Agent Orange exposure during his tour of duty in the Vietnam War.

Mother: Gloria Blane. Resides in Happy Sunrises Assisted Living Home in Jacksonville, Florida. Dementia patient.

Occupation: Computer programmer at Leusta Enterprises, a legitimate IT company.

Suspected secondary occupation: Founding member of the Vita Obscura.

A group that wasn't picky, I discovered. Apparently Holland had been telling the truth, at least about that. The Vita Obscura stole any technology they could find—especially military and defense—and then sold it to anyone who handed over the cash. Terrorists included. I pictured the two men from the motel and shivered. Had that been their plan, to sell me to some terrorist organization? So they could use me for . . . what?

As disturbing as all of this was, I still didn't understand what the Vita Obscura had to do with my test.

When I finished gleaning the background file for any tips, I sent the pages shooting back into their folder. I barely thought the command before the photo folder whipped up to replace it.

Open file.

The first photos that popped out were all of posed shots of Trenton. Besides the description before, he was pale and square jawed, with a mustache.

Then surveillance photos. Lots of them. In an office, jogging outdoors, eating in restaurants, by a silver Lincoln Navigator, in front of a tall, narrow house with a red door. Outside a sign for Tommy's Executive Three-Hole Golf Course, Fit! Gym, and Reynaurd's grocery store.

A whirlwind of images, many of them with other faces besides Blane's. Several over plates of burgers with an older, balding man, with a young, uniformed male trainer at the gym. A young brunette, helping him with his golf swing. A couple of different men getting into his car.

I sifted through more icons, more files, and discovered that they'd just about had enough on Trenton to seize him, when *Poof!* He vanished, like he'd known they were coming.

When I read the title of the next file, I thought I knew why.

VITA OBSCURA MOLE.

Apparently Holland was convinced that someone had infiltrated SMART Ops, just a few weeks before Mom left. His suspected goal?

Me.

There was no name associated with the mole, which I found odd, but they did have one photo. Not his military one—apparently he'd erased that off the computer before he'd escaped. No, this was a casual shot, taken with two other soldiers. I recognized one as the mustached soldier from the car—the one who'd touched my face, and the other a stocky blond I hadn't seen. They were identified as Mitchell Jennings and Ray Haynes.

The mole was wearing sunglasses, but I memorized the shape of his nose, his chin, his hairline. That way, if Mom and I ever did escape, we'd know who to look for.

I closed my eyes, blocking out the glowing square so I could analyze what I'd learned so far. I still had no idea how this information played into my test, and time was almost up.

Reopening my eyes, I sifted through the files faster.

But there was no specific information to extract. Desperation steered my fingers as the files shifted in front of me again. I had to have missed a connection somewhere. I went to flip a folder open for the third time when beyond the glimmering green enclosure that formed my temporary world, I heard footsteps. Beeps. The whoosh of a door opening. People were entering the room.

Holland was one of those people, and he was smiling.

TWENTY-EIGHT

gritted my teeth, hoping the action would stop my hands from trembling. I kept sifting through the data as five people approached, four of them on surprisingly quiet feet, the fifth one with footsteps that weren't quite even. Lucas was with them.

They drew closer, and closer, until I felt Holland towering just a few inches behind me, until I could feel their collective breath fluttering my hair.

My heart stuttered as their nearness burned into my skin, begging me to step forward to a safer spot, but I held my ground.

Determinedly, I waved my hand and commanded another glowing file to open and spill its documents along the virtual wall before me. I could do this. I could tune them out and finish my assigned task. This was just another part of the test, an attempt to unnerve me.

I'd almost convinced myself of that when two sets of rough hands latched on to my upper arms and yanked me backward. I tried to break free, but something cold and sleek molded itself to my wrists. Handcuffs. Chains.

With a flicker, the glowing files in front of me vanished as I jerked my arms against the restraints.

Tensile strength: 1000 lbs.

These were no normal handcuffs.

An icy knot formed in my chest as a sharp jab in the back pushed me forward. If they'd been trying to unnerve me, then they'd succeeded.

Hopefully, I hid it well.

I was silent for the first part of the march across the room, then finally blurted, "Is this part of the test?"

No response, other than a hard shove to propel me forward. I stumbled once, regained my footing, then continued walking. No talking. Check.

Good thing Holland couldn't look into my brain right now. If so, he'd probably fail me right then and there, based on the elaborate revenge scenarios I was plotting.

Two steps later, when I realized exactly where we were headed, my artificial veins went frigid, my legs turned to stone.

No emotions. No emotions. No. Emotions.

My mental chant was the only thing that kept me from gasping.

A few steps and harsh pushes later, and they'd shoved me over the chains in the floor and secured my hands.

The same chains they'd used on One when they'd put her through the torture test.

And there, on the table beside me, in the middle of the artful fan of tools, was the drill Holland had used to bore a hole in her chest—while her screams lingered on.

"Surprise," Holland drawled softly as he reached across and picked up the drill. "So here's how this test goes. You know all that intel you just studied in the files? It's all classified. If you give me even one tiny piece of information, you fail."

As he talked, I tore my eyes away from him and searched the soldiers' faces behind him—I recognized Haynes and Jennings—but there was no help there. Their eyes slid from mine, to stare at their feet. Holland's men were scared of him.

And Three, well—watching my own face look on without a hint of concern as I was prepared to be tortured sent a flurry of goose bumps across my skin. I told myself to take comfort in her unfazed expression, to use it as a guide.

But when Holland pushed a button and the drill buzzed to life, all logic vanished.

Oh, god. This was it. And even though I knew I

shouldn't be scared, because my pain sensation was so limited, I couldn't help it. That grating whir of the drill, it made the horrible memory crash over me with galelike force. Of another Mila, screaming. One who had felt every single thing they'd done to her. Just like a human.

A girl they'd tortured into sealing her own fate.

The drill spun, a silver whirlwind under the fluorescent lights. Almost pretty, in a deadly way. I couldn't bear to look at it, to anticipate the bit digging into me. I was too afraid my fear would show on my face.

Instead, I craned my head and focused on the last person in the room. Lucas. He stood several feet away from the others, his hazel eyes troubled but steady on mine. Intense. As if he were trying to will the strength into me. I found myself grasping for something, anything, to distract me from the drill that Holland was lowering toward me, and I concentrated on the dots of blue and gray in his eyes. I counted them over and over again as the drill drew closer, until I could feel the breeze it generated whispering against my neck.

No emotions. No emotions. No emotions.

"Look at me," Holland commanded, and with a shaky breath, I complied. But I looked right through his craggy face and pictured my mom, in a cell, depending on me to pass. I pictured Hunter's face. I even pictured Bliss. Anything not to focus on the drill.

I braced myself for whatever question Holland was going to ask. No matter what, I wouldn't answer. The drill was so close now, the tip grazed my skin, and it took everything I had not to flinch. My pain reception might be low, but the thought of that blade piercing my flesh, tunneling inside, tearing a gaping hole and exposing my insides for everyone to see, flooded me with an overwhelming sense of violation. We stood in that stalemate position for what felt like an eternity but probably only amounted to a few seconds. Every second, though, was a small triumph in willpower.

I would not move. I would not scream. I would not give Holland even a hint of satisfaction.

With a quick jerk of his hand, he moved the drill toward my ear, but I was prepared for whatever he could dole out. I didn't move, not even when the tip vibrated inside my ear canal, coming perilously close to plunging toward my brain.

One second the drill was whirring; the next, it wasn't. I watched in confusion as Holland stepped back, taking the drill with him.

"Good," he said, but his eyes didn't match the word. When he walked behind me, I waited for the drill to restart, but instead something tugged at the metal encircling my wrists, then clicked. With a jolt, I realized my hands were free.

I shook my head. "I don't understand . . . what—?"

Two soldiers slipped behind Lucas and grabbed his shoulders. From the widening of his eyes and startled protest, he was just as clueless as me. Then Holland strode over to him, and an instant later, Lucas's wrists were bound by the handcuffs I'd just vacated.

"What's going on?" Lucas asked, his voice impressively calm.

"Change of plans," Holland said.

"Uh . . . sir?" Lucas asked, not alarmed yet, but a confused line formed between his brows. My trepidation, however, rose with every passing second as they led him over to the steel chain and attached it to his cuffs.

While I watched Lucas, I felt Holland's steely gray eyes watch me. "Sometimes in the field, you have to resort to extreme methods when obtaining information. We need to know that your emotional responses won't get in the way."

He turned back to Lucas, and the relief from having his attention directed elsewhere eased the tightness in my chest, just a little. But it returned with a vengeance a moment later. "Lucas, I edited the files you gave to Mila and took out the name of the mole. In order to pass this test, Mila's job is to forcibly extract that information."

Extract. *Extract.*

The only sound that broke the bleak silence that followed was the uneasy shifting of the soldiers' feet. My stomach roiled with a toxic combination of disbelief and horror.

I wanted to shake my head—no, to shake Holland—to scream that no way would I be a part of this, but I felt his eyes on me again, watching, searching, waiting to pounce on even the slightest hint of a reaction.

This couldn't be real, I told myself. He couldn't possibly expect me to torture Lucas for information. That was too insane, even for Holland.

But the color that slowly drained from Lucas's already pale face told another story.

"Now, I realize this might sound cruel, but I'm being realistic," Holland said, gesturing with his age-creased hands for emphasis. "When you're on an assignment, you'll meet people who seem halfway decent. Hell, you might even like some of them. But none of that matters."

His eyes flashed. He stepped toward me, as if physical proximity alone could somehow persuade me to accept his logic, might make me agree that torturing people, torturing Lucas, was simply a necessary part of life. "The only thing that matters is the end goal—getting the intel. Intel saves lives, and that's the bottom line."

He inched even closer, and his voice dropped to a whisper, one that I was sure only I could hear. "You understand, don't you, Two?" he said, the silky-soft words slipping under my skin and turning everything inside me into a chunk of ice. A chunk of ice that was trying not to choke on his peculiar peppermint-and-alcohol scent, with only one thought piercing my shocked ice brain.

Holland was serious. This was real.

He straightened, smoothed his hands over his unwrinkled shirt, and increased his volume. "To pass this test, you need to obtain the identity of the mole. Lucas," he barked, eyes still trained on me. "Your job is to keep that information confidential as long as you can. Are we clear?"

Over Holland's stiff shoulder, my eyes pleaded with Lucas. *Say no. Say no and end this thing right now.*

"But, sir—"

Holland held up his hand. "We had a deal, remember? You follow orders and I help your chickenshit brother. Now, let's try again. Are we clear?"

Help his brother what? What could possibly be bad enough to make Lucas agree to this? Because one thing was sure: Holland wasn't the type of man who tolerated a refusal from an inferior, not publicly.

Even knowing his answer, Lucas's "Clear" was a sharp twist in my chest.

Whatever Holland had on Lucas's brother, he was going to use it to make Lucas a pawn in this latest bout of insanity.

"Now, we like the boy around here, so don't kill him or do any serious damage—just make him talk. Oh, and how's this for a little additional incentive?" He glanced at his oversized watch. "If you get the info on the suspected mole within ten minutes, I'll let you see Nicole."

Up until then, I'd been tempted to open my mouth and tell him exactly where he could go. Tempted to refuse to budge, fail the test, and pray that I passed the next one with flying colors. But his words whipped my head up.

A triumphant smile tugged at his thin lips, but I didn't care. Mom. He'd let me see Mom. Before I knew it, I'd taken one, two, three steps toward Lucas, on legs practically buzzing with hope.

"See? I knew you had it in you. You just needed the right motivation."

The satisfaction oozing from Holland's words should have stopped me in my tracks. It should have made me feel ashamed of my instant eagerness to comply.

But all I could think of was Mom. Where were they keeping her, how was she holding up? Was she even really still alive?

I crossed the rest of the short distance that separated me from Lucas, noticing that the closer I got, the more my pace dragged. Desperately I reminded myself that he worked here. No matter how kind he'd pretended to be, he was a part of this covert, sadistic operation. Willing or not, he was a part of the group keeping me away from Mom. The group that would terminate my existence without batting an eye.

When I finally stood right in front of him, though, and looked into Lucas's eyes, my breath hitched in my throat.

I don't know what I expected, but it wasn't his oh-so-subtle nod. As if he were giving me permission to get on with it.

Just like that, my resolve faltered. The fierce need to see Mom warred with stark loathing of hurting a bound man, and it felt like the conflicting emotions would rip me apart. I looked away, fighting off the burn behind my eyes.

I couldn't do it.

I had to try.

"Tell me who the mole is," I said, without even looking at him.

"Pathetic."

Lucas spit the word out like it tasted bad, startling me. Gone was the soft expression I thought I'd seen earlier, replaced by narrowed eyes and a scowl.

"What? If you can't even hit the guy who helped design these tests, you'll be hopeless in the field. You deserve to be terminated."

I gasped before the truth registered. Lucas was trying to goad me into hitting him.

Terminated. Design these tests.

And it was kind of working.

"Lucas—stay in character," Holland warned, his drawl clipped short.

"Sorry." But he didn't sound sorry at all.

"Tell me who the mole is!" I shouted this time, mere inches away from his face.

Overhead, the fluorescent bulbs glared without mercy, highlighting all of us like we were in some kind of macabre play.

He shook his head and exhaled in a loud, overblown sigh. "No matter what you do to me, the mole will track you down. He'll tear you apart for scrap pieces, and who knows what he'll do to your mom? Kill her, I suppose, but she's pretty, so I imagine he'll—"

My fist flew forward before he could finish the sentence, headed straight for his left cheek.

When my knuckles first touched his skin, realization crashed over me. I pulled back. Too late. There was still a sickening smack, and his head whipped to the side. Without his hands to steady him, his body followed. He crashed to the ground, and his stifled cry filled the room.

Horror spread like an oil spill through my body, heavy and thick and dirty. Both of the soldiers standing near Lucas shifted their feet uncomfortably in his direction, like they wanted to help him up but weren't sure they were allowed to. One of them even swore under his breath. No one was happy with this situation. No one except Holland.

On his back, Lucas groaned before shaking his head and rolling awkwardly to his side, his bound wrists hindering him. I moved forward to help him when a big hand landed on my shoulder. "You're going to have to do better than that. Lucas is tough, aren't you, boy?"

My skin crawled where his hand rested, but I didn't shrug

it off. Channeling every ounce of self-control I possessed, I kept my voice calm, my body steady. "I can handle it," I said. Even as something inside me shattered as I watched Lucas clumsily regain his feet.

"Can you? Or do you need a little help?" He turned and nodded to someone behind me. A moment later, Three glided forward.

"I prefer to use less violent and more painful methods. The drill. Or the pliers, for fingernails. They tend to be effective more quickly," my mirror image said, nodding serenely at the instruments on the steel table like we were discussing the best brand of nail files.

My stomach turned at her blasé response.

Lucas's cheek bloomed red, and swelling was already setting in, shrinking his right eye into a forced squint. He didn't say anything, but his gaze cut to the table and back to Three, and as I watched, a tiny dot of sweat beaded on his forehead and slowly, slowly, trickled down his nose.

Lucas might not be afraid of me, but he was definitely leery of Three.

Three reached for the pliers, and I knew I had to do something to keep her away from Lucas. I moved in front of her.

"Are you going to tell me about the mole, or do I have to hurt you again?"

Please, just tell me, I begged him silently. *Please.* Please.

Lucas hesitated, and for one glorious instant, relief swelled in my chest. Then Holland cleared his throat, and Lucas's jaw tightened. "Give it your best shot."

Damn it.

Trying to apologize with my eyes, I pulled back my fist and delivered a swift blow to his kidney.

I'd muted the punch as much as I could without making Holland suspicious, but it wasn't enough. Lucas doubled over and stumbled back, tripping over the chain. Once again, he fell to the floor, this time landing on his knees with a thud that echoed throughout the barren room and made me cringe.

With every punch, I became less of the girl Mom had risked everything to save and more of the monster Holland desperately hoped for.

"Well done . . . though I still would have gone with the pliers," Three mused, tilting her head and watching Lucas with a childlike curiosity as he moaned and slowly tried to straighten.

This time, the two soldiers darted forward and helped him to his feet, even steadying him when he swayed.

"Hands off the prisoner," Holland barked. The soldiers hastily released him and backed away.

This had to end, now. Surely Lucas would talk, and no one would fault him for it. But as I chanced a peek at Holland, my phantom heart dropped like a stone. He crossed his arms while his eyes wandered over the barely upright Lucas, and even though it vanished almost the moment it appeared, I saw the quick smile that briefly curled his lips.

In that instant, I realized this whole sadistic test wasn't just about me.

A fire kindled in my gut, the flames picking up pace and coursing through my body like it was a forest of brittle trees.

"Three, hand Two the pliers."

The fire roared louder.

Three passed the pliers to me, and my fingers curled around them. *Mom,* I thought. *Mom.*

I grabbed the front of Lucas's shirt, yanked him toward me, barely believing what I was doing. I hated myself, I even hated Lucas. But most of all, I hated Holland.

Lucas landed hard on his weak foot, regained his balance.

"You see these?" Obviously he did, because I was waving them about an inch away from his face. I dropped his shirt and grabbed his left hand instead, squeezing it harder than I'd intended. "Tell me about the mole, and I'll leave your fingernails alone. Otherwise, I'll have to pull them off, one by one."

Who was saying these terrible things? It couldn't be me.

I relaxed my grip. "Please. Just tell me, and this will all be over."

Lucas stared right through me, even as another drop of sweat trickled down his nose. The same as before, only different. This time, Three wasn't the one causing it.

I looked at his hand, at his strong, callused hand with

the short, clean nails and wondered how this was possibly happening.

"Two, I need to know you're one hundred percent committed. The pliers," Holland urged.

My fist tightened around cold metal while Lucas blanched. But he didn't so much as tremble. His chest expanded as he inhaled a deep, shaky breath and blew it out through pursed lips.

And then his shoulders sagged. His hazel eyes met mine, and it was like someone reached inside my chest, grabbed my phony heart, and squeezed it until it exploded. He expected me to do it.

"Go ahead, Two," Holland insisted, with a breathless anticipation that sickened me.

All at once, the fire from before blazed to life, consumed me, whipped down my arm and into my hand. My pulse pounded out a frantic beat.

Pliers.

Lucas.

Mom.

With the pliers still clutched tight, I whirled on Holland. The shock was still forming on his wrinkled face when I slammed the tool across his ribs.

TWENTY-NINE

His shout rang out, and for a split second everyone was still, even Three—right before chaos erupted. I backed away as reality crashed over me, a little too late. I'd screwed up. Big-time.

Three darted to Holland, while the soldiers rushed toward me and paused warily a few steps away, like I was a wild animal.

Actually, that felt exactly right.

The pliers slithered from my fingers and clattered to the floor. I raised my hands, palm first, while Holland hacked.

"Sir?" The mustached soldier glanced over his shoulder. "Do you want us to apprehend her?"

Holland wheezed once more, dashed a hand across his watering eyes. I waited for whatever punishment he might dole out, but instead he started laughing, a gasping, pained laugh that sent shivers down my back.

"Now, then—there's the Two I remember."

"Sir?"

"What? Oh, no, no," he said, waving them away with a dismissive flick of his hand, one that made him wince. "Leave her. It's my own damn fault. I knew she'd snap—I should have stood farther back."

"You will punish her, won't you, sir?" This was Three, sounding more curious than angry.

Holland's eyes narrowed on me. Even though he didn't say anything, I knew exactly what he was thinking. There was no punishment he could give me that would hurt worse than what I'd inflicted on myself.

Test number two had been an abject failure. Which left me only one more chance to save Mom. And right now, my odds were looking pretty slim.

I watched, in a blur, as Holland said something to the soldiers about the infirmary, and then Lucas was released, and staggered away with Three and Holland. Then the two soldiers led me to a tiny cell, no bigger than a closet. A set of camos was on the bed.

"Put those on," the shorter, buffer one said, not unkindly. Haynes. "Someone will be back to get you within the hour."

He exited the cell, and the door locked behind him. I sank against the wall and slid to the floor, burying my face in my hands. But I couldn't block out the dark thoughts that swarmed over me. My breaths came faster and faster, until I was practically hyperventilating and then fighting to keep the gasps hidden from the camera.

When Holland had said that was the Two he remembered . . . what did he mean? Had I tortured people in the past? Was that the future I had to look forward to, even if I did somehow manage to pass the tests? If so, maybe I should just give up.

Maybe termination was for the best.

I clenched my fists, pushed at the darkness until I could feel a glimmer of light. Of hope. I couldn't allow myself to think like that. If they terminated me, Mom's life was over. And what good would it do? They'd just make another MILA, another like Three, who would feel absolutely nothing as she picked up pliers and tortured a person until they begged for mercy. Yes, I'd let Holland scare me into hurting Lucas, but at least I'd stopped. I'd stopped before the point of no return, come to my senses before inflicting any permanent damage.

It was small comfort, but it was better than nothing.

Far too soon, Lucas was leading me down a new hallway. We hadn't spoken since he'd arrived at my door, asking if I was ready, his cheek a colorful blend of purple and black. His strides seemed heavier, more off-kilter than normal, and every one of them was a painful reminder of what I'd done.

Finally I couldn't take it anymore. I blurted, "Lucas, I'm sor—"

He cut me off. "Don't. You're trying to save Dr. Laur . . . your mom, I get it. Trust me, I've done things just as bad to help my family. Worse. Now, let's just get to where we're going, okay?"

Despite his words, I thought our silent trek down the hallway meant he was angry with me. Only later would I realize it was guilt.

Lucas led me down a network of dim corridors, through concrete doorways. We passed three unfamiliar soldiers, all of whom nodded at Lucas but gave me a wide berth. I kept my gaze averted. I was struggling enough without seeing condemnation of my attack reflected in their eyes.

We stopped in front of an elevator. After supplying his DNA—*DNA Scan verified: Lucas Webb. Please enter your pass code*—and his code, the doors parted.

He pushed B, and we sank farther into the concrete dungeon.

Unlike before, Lucas didn't attempt any small talk. He stared straight ahead. The quiet stretched out between us, filling the metal enclosure with a tension so tangible, I could swear I felt its frigid pressure boxing us in—android or not. Those doors would open, and then I'd have one last chance. For me, and for Mom.

The elevator stopped. A breath I didn't need froze in my chest as the doors slid open, exposing the unexpected glare of bright lights. Also unexpected was the massiveness of the space, and the high ceilings.

Height, 30.25 ft.

But as far as surprises went, the basement's architecture rated low in comparison to its contents.

Stretching out before us was a re-creation of an idyllic downtown square. Green and red awnings topped brick buildings, which lined wide, neat sidewalks. Nestled along the sidewalks were metallic-blue streetlamps, strips of grass, four potted trees, and even the graceful arch of a blue mailbox. Cheerful signs proclaimed each building's purpose: Inn! Café! Bank!

A tiny faux city, over thirty feet below the earth. Bizarre, but not especially terrifying.

Images from the last test came flooding back—Lucas's face when he was sure I would torture him, Holland, the pliers—to serve as a warning. Looks could be deceiving.

Directly to our left was a huge concrete wall that featured a large window overhead. Beyond that was an oval-shaped room, one that extended all the way to the far wall. It was completely enclosed in silver metal.

Nothing to see there, so I turned back to the cityscape. "What is it?"

Beside me, Lucas shuffled his feet. "*It* is a modified version of Hogan's Alley, the training area at Quantico that FBI agents and sometimes military forces use for urban combat training, to simulate maneuvers in populated areas. We sort of, uh, borrowed the concept. Obviously, those with special clearance for the MILA project are allowed to use it."

"Special clearance. Am I supposed to feel special?" I joked, if only to alleviate the steady pulse of anxiety awakening under my skin.

A ghost of a smile lit his plain face, but it vanished much too quickly, like a cloud blotting out the sun and dousing the warm air with an unexpected chill. He shoved his hands into his pockets and refused to look at me.

"All I'm authorized to discuss is this last test," he said, each word clipped.

I nodded, ignoring the sudden tightness that clutched my throat.

"Beyond the city is what the men around here call the Run."

I followed the trajectory of his pointing finger, past where the makeshift city changed, where the buildings turned from quaint and elegant to piles of deserted boards and dirt that pretty much screamed "war zone." I followed it to where the sidewalks dead-ended into the imposing concrete wall that formed the room's far boundary, to where the street met a dark, horseshoe-shaped opening. A tunnel.

"The Run?"

Lucas toyed with his shirt collar. "An obstacle course General Holland uses to make sure the soldiers here are . . . prepared for any eventuality."

I stared at the entrance, trying to ignore the dread curling around me like a dark, cold tentacle.

"In this test, your one and only task is to get through the Run with the highest score possible. You'll be competing against Three. Since she's performed the course before, I've been authorized to give you a brief breakdown of what to expect."

Three? The dread squeezed tighter.

"You'll be expected to navigate a series of obstacles, first in Hogan's Alley, then in the Run. The obstacles include barbed wire, vertical climbs, rope work, tunnels, and land mines—simulated, of course," he added, at my startled gasp.

"Along the course, you will encounter soldiers who are simulating enemy forces. They should be treated as real threats. They might have simulated weapons, and if they hit you, points will be deducted from your overall score."

It could be worse, I comforted myself, trying to relax the growing knot in my stomach. Way worse, given the horrors Holland could have invented.

"Whenever you trip up over an obstacle that could do real damage, points will be deducted. There will also be simulated civilians on the course," he said. "If you hurt a civilian—"

"Let me guess—points will be deducted."

Lucas spun to face me, fists clenched. "This isn't a joke, Mila! You need to focus." No smile, and his harsh words served as a wake-up call. As Lucas stared directly at me for the first time since we'd left my cell, his eyebrows lowered in an uncharacteristically fierce expression, I realized something was wrong, very wrong. The knot in my stomach twisted.

"Now, please turn your head to the right—I have to insert the blocking mechanism."

He positioned himself at an awkward angle, almost as if blocking my head from view. His fingers were gentle as they bent my earlobe. Cool metal slid into my skin, followed by a quick buzz of electricity.

Security Chi—

My internal voice cut out and then . . . nothing. When he stepped back, my hand immediately flew up to trace the thin line that marked the presence of a computer chip.

"Some of your android functions will only work for the first minute, to simulate a short."

Wait, which functions? But before I could ask for specifics, a light flickered on to our left. High on the wall, the spectator window illuminated, revealing a room set up like a theater. Three rows of chairs lined up across the space, and in front of them—an oversized TV screen. I saw four heads pop into view, but none of them had Holland's salt-and-pepper hair. No Three, either.

As if on cue, the elevator door beeped and slid open behind us.

When Lucas glanced over his shoulder, the tense set of his jaw relaxed ever so slightly. "Where's General Holland? Did he change his mind?"

I turned and watched Three glide across the concrete floor in our direction, decked out in camos identical to mine. Without my consciously summoning them, my hands ended up sifting through my hair, rubbing the short jagged edges as proof that we weren't one and the same.

"No, he's just setting up Two's"—Three's familiar green eyes, *my eyes*, shifted to me—"special challenge." She smiled that same serene smile, but the way she scrutinized me with more curiosity than usual didn't bode well.

Enough.

"What special challenge?" I demanded. I crossed my arms and faced him—just in time to watch Lucas's hands rake through his own hair. He closed his eyes and inhaled an unsteady wheeze of a breath.

Three had turned to watch him as well. "Peculiar" was all she said.

Mindful of the video cameras, I forced myself to relax by smoothing my suddenly clammy palms down my pants, once, twice, three times. "Can someone please explain what's going on?" I asked. "Why are we just standing here?

When are we going to start?"

A loud whir answered for him. All three of us turned to the left, where the oval-shaped metal wall I'd noticed earlier was lifting, revealing the gleam of glass beneath it. At first, when the metal slowly groaned its way upward, I thought the room was empty. Until my gaze slid right, near the far wall. A pair of women's tennis shoes was revealed. White tennis shoes with blue laces.

A sickening mixture of hope and fear twined up my throat, making it impossible for me to swallow. For a moment, I forgot everything—the Run, Three, Lucas, this room—while I waited as her legs, her torso, her neck, her chin were exposed, my non-heart beating with quick, urgent thuds. And then finally, her face; the first time I'd seen her in person since we'd been separated at the airport.

Urgency flooded my limbs, and I took a jerky step forward. "Mom?"

"No!"

Lucas's harsh command made me falter. "You should know that even your pretesting performance will count in your overall score," Lucas continued.

For one brief, desperate instant, I considered ignoring him, but reality froze me in my tracks. If my overall score dropped too low . . .

Trapped, I focused on Mom's still form, taking in the dilated pupils that almost obliterated any trace of blue from her eyes, her sluggish movements, the way her arms were taped to the chair behind her. Her head turned, and her lips pressed together. *"Mila,"* she mouthed, but no sound came out. One of her hands fluttered against the tape before she sagged into the chair, her head lolling forward like a doll's.

And here I was—as helpless as the doll she resembled.

A distinctive gray-haired figure emerged from the far side of Mom's room—Holland. His left hand was clenched around something I couldn't see, and he walked with more precise steps than usual, his shoulders rounded out of their typical erect posture. I noticed he winced a tiny bit with each inhaled breath.

My gaze shifted to his left side. The spot where I'd bashed him with the pliers.

Force of impact, 720 lbs. per square inch. Fracture to ribs 5 and 6 highly probable.

I had trouble mustering even an ounce of shame.

"What's he doing in there?"

"Part of the test," Lucas said in a strange, flat tone.

With those words thundering like an approaching train in my head, Holland turned to face us through the glass. His drawl echoed around us through hidden speakers. "So I know Lucas there gave you the basics, but I thought we'd add a little something extra, spice things up. There's no satisfaction in winning if the game's too easy, right?"

Wrong, I wanted to scream, and Holland's eyes narrowed

on me. The corners of his mouth twitched, like he knew what I was thinking and dared me to say it anyway.

I clenched my jaw against the temptation.

"I thought you and Three needed more of a real competition. While you're doing the Run, your job is to locate and retrieve a simulated explosive device. Now, you want to make sure you find it, because there's only one, and whoever brings it back to the finish line will receive a hefty bonus. I'm feeling generous, so I'll even tell you where to look—it'll be buried under a pile of worthless junk once you pass the tunnels. How's that for helpful?"

He paused to glance at the mystery object in his hand before continuing.

"Now, in real life, a bomb goes off and that's it, game over. Lucas there wanted to make dropping the simulator a point penalty, but me? Hell, I figured it should be *the* penalty." A hint of a smile crept over Holland's weathered face. "Lucas, why don't you do the honors and explain the rest?"

Lucas wouldn't meet my eyes. "If you drop the simulator, it's an automatic loss."

Everything inside me plummeted toward the floor. Absolutely, positively, no dropping the simulator. "What does any of this have to do with Mom?"

"You will have exactly fifteen minutes to enter the Run, find the phony bomb, and complete the course with it in your possession. Three will be completing the course alongside you, and part of your score will be determined based on the discrepancies in your performances."

We'd covered this already, but he had yet to answer my question.

My gaze flicked back to Holland to find his steely eyes focused on me. As soon as he saw me looking, he deliberately uncurled his hand, revealing a bright-yellow rectangular object.

A lighter.

I glanced at his hand, then across the room to where Mom was drugged and restrained. A horrible thought whispered through my head. No, there was no way.

"This test is meant to challenge your focus on the task at hand, under extreme emotional duress," Lucas continued. "You cannot, for any reason, veer off the objective. Any. Reason."

Now Holland was rolling his beefy thumb against the rounded edge of the lighter. The lighter burst into flame.

My scalp prickled with tiny pinpoints of fear.

"In order to assess your resilience to such pressure, General Holland added an extra facet to this test," Lucas said, each word sounding like he had to force it out through gritted teeth. He fumbled with something in his pocket, and for a moment I was distracted when the oversized digital red numbers glowed to life on the screen that sat atop the faux post office.

"Timer set for fifteen minutes," a detached, digitized male voice announced overhead.

Lucas withdrew his hand from his pocket. I thought I saw it tremble. Then his hand fisted—so tightly, his knuckles looked ready to pierce his pale skin.

"Fifteen minutes is the maximum time you're allowed. If you don't . . ."

"If I don't, what?" In the glass room, Holland bent his head as he searched for something on the floor. The lighter glowed.

No. This couldn't be happening. He was messing with me, as part of the test. That had to be it.

"General Holland has been testing out a new . . . information-gathering device. It uses a computerized set of fans and fuel to control the timing of the fire. It's currently set at fifteen minutes. After that . . ." Lucas trailed off. Unable or unwilling to finish.

Holland squatted, touched the lighter to the floor. A tiny red spark ignited. As Holland backed out of the room through an interior door I couldn't see, the spark burst into a wall of full-fledged fire, one that quickly soared to chest level, then higher. The flames swayed back and forth like red-orange dancers.

Flames—just like the ones I'd been told ended my fake father's life.

With my entire world shattering around me, I completed

Lucas's sentence in my head.

After that, your mom will burn to death.

"Twenty seconds to start," the dispassionate digital voice announced.

It felt like everything inside me had turned to stone. I couldn't move, I couldn't breathe. Choices flickered through my head in fragments, as if mimicking the dancing flames.

Shatter glass wall, yank Mom from chair. Fail test three, lose everything.

Focus. Complete the test. Don't go over time.

Everything in me strained to lunge, to break through the glass. To pick choice one and grab Mom. But that would mean game over. Holland would win, and Mom and I would lose.

Only the second choice gave us a fighting chance.

I had to compete in the Run, and I had to win.

"Step to the starting line, please," Lucas said. Still reeling, I followed Three in a daze to the bright-yellow line that bisected the floor. I felt the weight of Lucas's eyes on me, but I didn't look at him. I didn't look at Holland or Mom.

My control over my emotions was slipping with every breath. Unacceptable.

"Ten seconds to start."

Beside me, Three stretched her arms over her head, no more concerned than a runner at a track meet. "I hope you're ready," she said.

I ignored her. Ahead of us sprawled the town scene and, beyond that, the tunnel that led to the Run. That was where my chance—Mom's chance—at survival resided. My body tensed, and I leaned forward in preparation.

"Test starts in three . . . two . . . one . . . go!"

I was off and running before the "go" finished ringing in the air.

THIRTY

I raced into the intersection, my gaze sliding along the storefronts, the windows, anywhere that might reveal a sign of movement. At first I didn't see a single person out here, which sent my internal jitters into an uproar. Besides Three keeping abreast of me to the left, nothing stirred. It was like a ghost town we'd read about in history class.

My feet had just struck the concrete sidewalk when I saw the words, heard the digital voice:

Motion detected.

A man in a red Windbreaker emerged from the pseudo post office, head down, hands bunched in his pockets. Without breaking stride, I perused his clothing. A gun, did he have a gun, or a weapon of any kind?

No weapons detected.

I shot past him.

Motion detected.

Another man lunged out of the alley between the two brick buildings to my right.

I feinted to the left before the laser sight of his gun could bull's-eye my head, then sprinted at him. As he resighted his gun, my foot whipped out and, even though I held back, slammed his ear with enough force to send him careening backward. He landed with a scream, cupping his ear.

Impact, 865 lbs. per square inch. Ear ringing, nausea, dizziness, and temporary disorientation probable.

A pang hit me at his moan, but I shook it off. That guy had signed up for this.

My mom hadn't.

I snatched up the fallen gun, chucked it down the alley, and hurried on. Ahead was an awning with big white letters spelling out DRUGSTORE, but behind my eyes, all I saw were flames.

All those times I'd struggled to remember the circumstances around Dad's death, been so frustrated to draw a complete blank. Now I'd give just about anything to be blank again. To rid myself of this scorching, paralyzing fear that the fire would devour the one person on the planet who knew what I was and still cared about me anyway.

I passed a blue metal trash bin attached to a streetlight, a red fire hydrant, and a tiny patch of artificial grass. A slim alleyway appeared just ahead, between the bakery and the bank. A perfect place for a trap, I realized. Any second now, my motion detection function would sound an alert.

Nothing.

It took a soldier plummeting down a rope at my head for me to realize: my free minute was up. No more special functions.

He came fast, one hand on the rope while the other aimed a gun. I dived for the sidewalk at the last second, too late. The beam snagged the tip of my toe.

"Laser hit to foot. Minus ten points," the speakers blared.

Meanwhile, on my right, Three's feet pounded the concrete as she darted past.

That sent a blaze of determination through me. I had to catch her. When the soldier hit the ground, I was already bounding to my feet. I rushed forward, ducking my head.

My skull caught him right in the chest.

The momentum launched us both onto the ground, me on top. I twisted his gun hand until his grip released, then rapped him sharply on the head so he wouldn't follow.

I was barely upright when something glittered behind an open doorway across the street. The gun roared and I dived for the asphalt, thrusting myself into a hard roll to the right. I regained my feet and surged forward in one smooth motion, throwing a quick glance over my left shoulder as I zigzagged. The street remained empty.

A moment later, I was sprinting past the rubble of abandoned buildings and plunging into the yawning mouth of the tunnel. The computerized voice erupted around me.

"Twelve minutes remaining."

And then the dark musty cavern swallowed me whole.

Someone had been extra stingy with the light bulbs. With my night vision out of commission, I couldn't see more than five feet in front of me, but I could hear Three's shoes slapping the dirt ground ahead. Then they stopped abruptly, replaced by a strange, dragging noise.

She must have reached the first obstacle.

I sprinted into the darkness, desperate to catch her. With the visibility so low, the wall of tangled metallic wires seemed to rise out of nowhere. I skidded to a halt with my nose only inches away from kissing one of the sharpened points.

Barbed wire, as high up as I could see. Too tightly woven to slip between the strands, too high to go over. But there, between where the wall started and the ground, was a slender opening. Another twisted mass of wire extended horizontally, forming a bristly canopy that covered the path a little below knee level. Once again, I noted the rhythmic drag of a heavy object across the ground. But where?

With images of laser guns and other booby traps flitting through my head, I searched the terrain ahead. My hands curled in frustration. Nothing, nothing, noth—

There! I finally spotted the source of the noise, a little way up and to the right. Through the small gaps in the barbed wire walls, I could just make out the shadowy shape of Three's legs as she dragged herself through the dirt.

Crawling was the only way.

I dropped to my hands and knees, then my stomach, and wormed my way under the patchwork of wire. Maybe if I abandoned finesse in favor of speed, I could catch her. It wasn't like a few scrapes would kill me.

Pushing up higher on my arms, I surged forward. I'd made it only a few feet before a razor-sharp point sliced the back of my scalp.

No big de—

A jolt ricocheted through me; that, and a loud buzzing. For one long, terrifying moment, the cave plunged into absolute darkness, and my limbs froze. My internal voice issued a warning:

Impact: 75 volts

Perfect. Holland had allowed me to keep the useless functions. And booby traps, after all—only, they were in the fence itself. On the heels of that disturbing realization came Holland's computerized announcement.

"Barbed wire triggered. Minus ten points."

Behind, and down by twenty points.

I flattened myself to the ground and, snakelike, wiggled under the barbs. Escaping their jagged points took time, way too much time, and I had none to spare.

With an earthy, dank smell filling my nostrils and pebbles digging into my lower arms, I ducked my head and propelled myself forward. Surreal, this was all so surreal. A few days ago I'd been at school, fighting with Kaylee. Almost kissing Hunter. And now I was crawling for my life in some kind of macabre game.

After slithering for what felt like forever but must have been only a few seconds, my wiry cage ended. I shimmied out from under the canopy and jumped to my feet. What next?

I sprinted forward, flinching when a TV screen I hadn't realized was there burst into color overhead. No, not screen—*screens*. Because two, three, four more lit up in the distance.

More light, great—I could finally see more than two strides ahead of me. Until I realized that Holland wasn't broadcasting cartoons for our viewing pleasure.

Flames. He was broadcasting flames. And as if their red-orange flicker wasn't disturbing enough, there was Mom, still taped to the chair but now with her head up. She was awake, her eyes open and riveted to the wall of fire that was a good four feet closer than before.

I stumbled when it hit me. Four feet closer—one foot for every minute that ticked by.

The force of my phantom heartbeats filled my chest, my ears; a pump fueled by the same panic that threatened to flatline all remaining hope. A noise, somewhere between a strangled cry and a growl, filled my throat. These emotions, they were only making things worse. Frantically, I plumbed the depths of my own mind, searching for even an instant of control, of calm. A mere hint of the android I knew resided in me. And somehow, some way, I found it.

Don't look.

There, ahead. Focus on the next obstacle—that's the only way you'll see her again.

It still took a massive effort to tune out the monitors, but I did it. I clung to the smooth logic and ran hard as I focused on the behemoth of a barrier ahead—a massive, lumpy wall. It was so tall, I had to crane my neck to see to the top. A light mist fell from an overhead sprinkler system, the droplets catching in the dim light like dust. Between the uneven surface and the damp, rich scent, I realized I was looking at mud. The wall was completely covered in it. Overhead on my left, Three was already a little over a third of the way up the perpendicular climb.

As I sprinted the last few yards, I waited for my internal monitor to measure the height. Silence. Another jammed function. My fingers flexed in frustration. Not exactly the most optimal timing to start missing my android traits. I glanced upward again and estimated twenty, no, thirty feet. At least.

Then there was no more time to wonder as I reached the base and launched myself into the air. My jump landed me a few feet up the wall. My fingers sank into the slippery-cold mud and scrabbled for purchase, my sneakers doing the same. Neither could stop my slide back to the ground.

Red flickered on a monitor to my left. I caught myself just in time.

Focus.

Seven feet overhead, Three defied gravity and continued to climb, her legs spread wide. She looked like she was clinging to the wall by force of will alone. Then I noticed the way she carefully moved one hand at a time, her fingers searching under the mud before she attempted to move another part of her body.

Searching.

That was it! Under all that mud, there must be crevices, hand grips. *Something.*

I shoved both my hands into the mud high overhead, digging into the slimy muck until my fingers skimmed the firm surface underneath. Smooth, it was too smooth. I looked up and saw Three gain another handhold while my fingers worked their way along a surface that felt as slick as metal. Desperation clawed at my chest as time continued to tick away.

Smooth. Smooth. Smooth.

Wait.

My left pinky finger skimmed a small, rounded protuberance. Tiny, but enough.

It had to be.

Grabbing it as firmly as I could with my mud-slicked

hand, I hoisted my upper body, followed by my right foot, then my left. Mimicking Three's posture, I kept my legs splayed and was thankful for it. The wider stance gave me a bit of extra support.

The next handhold was quicker to find. And the next. I could do this. I could—

A flutter of motion on my left. From a hidden door halfway up the wall, a figure emerged, covered from head to toe in a padded black jumpsuit, only his eyes exposed behind a rectangle of clear plastic. The next instant he'd launched himself at Three. Two gloved hands wrapped around her right foot.

I kept climbing during Three's frantic stretch for the top of the wall, only inches away. But the soldier's weight proved too much. He braced his shoes against the wall and yanked again. A second later they both tumbled to the ground.

Thud! I stiffened at the sound of impact, then reached overhead for another grip, refusing to look down when I heard a scuffle follow. I finally had the lead, but I wasn't stupid enough to think that soldier would hold Three off for long.

My right hand was squishing through the mud when gloved fingers closed around my ankle. Before I could locate a handhold, the soldier was yanking me, down, down, down. As my body slipped, all I could think about was fire, eating away at Mom's skin.

No! Just as the gloved fingers tightened their grip on

my ankle, I bent my left knee and flattened my left foot against the wall. Then I lashed out as hard as I could with my right.

My shoe connected with the soldier's face—so hard, he released me instantly. Where was Three? I chanced a quick glance down and spotted her, leaving her attacker motionless in the dirt as she resumed her climb.

Our eyes connected briefly in the dim light, green on green. And then I turned and pushed myself higher. I tuned out Three, the soldiers, everything but finding the grips and not slipping, taking an odd comfort in the monotony of the motions. Find grip. Pull. Walk legs. Repeat.

I looked up and my heart surged. Only six handholds away. Now five, now four. Only three handholds away from the top when, with a rumble like thunder, the wall began to quake.

The unexpected and violent jerking upset my right hand. My feet bicycled in the mud with no chance at traction. The shaking increased in magnitude, and oh god, now my left hand was sliding. I curled my fingers and caught the end of the notch.

Only my fingertips were saving me from a twenty-foot plunge.

The wall shook and my grip weakened. Terror washed over me. I couldn't fall, not now. Falling meant lost time and, from this height, probable damage. If I injured myself, Mom was as good as dead.

The fingers on my right hand tunneled through the mud, searching for another grip. Come on. *Come on.*

I found another grip just as my left hand lost contact completely, and with a deep breath, I inched my body upward. Those last two feet were nearly impossible, with the slickness of the wall and the shaking and gravity resisting my every move, but somehow I did it. The second my right arm curled over the top, the shaking stopped and the speakers bleated.

"Nine minutes."

Too long, I was taking too long. Some way, somehow, I needed to pick up speed. I hoisted my right leg over the wall. The second I looked down, a gasp slid from my lips. No more mud. This side of the wall was pure metal—silver and sleek—and so was the wall opposite. Three thick lengths of rope spanned what had to be at least a twenty-yard gap between them. And way down below was a deep hollow, undulating with murky brown water.

If I fell down there, I didn't have a chance in hell of climbing back up.

Falling definitely wasn't an option.

I slid a few feet to my right until I reached the closest rope. A moment later I was dangling over the thirty-foot drop.

THIRTY-ONE

Carefully I shifted my grip and turned, so that I faced the way I'd come. I walked my hands backward one at a time. Instead of being grainy and easy to grip, this rope was slick. And when I lifted my legs to curl my feet around it for additional support, the entire thing bounced.

I swallowed, hard. Slick and not especially taut. Perfect.

Then, letting my head fall back, I stared up at my hands and started picking my way toward the far wall, one hand at a time.

I was only a few feet out when a flicker of orange caught my eye. Before I could stop myself, my head rolled to the right. For three agonizingly long seconds, I watched as Mom struggled against the tape while the fire writhed before her, much closer now. Then I squeezed my eyes shut and continued, concentrating only on the steady rhythm of my hands.

Pull. Pull. Pull.

Halfway to my goal, I heard the first clicking noise. My head rolled left, too quickly, and the entire rope swayed. A window in the wall had slid open, allowing a black barrel to poke out. One that was aiming at my shoes.

I unhooked my feet, just in time. The laser missed, but even so, I could feel the scorch of the heat it left behind, and my stomach turned. Another of Holland's special modifications, no doubt—laser guns that would actually inflict damage.

I couldn't afford to get hit.

Without wasting precious time to rehook my feet, I worked my way toward the other side, muscles taut as I listened for another telltale click. The rope bounced way too much for comfort. Was this how the regular soldiers performed the Run? Why did they tolerate it? Why did Lucas? All of my conjecture vanished when, out of the corner of my eye, I saw the rope to my left dip.

Three. Behind me and coming on fast.

The gleaming steel wall loomed ahead, like something out of an industrial nightmare. So much closer now. I surged forward with my right hand, then my left, shrinking the distance one grab at a time.

Click. Click.

Windows flying open, on both sides.

My threat came from the right. I had only an instant to see the barrel aim for my hands and less time to react. Arching my back like a gymnast, I swung my legs up hard and released my grip at the same time. For a terrifying moment, I was flying through the air with nothing to stop me from plunging into the murky water below. I whipped my head down, and the laser streaked past. Right by the spot my hands had been just moments before.

The rope jerked hard as my feet locked around it. The laser had nicked the rope.

From my upside-down and backward position, I saw Three emerge unscathed. She was lurching her way toward me at an impossibly fast pace. I swung back and forth, gaining momentum until finally my hands curled around the rope again.

Click, click.

My hands kept moving while my gaze darted right, then left. Not a window in sight. The rope jerked, hard. And then it went slack. As I plummeted backward toward the far wall, I saw the other severed half swinging for the opposite side.

Nice shot.

That was my last thought before I slammed headfirst into the steel wall. The impact reverberated down my spine, jarring the rope loose from my hands. I rebounded, slid two feet in midair before regaining my grip, then braced myself and *slam!* hit the wall again.

I slid until my left hand was holding air and I was dangling like some kind of offering to the patient water below. It would have to wait.

I reached up and grabbed the rope with my empty hand, carefully turned myself around to face the wall, and braced my shoes against the metal. When I reached the top, I allowed myself a brief backward glance and elation rushed through me. Three was clinging to her severed rope, but her piece was connected to the far wall, and I realized *I could actually beat her.*

Now, I just had to finish the course in time.

From my perch, I saw that yet another wall blocked my path, about eight, maybe nine feet away. Rocky instead of steel. But the rocks extended all the way up to the ceiling. The only way through was via two round metal tunnels that protruded a good twelve feet above ground. And they weren't especially wide.

As I started my descent, the choice flashed through my mind, quick as lightning.

Climb down this wall, run across, climb back up, or . . .

Climb down to tunnel level and dive.

I skidded down the rocky face, the tunnel's dark mouth drawing my gaze like a moth to the flame.

Safety or time, safety or time?

"Six minutes."

Decision made.

I didn't give myself time to second-guess. I balanced on a rock that protruded slightly above the level of the tunnel's floor, wishing once again that my android measurements weren't jammed. Then I lifted my arms overhead, bent forward, and, with a silent prayer to whoever might be listening, dived.

There's nothing like realizing you've miscalculated a split second too late. Wind whistled through my ears while panic filled me as I dipped too low and saw the rocks jut out to greet my face. I twisted, threw my left hand up, and managed to grab a handful of metal with little more than my fingertips.

After a wild swing during which I almost lost my grip, I hoisted my body up onto the cool metal surface of the tunnel. Then I was inside.

Besides darkness, the first thing I noticed as I started crawling was the fetid, rank smell. The deeper into the tunnel I went, the stronger it got. The aroma matched something in my memory banks.

Flesh. Rotting flesh.

I shook my head, as if that could banish the terrifying thoughts of what might be lurking ahead.

Don't think. Just move.

I rounded a corner, and what little light penetrated the narrow hole vanished. The air inside was chilly, the metal slightly damp under my hands. In here, it was like I was sealed away from the rest of the world. Just the dark and the sound of my own breathing and the rhythmic strike of my hands and knees. But I knew somehow, somewhere, Holland was watching, just waiting for me to falter.

I turned another corner, and it was like the floor fell out from under me. I was sliding, sliding, my hands scrabbling for something to slow me down, but the walls were too slick. I landed with a thud.

As if pressure-sensitive, a tiny, dim light flickered on in the middle of the tube. The space narrowed ahead, so much so that I could no longer crawl on my hands and knees. Without pausing, I plopped my forearms down, gritted my teeth, and moved as quickly as possible.

The stench grew stronger.

Ahead, the tunnel curved sharply to the left. I rounded the turn, hoping the end would appear. Instead, I saw feet. Bare feet, attached to a body—a body that reeked of death. I wasted precious seconds staring at those soles, the same size as mine, and breathed through my mouth to lessen the stench.

Had Holland planted a dead person as part of the challenge?

Don't think about it. Just go.

My head swam with borrowed dizziness as I pushed forward. I reached the body's feet, realizing with dawning horror that the tunnel was so narrow here, there was no way to pass without touching it. My chest dragged across the unmoving legs, the T-shirted torso. She was a girl, with a tangle of long brown hair. And then I reached her face, and my entire body went rigid.

This girl was my age, my height, my complexion. And her eyes, which were wide open, were startling green.

Three. Had she gotten ahead of me somehow to trap me? But wait—that was impossible. Then my gaze fell to the side of her head, where a wicked incision traveled the entire length of her hairline. That, and a bullet hole.

Oh my god. Not Three. One. Only not the version from my shattered memory. That girl had been vibrant, alive, whereas this girl . . . she was an empty shell. Vacant. And in her terminated state, so obviously not human.

A buzzing filled my ears, so loud at first I thought it was emitting from a speaker. But no, it was coming from inside my head—a phantom emotional reaction. I choked back the scream barreling up my throat at the last second.

Regret, sadness, and anger: they swelled into a bitter symphony in my chest as I left my predecessor behind like a discarded toy. I hurried past the slaughtered rat a few feet later—the source of the stench. Another one of Holland's tricks.

The tunnel curved again, and finally a circle of light showed.

When I neared the exit, the lights vanished, but I couldn't let that slow me down. I surged forward and plunged into empty space, but I didn't land on the dirt floor.

No, I landed in a pile of lumpy, loose parts—firm and awkward, but not too hard. And as the lights flickered back on, I knew.

Body parts, everywhere I looked—android, not human. Holland's pile of junk.

For a second, disbelief held me in place, sprawled belly down on top. Then I pushed to my feet and jumped, wobbling on the uneven surface. I barely cleared a haphazard cluster of arms.

If only I could vomit. Maybe then this sickening twisting of my stomach, this unrelenting nausea that made my mouth fill with unnecessary saliva, would finally cease.

But I couldn't vomit. I couldn't run. The simulator was here, somewhere—buried in a sea of discarded limbs. Limbs just like mine.

"Three minutes remaining."

The computerized reminder jolted me into action. I leaned over, grabbed an arm. Forced myself to glance inside. Hollow, except for a few left-over wires. I shuddered at the shell and tossed it aside, grabbing an abandoned lower leg next. The skin felt artificial, desiccated, as if separating the leg from the rest of the body had dried up any residual traces of humanity.

I dropped it and grabbed a torso. A thin incision split the body into two halves, and with grim determination I separated then, scanning the contents as fast as possible. Wires, and metal plates, plastic. But the thing that captured my attention was the small, fist-sized object. Not the simulator, but a pump. Black, smooth. Mechanical. A fake heart for a fake person. And nothing at all inside that resembled a soul.

I drew in a harsh breath. *I* might not have a soul, but if they existed, then Mom surely did.

Fueled by renewed determination, I became a parts-screening machine. Beyond the pile, I heard a whisper of a noise, then banging. The other tunnel. Three.

I had to find that simulator, fast.

The sea of parts grew shallower and shallower as I discarded hands, feet, arms, and legs, even as the banging grew louder. Despair clenched me in an unyielding grip. I wasn't going to find it in time. Three would get here, and then—

I moved yet another useless limb and saw it—a small, round, red device, about the circumference of the coffee mug Mom used to guzzle from each morning. A picture of a dynamite stick was etched into the top.

Above me, I heard Three reach the end of the tunnel. My fingers curled around the sphere at the same instant Three hit the ground, sending parts smashing into my legs when she landed. I gripped the simulator protectively, Holland's warning all too clear.

If I dropped it, I lost everything.

I whirled and pushed forward onto my right foot, ready to sprint my way to the finish.

A viselike grip on my arm yanked me back.

THIRTY-TWO

lurched backward, my thoughts pounding a frantic beat through my head. No time for a scuffle with Three. Maybe I could reason with her.

"Please—I have to save my mom."

I whirled to face her while my pulse thundered. Running. Out. Of. Time.

She tilted her head to the left in that puppylike way of hers. "You don't have a mom."

Something pained must have flashed across my face, because a small frown creased her brow. "It's not that I'm unsympathetic—they programmed me for that. But I'm required to obey orders."

"Orders? Don't you want to do more than that? Be more than an android?" As I said the words, I gave a surprise jerk of my arm. Nothing doing. She wouldn't let go.

How much time was left now? Two minutes? One?

"That's the difference between us. I'm content with what I am, and you're . . . not. It's a shame. There's nothing wrong with being an android."

I tightened my hand on the device, a desperate, insane plan beginning to form. "Unless at one time you thought you were human." As she mulled that over, I relaxed my arm. "You want the simulator? Then here, catch." In the next instant, I chucked the round device straight up over our heads, as high as I could.

I caught the brief widening of Three's eyes—shock that I'd do such an illogical thing—before she looked up. She didn't see my fist coming for her face until it was too late.

I put everything I had into that punch. My knuckles cracked across her familiar nose, and then she was flying back, airbound, toward the far wall.

The explosive!

I dived low and caught it, mere inches from the ground. And then I was on my feet and running. I knew I'd have only a short lead on Three, but it'd have to be enough.

At the end of the tunnel, I saw a circle of light, and beyond that, the glorious sight of a red stripe—the finish line.

"One minute remaining."

Three's footsteps pounded somewhere behind me, but I

was almost there. I was going to win, and then they'd free Mom and—

Wait a minute. Why was this stretch of obstacle course completely clear?

The thought hit a millisecond too late. My foot struck the ground, and the resulting explosion blasted my ears. At the same time, a perfect circle dropped out from under me and I was falling. I hit the ground with a thud, just in time to hear:

"Land mine triggered. Minus ten points."

At least I hadn't dropped the simulator. I braced my hands and feet on opposite sides of the narrow hole and climbed my way out. From behind, Three was barreling down on me. I glanced the other way, toward the finish. Only one chance to do this right. If I fell again . . .

Tucking the device to my chest like a football, I sprinted forward, propelling my legs as fast as possible. I had to build up speed, as quickly as possible, so that—

Another explosion cracked: the ground rumbled. Desperately, I ran harder, felt my left foot try to push off a dirt floor that was no longer there. But my right foot landed on solid ground, so I kept on going. I ran straight for the horseshoe of light that marked the tunnel's end.

"Land mine triggered. Minus ten points."

A few feet from the opening, I hit one last land mine. The simulator slipped in my hand. For a terrifying moment,

I juggled the simulator while I lurched forward.

Don't let go.

My fingers reached, curling around the slick surface before it fell. I craned my head over my shoulder, saw Three saving time by leaping the exposed holes I'd left behind. Cheater. But she wouldn't catch me. I was going to win.

"Ten seconds remaining."

Keep running. Just a few more steps.

I burst through the tunnel and into the light.

"Six seconds."

And then I looked to the left, and my remaining hope fell into a bottomless chasm. Somehow, the obstacle course had horseshoed and brought us out on the far side of the glass room. And there was Mom. A hungry trail of fire, taller than me, was now only a foot away, inching toward her and slowly picking up speed.

No! I looked at the finish line, some thirty yards ahead.

"Three seconds."

I wasn't going to make it.

I wanted to break down, right then and there. This entire test for nothing.

Mom.

With a howl I barely recognized as my own, I veered left, then dived. As my outstretched hands smacked the glass, the wall shuddered, then shattered, the sharp fragments scraping at my skin and yanking at my clothes. I hit the floor, rolled, and lunged to my feet, all in one fluid motion.

The flames were only inches away from Mom's feet when I reached her. With two vicious yanks, I freed her from the tape.

"Mila, no!" Mom coughed, half deliriously, while the fire's heat seared us from behind.

I picked Mom up, backed away from the flames, throwing a desperate glance over my shoulder. Was there a door back there? I could tolerate the broken glass, but Mom . . .

She moaned again, and to my surprise, tears slipped from under her eyelids.

"It's okay, Mom. I've got you."

Her eyes opened, but their blue irises looked glazed. "You always were so brave, Sarah. So brave," she murmured.

Sarah?

"Look," she said, pointing behind me—just before she passed out.

I felt the heat dissipate before I ever turned. The flames were gone. Vanished completely, without a trace, though the faint smell of smoke lingered. Just behind where the fire had raged, six soldiers waited—Haynes, the blond, two from the hallway earlier, and one I'd never seen, along with Lucas. Holland wasn't with them, and for that I was thankful.

Trusting Lucas's softly spoken promise that they would take Mom to the infirmary, I handed her over to the soldiers. I didn't know why she'd passed out, but if it was smoke inhalation, it could be bad.

My muscles tensed, readied. At this point, I had nothing to lose.

"Dr. Laurent will be fine. I promise you," Lucas said.

Maybe she'd be fine from this, but for how long? My last chance, my last test . . . and once again, I'd failed.

If Mom died—if I died—it was all my fault.

The urge to run after Mom, to tear apart anyone who stood in my way, was almost irresistible.

Maybe I shouldn't resist.

"If you fight, it will go badly for her. For both of you. The second you attack, the men with Dr. Laurent will be alerted. They have orders to eliminate her if you resist." The harshness in Lucas's voice left me no doubt that he was serious.

Hot fury erupted inside me. Eliminate? How could he so callously dismiss Mom's life? In that instant, every bit of past kindness he'd shown me was swept away. I wanted to lash out, hurt him. But I couldn't move. I was too terrified that if I took even a step in the wrong direction, Mom would die.

The inescapable logic in my head materialized. She might die anyway.

Overhead, the lights glared down on us, casting everything in a harsh glow. The unnatural brightness gave Lucas's skin an unhealthy pallor. "Look, come with me. Before General Holland comes back to fetch you personally."

The remaining soldiers held their ground. Their guns remained poised for action.

I lifted my arms, palms up. "You'd better be telling the truth about Mom being okay."

When the soldiers stepped forward, Lucas surprised me by shaking his head. "No, I don't need her restrained. You two are dismissed."

The two men exchanged a glance. The shorter one shrugged. They turned and preceded us into the street, the door swinging shut behind them.

Lucas motioned me to follow him. As I watched his back, one word kept slithering through my head.

Eliminate. Eliminate.

Eliminate.

PART FOUR

THIRTY-THREE

Lucas's lopsided gait was more noticeable than usual in the empty hallway; his left foot struck harder than before, with a slight scrape of shoe on concrete. I focused on that detail in an effort to regain control.

The elevator ride was silent, as was our exit into the hall.

A sudden thought snaked into my brain as I took in the stiff set of his shoulders, the hand-raked hair that stubbornly refused to lie flat. What if he wasn't talking because he was distancing himself? I mean, it wasn't like he needed to stretch that MIT brain far to realize I'd failed. So maybe he was just preparing himself for when I was gone.

Gone. A harsh laugh pulsed up my throat. I guess I'd resorted to euphemisms. By "gone," I meant "repro-grammed," or even worse, "terminated."

Either way, with the flip of a few switches, the me I

knew now would disappear forever.

If they reprogrammed me, would I still remember Mom afterward? No, she'd mean nothing. Just another face in a sea of them. I wrapped my arms around my waist and shivered. Worse—she'd be punished for my failure; Holland had said as much. Stealing from the U.S. military—she'd be jailed for life. If only I'd aced all the tests . . . I'd been so close, so close to saving her. . . .

I stopped, stared at the ground, tried to calm myself even though I wondered why. It was over. Hiding my emotions now would do nothing to save us.

In a rising panic, I lurched closer to Lucas and grabbed the front of his shirt. His heart beat strongly beneath the fabric, as if testifying to his humanity, his inner decency.

But I knew all too well how that steady rhythm could lie.

"I know that last test was like signing my death warrant . . . although I guess you can't really kill what was never alive, right?"

A sound suspiciously like a sob escaped my mouth. And then my throat constricted. No matter what they said, I was alive. I had to be. At least in part. Because the one clear thought screaming through me right now was: *I don't want to die.*

I didn't want to die. Not when I'd barely had a chance to live.

I clenched my fists, waited for the feeling that clutched

at my chest to ease a little, until I could talk without completely losing it. "Look, I know there's nothing you can do for me," I finally said, "but can you please try to keep my mom safe? If I'm gone, she won't cause you any more grief. There won't be any reason to."

Lucas stared into my eyes so directly, so intensely, it was like he was seeing beyond them, searching for something deep inside. Like he could see past my exterior to what lay underneath. I wanted to tell him that if he found anything unexpected, he should let me know. Because despite the undeniable knowledge that I wasn't human—or mostly human, anyway—despite the proof the computer screen had shown in the repair room, I still pictured my interior just the same as any other sixteen-year-old girl's. Blood and guts and bones. A brain, and a functioning heart. Hopes and dreams, fears and sorrow. They could tell me the truth, but they couldn't force me to accept it.

Lucas lifted his hand, let his fingers hover in midair before shoving them into his pocket. "I need to take you to your holding cell so I can get to my computer," he said, staring blankly at a point just over my head. "General Holland will be expecting a report soon."

I nodded numbly.

"You . . . you'll have to let go of my shirt first."

An awkward moment hit when I realized that I still clutched his shirt like it was a life raft. With a mumbled

"Sorry," I hastily released the starchy fabric and stepped back, and saw the nasty brown streaks I'd left all over it. I'd forgotten. Somehow in all the chaos I'd forgotten that I was covered in mud.

"Your shirt," I said, inadequately.

He looked down like he hadn't noticed either. "It'll wash," he murmured.

Lucas led me down two corridors, the second full of doorways. My feet slowed, my attention captured by that first steel rectangle. Could Mom be on the other side of that door? Or the next one? Or the one after that?

"She's not here," Lucas said softly, slowing his pace to match mine. "The infirmary's in a different part of the building."

My gaze slid from the door in defeat. He could be lying, but somehow I didn't doubt him.

We passed five more identical doors on the right before he halted to push a narrow door open.

"Shower," he said. "Take your time."

I emerged about fifteen minutes of harsh scrubbing later, finally clean and wearing my old clothes again, which had been neatly piled on a tiny stool in the corner.

After passing two more doors, he performed the passcode ritual.

Once the beep sounded and the door lumbered open, I walked inside without prompting, taking unenthusiastic note of my surroundings. It was tiny; smaller even than my room back at Greenwood Ranch.

Dimensions: 7 ft. by 7 ft.

This time, I couldn't drum up enough feeling to get annoyed by the voice. Even if, once again, I could have lived without knowing the exact dimensions.

Not much to see inside. A narrow cot against the far wall, one olive-green blanket folded in a neat square on top. Small steel toilet attached to right wall. Barren concrete floor. And the pungent scent of bleach, burning away any traces of previous occupants.

It was a room without pretensions, a room unconcerned with masquerading as something fancier than what it actually was: a prison cell.

Possibly the last place I'd ever "sleep."

Weariness settled over me, my reminder that humans—even pretend ones—needed rest. I walked the two steps to the cot and sat down. I wondered if it was real fatigue, or if somehow my brain knew when to trigger a fake signal. Maybe it was based on the amount of activity my body performed—like an exercise equation—because it certainly varied too much to be based solely on time.

I no longer cared enough to ask.

Ignoring the way Lucas hovered in the doorway, half-way in, halfway out, I collapsed onto my side. My eyelids closed. Wetness pooled beneath them, but I didn't bother wiping it away this time.

A harsh, indrawn breath. Hesitant footsteps. The sound of a joint cracking. "Mila?" Lucas's voice, soft, like he was afraid to startle me. Emitting from very close by. "Are you okay?"

I opened my eyes, unsurprised to find him squatting beside the cot.

When he reached out this time, his hand didn't stop, not until his fingers touched the traces of wetness left on my cheeks. I froze in place, unmoving, feeling the gentleness, the warmth, of his skin on mine. If I had any real air in my lungs, it'd be catching right about now. "You were crying," he said, in a hush.

I stared. Did that mean he actually cared? That someone in the world, besides Mom, besides a boy I'd probably never see again, thought of me as more than an expensive piece of machinery? Because I was starting to lose faith myself.

He wiped first one cheek, then the other. Just that simple act, that tiny show of compassion, felt like a miracle.

And then he shattered the illusion by looking over his shoulder and stiffening, before lifting his hand up to eye level, staring at the liquid, and rubbing it beneath his fingers. As if to assess the liquid's physical properties.

Which was exactly what he was doing. Lucas was awed by what an amazing work of science I was, no more, no less.

I rolled onto my other side and faced the wall. Hoping

he'd take the hint, run along, and examine his data.

When the door slid shut behind him, I tucked my knees up to my chin and hugged them tight. The fetal position; something I'd never known firsthand. The womb I'd experienced hadn't been a living body but a lab, one probably as cold and sterile as this room. I should feel right at home.

I closed my eyes, hoping for reality to fade away, at least for a little while. I imagined that I was protected. Safe. Imagined I could smell Mom's rosemary lotion, feel the soft slide of her hand down my hair, hear her heart beating above me as a gentle reminder that I wasn't alone.

I didn't want to be alone.

Footsteps approached down the long corridor leading to my room, much sooner than I'd anticipated. Lucas's lopsided strides, along with two more even sets of steps.

I jerked into a sit. Was this good? Bad? Indifferent? Surely Lucas couldn't be finished analyzing data on that last test so quickly. And if he was . . . what did it mean?

The door beeped and slid open to reveal Lucas's tall frame. In addition to the wrinkles and mud I'd inflicted on his shirt, the tips of his collar now flipped upward, as if mauled by stressed fingers. But in spite of that, his expression was carefully blank. No hint of emotion in those hazel eyes.

"General Holland is waiting," he said in clipped, precise syllables.

Holland. Holland was waiting. I wasn't ready to face him. I'd never be ready. "You finished the report?"

He shrugged and stared at the blank stretch of steel wall behind my cot.

I stood on heavy legs, commanded myself to walk. Every step felt impossible, like my feet had morphed into granite.

Lucas seemed strangely cold, distant. Not that it mattered.

I had more pressing worries.

Namely, my survival.

THIRTY-FOUR

Our march down the hall was both nerve-rackingly long and unbearably quick. The thought that this dank, barren hall might be one of the last things I saw filled me with such an overwhelming bleakness, it was a wonder my legs functioned at all.

As I followed Lucas and the pair of soldiers followed me, I remembered a documentary we'd watched in civics class, about death row prisoners. I wondered if this was how they felt on their march. Knowing that on the far end of the walk, death awaited. Yet still, in a tiny recess of their minds, they clung to hope that a last-second pardon would buy them more time.

Unfortunately Holland didn't seem like the pardoning type.

The extra-wide metallic door Lucas led us to was familiar. Too familiar. I watched, rigid, as he performed the Q-tip security ritual and punched his code into the security box, hesitating two full seconds before he punched the last number. I stood, unmoving, as the door whirred open.

I stumbled, numbly, when the blond soldier nudged my calf with a booted foot.

And then I was inside the repair room.

If hope were an object, it would be made of mesh, I decided, as I took another small step inside. Like a net, a sturdy one. One you expected to catch you from a free fall. But just as your body was inches from landing and bouncing exuberantly back into the air, someone came and ripped the fabric right out from under you.

All you'd hear as you fell through the gaping hole was that shredding sound.

For me? My shredding sound was in the form of a hum. The one emitted by the machine straight ahead, the one Lucas had programmed to perform my repairs.

The one he had told me they used to terminate us.

Lucas turned right, and there stood Holland and Three, facing a large computer monitor overhead. Holland, with his silver-streaked hair and his hands clasped behind his back . . . and my counterpart. The eerily similar follow-up version of me that was both better and worse than its predecessor, depending on whom you asked.

Three acknowledged our presence by glancing over her shoulder. Not Holland. He had to have heard us enter, but he didn't turn. A petty show of power, and a completely unnecessary reminder of his place in the hierarchy.

Lucas cleared his throat. "General Holland? I've brought Mi—Two," he corrected in that depressingly detached voice.

Holland forced us to wait one, three, five seconds before replying, while anxiety twisted my insides into a tightly coiled ball. Then he said, "Power off." Overhead, the computer monitor went black.

He pivoted, and Three echoed his movement fluidly.

He didn't say a word—just tapped his index finger against his mouth and stared. His hand was creased even more deeply than his face and sun-spotted with age, but immaculately clean, with neatly trimmed fingernails. Appearances were important to him.

Appearances, but not lives. At least, not mine or Mom's.

Beside him, Three's lips lifted into a hesitant smile. Then she glanced at me and her smile widened, as if inviting me to share it.

I shuddered and looked away, struggling with the disconcerting reality of being repulsed by the sight of my own face. When I looked at Three, I didn't see a teenage girl. I saw my inner ugliness, the freak inside, staring back at me.

Of the four of us, the only one who waited expressionless was Lucas. "Sir, did you finish reading the summary I sent?"

"I did. Do you have anything you want to add?"

Holland stared at Lucas with one silvery brow higher than the other. Behind us, one of the soldiers coughed.

Finally Lucas's frozen mask showed signs of cracking. He glanced at me, and in his hazel eyes I saw uncertainty. He shifted his weight onto his good leg, and his chest rose and fell before he answered.

"No, sir."

"Nevertheless . . . I read your report." Holland shook his head, and suddenly his eyes narrowed. "Exactly what kind of crazy bullshit are they teaching in colleges these days? I asked for a summary of how Two's emotional programming affected her performance in these tests, not on her—what did you call it? 'Ingenuity.'"

Lucas's left hand twitched, but other than that, he stood very, very still. "But sir—"

Holland smacked his hand onto the desk, and the sudden, sharp slap made the soldiers jerk into stiff postures, made me flinch. "I'm talking, not you. Your father always was too easy on you. I kept telling Joanna that he'd never be able to raise real men, but she didn't listen. And look what happened. One son I had to rescue from a dishonorable discharge, and the other—" His contemptuous gray eyes slithered over Lucas and landed on his foot, and he didn't need to finish the statement for anyone to know what he meant.

Worthless. His look said it all.

And wait—Joanna? Was that Lucas's mom? Was protecting his brother from a dishonorable discharge the way Holland had roped Lucas into this mess?

Beside me, I felt Lucas stiffen, watched his lips tighten and his fingers curl into his pants legs. Despite all that, his voice was amazingly calm. "You asked for my honest assessment, and I gave it to you. I can't help it if it doesn't mesh with what you wanted me to say."

Was Lucas actually defending me? But that didn't make any sense. The momentary stun of his words morphed into a flicker of disbelief, followed by a rush of warmth.

Lucas.

I couldn't do more than think the name, because Holland breached the distance between us with two swift strides. When his thick hand clamped on my shoulder, I was prepared. This time I didn't so much as flinch. Even though that same revulsion crawled over me at his possessive grip. At the feel of those old, wrinkled fingers, trying to claim me as a thing. At the overpowering stench of peppermint and alcohol.

The revulsion was there, but the celebration of emotions inside me was far more powerful.

I tilted my chin up and met his eyes, fighting to keep my

expression neutral. Even as the incredible realization continued to warm me from head to toe.

Lucas had tried to save me.

"Lucas might be impressed by your little antics, but I'm not."

Holland's nostrils flared as his hand squeezed tighter.

"Well, here's the thing. . . ." He released me to expel a long-suffering sigh.

"Sir?" With my peripheral vision, I could see Lucas's hands twitch. A tiny motion, but I caught it.

Three remained in her same spot. Calm. Neutral. Unfazed by any of this. But her careful gaze was assessing.

"Good for you, Lucas, for sticking to your guns. You're tougher than your father already." Holland's gray eyes bored into mine, as if trying to drill a hole through my lenses and see what made me tick. "However, I'm sorry to say that I don't share your views. Two's inability to keep emotions out of the task at hand makes her a loose cannon in the field, and that kind of uncertainty can translate into dead operatives. Not something I'm willing to risk."

He gave me a brusque nod. Terrifyingly enough, the logic behind his reasoning was inescapable.

The thing was—I didn't want to work for the government. I just wanted to live. But he'd never understand that, not in a million years. Military was his life. When he looked at me, he saw a huge liability. A reminder that he'd screwed up. And to a man like him, appearances were everything.

"I'll forward your summary to my superiors, but I have the ultimate veto power. And I'll be letting them know that my first assessment was accurate."

Holland's tiny, smug smile said it all. Forget the tests, the talk of second chances—he'd never let his superiors suspect he'd blown it, not after the failure of MILA 1.0.

He'd rather scrap me and be right than save me and be wrong.

And honestly, I couldn't even say he was wrong. Based on his criteria, I had failed. Mom had warned me, made me promise, not to show my emotions, and I hadn't been able to do that.

And now it was costing us both.

"Sir?" Lucas said.

"Don't worry, Two won't go to complete waste."

A crazy hope flared.

"We'll be removing her nanobrain and implanting a new one—one exactly like Three's." And with those words, Holland snuffed the hope dead.

Even though I'd prepared myself for this moment—for hours now—the reality threatened to break me.

Remove my brain. They were going to remove my brain. Strip away everything I was, everyone I'd ever cared about, with one procedure. No more phony Dad, Clearwater, or even Kaylee.

No more Hunter or Mom. No more Lucas.

No more me.

I'd been so focused on the horror of being less than human that I hadn't stopped to appreciate the humanlike qualities I did possess. Sure, maybe Three's existence would prove easier: no worrying, no caring, existing only to follow commands. But it wouldn't be living.

And now it was too late.

I waited for Lucas's protest, but none came. He stood stiffly, fists balled, but silent. Not surprising. I'd been a novelty for him, nothing more. Still, I couldn't fault him. Overall, he'd been more than decent.

I drifted off as Lucas and Holland discussed specifics.

"When will this procedure occur?"

I'd miss Lucas's inimitable multicolored eyes.

"We'll strap her into the machine, but we'll have to wait until tomorrow, when Lieutenant Barry gets back, so he can perform the procedure."

I'd miss the slippery-rough sensation of Bliss's mane under my hands.

"I see."

I'd miss the anticipation that had filled me when Hunter lowered his lips toward mine.

Most of all, I'd miss Mom: her fierce hugs, the way she fidgeted with her glasses when she was stressed, the rosemary scent of her lotion.

Mom.

That final thought snapped me out it. I lunged forward, grabbed Holland's sleeve. Screw decorum—let him be as disgusted as he wanted over my shortcomings. None of that mattered now. "My mom, can I please see her again? Just one more time? Before . . ."

. . . *you terminate me.* But that sounded so cold, so impersonal, that I couldn't force the words out.

"She'll be okay, right?" I demanded instead.

I saw a rush of movement on my right, then tumbled backward to the floor when Three jerked hard on my shoulder. "Don't touch General Holland without permission."

I regained my footing and surged forward, only to have her push me back again.

My eyes narrowed, and my hands curled into fists. "Move," I said. Nothing could deter me from this one crucial answer.

She shifted her feet so they were shoulder-width apart, bracing herself.

We eyed each other much like we had during the first test, each waiting for an opportunity to strike.

Holland smoothed the fabric on his sleeve back down before clamping a beefy hand onto Three's shoulder. "No, no, it's okay, Three. Step aside."

I didn't know if it was just me, but I swear it took an extra second for Three to obey Holland's command. And her expression definitely looked less than pleased. But then I wondered if I was mistaken, because after I blinked, she'd shifted to the side, looking completely neutral.

Holland smiled, that smug curling at the edges of his lips. "See, this is exactly what I'm talking about. Nicole did you a disservice. No matter how you *feel*, you're not real. You're not a girl, you're a replica of one. You're nothing more than an extremely accomplished mimic—one that I helped create. The fact that you can't tell the difference is a huge liability."

I held my breath and waited for a bomb to drop.

"Nicole Laurent isn't your mother, she's your creator. It's unfortunate, but she leaves us no choice. Given her act of treason on a highly classified military project, she's to be execut—"

It was like rage slammed me and gave my hands a life of their own. His sentence ended in a strangled gasp when I lunged and wrapped them around his throat.

I squeezed, hard. The same instant he started to choke, I slithered behind him, slipping one hand under his jaw and shoving it to the right in one smooth motion. My other palm cupped the back of his head.

All this before Three could so much as move.

He jerked against my hands once, and I dug my fingers in mercilessly. "Move again, and I break your neck." His entire body went rigid.

The two soldiers in the background jerked to attention, but there was nothing they could do. Beneath my fingertips, I felt his pulse soar and his skin dampen with sweat. "Take one step this way, and he's dead." *I should do it anyway.* My fingers tightened.

He deserves it.

My fingers tightened.

This awful man is going to kill Mom.

My fingers tightened.

The soldiers exchanged panicked glances but didn't dare move.

Three frowned. "Let him go. Even if you kill him"—I felt Holland twitch at that—"it won't change anything. Why bother?"

Why bother? Because, you completely ignorant half-sister, it will feel good.

Sweat poured from Holland, making his shirt cling to mine. Its sour smell gave me a triumphant rush. Screw logic. I didn't care about logic. At this instant, all I cared about was seeing Mom, and barring that, making Holland pay.

"Mila, no!"

I turned my head an inch, keeping one eye on Three and the soldiers. Lucas eased toward me, like he wanted to whisper in my ear.

His hand lifted.

I barely saw the Taser before the shock hit.

Electricity exploded through my body. My torso, my limbs, everything erupted into convulsions. A barrage—wavering images—patches of black. My thoughts—slipping—

And then I——————————————————

———————————————————————

———————————————————————

———————————————————————

———————————————————————

———————————————————————

———————————————————————

——

THIRTY-FIVE

My eyes jerked open like someone had flipped a switch. The black void shifted into shrill static.

First just that relentless buzz, filling my head. Then an occasional crackle as lights flashed behind my closed eyes.

Reboot. The word flickered red through the static. A familiar voice—mine?—echoed the word, but it sounded distant. Distorted.

A warm substance melded against every curve of my body. Locking me in place. The sensation sent an image flashing through my head, also distorted, too distorted to decipher.

I pushed through the static, now deadened to a hum, to open my eyes. That tiny motion sent shock waves pulsing through my head. One, five, twenty times.

The moment they ceased, panic set in. Those shock waves, I knew what they were—zaps of residual electricity trapped inside me.

And now I knew where I was.

The chamber, from earlier. The special machine Lucas had used to repair my injuries.

The special machine Holland now planned to use to reprogram me into Three.

Reprogram.

Within my heartless body, a pulse slammed through my ears. No endocrine system to speak of, and yet adrenaline surged, demanding that my equally nonexistent muscles contract and propel me out of here. No lungs and yet mine were thick, heavy, too solid to suck down air.

I fought off the panic, tried to banish it with logic. It wasn't real. None of what I was feeling was real.

A coldness originated in my core and spread outward, gathering strength as it poured through layer after layer, until it culminated in an icy sheet across my skin.

I had to stop this. I had to stop this and *assess.*

My surroundings. I'd focus on my surroundings. Search for a clue as to how I could free myself from this seemingly inescapable barrier. I scanned the area and saw nothing.

No motion detected.

Despite the hum of machines, this room was devoid of

life. Free of human sounds. Empty.

Was that how I'd feel once the procedure had been performed? A permanent silence inside me, where thoughts and feelings used to rush around like traffic on a busy street?

Maybe it would be peaceful. Maybe not. I'd never know for sure, because the current version of me would cease to exist.

No. *No!*

I thrashed against the plastic, pushed with every bit of my power. The material remained resistant, didn't yield even a fraction of a millimeter.

Hopelessness sucked the energy out of me. According to Lucas, the only way out was via reprogramming the machine. An action that occurred from outside my impenetrable enclosure.

Lucas. Lucas had Tasered me.

As if the bitter taste of betrayal had summoned him, his voice echoed in my ears.

Mila.

My gaze darted around the room, but he wasn't there. No one was.

That's when I realized his voice really *was* directly in my ears, like during the first test.

And despite his betrayal, I couldn't help the desperate whisper that escaped my lips. "Lucas?"

Blink twice if you can hear me.

I blinked.

His relieved sigh rustled through my ears.

I'm sorry about the Taser—I had to make sure Holland wouldn't suspect me. We have to be quick. I used a minimal setting—enough to make you black out for Holland's benefit, but not enough to mess up your functions for long. They should all be working soon, if not already. I'm going to get you and Dr. Laurent out of here. But you need to do what I say. Can you do that?

Lucas was going to help me and Mom? Another blink.

You're going to have to make it look like a real escape. I'm going to be your hostage.

Hostage? Something inside me rebelled, even as I realized the necessity of his words. Using Lucas as a hostage was the only way to ensure he didn't get caught for helping us.

Blink.

First thing: you need to free yourself from the machine. If I help, they'll be able to track my security code on the door. I don't think they're monitoring me, though. Not yet.

Hopeless. This was totally hopeless. Didn't Lucas realize that if I could free myself from this plastic cage, I would have by now?

But Lucas must have a potential solution to my imprisonment in mind. He was too methodical to bring it up otherwise. But what?

Um . . .

His reticence, especially given the urgency of the matter,

didn't bode well. What was I missing?

There was no way to break out, no way to solicit help from the outside. No, I had to make this thing open from the inside. I shoved against the walls. Nothing. The material was too strong.

Counterpressure: 2000 lbs. per square inch.

Way too strong.

Despair erupted in my mind, overpowering my logic, hope, everything. There was no escape if Lucas couldn't get in and I couldn't get out. No escape.

No escape. But wait . . . Lucas knew that. He knew the parameters of the machine better than I did. He couldn't expect me to break through physically, which meant . . . I had to break through mentally.

Lucas confirmed my conclusion a moment later.

You're going to have to communicate with the machine.

The acrylic tube absorbed the earthquake of tremors that erupted inside me.

Communicate with the machine. On a machine-to-machine level. Like we were one and the same.

A silent scream built in my head. No escape meant Holland cracking open my skull, extracting my brain, and replacing it with a new one, turning me into an exact replica of Three. A true machine. And now Lucas was telling me that to escape, I'd have to turn into a machine anyway.

You already have the permissions—I enabled them the first time you went in, just in case. You need to open your ports.

Open my ports—he made it sound so easy.

I didn't even know what that meant exactly.

Still, I had to try.

I scurried through my mind, searching for the command until I found it.

Open ports.

At first I felt nothing. Not a hint of electricity, nor of a green glimmer. It was more gradual. Like a slowly building roar that wasn't there one second and was the next. A roar that slithered into me and vice versa. A presence all around me, one that I could reach out and touch. Only I didn't have to move my hands.

I'd been terrified it would feel stark, empty. Desolate. Like a wasteland. It didn't. While the presence wasn't quite alive, it didn't really feel dead, either. More like an all-encompassing energy.

The code glimmered into being—inside my head or not, I wasn't sure at this point. But it was everywhere. An endless stream of letters, symbols, numbers.

For once, I knew exactly what to do. I reached out tentatively with my mind, feeling the code sifting by like sand pouring between fingers. From the stream, the characters slowly shifted to re-create my command.

Override lock.

A hesitation; a shimmer in my head. And then a door slammed shut.

Verify user.

Frustration roared through me like a massive wave. I couldn't verify the user, because I wasn't supposed to be there. If only I could talk to Lucas. But no. Lucas's permissions had gotten me a connection to the machine in the first place. The rest I had to figure out on my own.

Determination uncoiled within me, spreading and spreading until every last cell burned with conviction. No matter how big my attempts to hide from my true nature, it still existed. I was a machine, and a powerful one.

This inferior specimen would not deny me.

This time the command burst from me like an explosion.

Override lock!

A minuscule hesitation, one that cracked my confidence. And then I felt a shift in the energy, a change in the roar. The door whooshed open.

Five seconds later, I was free.

By the time I got to the door, forcing the code to cede to my demands was simple. A quick override, and the door beeped.

Metal parted, and I saw Lucas. Standing with his hands in his hair, his hazel eyes wide and stunned. He didn't talk, just stared in that dazed manner before reaching into his pocket to pull out the Taser and push it into my hand.

Lucas started loping down the corridor, but I froze, my eyes on the video camera at the end of the hall.

He shook his head. "I've got them on a loop for now, but we have to hurry. It won't take the men on security duty that long to figure it out."

My fingers curled around the Taser as I followed Lucas. I didn't hear any guards, but even a single mistake at this juncture would mean show over.

Ten feet ahead, another corridor bisected our path. Lucas veered toward the left, and I followed. Flattening himself to the wall, he inched his way toward the opening.

"Do you hear anything?" he whispered.

I closed my eyes, focused. From the opposite direction I heard the murmur of voices, a man and a woman. Then canned laughter. A TV, probably from the guards' station.

Ahead of us . . . I heard nothing. Just the faint buzz of the lights and the hiss-and-sigh rhythm of Lucas's breathing.

"Clear."

Despite my reassurances, he poked his head around the corner and looked both ways before hurrying down the path to the left. This hall was narrower than the last, and darker, with only tiny dots of emergency lighting flickering along the wall. My vision brightened instantly, but Lucas would have to manage on familiarity.

He pulled up short in front of a narrow gray door on the

left and began the DNA pass-code ritual.

I rushed to the door, stood so close that my nose almost touched the smooth surface, curled my fingers into my legs to resist the urge to try to rip it open myself. Mom's room, this had to be Mom's room.

Every tenth of a second Lucas took to key in his numbers felt like torture. Finally the beep sounded, followed by the click. I shoved my way inside before the door had opened even halfway, its unhurried glide much too slow.

I rushed straight for the unmoving figure on the bed. "Mom?" I whispered.

In a flash, Mom rolled away from the wall and sat up. "Mila?" She fumbled for the glasses on the tiny, rickety table.

"Yes."

She bolted to her feet. In the next instant, my face was mashed against Mom's shoulder as she yanked me into a hug, squeezing with every bit of strength her thin arms could muster.

I allowed myself one, two, three seconds to bask in her warmth, in the flash flood of relief that made me sway. She was still whole. Alive, and exactly how I remembered her.

After one more brief squeeze, I gently untangled myself. "Save your strength."

I stepped to the side, revealing Lucas, who stood guard at the door. "Wait, what's going on?" she said.

"Lucas is helping us get out of here. Now."

Surprise widened her eyes. "I don't understand, how—" She shook her head, as if in a daze. "Can we do it?"

"We're out of options."

As usual, Mom's uncanny power to maintain calm under extraordinary circumstances amazed me. "Right. Let's go."

She swept for the door, leaving me to follow. "The south halls? No one uses those much."

Lucas nodded. "That was my plan," he said, and he turned to lead the way.

But not before I saw Mom grab his upper arm and lean in close to his ear. "Thank you," she whispered.

And not before I caught the red bloom in his cheeks.

Then Mom darted down the hall and Lucas loped after her. I curled my fingers around the Taser and followed.

We headed in a direction opposite the way we'd come, and eventually the hall ended in a left turn. We were only three steps into it before Lucas cursed softly.

"What?"

He nodded up at the far corner. "The cameras, they're moving. Either the loop stopped functioning, or . . . they figured it out."

We all froze, watching the camera make its sweep up our hall and then down the adjacent hall.

"So they've seen us?"

Lucas shook his head. "Not necessarily. It just depends

how closely someone is monitoring that particular camera at the moment. The Vita Obscura mole has made them more vigilant than ever, but if we hurry, we just might make it. . . ."

We picked up our pace, jogging down the halls at just short of a run, trying to balance the need for stealth with the need for speed. Lucas's bad foot was more noticeable now, but he never once mentioned it.

Mom led the way as we made another left turn, followed by a quick right. "This pops out right near the guards' station. If they're distracted by the monitors, we may be able to sneak by."

As I was nodding my agreement, a whir of overhead motion caught my eye. The camera. It had shifted to the left, so that the circular lens now pointed directly at us.

I waited a heartbeat, to see if the camera would continue moving on its regular sweeping path, but it didn't. It stayed steady and focused, and for a split second, it was almost like I could feel Holland's cold gray eyes on me.

"Run!" I said, and Mom and Lucas didn't hesitate. Still, we made it only a few steps before the siren screamed overhead.

THIRTY-SIX

With our plan to sneak out in shambles, the three of us bolted down the hall, heading right toward the newly alerted guards.

Mom and I kept our pace even with Lucas's. He was surprisingly swift, but I could tell the speed was uncomfortable, based on his heightened limp. Still, he didn't complain, and I stayed one step behind him, knowing I needed to make this look real, because I was sure our entire run was being recorded. I didn't say anything. I just shoved the Taser into the small of his back and urged him forward.

We burst into the wide corridor that led to the car bay with Lucas just a step ahead of me, the guards' station directly on our right. Two guards gestured wildly with raised guns.

"Behind me," I hissed to Mom. Pushing to my tiptoes, I flung my right arm around Lucas's throat. The Taser now indented the skin just over his jugular.

"BACK OFF!" I shouted at the guards. Both had dropped into a shooting stance, trying to aim at me. "Back off or I fry him!"

The taller guard's gaze flicked to his partner. "We're under orders." His voice wavered, but he didn't lower the gun.

A burst of completely inappropriate laughter rushed up my throat, one that turned into a small, choked cry. Orders. Of course. Holland didn't care what kind of casualties he incurred, so long as it prevented Mom and me from escaping. So much for his heartfelt speech about saving lives.

I felt Lucas tense under my arm, felt his pulse race. "Please," Lucas said. "She'll do it, I know she will."

I flinched. After that second test, I didn't know if he was acting or if he actually believed I'd shock him.

The guards shifted uneasily but held their ground.

Any minute more soldiers would appear. Even now, I heard a set of booted feet pounding concrete in the distance. Time was running out.

Mom's voice rang out behind me. "So you're going to shoot a hostage in cold blood?" she said, jabbing me in the back. Taking her hint, I urged Lucas forward. The footsteps grew louder.

"You realize bullets won't stop her, right?" Mom

continued. "If you shoot, she'll take both of you down. Didn't you hear what she did to Holland?"

I think the serene Three-like smile I summoned to my lips was what did it—that smile made them *believe*. They lowered their guns.

Good thing they couldn't feel the tremor in my Taser hand, or know how wrong it felt to hold it to Lucas's neck. They had no idea that I'd never, ever let anyone force me to kill. Or torture someone again, just to test my reactions. I wouldn't become a monster.

I wouldn't become a Holland.

I pushed Lucas forward again. One step, two steps. That's as far as we made it before the shorter guard uncovered the weakness in our plan. The moment he had a clear shot, he raised his gun and aimed at Mom. "Let him go or I shoot Dr. Laurent."

Lucas and I froze in unison. The guard's cheeks were pale, and a sweat droplet trickled down his cheek. Yet his gun hand was all too steady.

He would do it. He would pull the trigger and shoot, and everything up to this point would be for nothing.

"My other side, now!"

It all happened at once. Mom slid to my left and the gun exploded. Lucas jerked backward into my chest.

I looked down, stunned at the blood just starting to stream from his left thigh.

His good leg.

Guilt cracked me like a lightning bolt.

"Just go," Lucas rasped through gritted teeth.

But we couldn't. As the tall guard screamed at his partner, the pounding behind us closed in. I turned my head, and what I saw made my remaining confidence crumble. Three raced toward us—less than twenty feet away, and gaining rapidly.

"Two, stop Two!" From way off in the distance, Holland's order barreled down the hallway.

Ahead of me the steel door gleamed, marking our path to freedom; so close but not close enough. We weren't going to make it in time.

"Get him to the door—hurry," I snapped as I transferred Lucas's weight to Mom. I cut her off when she opened her mouth to argue. "Do it!"

While Lucas draped his arm around Mom's neck and they stumbled forward, I focused on the locking mechanism, linked with the computer, and overrode the code. The door beeped and was starting to slide open when I whirled and ran straight at Three.

The original two guards reached me first. I dropped to the floor, barely dodging the bullet that whizzed over my head. Faster than they could aim again, I rolled, pulled back the Taser, and *wham!* smashed the device against the shorter guard's knee.

He crashed sideways into the taller guard, his scream drowning out the clatter of his gun striking the ground. Before the second guard could steady himself, I jumped to my feet, reared back with my right hand, and punched him hard in the gut.

When he doubled over, my knee was there to meet his nose.

I turned in time to watch Three sprint past without even glancing at me, her eyes trained on someone else.

Mom.

No, oh no. I sprang after her, the chill of desperation pumping through my limbs. Ahead, Lucas and Mom were just now hobbling through the open doorway, but Three was gaining. My plan had been to Taser Three before diving through the door and locking it behind us, but fighting the guards had wasted valuable time.

Even though I knew I'd never cover the distance in time, I linked to the computer and commanded the door to close. It was the only way to keep Mom safe.

As I raced after Three, I had a horror-stricken moment when I thought she'd fly through the door before it closed, leaving me stranded on the wrong side, with no way to help.

Close, please close.

I caught a glimpse of Mom's face, her expression frozen and her gaze glued to Three like she was staring down the barrel of a gun. Three flung her hand toward the narrow opening, her fingertips reaching, reaching, and oh god, if she got them inside, she might pry it open and then—

Three's hand hit metal as the doors clicked shut.

With her back still to me, I raced the remaining distance between us and lifted the Taser. She whirled, a blur of motion and whipping brown hair. Her fist knocked my hand and the Taser went flying. The next instant, so did I—against the steel wall.

My head cracked hard. Her fist flew at me and I feinted right. When her knuckles slammed metal, I grabbed her outstretched arm with both hands, yanked it down onto my knee. The crunch reverberated up both of my hands.

"You . . . you damaged my elbow joint!" Her green eyes widened and then narrowed. Was Three actually angry?

No time to wonder, because her booted foot lashed out and hit me square in the chest with devastating force. I flew back until I crashed against the far wall.

Impact: 1200 lbs. per square inch.

At least some of my functions were returning.

The thudding from Holland and the soldiers drew closer now. From my position on the floor they looked bigger, more menacing. And they'd be on us in a manner of seconds. Last chance.

My gaze caught on the Taser, several feet away. Three saw it at exactly the same time. We both dived, hands outstretched, only I was quicker. I grabbed it and fumbled for the button. Her fingers closed around the edge right as the prongs shot out.

I shuddered when her entire body spasmed. And then she collapsed to the floor, and I vaulted over her while simultaneously ordering the door to open.

I slipped past and turned to face the oncoming soldiers. "Stay down!" I hissed at Mom and Lucas. They were too far back to follow, but I didn't trust Holland not to take back his order to hold fire. Not now—not when his prize experiment was escaping once again.

"Mila, the other door," Mom said. Without turning my head, I ordered the computer to open the door leading to the car bay. At that same time, the lights began to flicker.

A smooth computerized voice followed. "Emergency override activated. All locks will be disengaged in thirty seconds."

Which meant no matter what I did, soldiers would be pouring through these doors way too soon. We were safe for the moment, though. But as the door leading into the compound slid shut, I saw something that made terror clutch me with an unyielding grip. Through the narrowing gap, I saw Three move her legs before slowly rising.

I turned away, shaking. How was Three's quick recovery possible? Was that another of her so-called improvements—resistance to electrical shock? Not that the how or why mattered. No, the only thing I needed to know was—she was coming.

We burst into the car bay. I ran for the black Suburban nearest the door and shoved at the trunk.

It wouldn't budge. Had I overestimated my android strength? The shouts inside the door drew closer.

Come on. If ever I needed an android ability to step up to the plate, now was the time.

I shoved harder. Like a miracle, the car groaned; the trunk began to swing around. Just as the guards started to open the door, I gave a final push, and the side of the car smacked right up against it.

Locked in, for the moment. Until they exited a different door.

I ran back to Mom to help. "Where's your car?" I yelled to Lucas, for the camera's benefit. Softly, I whispered, "Are you okay?" But of course he wasn't okay. His stride grew weaker with every step, and more of his weight sagged against me, until I was sure that I was the only thing holding him upright.

"F-fine," he whispered back, but the hitch in his voice tore at me. I should stop and get him help. This wasn't right. "Don't . . . you dare stop now," he continued, as if reading my mind. He grappled through his pocket and pulled out the keys.

"The Camaro," he said, pointing past a fleet of Suburbans

to a classic car to our left, toward the exit ramp.

Mom raced around to his other side, and with her assistance, I hauled Lucas toward the car.

"We have to bind his leg," I said. Mom paused with her hand on the door, looking at my flannel shirt.

Without a word, I ripped it off and tossed it to her. "Here," I said with barely a ripple of regret. Lucas needed it far more than I did.

I lifted him and placed him on the hood of the Ford truck parked next to the Camaro. When I stepped aside to let Mom bind his leg, I saw the blood streaming from it, darkening his gray slacks like he'd waded in a pool.

"Don't bother," he whispered. "They'll fix me in a second anyway."

I shook my head in response, my throat too tight to speak—while Mom finished tying the shirt around the wound. "That should stanch the bleeding for a few minutes, until help gets here."

Mom wrenched open the driver's side door while I stared at Lucas's face, his cheeks pinched in pain. I couldn't leave him like that.

"Mila, come on!" Mom yelled.

"Wait," Lucas panted. Then he swallowed hard and said, "For the record, I think you make an excellent human."

And then his eyes glazed over in a haze of pain.

My throat clogged. Even now, he was thinking of me. I

wished there was time to do more. To thank him for everything. The *"Sorry"* I mouthed wasn't close to adequate. Then my hand snaked out, and I jabbed him right in the sensitive spot in the neck. I caught him under the armpits when he went limp and pushed his unconscious body onto the hood.

At least I could spare him the pain until help arrived.

"Mila, hurry!"

With one last wince at Lucas's motionless form, I jumped into the driver's seat and reversed us out of our spot.

I slammed my foot on the gas, and the rev of the engine competed with the siren's continuous screech. I searched the rearview mirror one last time for Lucas. Instead, I saw the Suburban I'd used as a barrier shudder before slowly moving away from the door.

The top of Three's head emerged just as we rounded the first turn.

THIRTY-SEVEN

We raced through one, two, three rotations of the parking garage, finally getting to the security gate where we'd entered. And just in time.

From down below us, I heard the slam of car doors. They were coming.

Three was coming.

An armed guard blocked our way, standing with his gun aimed at our windshield.

"Duck!" I yelled, swerving wide to the left and pumping the gas. The Camaro surged for the bar that blocked the entrance, taking a hard smack that cracked the windshield. The bar shattered off at the base. A gunshot fired, but it plunked against metal.

The impact reverberated through the car, but I didn't

stop. We pushed on through and revved our way up and out, into another parking garage.

A few turns later we were in fresh night air. Just outside the John F. Kennedy Performing Arts Center.

The Camaro's tires caught air, and Mom and I bounced in our seats as we hit the street hard. Her hand latched onto the back of my seat for support, her knuckles taut under the skin. Her head bowed and I saw her lips moving, but no sound came out.

Mom? *Praying?*

That wreaked havoc on my confidence, so I focused on the road. I followed the curve left, glancing in my rearview. No one behind us yet, but I was sure that would change in a matter of seconds. And I had no idea where I was going. But I could fix that now that we weren't locked away underground.

GPS.

A light burst behind my eyes, followed by a low buzz.

GPS.

Nothing.

Lucas's voice replayed.

". . . your functions shouldn't be out for long."

All except for my stupid GPS . . . the one I needed the most right about now.

"My GPS is out . . . ideas?" I said. Of course, Lucas just had to have a classic car that way predated that technology.

My eye caught on the long, curved line in the windshield. Oh, god, Lucas was going to kill me.

"Left at that main street ahead, Rock Creek Parkway," Mom said. Thankfully her voice was steady as ever.

I accelerated the Camaro hard through the curve, pumping the clutch and downshifting before we hit the intersection. Holland's men would be after us any second now.

As we headed south on Rock Creek Parkway, I glanced out the driver's side window, back down the street we'd used to exit the Kennedy Center.

In the distance, behind the bushes, Suburban-level headlights pulled onto the street from the parking garage exit.

I pressed harder on the gas pedal.

We'd never lose them on the highway. The roadblock probability was way too high.

Mom saw them coming in the sideview, too, and said exactly what I was thinking. "City."

I edged the speedometer up higher and higher as we raced down the road, trying to put distance between us and the slower Suburbans while I had the chance.

Only a few yards over on our right, the Potomac glowed a dark greenish black under the moonlight. Mom glanced over her shoulder.

Her hand flew to her glasses.

"How many?"

"It's pretty far back, but I think—two. Three, maybe."

As we went under an overpass, I swerved past a Dodge Neon, noticed an open stretch was ahead of us, and chanced a quick look in the rearview.

My heart seized. Three Suburbans, not nearly as far back as I'd like.

One driven by Holland, another—by Three.

"Stay left," Mom commanded when the road split. "Then right up ahead."

I cursed under my breath, a word I knew would get me grounded if we survived this night, and then cursed again, in my head. After fighting against my special functions time and time again, right now I felt the absence of my GPS sharply. Sure, we had Mom to navigate, but Three had a computerized navigational system in her head.

"I heard that."

"You can't get mad—it's my evolution talking," I said, parroting the idea she'd brought up at the airport.

Her hand squeezed my right arm. Hard. "It's no joke, Mila. Answer me this. Do you remember anything about the compound from before, anything at all?"

I swerved around a car, wondering why we had to talk about this now. But I knew Mom better than to argue. I never won against her stubborn streak. "A little. I remembered the white door into the lab. And Mila One getting tested."

Mom's grip tightened. "I erased your memories from here, Mila—all of them," she said, with a peculiar breathlessness.

"You must have missed some."

Mom's blond hair flew as she shook her head. "No. I erased all of it, Mila—I'm sure. Which means you managed to store those memories on your own. That's what evolving means. You're becoming more human every day . . . even if you don't realize it. Whatever you do, don't forget that."

"Fine. And you can tell me all about it—later." Right now, I was a little busy. Besides, her telling me now . . . it almost sounded like she expected something bad to happen to her.

A shiver passed over me, but I shook it off.

I wouldn't think about what would happen if they caught us.

I wouldn't.

My chest heaved and I gripped the steering wheel harder.

"Once we pass the Lincoln Memorial, veer east toward the Kutz Bridge," she said.

"I don't know where the Kutz Bridge is!"

"Just veer east, then."

Amid a cacophony of car horns, I slid onto a street called Independence, the Kutz Bridge looming in the distance. The Suburbans had fallen back, but they were still there. Well, only two of them.

Where the hell had the third one gone?

Through the windshield I caught the glitter of lights reflecting off water. "What are we crossing?"

"The Tidal Basin."

We hit the three-lane, one-way bridge at 105 miles per hour. I braked sharply as a red Lexus pulled in front of me, yanking the wheel hard to the right. Then frantically back to the left to avoid smashing into the back of a limo.

We flew off the Kutz Bridge, back onto Independence.

I headed east, hoping to speed away from them around twists and turns. Mom dug through the glove box as a stoplight turned red in front of us and cross traffic began to flow.

"Lucas, you're a genius," she breathed when she pulled a white envelope out and peered inside.

"What?" I said, accelerating. A taxi flew by in front of us, and I whipped the wheel to the right, skimming by its bumper with only a few inches to spare. Horns blared behind us, brakes squealed. We kept right on going.

"He left us money. Eight hundred dollars."

Hopefully we'd live long enough to need it.

I tore my gaze off the road for a quick glimpse in the rearview mirror. My hands ground into the wheel. One of the Suburbans was just a few car lengths back.

Bad enough, and then the third Suburban pulled onto our street, a block ahead of us. Heading our way.

"Turn left!" Mom said as we were almost upon the intersection.

A quick yank of the wheel, a tap of the brakes, and we

were sliding into a left turn. Right into the path of an oncoming pickup truck.

The headlights blinded me with their brightness. My hands froze as my body braced itself for impact. Then I snapped out of it and accelerated even harder. Oh, god, it was going to be close.

Its brakes squealed, its loud horn blared. By some miracle, we squeezed past it. Clear until the truck clipped our rear bumper.

The Camaro tried to lunge right, but I held on tight, refusing to let it spin and send us crashing into the truck's wheels. We straightened and rushed down the side street, listening to the brakes and crashes that piled up behind us.

Mom craned her head over her shoulder and winced. "That SUV's out of the picture—they tipped."

Two more to go. And I'd barely gotten us through that one.

The two remaining Suburbans found us again two streets over, only one block behind. Holland and Three.

Our car was faster, but in these kinds of streets that wasn't much of an advantage, if any. Plus they both had navigation.

But I'd defeated Three before.

And then it hit me. I'd beaten her with a completely crazy, humanlike move. Maybe I could do it again. We might look identical, but despite my fears, we weren't the same, not underneath that superficial outer layer. Holland might see my emotions as a flaw, and maybe they were—at least in terms of being a perfect soldier or spy. But I didn't want to be either of those things. I just wanted to be a girl.

And according to Lucas, I was a girl capable of ingenuity, a girl capable of defying logic if the situation warranted it— something the more rigidly obedient Three would never understand.

I pulled a sharp right at the next intersection, the Suburbans following way too close behind. The light ahead of us had just hit yellow, and the two cars in front of us slowed. Trapped. I swerved into the southbound lane and zoomed past them going the wrong way, racing under the light as it flashed red.

"Mila, what are you doing?" Mom said. With my peripheral vision, I saw her left hand latch onto the side of the seat, her right one braced against the passenger door.

"I have a plan," I said, my steady voice contradicted by my squeeze-squeeze-squeeze grip on the steering wheel.

A moment later, I cut back onto eastbound Independence, except we were heading westbound. Straight into the oncoming traffic.

Turn around. Collision likely.

Except I couldn't turn around. That was the whole point.

I braced myself as the first blaze of headlights collided with ours. I couldn't believe I was doing this, when every impulse screamed bloody murder and insisted that I turn the Camaro around, that this was the stupidest plan ever. But it also happened to be the only plan we had. So I clenched my jaw and clung tightly to the wheel, and tried to ignore the logical part of me that yelled we were going to crash and burn in a horrific and incredibly literal way.

A Hyundai sedan blared its horn and swerved out of our lane. The Suburbans still followed, but fell farther behind as the drivers struggled to navigate the heavy trucks. I eased my foot off the gas, just a little. Timing here was crucial to give this plan a chance in hell of working.

I tried to swallow, even though it felt like my heart had lodged in my throat.

Timing, and one gigantic helping of luck.

Ahead of us, I saw the land on either side of the road fall away, air taking its place with dark water lapping below. With only a ten-car-length lead to spare, we hurtled back over the Kutz Bridge.

Head on into the sea of oncoming cars.

Car horns blared from all sides in a discordant symphony as I gunned the Camaro.

Collision imminent. Veer right.

I'd barely swerved that way when another command popped into my head.

Collision imminent. Veer left.

I yanked the wheel left, narrowly missing a shocked motorcyclist. I tuned out Mom's harsh gasp, tuned out my own doubts, and pushed the car onward.

We were three-quarters of the way across the bridge when an Explorer and a truck sped by, swerving wildly. I made a last desperate grab for my waning courage.

Here went everything.

"Mila, now!" Mom yelled, right as I yelled, "Hold on!"

I grabbed the power brake to slide into a one-eighty-degree turn. The Camaro's tail swooped in a wild arc behind us, brakes squealing; ours, and the cars heading our way. My head roared. As soon as we straightened, I hit the gas.

Everything happened so fast, even I could barely discern the individual parts. Us, heading dead-on for Holland's Suburban, seeing the shock on his face. Veering to the left at the last possible moment, the Camaro's driver side mirror smacking the barrier. Three's crash into the opposite barrier, as she tried to turn sharply and failed.

The back passenger window bursting inward, raining shards of glass everywhere. Shattered by a gunshot from the soldier in Holland's passenger seat. Right before they took the turn too fast in a horrible screech of tires and tipped over, the Suburban crunching against the ground.

My victorious shout, my hand pumping in the air. Right before I noticed Mom's gasp as she clutched her side. Before I noticed the red liquid already pooling on her shirt.

THIRTY-EIGHT

fought off a sickening wave of dizziness—yet another physical response to emotions that I really questioned the necessity of—and tried to stem the panic shuddering through me like an earthquake.

Bleeding. Mom was bleeding.

"Mom! Are you okay?"

I yanked the wheel to the side, ready to pull off the street right there.

"I'll be fine, Mila," she gasped. "Just get us out of here."

Just get us out of here.

Her labored breathing sent a reaction right down my leg, shoved my foot harder on the pedal. We'd get out of here.

If only I knew where to go.

Already, sirens wailed in the not-too-far-off distance.

Where would they not think to look?

An image of the green river we'd passed earlier appeared in my head.

The Potomac. A dead end, and therefore the last place someone with half a brain on the run would want to go. My android logic insisted I avoid it at all costs.

That was our spot.

"Still okay?" I said, sparing a quick glance for Mom as the Camaro tore down the street.

I swerved, and the car's front passenger tire veered off the road, just for a second. She didn't look okay, not at all. Her face was pale, and her teeth ground into her lower lip. As if she were biting back a scream.

"I'm okay . . . just keep going." But she didn't sound okay, either. Her voice sounded strained, exhausted, the way it did after she'd stayed up all night bringing a new foal into the world.

I steadied my hands on the wheel before turning to face her. My eyes scanned her body, and in front of me, a shimmering 3-D replica appeared, just like with the man back in the motel room. Only this wasn't some stranger bent on capturing me . . . this was a replica of *Mom*.

I inhaled deeply, felt my chest rise and fall, let the motion steady me before I focused.

On the green image, the two bullet holes pulsed red, both on her left side. Mentally I pulled back layers of skin and muscle to expose the location of the organs beneath. The first thing I noticed was that based on the entry wounds, the curved model of the kidney and the much smaller gallbladder were too low to have been hit. They were safe.

Then my gaze traveled upward, and my gasp ricocheted through the car.

The upper portion of her liver. Her liver, and no—no, no. Her lung. Her *heart*.

"Hospital, where's the hospital?"

"Mila, no. No hospital, it's not safe. Just . . . go."

"What? No! You need help!"

Mom clutched my arm again, with surprising strength. But her skin—did it feel a little cooler? "Listen," she said fiercely. "When we made you, we crossed a line . . . and created a miracle. I knew the risks when I stole you, and I took them anyway. Willingly. Happily. If you want to help me, you know what you can do? *Live*."

Her grip slackened, and my heart froze. "Mom?"

"Keep . . . keep driving."

And so I did. Around every turn I tensed, anticipating another shattering window, another gunshot streaking its way to Mom, who stayed huddled as close to the floorboards as she could.

We finally made it to the river, racing across an old abandoned construction site that led to an abandoned pier. I parked the car behind a rusting metal shed.

"Mom, we're here. You can sit up now."

Nothing. "Mom?"

Mom slowly hoisted herself back into the seat. Crimson soaked her entire shirt now.

No. Oh, no.

Just then, Mom's eyelashes fluttered and I heard a low moan. Deciding it was kinder to move her without warning, I counted to three, then picked her up and lifted her out of the car. She screamed, and my echoing sob clogged in my throat.

I laid her on the ground before flipping her partway onto her stomach. Her shirt back was soaked in blood. I pushed it up, then had to wipe the area near the wounds clean with my shirt just to see. And there they were, two dime-sized holes.

Wiping my finger as clean as possible—when we got out of here, the first thing we'd need to do was find some antiseptics and antibiotics— I gingerly slipped it into the more concerning hole, the one that tunneled toward her heart.

Mom jerked, but I steadied her with my free hand and pushed on. Metal. I just needed to hit metal. Find the tiny ball being held at bay by the bony cage of her ribs.

As I probed, the 3-D image appeared again, showing me every layer I passed even as I felt it. The easy yielding of skin, the tougher striation of torn muscle. And then my finger slid between two solid, slick surfaces, while the image flashed in front of me. Ribs.

No bullet, and the tunnel went deeper—to the heart. I didn't dare press farther.

My feet started shaking first. Then my legs. I barely had time to pull my fingers away from her body before my hands started spasming, too. There had to be a solution for this. Somewhere, somehow.

The bullet was obviously lodged somewhere deep inside Mom. And I had no way to dig it out. No tools at all, unless . . .

"Mom, was there anything else in the glove box?" I yelled, giving her shoulders a swift shake when her eyelashes barely fluttered. Or maybe the trunk. Maybe Lucas kept supplies in the trunk.

If I could get to the damn trunk. I tore off her shirt and bunched it up against the holes, which were hemorrhaging blood way too fast.

Mom finally spoke. "Mila, stop. It's . . . over."

No. I refused to accept that. "I'm a machine, remember? I can fix anything."

"You can't fix . . . what's unfixable."

"Don't say that," I whispered fiercely. The need to look in the trunk, to find tools, burned brightly, but right now, I was too scared of her bleeding out. "Can you hold this shirt? Just for a few seconds?"

"Mila, you know better." She lapsed into a coughing spasm before continuing. "We need to think about you."

About me? No, us. We needed to think about *us*. This whole thing, from the beginning, had been the two of us, against all odds. She couldn't just ditch everything now—I wouldn't let her.

If it weren't for me . . .

"You should have just left me there to begin with. Then none of this would have happened."

Her pale blue eyes burned with a feverish light. "Do you think I regret any of this? Do you? Because I don't. Not for a second. I wasn't sure I could at first, I didn't . . . but I was wrong."

The words both warmed me and chilled me to the core. Because this person spouting gibberish, this wasn't my mom. My calm, practical mom. Which could only mean . . .

With a rapidly expanding knot sealing off my throat, I turned to stare into the dark depths of the Potomac. Furious at my lack of control. How useless, programming a droid with tears. With a violent flick of my hand, I swiped at the liquid that spilled down my cheeks.

Mom heaved a big, ragged sigh. I whirled to her, in time to see her pale eyelids flutter closed.

"No—don't close your eyes!"

Her fingers, once so strong and warm, chilled on my arm.

Critical blood loss: Probable.

Heart failure: Probable.

451

Organ failure: Probable.

This time, the voice was anything but a comfort. I got it, I did. The clinical explanation was blood loss, robbing her muscles of the oxygen they needed to sustain forceful contractions until they finally stopped altogether. But there was another, more lyrical explanation: her soul was fading, drifting away to some better place.

While logic insisted the former was correct, I desperately wanted to believe in the latter.

"Mila," Mom said, her voice soft, a faint smile on her pale, pale face. "I know you worry that you experience the world differently than regular people. But . . ." She paused, panting for a moment before gritting her teeth. "No two people ever view the world from exactly the same perspective, understand things the same way, human or not. The best . . . the best . . ." Her voice petered out, her eyelashes fluttered shut. Her chest expanded with the force of her next inhalation, an exertion that turned the red stream seeping from her wound into a river. The rest of her sentence slurred together. "The best we can ever do is try."

With her eyes closed, her hand fluttered toward her throat and closed around her oval pendant. My phony birthstone. She yanked, but with so little strength that the necklace refused to give.

"Here." I reached up, cupped my hand around hers, and pulled. The necklace tore free as easily as a sheet of paper.

Mom pushed the pendant into my hand. Her voice lowered to a raspy whisper. "Find Rich—Richard Grady. He knows . . ."

The last word drifted out on a sigh. After she uttered it, her head lolled to the side. Her hand went limp, and in that moment, I felt something deep inside me die, too.

Overhead, birds squawked to herald that dawn was just around the corner. The Potomac rushed past. The smell of doughnuts wafted from a bakery somewhere in the distance. And here, on the dirty asphalt, my mom's all-too-human heart stopped beating.

"We were supposed to be a team, remember?" But of course my choked whisper fell on ears that could no longer hear.

A hole ripped open in my chest, spilling a corrosive mixture of darkness and pain and loss, one that filled me until I thought my skin would explode from the terrible pressure. My throat clogged again, and it ached, oh, god, it ached, in a way that made me think I would never swallow or talk, laugh or sing, or utter a single sound ever again. And why would I want to? It had always been Mom and me, yet now, suddenly, it wasn't.

I was alone in a world I'd barely experienced, one that looked stark and empty.

Without her, everything seemed stark and empty.

I didn't bother feeling for a pulse I knew wasn't there, or

trying frantic CPR, or throwing her into the car and rushing her to a hospital.

None of those things would bring her back.

Instead I smoothed her hair away from her forehead. Her beautiful hair. Then I curled up next to her. I slid one arm around her waist, pressed my cheek against hers. Her skin still smelled of rosemary lotion.

I closed my eyes. Tried to imagine we were just back in Clearwater, snuggled on the couch. Watching some ridiculous show on TV. She'd ask me if everything at school was okay, and I'd say yes.

If only I could will it into reality, make it true.

But I couldn't pretend. This was wrong, wrong, all wrong. Mom's skin was still warm, but there was no gentle stirring to indicate breathing, no faint thrum of a pulse. No movement inside her at all. Nothing to contradict the chilling reality.

In death, Mom was more like me than in life.

I shot up, a horrifying thought tearing through me. I couldn't leave her here. They'd find her, and what if . . . what if they harvested her cells, or whatever they'd done to make me?

Mom might want me to live, might have died giving me the chance, but I couldn't believe she'd want this to happen to anyone else. And I refused to allow it to happen. Not to her.

If it were up to me, I'd stay here, with Mom's body, and wait for them to find me. The thought of leaving her behind felt so wrong, so traitorous. Yet I knew the last thing Mom would have wanted me to do was stay. She'd made that more than clear. She'd risked everything to bring me freedom, and if I squandered that, it was like I was squandering her life all over again.

Mom wanted me to fight.

To live.

I'd just never dreamed that I'd have to do it alone.

A sharp honk in the distance reminded me that it wasn't safe here. This tiny, run-down area that edged the Potomac appeared secluded, but it was literally minutes from downtown D.C. Holland and his underlings could stumble upon me at any time. Or for all I knew, even the Vita Obscura. To honor Mom's last wish, I needed to run. But to honor *her*, there was something else I had to do first.

I looked at Mom's still body for a moment, watched her hair flutter gently in the breeze. I smoothed it off her pale face, bleakness threatening to overwhelm me. Then I hurried into the shed.

A few minutes later, I'd tied the rusty old anchor I'd found to Mom's body with the jumper cables in Lucas's trunk. After scooping her into my arms in one efficient motion, I carried her toward the river. Away from the buildings looming behind us, away from D.C. Away from Holland's reach.

I carried her to the edge of the river, watched the water churn below.

I hated the thought that the briny liquid would swallow her rosemary scent once and for all. Cradle her blue eyes, her soft hair, her thin yet steely body within its depths, where I could no longer see. I knew she was dead, that whatever had made her alive was gone from the shell in my arms. I knew it, but still I whispered, "Good-bye, Mom."

I looked at the dark, opaque water again, and my hands clenched on her skin. How could I do it? Just toss her into the water like so much unwanted garbage? She deserved better than this. A real funeral, with mourners and flowers and a priest to say last words, the kind of funeral she'd implanted in my head for "Dad."

Then I pictured Holland finding her, taking her back into the depths of that hellish place, and I shuddered. I couldn't let that happen. A proper funeral would be just one more thing he'd stolen from us.

I inhaled deeply. And then I tossed her ruined body into the greedy water below, and it was like I'd ripped out my heart and tossed it in with her, because surely nothing less could cause that kind of pain. But at least Holland could never have her now.

I turned away before her body disappeared, trying to accept what my logic was telling me. Right now, letting the complete android in me take over was a blessing—anything to help stem the pain. Mom was gone, and staring at the river wouldn't bring me any closer to her last request. I had to get out of here.

And I needed help.

THIRTY-NINE

After stuffing the money into my pocket, I headed away from the Camaro. With its blown-out glass and license plate and make probably known to every official with clearance in the state by now, it was a moving trap.

I tacked "new car" onto the mental list of things I owed Lucas. Not that I'd ever see him again. I jogged past the Camaro and back toward the streets, keeping my eyes open for any black Suburbans. Every step hurt, like I was abandoning Mom. I couldn't help thinking that I'd failed, and that Mom had paid for that failure with her life, no matter how much she'd tried to convince me otherwise. And now I was leaving her behind. Forever.

But I made my feet keep moving, and I didn't allow

myself to look back. The only way to honor her now was to fulfill her dreams for me. If I got caught, everything she'd sacrificed would be for nothing. That was the only thought propelling me forward, but for now, it was enough.

If finding this Richard Grady was what Mom wanted me to do, then I'd find a way.

I couldn't fail again.

I needed a phone, but first, I needed new clothes. Along the way, we'd passed a huddle of homeless people staking out a spare patch of grass. I retraced our path until I found them.

They turned to look up at me from their dirty blankets, huddled against the cold. A couple of faces were blank, others bright with curiosity. I studied their group before finding an older woman close to my size who wore a thin hooded jacket.

I dug into my shoe and extracted two twenties and a ten. "I'll give you fifty dollars for your clothes. You can have my clothes, too." I glanced down. Bright-red spots stained the front of my shirt.

Mom's blood.

My throat tightened again, and in my head, I saw an image of her face. Her pale, unmoving face, with her blue eyes closed for good. How could she expect me to do this, how?

I reached up, and my fingers curled around the emerald

pendant that had rested around Mom's neck until recently. I could picture Mom doing the same, and somehow, the coolness of the gem soothed me. "The shirt's a little stained, but—"

I didn't even get to finish before the woman stood up and started unbuttoning her dirty beige jacket. Her gaze clung to the money in my hand like it was her salvation.

"You got more money, girlie?" A thirtyish man sidled up to me, one of his teeth rotting in his mouth, fingers trembling and stained from nicotine.

I grabbed his hand just as it reached for the money, squeezing hard enough to let him know I meant business but not hard enough to do any real damage. "The money isn't for you." I didn't even bother glancing at his face.

He gasped in pain and lurched back when I released him. The others around him muttered, but no one approached. Good. I didn't have the time or inclination to fend off a desperate crowd.

The woman tossed me her jacket. A brown stain streaked the front, and it smelled like stale sweat. Still, my choices at the moment were limited, and the hood would come in handy. Every single thing brought me a little closer to achieving my—*Mom's*—goal.

I turned my back to change, confident I'd hear anyone if they tried to approach. The jacket was long, hanging halfway to my knees, so I went ahead and stripped off my pants while she removed hers, a pair of ripped-up black jeans.

They didn't smell any better than the jacket; worse, in fact. Gritting my teeth, I pulled them on. Androids couldn't afford to be squeamish. The pants hung low on my hips, even after I buttoned them, but they'd stay up. Good enough.

I pulled the hood over my head, tucking all my hair inside. Hopefully, from a distance, I could even pass for a boy.

"Here you go," I said, handing the woman the money.

She gave me a wide grin that wrinkled her face, revealing two missing teeth, but didn't utter a word. She just grabbed the money and tucked it in up under her new shirt in a flash, like she was afraid I might change my mind.

I glanced over my shoulder, caught a flash of the rising sun glimmering off the Potomac. I did want to change my mind, but that had nothing to do with the money. As I turned to walk away, I stopped by the guy who'd tried to hit me up for money, who was still eyeing me with a wary look. "Here," I said, shoving a ten into his hand. "Next time, don't grab."

Then I took off at a brisk pace, hands in my pockets, head down. Heading into the city.

A block away, I found a red bike locked with a chain outside a building. Uttering a mental apology to the owner, I twisted the lock until it snapped and hopped on. I needed to make better time. Plus I figured a lone person on a bike was the last thing they'd be looking for.

I pedaled down the streets, keeping my head down but my eyes open for the black Suburbans, or any cars whose passengers looked a little too interested in checking out other drivers. A few blocks later, I stopped at a convenience store.

When my hand touched the door, I remembered the last convenience store I'd been to, not very long ago, outside the motel. Back then, Mom had still been alive.

I felt a sharp stab to the gut, followed by a strange, almost welcome numbness. Then I darted inside to buy a prepaid phone card and a frozen coffee drink—again, for camouflage effect.

Once I paid, I headed to the pay phone just outside. In the distance, the Lincoln Memorial rose up against the dawn-streaked sky, its wide white columns and huge rectangular top looking stately and powerful. Abraham Lincoln, abolisher of slavery. Abraham Lincoln, assassinated for his beliefs.

I searched the streets for any signs of pursuers.

No threat detected.

Turning back to the phone, I lifted the receiver, punched in the numbers. And then gripped the phone like it was the only thing keeping me standing.

Three rings later, he answered in a voice still groggy from sleep. "Hello?"

"Hunter?"

"Mila? Is that you?"

I closed my eyes and clenched the phone even tighter. It was unbelievable, just how much I'd missed the sound of his deep voice. No matter how high the quality, memories couldn't compare to the real thing.

"It's me. Listen, I don't have much time but . . . I need your help." I squeezed my lips together. If he said no, that was it. I'd be completely on my own.

That fear barely manifested before his quick reply banished it. "Of course I'll help—what's wrong? Are you okay?"

Mom's limp, broken body filled my head. I bit my lip and stared back at the memorial, at the tiny birds flocking around it, like today was any other day. Nothing was okay, not for me—but my reality wasn't theirs.

Maybe it was like Mom said. No one could experience life through someone else's eyes. Not me, and not them. Maybe we weren't that different, after all.

"Mila?"

"No," I said softly. "I'm not okay."

A pause. "Where are you?"

Hunter was the only person I had left who I could trust, besides Lucas—but contacting Lucas would be impossible. And I didn't want to have to do this alone. Plus a steady fear had been gaining strength inside me, ever since I'd let the

Potomac take Mom. If I lost all contact with people I knew, people I cared about, would I lose the things about myself that made me more human and less machine?

I needed Hunter. But he deserved a choice.

"Are you sure you want to know?"

I pictured Mom again, the crimson spreading across her shirt, and felt my eyes well up. For Mom, those people had proved deadly.

"Yes, I want to know. Let me help you."

"Thank you. Mom's . . . gone. I have some things to tell you, but I can't over the phone, and I can't go back to Clearwater. But I need help."

He didn't even hesitate. "Don't worry, Mila. I'll come to you."

"Come to me? But your parents—"

"Are so busy, they could care less. I've traveled by myself tons of times. Besides, I'm eighteen. I don't need their consent. Just tell me where."

Oh, god. Between the sweet sound of his voice and his eagerness to help, he was going to turn me into a big weepy mess. And I didn't want to cry. Not again.

I twisted the metal cord between my hands, completely torn. It was selfish of me to ask, I knew that. What if just meeting me put him in danger? And yet . . . Mom wouldn't want me to be alone.

"Mila—tell me. Please."

I should have said no. I should have, but the relief coursing through me was too strong to resist. With no Mom and no Lucas, I had nobody but Hunter to depend on for help. Plus I couldn't deny that I wanted to see that lopsided smile again. Even if it was only for a short time.

In my head, one of my implanted memories replayed, a fabricated vacation that had always seemed so idyllic. "Okay. Meet me in Virginia Beach in two days. I'll call you when I get there, to give you more detailed directions."

Virginia Beach. A wave of longing washed over me. I might never, ever get to visit that beach with Mom for real, but maybe digging my toes into the sand, listening to the crashing waves, and people watching on the boardwalk like in my phony memory would help me feel a little closer to her, somehow.

A siren wailed off in the distance. "Gotta go. And Hunter? Thank you." I hung up the phone before I heard his reply and headed for my bike.

Yes, Virginia Beach might be the perfect place. All I had to do was make sure I got there in one piece.

FORTY

The young waitress looked out of place. With her long chestnut hair, pulled back into a ponytail, wide-set blue eyes, and perfectly symmetrical features, she could have been a model. I wondered what made her choose a job as a waitress in this grimy café, serving sunburned parents and screaming children and cleaning up dirty dishes.

I wondered if she had any idea how I envied her. She had the freedom to do whatever she wanted, to be whoever she wanted to be. I planned on having that kind of freedom. Soon.

A man's shout rang out from somewhere down the boardwalk, and I stiffened in the wooden chair. I glanced out the window, and faster than ever, my android functions took over.

Target: Located.

A zoomed-in image of a short, potbellied man wearing a wide-brimmed hat appeared before me. I watched as he shouted again at two kids, who were down on the beach and running for the waves, fully clothed.

No threat detected.

If I'd learned one thing in all of this, it was that fighting the reality of my capabilities did me no good. It was better to just accept them. They made things easier.

Sometimes I wondered if being less human would make things easier.

My hand clasped around the pendant that dangled from my neck. I'd never understood why a phony birthstone had meant so much to her, but she'd wanted me to have it, and I was glad. It was the only physical reminder of her I had, and while my android logic fought against getting attached to an inanimate object, the gemstone offered me some small measure of comfort all the same.

My eyes stung, so I stared outside at where the sun burned bright, refusing to allow the tears to fall. The beachfront café's open windows allowed the scent of salt and fish to waft inside. Seagulls screeched, the ocean rumbled, and everywhere, the sound of chattering tourists.

I toyed with the cold french fries on my plate, sipped at the iced tea the waitress had already refilled twice. Much longer, and I'd probably need to order something new to justify the booth. This was the first time I'd even attempted to eat anything since I'd escaped Holland—it seemed ridiculous to waste money on food that I didn't really need. Plus my programmed appetite obviously responded to my emotional state, because it was nonexistent. And now that I hadn't eaten in so long, the whole process felt . . . unnecessary.

A hint of anxiety niggled at me, as it had when I'd first ordered and found I didn't really want anything. Like maybe when I stopped doing human things, the humanity in me would just fade away.

A few tables over, my waitress interacted with another group of customers. I watched the way she laughed down at a squirming child. She'd been nothing but friendly, smiling every time and asking me to flag her down if I needed more. She must have a wonderful life away from work to be so cheerful, I'd decided.

I looked out the window again, not expecting to see anyone I knew. He'd probably decided not to show. I couldn't blame him. Who in their right mind would fly from Minnesota to Virginia Beach to meet a girl they'd only known for a few brief days?

With or without him, I'd evade Holland, Three, and the Vita Obscura, if they really existed, and I'd track down this Richard Grady, whoever he was. He'd tell me what he knew, and after that, I'd try to get on with my life.

I really, really hoped that life involved Hunter. But my chances weren't looking good.

I reached down to brush a few lingering grains of sand from my flip-flopped foot. When I sat back up, I saw him. He walked down the boardwalk, his hair as long and wavy as ever, hands stuffed into the pockets of his green hoodie, his calves bared by a pair of cargo shorts. Just outside the door, he hesitated and looked over his shoulder, and for a heart-stopping moment, I thought he was going to turn around and walk away. My breathing quickened. I wanted to shout out to him, but instead I sat there silently, clinging to my iced tea glass like it was my only salvation.

He had to make this final choice all on his own. And it wasn't like I could blame him for having doubts. He had to be wondering what the heck was going on. What kind of trouble I'd managed to get myself into.

And then he was looking into the café, and his hand was pulling open the door.

I'd meant to stay reserved, so that I didn't freak him out as soon as he walked inside by assaulting him with one hundred and twenty pounds of emotionally flawed android enthusiasm. But somehow I'd propelled myself to my feet and pushed away from the table, and by the time he entered the cafe I was running.

I paused just before I reached him, suddenly realizing what I was doing and how everyone was staring, and good grief, that he was probably expecting a handshake and here I was, about to plow him to the ground. But then he opened his arms, and I flung myself into them.

Well, carefully flung, of course. Tackling my dream boy with the force of three juiced-up linebackers, as Kaylee used to say, probably wasn't the best way to make an impression.

"You made it," I whispered into his neck, breathing in the familiar scent of him. Suddenly, my earlier anxiety about fading humanity seemed sillier than ever.

He squeezed me tight. "You still owe me another date, remember?"

I choked back a laugh as we stood there in the middle of the café, me hugging him like my life depended on it. And maybe it did.

Now that he was here, I felt like the reasons behind this impromptu meeting could wait.

Maybe forever.

ACKNOWLEDGMENTS

Holy cow—I wrote a book! But I didn't do it alone. Since writing can *feel* like such an incredibly solitary pursuit sometimes, it's amazing how much help and support (and sanity checks!) are required to make a book possible. Luckily, I've surrounded myself with some of the most helpful and supportive people on the entire planet.

Thanks to Kathleen Peacock, Lindsey Culli, Rachael Allen, Kara Taylor, Stephanie Kuehn, Sarah Harian, Vahini Nadoo, Elyse Regan, and all of my fellow YAWNers for assuring me at various points along the way that I wasn't writing complete gibberish.

To the amazing writers at LB, WN, and the Hopefuls—thank you for listening and keeping me (relatively) sane (and trust me—I know what a difficult task that is!). Ditto to the Apocalypsies, Luckies, and Classes—much love to you all.

Special thanks to my amazing and talented writer friend Kathleen Peacock, who is equal parts Cheerleader of Awesomeness and Purveyor of YouTube Distraction. Joss lovers, UNITE!

To Absolute Write, for showing me how to become a serious writer, and especially to my Purgies for offering endless support—Sweet Cartwheeling J, y'all!

Huge thanks to the SoCal writing gang—you know who you are, and you make me proud to be part of the local writing scene. (Also—More. Lunches. Just saying.)

A special shout out to the YA community—writers and bloggers and everyone else. I know we have our ups and downs, but overall, I think we're part of something pretty amazing.

To the wonderful team at HarperCollins and Katherine Tegen Books, who made this all possible: my fabulous editor, Claudia Gabel—there'd be no *Mila* without you—Melissa Miller, Katherine Tegen, and Katie Bignell in Editorial, Amy Ryan and Erin Fitzsimmons in Art, and Sarah Hoy and Benjamin Delacour, who aren't technically Harper but who helped make the cover (OMG, you guys—THE COVER!!!!!), Renée Cafiero in Copyediting, Lauren Flower and Megan Sugrue in Marketing, and Casey McIntyre in Publicity. Also, thanks to all the wonderful Harper folks I met at ALA and Comic Con, for making me feel so welcome, and everyone else at Harper who helped with *Mila* in some way, big or small. I can't even begin to tell you how much your enthusiasm for this book means to me.

To my friend/cheerleader/ledge-talker-offer/agent extraordinaire, Taylor Martindale, for handling all my random and angst with utter grace. Also, to SDLA and Full Circle Literary Agency for their support.

Thanks to Kat Post, for the no-stress author photo and for watching my little darlings when I needed to snatch a few extra writing hours.

To my nonwriting friends, for both your support and your

infinite patience in putting up with all of my book babble over this past year. Plus, emergency revisions babysitting, WOOT!

Special thanks to Tom Wyatt, for making the trek to Clearwater. I owe you a Blizzard.

An enormous thank-you to my mom for getting me addicted to reading and YA in the first place. To all of my family in Colorado for their unlimited support and kid-watching assistance (although I am still waiting on that Ivory Tower), with a special thanks to the Jerhound, for flying and/or driving to CA at a moment's notice. Thanks to our Chicago family for your enthusiasm, and to Dawn for letting your house double as my writing cave.

(On a similar note—thanks so much to the San Marcos Starbucks, Boudin and Panera, for allowing me to write without turning into a hermit.)

To Shani and the rest of the hounds—see how I snuck that Ridgeback in there?

To Finley and Connor, for (sometimes) understanding that while Mommy would love to play MineCraft and ponies 24/7, she needs writing time, too. Also, for filling the house with hugs and laughter (and the occasional scream, but we'll forget about those for now).

To Scott—thank you for being a kid wrangler extraordinaire, for giving me the gentle boot out the door when I have deadlines to meet, for never complaining and always believing. Your support makes all the difference in the world and, just so you know—tidy houses are overrated.

And finally, thanks to you, lovely reader, for picking up my book—because stories aren't much fun if you can't share them.